I0613751

Orion's Foot: Myth, Mystery, and Romance in the Amazon

by

M. S. Spencer

This is a work of fiction. Names, characters, places, and incidents are either the product of the author's imagination or are used fictitiously, and any resemblance to actual persons living or dead, business establishments, events, or locales, is entirely coincidental.

Orion's Foot:
Myth, Mystery, and Romance in the Amazon

COPYRIGHT © 2019 by Meredith Ellsworth

All rights reserved. No part of this book may be used or reproduced in any manner whatsoever without written permission of the author or The Wild Rose Press, Inc. except in the case of brief quotations embodied in critical articles or reviews.
Contact Information: info@thewildrosepress.com

Cover Art by *Debbie Taylor*

The Wild Rose Press, Inc.
PO Box 708
Adams Basin, NY 14410-0708
Visit us at www.thewildrosepress.com

Publishing History
First Crimson Rose Edition, 2019
Print ISBN 978-1-5092-2777-8
Digital ISBN 978-1-5092-2778-5

Published in the United States of America

They went back down the path they'd come, surveying the ground and vegetation for any trace of a large animal. They had reached the mahogany tree when Petra checked her watch. "Winston's been gone half an hour. Maybe we should—" Her words were cut off by a low snarl. "Emory? Is that you?" She whirled around. "Where are you?"

For answer, the growl grew deeper and more menacing. *Sounds like a gorilla—but they don't live here, do they?* She whispered, "Emory?"

"*Shh.*" She looked up. Emory clung to a low branch of the mahogany tree. He held a hand out. "Quickly."

She grabbed a liana, hoping fervently it wasn't a curare vine, and scrambled up. The growl came again, closer. They climbed higher. Something crashed through the woods, puffing. Whatever it was entered the clearing, and the noise stopped. Petra held her breath and Emory's hand. *It must be looking for us.* After a lengthy pause that left her feeling chilled to the bone in the torrid heat, the puffing started again, gradually diminishing into the distance. She waited five more minutes to be sure it was gone before whispering, "Did you get a look at it?"

"No, the foliage was in the way, but it sounded awfully big. And grouchy. I'm going to—" As he started to climb down, a twig snapped below them. They froze.

Something's being dragged through the underbrush.

Dedication

To my beloved son Spencer,
who led me down the jungle path to adventure

Chapter One
In Darwin's Footsteps

September 25

"Okay, that's dictionaries done." Petra sighed. "Gawd, I do *not* look forward to the encyclopedias. They are such a bitch. Come on, Eloise. Let's get some lunch." She pushed the little tortoiseshell cat off her lap and headed toward the kitchen. The doorbell rang.

She opened the door to a blast of cold air and a shivering mailman.

"Hey, Petra, I have a package for you. Your car's not out front, so I thought I'd check to see if you were in before I left it."

"Thanks, Murray. The old dune buggy's keeping warm in my neighbor's heated garage." Petra took the thick manila envelope from him. "Winter hitting right on time, huh?"

"Too right. This is my last year for sure. Me and the missus are heading to Boca Raton next February. Sixty years of Chicago's deep freeze is enough."

Petra looked past him to the drizzle of snowflakes floating in the wind. "Understood."

"Oh, and here's the rest of your mail."

"Thanks." She hated to shut the door on him, leaving him out in the frigid air, but hey, utilities weren't included in her rent. Apartments were scarce in

Hyde Park, the neighborhood surrounding the University of Chicago, and she was lucky to have found one with a parking lot and more than one room.

Petra dropped the pile on the kitchen counter and went to the cupboard. "Let's see…for you, Eloise, I think the seafood feast." She plopped the contents of a can into the bowl labeled ME ELOISE. Her pet sniffed it suspiciously. "Come on, sweetie, it's your favorite."

Once the cat started to eat, Petra put a wedge of quiche Lorraine in the toaster oven to warm and took her mail to the table. "Ah, the materials for the Galapagos trip." She ignored the pulsing nerve in the pit of her stomach. "You're going to do it, Petra. You wimp out, I'll never speak to you again."

Accustomed to making empty threats to herself, she set the brochures aside and turned back to the pile. A business envelope with familiar angular handwriting caught her eye. "Nicky? I wonder what he wants." She tore open the flap. Two sheets of paper fell out. She picked them up and unfolded the first one. It was a handwritten note.

Dear Sis,

See enclosed itinerary. I'll pick you up at Lima airport.

Nick.

The second sheet was a printed copy of an email. It listed an Avianca Airlines flight, leaving Miami at 3:00 p.m. on October 2, arriving Lima, Peru, at 7:00 p.m. "Peru! What the hell?"

The phone rang. "Petra? It's your mother."

"I know it is."

"What? Oh. Well…uh, how are you?"

Why does she sound hesitant? "I'm fine, Mom.

Why are you calling?"

"No need to be snippy. If your father heard you use that tone of voice, he'd—"

"I'm sorry, Mother. Isn't Daddy there?" Her mother tended to get flustered when her husband was traveling. They had been married for fifty years and still had trouble being apart for more than a day.

"No, he's not." Her voice rose. "He's flying down the Colorado River in a teeny tiny airplane. I think it's the same one that crash-landed on his trip to North Dakota." She hiccupped. "What I want to know is, why won't the Bureau of Reclamation spring for a new plane? That Piper Cub must be thirty years old."

"Mom—"

"I called Carol over at the procurement office. She says it's not even in the budget. I pointed out that it's kind of important that the director of the Bureau of Reclamation be safe in the air, you know, since he has to fly all over the West. But no…"

"What's he doing in Colorado?"

"He's taking the new public affairs person for the Bureau on his annual inspection tour of the dams. He'll be gone for *weeks*."

"That's such a wonderful trip, though. Remember when we got to go? I think I was fifteen and Nick twelve." Petra closed her eyes. "Shadowing the course of the meandering river in a single-engine plane, landing way out in the desert with nothing but tumbleweeds to steer by." She opened her eyes. "I've always said our dams are much more beautiful than the Grand Canyon. The canyon's just a big brown hole in the ground."

Her mother sounded bleak. "You won't get an

argument from me, but a lot of so-called environmentalists would sell their souls to see any man-made construction torn down, even one that powers their houses. And waters their farms. And makes for great white-water rafting…And…Where was I?"

"Well, dams *are* huge. Remember poor Nick? He couldn't handle Hoover Dam. He freaked in the elevator going down, and they had to take him out through the turbine room."

"Your father was mortified. His only son—scared of a measly seven hundred sixty tons of still-curing concrete over his head. I'm glad I persuaded him not to stop at Parker, though. It was a hundred and fifty in the shade that day. We would have put Nick off dams forever."

"Sorry, Mom, but I think we did anyway. He hasn't photographed a single building since then. Just animals."

"I'm sure it's only because we never let him have a dog."

Petra took the quiche out and set it on a plate. Cradling the phone, she got a liter of cheap wine from the refrigerator and poured herself a glass. "So, you're alone? Do you want me to come visit?"

"Aren't you in the midst of that book on reference works?"

"It's okay. I finished the section on dictionaries today. I can take a break before I hit the encyclopedias." *A long break.* "I still have six months on the sabbatical."

There was a pause. "Actually, *I'm* fine."

No, you're not. "What's up?"

"It's your brother."

"Nick?" She glanced at the printout on the counter. "I just got a note from him."

"He wants you to come to Peru."

"That's what he says. I thought he was with that group photographing wildlife in the Amazon. Isn't that in Brazil?"

"Some of it is—not all of it. Nicky says Amazonia includes parts of Brazil, Peru, Colombia, Venezuela...and let's see, I think he mentioned a couple more countries. Anyway, it's *huge*, dear. The far western portion of the river basin is in Peru. Nicky's on safari, or whatever they call it. It's not trekking...Now what..." The silence lengthened.

"Mother?"

"What, dear?"

"We were talking about Nick. Why does he need me?"

"No idea. He won't tell me. He called in a lather ten minutes ago. He says you're the only one who can help them."

"Only one...what does that mean?"

"You've got me. He sounded almost hysterical— more than usual. His voice was squeaky. You know, the way it was when he pretended he'd seen the ghost."

"Really?" Petra's brother was notorious in the family for practical jokes. Not to mention hyperbole and histrionics. "This isn't another one of his ploys to get me sucked into some magazine article about the haunted houses of Machu Picchu, is it?"

"No, I don't think so. He said it was earth-shattering."

"Earth-shattering."

"Yes. And you're indispensable to its success."

"Me! I'm just a librarian. I don't know anything about the Amazon. Or photography."

"That's what I said, but apparently your particular expertise is crucial."

"Reference?"

She could almost hear the shrug. "An encyclopedic knowledge of sources of information can sometimes come in handy."

"Okay. So did he give you any hint at all?"

"Only that he's found something."

"Excuse me?"

Her mother's voice grew testy. "Don't ask me, child. That's all he said. He was adamant that you come down. Now, what are you going to do with Eloise?"

"Eloise! I hadn't even made up my mind to go yet."

"Nonsense. I'm sending you a plane ticket to Alexandria. Drop her off here."

Resistance is futile. Petra said weakly, "Okay, but how do I get to Peru?"

"He didn't send you airfare?"

"Just flight information."

"Damn the boy. When will one of my children actually make enough money to pay for their own junkets?" She went on, clearly not expecting an answer. "I'll take care of it. You can fly to Lima from Dulles. It'll keep my mind off your father swooping around in midair with that hussy."

"Hussy?"

"The new PR director. Why are they always female? And young? Shouldn't they have more experience? A *lot* more experience? As in years? I mean—"

Petra said gently, "Most people who work with Daddy—both men and women—get burned out in two years. If they weren't young, they couldn't deal with the hours."

Her mother didn't respond. After a minute, she remarked, "You'd better get some tropical-weight travel clothes. Apparently this research station is pretty rustic. Before he went, Nick was all aquiver that they only used solar power, but in his last letter, he grumbled that that translates into cold showers and warm beer."

Petra laughed. "I happen to know that the Amazon averages more than a hundred inches of rain per year—not enough sun to power a toy car."

"See? Like I said—you know things no mortal person knows. Maybe they want a fact checker. Now, you only have four days to get ready, so I'll get off the phone. Send me an email with the reservation, and I'll pick you up at National. *Hmm.* Do you need a ticket for Eloise? I'd better check. I—" She hung up before she'd finished her own sentence.

Dad can't get home soon enough. Petra looked out the window at the now heavily falling snow and sighed. *All right, all right, all of you. I'll go.* She reflected that her mother fretted twenty-four/seven when her father was on the road but could send her daughter off to Antarctica without so much as a toodle-oo.

****

Lima, October 2

Petra waited anxiously at the security exit. Beyond it lay the main terminal. It had been crowded when she arrived, but by now, toward nine o'clock, only the uniformed guards paced the tiled floor. For the thirtieth time, she asked herself, *Where the hell is Nicholas?*

Frustrated, she plopped down on the hard plastic seat again. He hadn't answered her texts or calls since her arrival at the Lima airport. She refused to go through the gate until she saw him. *If he pulls his usual stunt and doesn't show up, I want to be able to turn around and get right back on a plane home.* She checked her watch. "Will you look at the time. I haven't eaten in ten hours!" She had gotten up to see if the newsstand kiosk was still open when she heard a shout.

"Petra!"

She spun around. "Nick!"

Her brother loped toward her, his six-foot-three frame towering above the little native Peruvians. The unruly shock of coffee-colored hair added a couple more inches in height. He skidded to a halt by the Do Not Enter sign. "Why are you still in there? Come on!"

"Nicky, where have you been?"

The question seemed to puzzle him. "What do you mean?"

"I arrived two hours ago. You said you were going to pick me up."

He blinked. "Well, here I am."

She knew better than to expect an apology, so she picked up her bag and walked through the gate. Nick swung a camera to his eye. "Hold it." He clicked the button five times in quick succession.

"What's that for?"

"Before and after. What a traveler looks like after schlepping across the globe. I'm doing a spread for Condé Nast. Come on, let's take a taxi to your hotel."

"We're not going to the research station?"

"Pacaya? No, no, not yet—I want to show you Lima. Besides, it's a fair distance from here. We'll head out day after tomorrow. The flight to Iquitos leaves at six a.m."

"Iquitos?"

"Jumping off point for our great adventure." He patted her on the back. "Northeast corner of Peru, near the borders of Brazil and Colombia. We'll spend the night there. Then it's a six-hour boat ride to the station."

"Three days just to get there? Nicky, you know I've only got two weeks!"

"All the more reason to get cracking. Places to go; people to meet." He flagged down a miniature white Fiat, its bumper tied on with twine, and spoke in rapid Spanish to the driver. All Petra caught was "MN Lima Hotel." He threw her bag in the trunk and hopped in. "Come on! I want to hit my flat for a hot shower before we go eat."

"You have an apartment here? Why am I staying in a hotel?"

"Not an apartment—just the spare room of a friend of mine. Besides, the hotel has a fabulous breakfast buffet."

She shook her head. *Brothers.* "All right. You can tell me why you sent for me on the way."

"Oh my God, sis. It's big! I…we…have found something."

"Big? As in mountainous or momentous?"

"Just wait." Nick refused to enlighten her even after they rendezvoused at her hotel. "Let's get some dinner. Then I'll explain everything."

Petra was too hungry to argue, until she noticed the time. "It's almost ten o'clock! Nothing will be open."

"Nonsense. Remember, this is Latin America. The

evening has just begun. Besides, that's the beauty of jet lag—we can use it to our advantage. You'll be awake for another five hours, mark my words." He pulled her through the revolving doors to the street. "Look, there's a cab." He whistled.

Nick told the driver to take them to Larcomar.

"Did you say 'Larcomar'? Sounds like a laundromat."

"Nothing so banal." Nick winked. "You'll see."

Petra watched out the window as they passed through a downtown business section, then a blighted neighborhood of broken sidewalks and graffiti-covered walls, eventually entering a European-style neighborhood with parks and cafés. "Look at all the fountains and flowering trees! It reminds me of Paris."

"More like Madrid. It's called Miraflores. This was a Spanish town before it was incorporated into Lima."

Larcomar turned out to be a brightly lit, modern shopping center overlooking the Pacific Ocean. Nicky led her to a restaurant. Even at that hour, it was packed with people. "Wow. They all must sleep late in the morning."

"Lima doesn't really come alive until after eleven," replied Nick. "Like Madrid."

The hostess took them to a seat by the picture windows. Petra bent over the table to look out. "Oh my God. Nick!" Just a few feet from their table, steep cliffs dropped straight down to the water. "How far down is that?" She pointed.

"More than two hundred feet. Great place for hang gliding."

She shrank back. "A little too much like an eagle's aerie for me. How safe *are* we?"

"Safe enough." Nick grinned at his sister. "Want a drink?"

She nodded vigorously. "Make it a double."

Nick called the waiter over.

"Good evening, señor. I am Domingo. What can I do for you?"

"Two pisco sours, *por favor*."

"Right away, señor."

A minute later, Domingo handed Petra a milky liquid in a martini glass. She held the glass up. "What is this?"

Nick toasted her. "Pisco sour. It's the Peruvian national drink."

She sipped. "I taste the lime juice, but what's the alcohol? It's not tequila."

"Pisco is a kind of brandy. It's made from a blend of grapes, some of which are only grown here. It's unique to Peru."

"And yummy." She munched on the crisp yellow nuts the waiter had brought to their table with their drinks. "And so are these."

Domingo smiled. "They are called *cancha*. Toasted corn. Would you like to order?"

She skimmed the menu before putting it down with an embarrassed smile. "I'm sorry. I don't speak Spanish."

He took pity. "We have several Peruvian specialties tonight. Perhaps you would enjoy a nice ceviche?"

Nick whispered, "Pickled fish." Petra gave him a dubious look.

"We also have *chicharrónes*. They are pork—fried belly."

"Belly?"

Nick screwed up his face. "It's…see, you slice the pork rind and then fry it in deep fat. Kind of like bacon?"

"Oh, you mean *cracklings*. Soul food—an American snack."

Both men disapproved. "Peruvian."

"Special."

Nick put his glass down. "Tell you what, let's get a tasting plate. After that we'll order entrees."

Domingo went off, to return with a large platter. He pointed at several small plates arranged in a circle. "Ceviches of different fishes."

In the center lay an elaborately sculpted cylinder, garnished with cilantro and olives. Petra admired it. "And this? Is it just for decoration or is it edible?"

"*Causas*. Mashed potato stuffed with chicken."

Nick added, "Very traditional. Everything comes with potatoes in Peru."

Petra tasted a little of each dish. "Lovely." She finished her drink. Her head was beginning to feel fuzzy.

Nick checked out her empty plate. "Still hungry?"

She gulped down some water. "I guess so."

"Get the *lomo saltado*. You'll like it."

Domingo explained. "Fried beef strips with french fries."

She frowned. "Doesn't sound very Peruvian."

"It's Chifa—Chinese."

She looked at Nick, but he just shrugged. Jet lag was definitely setting in—*or is it the alcohol?*—and Petra decided comfort food was preferable to more questions. "Okay."

After a few fries, she felt better. Traveling had never agreed with her, and she hadn't forced the issue. *I kept waiting for someone to go with...on a honeymoon.* Sure, Nick had dragged her on a few excursions—to Turkey and to England—but she always felt more comfortable reading about an exotic place than sitting in it eating unfamiliar food.

"For a reference librarian, you sure are a wuss, my dear daughter"—words imprinted on her memory the day her father blew up when she refused to accompany him to China. After that, she swore she'd make him proud. She thought of the brochures for the Galapagos still sitting on her kitchen counter. *Peru should qualify, right, Daddy?*

"Hello? Did you just nod off?" Nick touched her elbow.

She put down her fork. "No, I'm awake, but not for much longer. Now, once again, why am I here? I presume this is another one of your nutty ideas for solving world hunger."

"Sis! You wound me." He leaned forward, his eyes bright. "I told you it was big. Well, this is something that will turn the scientific world on its head."

"A third strand of DNA? Proof of evolution?"

"No, no. What are they always finding in the Amazon?"

"A new species?"

"Yes!"

"Yes? You've found a new species?"

"No. I mean...well, sort of."

"Sort of?"

"Look, it'll be easier to show you when we get there. Aguirre can explain it better."

"Aguirre?"

"Aguirre Tramposo. He's the one who made the discovery. A member of the team I signed on with. They're from the ITR—the Institute for Tropical Research."

"Institute for Tropical Research? I've never heard of it."

"I'm not certain how long it's been around. All I know is they received a significant grant to study the rainforest. And they're paying me enough to afford that '68 Mustang convertible I have my eye on." He beamed.

"*Hmm.*" Petra knew her brother well, especially his penchant for avoiding probing questions when money was involved. "Where are its headquarters?"

"Florida. In a town called Ocala." He nodded enthusiastically. "They've rented the research station for six months."

"Tell me about the place we're going to."

"Pacaya River Lodge."

"Is it affiliated with a university?"

"It's privately owned, but scientists can apply to do biological research on a first-come, first-serve basis."

"Wait a minute. Did you say *Pacaya* River? I thought we were going to the Amazon."

"We are. The Pacaya is a tributary of the Ucayali River, which runs into the Amazon." When Petra didn't respond, he added, "The Amazon River basin covers almost three million square miles and has thousands of tributaries."

"I see." Petra made a mental note to pull up a map when she had a minute. "So, the scientists. Who do they apply to?"

Nick shook his head. "Not sure—that's Ffoulkes's department. He's the director of the institute. He hired me."

"What do they study?"

"Well, it's mainly biology, but since this is the Amazon, there's research to be done in all the sciences—from paleontology to botany to medical research to anthropology. Our group is a real mixed bag—they all came down with their own projects, but now..." He stopped.

"Now you have this—whatever it is—to occupy you."

"Right." Nick's eyes flickered.

Petra knew better than to try to pry it out of him before he was ready. *He'll be forced to tell me when we get there anyway.* "So who's on this team?"

"Well, let's see...there's Dr. Lewis Gordon. He's a medical doctor, here to check out native cures for tropical diseases. He's been conferring with local shamans. Did you know there are a hundred and fifty thousand plant species in the Amazon? According to this one article I read, only one percent of the catalogued species has even been tested for medicinal properties."

"This Dr. Gordon has his hands full then. That's one. Go on." *Keep him on topic while I'm still conscious.*

"What? Oh. Then there's Alex, Alex...some unpronounceable German name. Hang on." He pulled a notebook out. "Let's see...yeah, here it is. Alex Bönickhausen—he's a herpetologist. Evidently, this very rare caiman has been spotted in the Pacaya area. Aguirre Tramposo—our current celebrity—is a botanist, supposedly searching for new orchids, although…" He drummed his fingers on the table.

"Although what?"

"I'll leave it until we get there. Now, let's see…I'm missing one…oh yeah, Emory Andrews, ornithologist."

"Whew. You weren't kidding about a mixed bag. Who's in charge?"

"Well, until Ffoulkes gets there, John *thinks* he's the leader, but everyone pretty much looks to Emory."

"John?"

"John Dillinger. Public relations. General factotum for the institute. He arranged the trip and wangled the grants." He grinned. "He's a piece of work."

"Just so long as he doesn't live up to his name."

"John Dill—? Oh, you're referring to the mobster." He chuckled. "Wait'll you see him. I doubt we have anything to worry about."

"So can you at least give me a clue about this find?" Petra felt her attention beginning to flag. "In ten words or less?"

"All right, all right. Here's a hint." Nick tossed off his drink. "The hoatzin."

"The *hoo* what?"

"It's a bird—a truly weird bird. They thought for a while it was most closely related to the pterodactyls, but they couldn't find any fossil record to link it to the Jurassic period. Until now."

"That's what you've found? A fossil?"

He nodded vigorously. Domingo took this as a sign to replenish his drink. "That's what he claims, anyway. The rest of us haven't seen it yet. Tramposo wants to keep it under wraps until Ffoulkes arrives."

"So why do you need me?"

He looked at her like she was eleven eggs short of a dozen. "Your research skills. Duh. We want you to search the records—find any reference to this creature."

"Does that mean I have to stay here? I don't get to go to the Amazon?" Despite her initial misgivings, she felt disappointed.

"No, no, you'll be on site. No worries. We have Wi-Fi at the station. Plus the place has got the latest top-of-the-line equipment—a lab, a darkroom. Everything."

"Mother said you were complaining because it doesn't have hot water. That doesn't sound very twenty-first century to me."

"Oh, well, amenities for the *human* tenants are pretty rudimentary—they only let us have the one solar panel."

"So she said."

"*But* the lab has its own generator and a small air-conditioning unit. And no, we're not allowed to sleep there." At her expression, he added hastily, "You'll be very comfortable. Luz has set up a room for you away from the men. It even has a fan."

"A fan." She drew her jacket around her in the sudden chill. "Why do I need that?"

"You're kidding, right? This is the Amazon we're talking about, sis. Average temperature year-round is ninety degrees. And humid?" He pretended to wipe his forehead. "Humidity's generally a hundred percent." He checked out her khaki slacks and navy blazer. "Let's hope you sprang for appropriate clothing. Something you can rinse out every couple of hours."

Uh-oh.

Chapter Two
Ecological Niches

October 3

The hotel room phone woke her. "Hello?"

"Señorita Steele? Your brother is on the line. May I patch you through?"

"Yes, please." Sun streamed through the large window curtained in chiffon. She checked the clock. *Oh my goodness, it's almost ten thirty!*

"Sis? Get a good night's sleep?" He didn't wait for an answer. "Meet me in the breakfast room."

Breakfast was served in a pleasant airy space with a line of chefs waiting to take her order. There were baskets of sweet, saffron-colored rolls, bowls of fruit—some recognizable, some not—and an omelet station. While they waited for coffee, Nick chattered about Lima and its history.

"So there are actual Inca ruins right in the middle of the city?"

"Uh-huh. And some sites are even earlier. I propose we work backward historically, though, starting with the cathedral. It's called the Basilica of Saint John the Apostle and is literally the center of the town." He rose. "You finished? Get your stuff, and we'll be off on a whirlwind tour."

"Didn't you do this when you first arrived?"

"Of course, that's how I know where to go. You might as well see the sights now—once we get to Pacaya we won't be communicating with the outside world for who knows how long."

How remote is *this place?* "So, we'll be venturing into Tarzan's lair?"

"Don't be silly—that was in Africa."

They took a taxi to the main square, Plaza Mayor, and wandered among the crowds over to the cathedral entrance. Petra read the marker outside. "Did you know Lima was founded by Francisco Pizarro in 1535? Says here he laid the cornerstone of this church the same year."

"Not surprising. After all, Pizarro conquered the Incas, and this was their playground." Nick led her through the massive, carved wooden doors.

An hour's tour of dark, looming choir stalls carved with the dour faces of saints, followed by a crypt piled high with skulls, was enough. She shook her head. "Too many skeletons."

He pulled a long face. "It's the Spanish soul. Here, I'll make it up to you." He led her out into the sun and pointed down an alley. "Hector says the best *anticucho* stalls are down there."

"Hector?"

"You'll meet him. He's our guide—the resident ranger at the station. *Anticucho* is another Peruvian delicacy."

I'm not going to ask.

Luckily, Nick refrained from elucidating until she was licking the last of the sauce off her fingers and weighing whether to order another plate. "*Anticucho*, in case you were wondering, is cow's heart. Although"—

his eyes sparkled with mischief—"if the heart's unavailable, cooks have been known to use the udder. The recipe was first created by black slaves in Peru, who, like slaves in the American South, had to make do with the parts their masters threw out." He surveyed the myriad shades of color of the customers happily eating. "The fact that it's one of the most popular dishes in Lima is what I call payback."

Petra considered responding but didn't see the point. "What now?"

"You were interested in the Inca ruins—want to tour a ziggurat?"

"A ziggurat? Weren't those Mesopotamian temples?"

Nick smirked. "Oh, right. My bad. Although, the Inca temples were so similar, it's gotta make you wonder—which came first?"

"I know, but I'm not going to tell you."

"What? Hey!"

"Shall we?" She rose and put her napkin on the table. "Where are these ruins?"

"In the Miraflores district where we had dinner last night. It's called the Huaca Pucllana."

The taxi rolled into a parking lot surrounded by office buildings and apartment houses. Before them rose what at first looked like a brown pile of rubble. Their guide led them to the top level. "Huaca Pucllana was a ceremonial center for the Lima culture. They disappeared some seven hundred years before the Incas invaded."

Nick drew back. "Hold the phone, I thought these were Inca ruins."

"No. The Inca weren't the only civilization in Peru.

Numerous distinct cultures flourished in this region for over five thousand years."

Looks like I've got some reading to do. The sun beat down as they roved the baked earth platform. Petra was ready to find some shade and order a cool glass of anything when Nick pointed.

"Hey, isn't that Ffoulkes?"

She peered at a retreating figure wearing a pith helmet. "How would I know? Who is Ffoulkes?"

"Denys Ffoulkes. I told you. He's the director of the Institute for Tropical Research." He gazed after the man. "I wonder what he's doing here? He's not supposed to arrive until next week."

Petra shrugged. "Considering how long it takes to get anywhere in this country, I suspect he's taking some time to explore Lima just as we are."

"Yeah, I suppose. Except he claimed he couldn't come down with the team because he was inundated with other projects."

"Whatever." Petra was beginning to tire. "You can ask him when he gets to the station. Now, may I go back to the hotel?"

"What? Oh, sure."

Nick dropped her off, and Petra headed to the bar tucked away in a side room and ordered a pisco sour. She was nursing it when he returned, carrying an overnight bag. He signaled the bartender. "*Cerveza, por favor.*"

Petra ordered another pisco sour. When it had been placed in front of her and Nick had his beer, she asked him, "When is the flight?"

"Six in the morning. We'll have to leave here by four." He finished his beer and picked up his suitcase.

"That's why I'm going to stay with you. It'll save time."

Petra remembered without fondness their childhood in bunk beds. "But you snore!"

"So do you."

****

October 4

As dawn broke, they drove back to the airport. They had handed their boarding passes to the agent and were about to head out to the tarmac when Nick stopped. "Damn, I need some coffee. I forgot they don't serve food on these little planes. Be back in a jiff."

She had found her seat when he came running down the aisle. He plopped beside her, panting. "You'll never guess who I just saw *again*."

"Your director?"

"Uh-huh. Odd. I called to him—I know he saw me—but he pretended not to recognize me."

"Probably just your imagination."

"He was talking to a man and pointing at a plane parked in the general aviation terminal."

"You mean, where the private planes are? Maybe he's negotiating a flight to Pacaya. We'll know soon enough."

"Yeah…you're right. I'm sure there's a perfectly legitimate explanation." He took the lid off his coffee and began to sip.

While the plane queued up for take-off, Petra pondered her unprecedented willingness to hop into a new adventure without even a parachute. *Is it because Nick is with me? Maybe. Face it, I really don't like traveling alone.* It wasn't much fun to eat at a table for one or explore places without a companion to share the experience. *Another reason George wouldn't have worked out, even if he hadn't dumped me. His idea of derring-do was the teacup ride at Disneyland.*

Despite that, Petra had never known a time when she didn't thirst for learning. She found everything fascinating—history, nature, archaeology, sports, languages, even cooking. It was probably why she'd never been able to settle on any particular field of expertise. *Like Mother said, I was fated to be a librarian.* That way she could dabble as much as she wanted in any subject. The plane rose in the air. She looked out the porthole at the rapidly disappearing land and felt a prickle of trepidation. *Just so long as I can do it from the comfort of my study. Oh, Mother, what have I gotten myself into?*

Two hours later, they circled a bustling city crouched next to a wide brown river. At the airport, a stout man, as round as he was tall, introduced himself as Joaquín. "Welcome to Iquitos, the Gateway to the Amazon! I am the local travel agent for all the Amazon tours. I'll take you to your hotel and escort you to your boat tomorrow morning."

Once they'd settled in the hotel, Petra picked up a brochure. "Says here Iquitos has a population of four hundred thousand, but it can only be reached by boat or plane. Wow, we really are in the boondocks."

"There are some local roads, yes, but if you want to go to Lima, you have to fly."

"How did such a huge city spring up way out here? Where did the settlers come from?" She looked out the window, which faced east. "Is the Amazon navigable all the way here from the Atlantic?"

"Questions, questions. From what I hear, most of it

is navigable, yes—on mid-size boats like those river cruise ships."

"What else do you know about it?"

"That's about it."

"Nicky!"

"Hey, I've only been here for a month, after all, and the team jumped right into research." When she continued to pout, he gave in. "The in-flight magazine said it was founded as a Jesuit mission in the eighteenth century and remained more or less a hamlet until the rubber boom."

"Rubber boom?"

"Started about 1870, but really kicked in during the 1880s. In ten years, Iquitos went from a population of little more than a thousand to twenty thousand. It was all over by 1912."

"Pretty short boom."

"I dunno. The California gold rush only lasted eight years."

"So how did it end?"

"Some British creep stole rubber tree seeds and set himself up in Malaysia where labor and transportation costs were cheaper. The whole industry moved there."

"Too bad." She looked out the window. "We have all day here. Let's explore."

They ambled along dusty streets lined with crumbling stucco storefronts painted in shades of green and pink. Quaint three-wheeled buggies swarmed the lane, jostling each other. The place had a fin de siècle air—the shabby elegance of dimly remembered glory. "It looks like it went downhill fast after the rubber boom."

"Yes, but it's regained some prosperity as a

jumping-off point for eco-lodges. Extremely popular with the hardier globe trotters." He broke off. "Joaquín said people come for some kind of hallucinogenic drug ceremony, too."

"Well, aging hippies gotta keep busy, don't they? What about where we're going? Is it an eco-lodge too?"

"No. Pacaya was originally a vacation home for a fellow named Wittersmith, but it was so remote he decided to turn it into a research station. He lets teams of scientists come down and stay, for a hefty fee."

"Does he still own it?"

"As far as I know."

They passed the docks, crammed with every kind of boat from large yachts to dugout canoes, then strolled along the corniche until the sun drove them into a cool café. A native family, dressed in startlingly colorful shirts and skirts, sat next to them sipping from bottles of a familiar shape.

"That's not Coca-Cola. What are they drinking?"

Nick glanced at the sickly yellow liquid. "Moche Kola. Very popular."

"Oh." Petra took the brochure she'd picked up at the hotel from her purse. "Maybe when we come back through we can take a tour. I want to see the Iron House."

"Iron House?"

"It says here the Casa de Fierro is the most famous structure in Iquitos. It's constructed entirely of iron panels. Local gossip has it the guy who built the Eiffel Tower designed it."

"Well, well. How did it end up in the Peruvian Amazon?"

"Good question." Petra read on. "It doesn't say."

"Well, you're the librarian—look it up."

"Remind me."

As the sun went down, they headed back to the hotel. Family groups and couples lingered on the esplanade, enjoying the last glimmerings of the sunset on the broad expanse of muddy water. It seemed strange to Petra to think that this jam-packed city could be so isolated, surrounded by vast jungles and waterways. *Rather like the Emerald City of Oz.*

Later, after supper in the hotel, she gazed out her window at the lights of the city. If she craned her neck, she could see boats floating past at the end of the street. *Tomorrow I will have my first brush with the great and powerful Amazon. Will she be a good witch or a bad witch?*

****

October 5

Early the next morning, Joaquín drove them to the docks. A launch about thirty feet long was tied up at the far end. He helped Petra on, and they motored out of the bay to the Amazon, then headed downriver. About five hours later, he turned the boat into a small tributary. On the far shore, an old sternwheeler listed on its side, stuck on a sand bar. Its elaborate scrollwork railings were rusted, and the white and red paint faded. Nick pointed at it. "I heard that ship was in a famous movie."

They headed south in the narrow channel. The jungle grew almost to the river's edge, huge trees and vines looming over them, scraping the boat's sides. The current ran fast, deep brown with silt.

Joaquín nodded at the riverbanks. "There are three types of forest in the Amazon. This is called *varzea* forest. It grows along our swift-moving rivers." He pointed at a gorgeous purple flower peeking from a branch. "Lots of air plants, lots of orchids. Many types of trees like the kapok, the Brazil nut, the mahogany. You find the *igapo* forest near the blackwater lakes."

"And the third?"

"The third is the dry upland forest. We call it *terra firme*."

"So do we." Petra laughed.

A troop of monkeys passed them, swinging along from tree to tree and screeching. Joaquín looked up. "Squirrel monkeys."

Nick shaded his eyes. "Sure are a lot of them."

The cries of the animals grew distant, and they motored in silence for a few minutes. Though the forward movement of the boat produced a tiny breeze, the humidity ground into Petra. "This is hotter than DC in August." She trailed her hand in the cool water.

"I wouldn't do that if I were you, sis."

"Why?"

Nick stifled the titter. "Piranhas."

She tore her hand out of the water. "Not funny, bro."

Around a bend, a large clearing opened up on the east bank. Several thatched-roof buildings clustered in the packed-earth yard, connected by long, covered walkways. A boardwalk led down to a wooden dock.

As the launch pulled up, a bare-chested man wearing nothing but a pair of cotton shorts ran toward them waving his arms madly. "Mr. Nick! Mr. Nick!"

Nick jumped off the boat and held his hand out for Petra. "What is it, Winston?"

"Come quick. Mr. Lewis…it's Mr. Lewis! Hurry!"

Joaquín called. "I have put your luggage on the dock. Good luck!" He reversed the boat and headed back upriver.

The two strode up the steps after Winston, Petra barely having time to take in the tapirs—large gray animals resembling baby hippos—grazing on the bank, and the blue-and-yellow macaws infesting a huge kapok tree in the center of the yard. She almost stepped on a toucan pacing the top step.

Winston swept the bird aside. "Get out of the way, Molly. Stupid bird."

He led them into a small lobby and down one of the covered walkways to a second building. Petra glimpsed a modern laboratory through one door. Winston stopped at the next room. It was filled with men. They sidled in. Nick put a hand on the shoulder of one young fellow, a blond whose pink face was covered in freckles. "Alex?"

Alex pointed to a man with a crewcut and heavy five-o'clock shadow who knelt by a figure lying on the bed. "Aguirre brought him inside." The man looked up, his eyes red-rimmed. "It's Lewis."

Nick whispered, "It's Lewis Gordon, the doctor."

Petra looked over his shoulder and sucked in a ragged breath. There wasn't much left of the man. His cheeks had been torn off, leaving bloody hollows. One arm was gone, and his stomach ripped open. Whatever had done this had taken—*eaten?*—the organs, so the cavity was almost clean.

"He didn't die in here, did he?"

"No." Winston spoke behind them. "I pulled him from the river. Many, many piranhas feeding."

Nick shook his head. "Piranhas don't usually kill

humans."

Now he tells me.

"No. They are carrion feeders. Mr. Lewis—he already dead when they started on him."

"But how?"

He shrugged. "Maybe jaguar. Maybe caiman."

Alex spoke up. "Not a caiman."

He must be the herpetologist.

A tall, powerful-looking man who had been standing silently at the foot of the bed added, "Nor a jaguar. Either one would have dragged the corpse away to feed on at its leisure."

Nick turned to him. "Then it's a good thing I asked my sister to join us, Emory. This is Petra Steele. She's a reference librarian—one of the best."

The man nodded absently.

Under the circumstances, Petra didn't expect her presence to be paid much attention.

On the other hand, her brother seemed to feel the need for additional clarification. "I thought, since we all have such diverse backgrounds, she can pull different disciplines together and help in our research."

Emory tore his eyes from the corpse and looked her up and down. Something—interest?—gleamed in his eyes but was quickly snuffed out. "Okay, Miss Steele. You can start by finding out what eats human organs and cleans up after itself."

There was a commotion at the door. Winston made room for a pudgy fellow of about sixty, whose skin had obviously not felt the sun in years. He wore crackling new safari gear and flip-flops. He approached the bed. "We've got to get him out of here."

Everyone goggled. "What on earth do you mean,

John?"

"We can't have anyone find him at the lodge."

"Are you saying you want to hide him?"

"How do you propose to move him?"

The questions gradually died down, and they were staring blankly at the corpse when Petra decided to take charge. "First things first. Are any of you doctors?"

No one answered. Finally, the tall man named Emory said, "Lewis was the doctor."

"Then we need to call one."

A short man in a khaki uniform came in. "Miss Steele? I have put your suitcase in your room. I can escort you there if you like." His flattened, dark features identified him as a local native, but unlike Winston, he spoke perfect English. His diction indicated a university education.

Nick interrupted impatiently. "Never mind that now, Hector. We need a doctor."

"The closest doctor is in Nauta. I can radio him."

The pudgy man named John intervened. "No! We don't want any bad press, Hector."

Emory huffed. "Don't be absurd. How's it going to hurt the institute? Lewis was killed by some kind of predator. It's not our fault."

Institute? Oh yes, the Institute for Tropical Research.

John inspected the body. "You sure it was an animal that killed him?"

Alex cried, "What else could it be? We're way out here in the sticks. You think some random killer is wandering around knocking people off?"

The older man scratched his head. "I dunno. Could be one of those native ritual executions…or maybe the…you know." He gave Petra a sly glance. "I mean, look at his gut."

Hector made a garbled sound. Emory put up a hand. "*Ribereños* aren't cannibals, last I checked. But we should probably call the police as well." He pulled out a cell phone and tapped it. "It's not working."

Alex did the same. "Neither is mine."

John started to speak, but Nick interrupted. "You need a special chip for the signal to work out here in the jungle. Here, I have—" He patted his pockets. "Now, where…?"

"We all have the cards." Emory began to fiddle with his phone. "It should still be good. I—"

Aguirre rose from his knees. "Never mind, John's right. We can't afford any attention. Not now…" He stopped. For the first time, he seemed to focus on Petra. "Who are you?"

Nick laid a protective hand on her shoulder. "Maybe you weren't listening, Tramposo. This is my sister Petra. I asked her to come help with the…research."

Tramposo took a step toward Nick. "You *told* her?"

"Not everything, but we'll need her skills. Until Ffoulkes gets here, we've got what—me, a photographer, and you"—he pointed at Emory—"an ornithologist. Alex is a herpetologist, Aguirre only knows plants, and John here is…" The words were clear if unspoken. *Of no use at all.*

Hector fidgeted. "Then what do you want me to do?"

The others faced the body on the bed. At that moment, a bell sounded. "It'll have to wait." Alex headed toward the door.

Petra whispered to Nick, "Where's he going?"

"Lunch."

"*What?*"

The rest began to file out. Nick held Petra back. "If we're late to a meal, Capac—he's the cook—refuses to serve us."

"But...but what about"—she gestured—"him?"

He shrugged. "He'll keep."

Petra, wiping her forehead for the tenth time with a now-wringing-wet handkerchief, wasn't so sure. *When in Rome, I guess.* She followed her brother down the hall.

She found a spot at the end of the long table and prepared to study her new companions. The fat fellow ate quickly, his chin nearly touching the plate. *He's the institute official...John Dillinger.* She wondered fleetingly why they needed a communications fellow out here in the wilderness—especially one who seemed so publicity shy. Next to him sat the hawk-nosed fellow. *Aguirre. Aguirre Tramposo. What kind of a name is that?* He spoke with a Spanish accent, larded with a slight Midwest twang. *Must have lived in the States for some period. And what a schnozz!* Big as an anteater's, with a curved tip that could double as a can opener. That brought her to the fresh-faced, freckled Alex. *Can't remember his last name. He's rather sweet. What does he do? Oh, yes, reptiles.* She'd always had a fancy for snakes. *Maybe we'll see an anaconda.* An anticipatory tingle went down her spine.

The ranger Hector wasn't at the table, nor was Winston. She wondered if the staff had separate quarters. Her glance swung past Nick to the big man—

Emory Andrews, wasn't it? *Nice name.* She examined him. Early fifties, she guessed. Just a touch of silver at the temples, the rest a full head of thick, black hair. Tanned. His large hand grasped the fork a bit clumsily, as though he were more used to holding bulky objects. A rifle? No, he was the ornithologist. *Probably binoculars.*

He must have sensed her scrutiny, for a side of his mouth turned up. He said sternly, "Can I help you, Miss Steele?"

She took a quick bite. "Delicious. This is ceviche, right? But it's got a different flavor from the ones we had in Lima."

Alex answered. "There are thousands of versions of ceviche. Depends on whatever fish the cook caught this morning."

She took another bite. "So what kind of fish is in this one?"

He grinned. "Piranha."

There was a general gasp. Petra realized that, for the past half an hour, she hadn't thought of the dead man once.

Finally, Emory said, his voice shaking a little, "Why don't we consider this as simple justice?"

She watched as the others struggled between amusement and shame. *Emory has a sense of humor— macabre though it may be.* She watched him eat. He seemed to savor every bite, as though he'd missed too many meals and appreciated the ones he had time for. He sipped the beer rather than gulping it down like the rest of the guys. At one point, he put down his fork and rubbed his lip pensively. She wondered if he were contemplating their next steps. *Didn't Nick say everyone looked to him as the leader?* She dredged up the study of physiognomy she'd been reading during her last bout with the flu. *Strong chin—thank God, no dimple.* Tendrils of dark hair almost hid his widow's peak. *Let's see—widow's peak means intelligence and breeding. Strong chin? Either perseverance or obstinacy.*

She was on her second warm beer—"Just pretend you're in England, sis"—when Hector came rushing in.

"What is it?"

"The police! The police are coming."

Chapter Three
Living Laboratory

October 5

"The police!" John glowered at Hector. "Did you call them?"

"No! You said not to. I don't know what they're doing here."

"How close are they?"

"Still half an hour away. My cousin Luis told me they're coming from the police substation in Nauta." He faltered. "I…uh…I did send for Don César."

"Don César?" Aguirre seemed confused. "Who's he?"

"He's the local shaman."

"What!"

"What do we need him for?"

No one seemed happy at this news except Petra, who felt her interest piqued. *A shaman! A real native witch doctor…Will he be naked? Or wear a necklace of shrunken heads?* Visions of scalp locks and tattoos swirling in her head, she barely heard Nick.

"Perhaps he'll be able to tell us what caused Lewis's death."

Aguirre laughed unpleasantly. "Great, he can chant and burn smelly plants. Maybe dance around the corpse jiggling shrunken heads on a stick."

Aha, see? It's not just me. She regarded Aguirre with approval.

Hector coughed. "Our shamans train in the arts of healing for many years. They know the flora and fauna of the rainforest better than anyone alive. Don César is a *banco ayahuasquero*—a master shaman. He is very skilled." His mouth set in a prim line. "We here in Peru do not shrink heads. At least, not anymore."

Ulp.

Aguirre said something under his breath.

Alex piped up. "What about the body? Should we leave it on the bed? Hide it from the police?" He looked toward John.

Emory wrinkled his nose. "He's already been exposed to the air far too long." He glanced at Petra. "The police will only have to follow the aroma to discover him."

John jumped up. "It doesn't matter. Let's hide it, at least until we hear what they want."

Nick ventured, "We could put him in the lab refrigerator."

Emory nodded, but the others chorused a loud "No!"

Aguirre whined, "I have specimens in there. There's one flower I think may be a new variety of bromeliad."

Alex added anxiously, "And I have two caiman eggs cooling. They were almost ready to hatch. I want to see if lowering the temperature at this juncture in the incubation period will have an effect on the sex."

"And what about my bottle of Stolichnaya?" This last question probably did not have the effect John anticipated. "What? I was going to share it during the celebration."

Petra surprised everyone by asking, "Celebration? What celebration?"

Aguirre glared at Nick. "I can't believe you brought her here."

"I told you—"

Hector interrupted. "Excuse me, but what shall we do about the police? The shaman cannot come until tomorrow."

Emory rapped the table. "Here's a crazy idea. We tell them the truth."

The sound of a motorboat pulling into the pier brought them to their feet.

****

Hector came up the steps, wiping the back of his neck. "They say they're looking for a fugitive, a *ribereño* who has been breaking into hotel rooms and stealing identification papers and valuables. He's wanted in Iquitos."

"Did you say anything about Lewis?"

"No." He looked at Emory, the question clear.

For answer, the big man strode down to the police launch. The officer listened to him, his face impassive. Finally, he followed Emory back to the lodge. In stilted but fluent English, he said, "I am Detective Montoya of the Iquitos police. May I see the body?"

After a cursory inspection, he left, coming back with his men and a stretcher. "We shall take him back with us."

"Do you want us to accompany you?"

He shook his head. "I will return after he's been examined." He surveyed their worried faces. "I shall have questions. Please do not leave the area."

Petra felt a chill at the back of her neck, a strange feeling in the stifling heat. They returned to the dining hall. Without a word, John went to the lab and retrieved his bottle of vodka. They passed it around, not bothering with glasses.

Alex put down the bottle. "You know, it may be for the best."

"Why?"

"It's out of our hands now. The police will take care of Lewis. We can get on with our research."

"What about Lewis's family?"

John answered. "I'll contact them. I believe he's only got a brother—his wife passed away several years ago."

"Let me. I'm the one who found him." Aguirre seemed eager.

"No, it'll be quicker if I do it. I can get the address from my files in Florida."

Alex took a swig. "What are we going to do about a doctor? Lewis wasn't just a specialist in tropical diseases. He was our whole medical staff. Where are we going to find a replacement?"

"Is it all that necessary to replace him?" Aguirre cocked his head toward the lab. "He wouldn't have been much use in our study of…you know."

Before Petra could ask what he referred to, Emory cut in. "We should at least have someone here with medical training in case of an emergency."

Nick said, "There's always the shaman." When no one responded, he said earnestly, "No, I mean it. Hector said he's well versed in jungle cures."

Emory scratched his chin. "Nick may have a point. We're only going to be here for five more months. I say

38

we make do. We can't afford to lose precious time looking for a new team member."

"Besides, we're all booked up as it is," said Alex. "Since we had to vacate a spot for Nick's sister, Lewis and I were stuffed like sardines in that little room."

"Agreed." They finished the vodka.

Petra put a hand on Nick's arm. "It's been a long day. Can someone show me where I'm bunking?"

"Oh, sorry! Here, follow me." He took her to a small room with a cot, a desk, and a chair. A sink and an open shower stall took up one corner. "I know you're not used to such luxurious surroundings, Petra, so don't let it spoil you."

Petra put her suitcase on the bed. "As long as that shower works, it'll do."

"Be prepared, then."

"What do you mean?"

Nick grinned. "You'll see. Let me know if you need anything. Will you be at dinner?"

Fatigue melted Petra's muscles. She caught the back of the chair with an unsteady hand. "I'm awfully tired after all the travel. Would it be possible to get a tray with a sandwich or something?"

"Already with the royal demands? Yes, I'll ask—or rather, beg—Capac to put something together for you, but don't get used to it. See you tomorrow."

As Petra said goodnight to her brother, Hector came down the walkway. She stopped him. "When does the shaman arrive?"

"Tomorrow. Late afternoon."

"Oh. Well." *I hope I didn't come all this way just to sit around and twiddle my thumbs.* "Perhaps I can spend some time working on my book." The prospect didn't appeal. She sighed.

Hector smiled. "I am leading some of the team on a hike through the rubber tree forest in the morning. If you like, you can come with us."

"Rubber trees!" Petra had a fleeting image of trees bending and swaying like air dancers at a car dealership. "What are they like?"

"Very tall. A hundred years ago, this region was blanketed by rubber plantations."

Nick leaned in. "I told her about the rubber boom."

"I'll show you how the workers tapped the trees for the sap." Hector's brow darkened. "Very hard work. It was a terrible time for our people." He blinked away the gloom. "Also, Winston saw a family of pygmy marmosets in a Brazil nut tree. We might catch a glimpse of them."

"Marmosets?"

Nick whistled. "I read about them. The pygmy marmoset is the smallest monkey in the world! Very rare."

"Sounds wonderful. When do we leave?"

"Six a.m."

Well, it's better than four.

****

October 6

The next day dawned just as hot and humid as the first. Petra had always disliked being hot—hated how it made her feel dirty and heavy. As she passed the door to the kitchen on her way to the dining room, the cook beckoned her. She went reluctantly, wondering if his reputation as a drill sergeant extended beyond meal hours. *Better try to humor him.* "Thank you so much for the tray, Capac."

"I happy to accommodate the lovely señorita." He caught her arm and, with a wink, cackled, "Before you go on your hike, Miss Petra, come find me. I have a gift for you."

Twenty minutes later, she poked her head in. "What is it, Capac?"

He opened the refrigerator and pulled out a frozen bottle of water. "*Shh*. Don't let the others know. For ladies only."

She held it against the back of her neck and sighed. "Thank you, Capac. Right now, this is more precious than diamonds."

Nick, Emory, and Alex were already on the pier. "Where are the others?"

"Aguirre is repotting orchids. John never comes on our outings."

"What does he do all day, then?"

"I think he writes press releases or reports or something for the institute."

Emory laughed. "Actually, he spends most of his time fending off the monkeys."

"Which ones?"

"All of them—squirrel, capuchin, spider—even the howlers. They hang around him—"

"And on him—"

"All day. It's weird. It's like he's monkey candy."

Alex chortled. "Or maybe he has particularly delectable fleas."

Petra looked back toward the lodge just as John appeared in the doorway. A tiny brown monkey immediately leapt from the roof, landing on his head. He tried to shake it off, but it hung on for dear life. Emory said, "Spider monkey. There's a whole family of them living under the lodge. Capac feeds them."

Petra watched John struggling. "It almost seems like the little thing was lying in wait."

Emory answered. "Yup. They love to leap out and surprise him."

The monkey finally sprang off, and John, possibly shocked at the sudden departure, fell over.

They crossed the gangplank onto the launch and motored about a mile to a spot on the west bank. Petra sat in the bow, watching the changing landscape avidly. Emory moved up to stand beside her. She could feel his eyes on her. *Why is he watching me?* The effect was disconcerting. "Did you want something, Mr. Andrews?"

"Emory. How much do you know about the Amazon, Miss Steele?"

"Only what I've read. And please, call me Petra."

He didn't respond. After a minute, he walked back to the stern and sat down next to Hector.

What was that all about?

Hector threw an anchor out and tied the bow rope of the launch to an overhanging tree. "This is dry forest from here—what we call *terra firme*."

"Yes, Joaquín described it."

They marched in single file along a path only Hector could see. When Petra held up an arm to brush a twig out of the way, he caught her hand. "What's the matter?"

He pulled a pencil from his pocket and prodded the twig. It moved.

"Oh my God, it's alive. Is it a praying mantis?"

"A walking stick." He prodded it again and the insect—which revealed itself to be a full foot long—

jumped to another branch. She watched it freeze again, turning back into a piece of the woodwork.

Hector stopped before an enormous, straight-trunked tree. "Here we have a fully mature rubber tree. *Hevea brasiliensis*. Quick-growing, it can reach heights of a hundred feet or more."

"So this was the source of all the frenzy."

"Yes. A nineteenth-century explorer noticed that the natives here wore ponchos and hats that seemed to slough off the rain. They showed him how to insert a small pipe into the tree to siphon off the sap, called latex."

Nick took up the narrative. "The substance made its way to Europe, where entrepreneurs started making tires, tubes, even shoes out of it. But they soon discovered it melted in the summer heat and hardened and cracked in the cold. The fledgling industry was on its last legs until—"

"Until Mr. Charles Goodyear added sulfur to the latex in 1839, and the industrial revolution took off." Hector pointed at a round mark on the tree. "You can still see the tap holes."

Petra raised her eyebrows. "The holes never heal? Does tapping kill the tree?"

"It does no harm if done properly." He took a penknife and cut a small sliver of bark away. Immediately a stream of milky white liquid began to seep out.

Alex chirped, "Just like tapping maple trees."

"Right, only the labor conditions weren't quite so pleasant." Hector shaded his eyes. "The *caucheros*—"

"*Caucheros*?"

"The rubber barons. They hired men from the West

Indies called *muchachos*, who sent the natives into the jungle for months at a time to tap the latex. It was backbreaking work, and they were severely punished if they didn't return with enough latex."

"Were they paid?"

"A pittance. It was basically slave labor. Many died."

Petra sighed. "Maybe it wasn't such a bad thing that the industry moved to Malaysia."

Alex wiped some of the sap from the tree. "What did they do with the latex?"

"It would be shipped downriver to the Atlantic ports. Iquitos's most famous son, Fitzcarrald, found a shorter route for the boats, saving much time and effort."

Petra was struck by the odd name. She whispered to Nick, "Fitzcarrald?"

"*Shh*. I'll tell you later." He pointed at their guide. Hector had halted at a tall tree with large pods hanging from the canopy of branches at the top. He put a finger to his lips before pointing upward.

Petra couldn't see anything but leaves.

He whispered, "Wait for them…"

After about five minutes, she saw a tiny face peek out of a hole in the tree. A fuzzy, gray-brown animal with huge eyes climbed out onto a limb, followed by two more. No more than five inches long, one would fit comfortably in the palm of a hand. "Are they the monkeys you talked about?"

"Pygmy marmosets. Very shy."

They watched the little animals frolic in the tree above them until Hector called them away. "Time to get back. Don César should have arrived by now."

Petra regarded their guide. Hector was clearly well educated and just as clearly raised in the rainforest. He could identify every plant, every insect, every mammal. He seemed to know his environment intimately. "Hector? May I ask you a question?"

"Yes?"

"Does your family live here? Along the river?"

He hesitated. "Yes. I was born and raised two miles from here, in the village of Nuevo Loreto. It's on the Ucayali River."

"But you went to college?"

"I went to University of Lima. I have a doctorate in biology."

Impressive. "Was this your first position?"

"No, no. I worked for the Forestry and Wildlife Agency in Lima for three years, but after an injury"— he pointed at his leg—"I was relegated to a desk job. That did not suit me." He gave her a wry smile. "I met Señor Wittersmith when he applied for a permit to open his vacation home for research groups. He invited me to join the staff as a field guide."

"It must be nice to be so close to your family."

His mouth twisted. "In a way. It is hard to remain single when you have so large a family. I get little peace when I'm with them. It is good that I have my own quarters at the lodge."

She racked her brain for anything she knew about Peruvian kinship but came up empty. "Are you required to marry a relative?"

"No, although they would like that. I would prefer someone who has traveled, who has some education…"

"Someone you can talk to. I understand." She gazed around her at the dense jungle. *I wish him luck.*

When they reached the station, a wiry old man in shorts and a torn T-shirt squatted by the steps, feeding a squirrel monkey. He rose in one fluid motion. He was thin as a sapling, his ribs poking through the holes in his shirt. Hector bowed to him. "Don César." He introduced the others.

Petra checked out the man's leathery, shriveled face and bald head and sighed. *As close to a shrunken head as we'll get, I suppose.*

Don César looked inquiringly at Hector.

The ranger led the way into the lounge, where Aguirre sat reading a book. Emory went to a side table. "The police took the body to Iquitos, but we have photographs of the dead man. Will you take a look at them?"

He handed the old man one of the pictures. His eyes widened. "This is Dr. Gordon!"

"I told you it was," said Hector.

"You only said one of your team had died." The shaman gazed sadly at the photo. "Dr. Gordon was a friend to the *ribereños* and was quickly learning the ways of our forest. I was readying him for the *ayahuasca* ceremony. It is with sorrow that I will inform Don Bernardo and the others."

Alex scratched his ear. "*Ayahuasca?*"

Hector took him aside. Petra drew near to hear. "It's a ritual in which you drink a potion made from the *ayahuasca* vine and other plants. It is a native method for cleansing the body and the mind."

Aguirre evidently overheard Hector and snorted. "You make it sound like a dose of castor oil. In fact, it's an extremely painful purgative coupled with hallucinogenic nightmares. Like a combination of an

LSD overdose and amoebic dysentery, only worse."

Hector glared at him. "You must, of course, have the properly prepared frame of mind for it to work. When applied by an experienced shaman like Don César, you will come away with your body purified and your soul healed of its troubles."

The shaman held a finger to his lips. "Please, I need quiet." He held his hand out for the other photos and studied them carefully before looking up. "Poison."

Chapter Four
Biodiversity

October 6

Everyone spoke at once. "Poison?"

"Are you saying he was poisoned?"

"With what?"

Don César replied, "*Ourare*."

"What's that?"

Aguirre interjected, "I think that's the local term for curare."

"Correct. See there?" The shaman pointed at the picture of Lewis.

Petra noted the wide-open mouth and staring eyes. "It's as though he was gasping for air."

"He was. *Ourare* contains an alkaloid that paralyzes your muscles. When the poison reaches your lungs, they seize up. You are unable to breathe and die of asphyxiation."

"Does it affect all of your muscles?"

"All."

Emory spoke up. "I guess that's why, when I tried to move his arm, it was as rigid as a steel beam."

Nick looked thoughtful. "Wait. Isn't curare the arrow poison?"

Hector answered him. "Yes. It is made from the bark of the *ourare* vine, but it doesn't have to be applied to an arrow to be effective. If you merely rub against the vine with an open wound, the poison can enter your system."

Aguirre added, "The plant he is talking about is called *Chondrodendron tomentosum*. It is a vigorous shrub that can climb as far as thirty meters up into the canopy." He gazed out the window toward the river. "On the day of his death, Lewis told me he was going up the river to study an uncommon variety of *Ficus* for potential medicinal uses. He may have touched the plant inadvertently."

"Or maybe on purpose—say, to get a sample." Emory looked at the shaman. "Does curare have any therapeutic value?"

"Some, but the toxic dose is so close to the pharmacological dose that it's easy to overdo it."

"So it must have been an accident."

Petra turned to Don César. "How long would it take for the poison to take effect?"

"It could take a while if it penetrated the skin through a small scratch. Death occurs much more quickly when you are struck by an arrow."

"Ah…" She pursed her lips. "So he might not have noticed it right away. He could have gotten into the dugout and started paddling home before it hit him."

"Possibly."

"Which would explain why Winston found him in the water."

Emory nodded. "Looks that way. However it got into his system, it eventually caused total paralysis. He fell out of the boat, and the piranhas bellied up to the buffet."

Petra rolled her eyes. "You certainly have a way

with words, Emory."

"What about his stomach cavity?" Aguirre turned to Don César. "Any idea what would have eaten the organs?"

The shaman shook his head. "I'd have to see the body, but the stomach could have been washed clean by the current. Or maybe"—he winked—"it was the Mapinguari." He gave the photographs back to Hector. "I must go. My apprentice, Acarapi"—he nodded to Winston—"is waiting for me."

Petra turned her gaze to Winston, who said proudly, "My oldest son."

The shaman boarded his canoe and poled away from the dock. Petra wiped the perspiration off her forehead and looked longingly at the brown water. "I don't suppose it's safe to swim?"

"Sure! It's fine. The fish are likely full—they won't need to feed for a while."

"Emory!"

"Just kidding. You'd have to be dead and bloated for them to want to eat you."

Petra was by now almost used to his little jokes and turned her attention to Hector.

"Yes, miss, it's perfectly safe. And cool!"

She went back to her room to put on her bathing suit and returned to the pier.

Emory sat on a bench by the water. "I'll keep an eye on you."

"No need."

"All right, I'll be honest—I'm hoping to see pink dolphins. Winston told me a pair was playing here yesterday."

"Oh, how wonderful! Are they really pink?"

"Uh-huh."

She surveyed the rushing river. *He's yanking my chain. They're probably not here...or not really pink.* Just as she stepped onto the ladder, he mumbled something.

"What was that?"

"Also, a couple of black caimans. Big ones."

She decided to ignore him and slipped into the cool, silty water. It felt so good on her burning skin. She held onto the ladder and kept her mouth closed to avoid swallowing any. Hector may have asserted it was safe, but who knew what floated in those chocolate depths?

Emory kicked his bare toes in it and watched her. "So, Nick tells me you're a librarian. What kind?"

"Reference."

"Ah. A dilettante. You must be pretty dispensable."

"I'm on leave from the University of Chicago."

He grunted. "Don't see why a librarian needs a vacation. It's such a restful job."

Typical scientist. He probably doesn't think any profession is as important as his own. "On the contrary. I have to deal with continuous unrealistic and inappropriate requests from the other departments. Particularly the hard sciences."

"Ow, that smarts."

She looked him over. Under the ebony hair tinged with silver glittered piercing green eyes and a mobile mouth. His broad shoulders strained at the thin material of his shirt. *Not bad-looking.* Good thing she was out of the mating pool. After George left her at the altar, she'd given up on finding a good man. *At any rate, the only ones available for a forty-year-old woman are usually divorced—and usually for a good reason. Still, I'm not going to ruin it by telling him why I took a sabbatical. Nobody needs to know about George.* Nick was sworn to silence. "What's your specialty?"

"I'm an ornithologist."

"Oh, that's right. Nick told me. How did you get into that?"

"Bass ackward."

"Pardon me?"

"I mean, my father loved to go bird-watching and dragged me and my sister along with him. We spent every spring and fall at the Chincoteague National Wildlife Refuge to watch the migrations. He'd roust us up at dawn to traipse through muddy swamps and sun-burnt fields in the vain hope of seeing some accidental gnatcatcher. Cathy and I used to tease him by pointing at a tree and yelling, 'Hey, look, Dad. It's something different!' He'd swing his binoculars to the tree and stand there like an idiot for maybe ten minutes, searching for a nonexistent bird."

"Not very nice of you."

"Hey, we may have had our revenge, but he had the thrill of the hunt." He swatted at a fly. "Once, on a road trip, we had to listen to a two-hour tape of warbler songs. 'Bout near killed me. Ruined my sister's life."

"How?"

"After the first hour, she got carsick, and from then on she couldn't ride in a car. Had to take the bus or train everywhere. Very expensive."

"You're kidding, right?"

"Duh. But it's true that to this day she loathes birds."

I can't tell if he thinks he's funny, or if he's just a

jerk. Still, she wanted to know more about the man...*not because he's handsome, or mysterious. Just natural curiosity.*

"How'd you end up in ornithology, then?"

"I guess I'm just contrary. Besides, it made my father happy."

When he didn't elaborate, she moved on. "What's your line of research?"

"For the past ten years, I've been working on migration routes—the Pacific and the Central Flyways."

"Huh. Why are you here, then? As far as I know, neither ends in the Peruvian Amazon."

The remark seemed to annoy him. "How the hell would you know?"

She was ready with her answer. *"Random House Atlas of Bird Migration.* Jonathan Elphick. I was helping a grad student with his thesis. Also, I'm an amateur birdwatcher myself."

Her response seemed to vex him even more. "Armchair quarterback. Pathetic."

"Oh, *real* mature." *He must be one of those cranks with a stick up his rear about librarians.* Petra decided to swim a bit. As she kicked off, keeping her head above water, she had a pleasant thought. *Maybe one dumped him.*

When she returned to the dock, he leaned down. "Sorry. That was uncalled for. Didn't get much sleep last night, after Lewis..."

"Were you close?"

"No. In fact, I didn't know any of these guys until a month ago."

"Really? How did you hook up with them?"

"Long story. I was giving a lecture at the ITR—"

"The what?"

"The Institute for Tropical Research."

"Oh, right. That's the research group sponsoring this expedition."

"Yes. Anyway, the director—Denys Ffoulkes—approached me. I…er…happened to be…between commitments, so I climbed on the wagon."

"What's the project?"

He squinted and looked over her head at the far bank. "There's always something to discover in the Amazon. I'm here to look for new species. Over forty have been found in the Peruvian Amazon in just the last thirty years. I aim to find me one."

"Seems to me there are enough already. Nick said there were more than five hundred species of birds in this region alone. He talked about one…what was it called? The hua, the hua—"

"The hoatzin?"

"That's it. What makes it so interesting?"

"Well, for one thing, it might have been put together by two chimpanzees and a robot."

"Excuse me?"

"Let me explain. Its body is about the size and shape of a turkey but with a tiny head bobbling on top. Add in a sky-blue face and a bald pate, topped off by this dorky little crest. Oh, and the tail is as big as a peacock's. Looks more like one of those flying dinosaurs than a bird."

Nick said Aguirre had found a fossil. I wonder…
"So it's kind of a living fossil?"

"Damn it, no! Everyone always jumps to that conclusion, as though the Jurassic period was still partying away in the middle of the rainforest. Sure, the hoatzin looks primeval, but as far as we know, it's only been around a few hundred years. No one's found any evidence of its connection to the dinosaur age."

Wait—didn't Nick also say, "until now"? What does my brother know that Emory doesn't? "Emory—"

Just then, Alex came running down the slope. "Come on, both of you. Aguirre wants us to come to the lounge."

Emory helped Petra out of the water and handed her a towel. Together, they walked up the steps. She turned toward her room. "I'll meet you there."

She dressed quickly and returned to find the others gathered around a table. She came up behind Nick. "What are you all looking at?"

"A fossil."

"Fossil?"

Nick spoke. "I persuaded Aguirre to show it to us now rather than wait for Denys. He thinks it's a fossilized forebear of the hoatzin."

Sitting on the table was a slab of reddish rock. Petra could just make out ridges and lines on it. Emory gave it a cursory glance. "Nonsense. That's no more an ancient hoatzin than my high school picture is."

"What is it, then?"

He looked more closely. "Looks like a skeleton. I can test it in the lab, but I'd say it's no more than a couple of years old." He pressed a thumb into the stone. "This is just semi-hardened river clay."

"Can you tell what kind of bird it is?"

"Most likely a guan. Or a chicken."

Aguirre huffed. "We all know your reputation, Emory. You're a cynic. I say, let's have Denys take a look at it."

Alex ran his fingers over the slab. "Exactly where did you find it, Aguirre?"

"Upriver. We walked inland from the junction with the Marañón."

"The understory there is really thick. How did you get through?"

"Hector was with me. He'd come across an orchid blooming there that might prove to be previously unrecorded. A *Prosthechea*. Very fragrant."

John pointed at the rock. "Doesn't look like a flower to me."

Aguirre snorted. "I tripped over this. We both immediately recognized it as a fossil. I'm sure Denys will confirm our hypothesis when he gets here."

"When does he arrive?"

"Should be here tomorrow."

"Good. We need to get started on the project."

Petra gave Emory a surprised look. "I thought you were already started. Haven't you been out searching for birds?"

He seemed at a loss. "I…uh…yes, but Ffoulkes has other ideas."

"Huh? I thought you each had your own research?"

Aguirre picked up the stone while Nick fiddled with his camera. John and Emory moved casually away. Alex gazed out the window. Petra had had enough. "Why don't you all tell me why you're really here?"

The quiet was deafening. Finally John cleared his throat. Fixing Petra with an unblinking stare, he said, "The ITR is exploring the possibility of purchasing this station from the owner."

People drifted back. "Yes."

"Yes."

"That's it."

She looked at Nick. "That's a lie."

"No, it's not." Emory spoke defensively. "It's not the only reason, but it *is* one of them."

"Well, then, what is your primary purpose?"

Alex looked for approval from the others before opening his mouth. "We—"

"Help! Help!"

The cook ran in, his eyes wild. He cried shrilly, "*Ayudo! Ayudo! Mi hermano*...my brother...he's gone!"

"What do you mean, gone?"

"He's disappeared."

Chapter Five
Cryptids

October 6

"Who the hell is his brother?"

Winston sidled around the cook into the room. "Capac's brother Manuel is the gardener. He provides us with our fresh vegetables. Capac says he went off to his plot this morning and hasn't come back."

The cook, tears running down his face, cried, "El Chullachaqui ate him. I know it. Manuel found an open space in the woods and planted some bananas there. It must belong to el Chullachaqui. Manuel disrespected him, and he tricked him."

Petra, baffled, turned to Emory. "What's he talking about?"

Emory pressed his lips together. "The Chullachaqui is a local legendary creature. Natives think he lures them to their death in the jungle. Manuel's probably just off on a bender."

"He's a drunk?"

"When these guys go into Nauta, they usually spend their whole paycheck on *chicha*."

"*Chicha?*"

"*Chicha de Jora*. A kind of beer. You wouldn't like it."

Winston tried to console the cook, to no avail.

Capac insisted his brother had angered the forest. "Sachamama, she no help him. Manuel, he never respected her. She sent el Chullachaqui to kill him. I know it!" He went off wailing.

Winston threw up his hands and followed him.

Nick gazed after them, his mouth open. "Does this mean we don't get dinner?"

****

October 7

A long, rather hungry evening passed eventually. By the next morning, Capac had recovered sufficiently to prepare a meal of cornbread and fruit. He dropped platters in the center of the table and left, sniffling. The team had settled on the food like a horde of ravenous bees when Hector and Winston came into the dining room with the cook in tow.

John seemed surprised to see them. "What are you two doing in here?"

The hint of disapproval in his voice struck Petra as rather jarring. *After all, this is their home. Who does he think he is?*

They didn't seem to notice. "We found him."

"Manuel?"

Winston nodded.

"Is he—?"

Hector spoke somberly. "Yes. He's dead."

Winston added, "He was in a clearing, about a half mile from here."

A second death in as many days? How safe is *this place?* "What did he die of?"

It was Winston who replied. "Fright."

The cook began to keen. "I knew it. Manuel was foolish—he defile el Chullachaqui's garden." He staggered off to the kitchen.

The rest gazed after him. Finally, Alex poured himself more coffee and muttered, "He's a nutcase."

Emory replied, "Not necessarily. Consider the power of voodoo, or witchcraft. Playing with a credulous mind can have tragic consequences."

Aguirre hissed, "What rot. I knew Manuel. If he were any dumber, he'd have to be watered once a day. Like Emory said, he probably fell into the river and drowned after a night in Nauta."

Petra stared at him. "Except he didn't drown."

Aguirre did not reply.

Nick asked, "What will happen now?"

Hector answered him. "They'll take his body to his home village."

John plopped a purple passionfruit on his plate and began to cut it up. "None of our concern, then."

"But…" The general lack of interest appalled Petra. "We don't know how he died. What if it was murder?"

"Murder! What a ridiculous thing to suggest!" Aguirre scowled, but there was a hint of fear in his voice.

When she didn't respond, Nick said, "It's because of Lewis."

"But that was an accident."

"Was it?" He gave his sister a side glance. "What if we have a killer on the loose?"

"I don't see any connection between them," John pointed out. "Manuel never came in contact with us. He just dealt with Capac."

"Not here at the station, no." Nick warmed to the debate. "But they were both out in the jungle when they died. They both work with plants. Maybe Manuel also touched the curare vine."

Hector scoffed. "Manuel is a native. He knows this land almost as well as I do. He would not have made such a mistake."

Petra took Hector's arm. "You say he died of fright. What made you think that? How did he look?"

Hector considered. "He lay face down in the middle of the clearing. When we tried to move him, his arms and legs were rigid."

"Simple rigor mortis." Emory picked up his napkin.

"Maybe, but then Winston turned him over." He shivered. "His mouth was wide open—as though he'd died screaming."

Winston added, "And his eyes. His eyes had rolled back into his head."

Aguirre's voice trembled. "Just like Gordon."

The scientists looked at each other. Alex spoke. "We have no one here with the expertise to diagnose cause of death."

Alex stirred. "What about you, Aguirre? You're the botanist."

The Spaniard took a step back. "I'm an orchid specialist. I know nothing about the toxic effects of such plants."

"How about the shaman, then?"

Hector shook his head. "Manuel's family has been feuding with another downriver. Perhaps this was a revenge killing. Don César will not interfere. It is best left to the families."

Emory stood up. "Then we shouldn't get involved either."

The room emptied except for Petra and Nick. She was glad for his company. "Nick, it's about time you told me why I'm really here."

"I can't. Not yet."

"Is it the fossil—or something else? You're keeping something from me."

He placed his palms on the table. "Yes. Like I told you, we can use your help with Aguirre's fossil, but its discovery was unanticipated. The reason Ffoulkes hired me was to document something else. If we find it, we'll need your expertise."

"Library science?"

"Anthropology. Well, both."

"But I only hold a bachelor's degree in anthropology! I'm no expert."

"True, but like I told the others, you have the research skills we need."

She paused. "None of you seemed surprised by the cook's allegation. Is it this chulla…el chacalaca…?"

"El Chullachaqui." He steepled his fingers. "No, no, but it's a good place to start. Can you find out all you can about him?" He lowered his eyes to his plate and spoke casually. "And maybe check out other legendary forest beasts while you're at it?"

"Not until you tell me what this is all about. You people are sneaking around here like you've discovered a secret gold mine…or pirate treasure or something. I don't like being kept in the dark. This had better not be illegal."

Nick started, surprised. "Sis, you wound me! You should know as well as I do that when a scientist is onto something, he likes to hold it close to his chest until he has all his ducks in a row. That's all this is. Trust me."

It's not much, but at least it'll keep me busy.
"Okay, but I don't have to trust any of the others."

"Deal." He grinned.

"You said there's Wi-Fi here. Do you have a laptop I can borrow?"

"I've got an extra netbook in my room. I'll set it up for you."

"While I'm at it, I think I'll do a little research on how a stomach cavity can be cleaned out slick as a whistle."

"I wouldn't spend a lot of time on that. The medical examiner will probably have an answer to that particular mystery."

****

An hour later, Petra sat, chin in hand, in front of the computer. Nick tapped her shoulder. "Anything?"

"Nothing that would explain how Lewis's stomach was cleaned out. Unless you count the monster that apparently sucks people's organs into his stomach."

Nick jerked. "Big guy? Hairy?"

She clicked a few times. "I can't find it now, but yes, I think so. Why? You've seen it?"

He drew back. "No, no. It's just..." He gulped. "Reminded me of Lewis, that's all."

Petra peered at him, but his face had closed down. "Oh, I did learn a new word today."

"Yeah?"

" 'Cryptid.' "

" 'Cryptid.' Sounds like a good clue for a crossword puzzle."

Petra rolled her eyes. "A cryptid is a legendary monster or a supernatural being, but it can also be an animal that's rarely seen, or thought to be extinct—like the Loch Ness Monster or the Yeti. There's a whole field called cryptozoology."

"Huh. So…do any of these so-called cryptids live in the Amazon?"

"Oh, dozens."

"How about our Manuel's nemesis?"

"Yes, indeed. The creature Capac was railing about is called el Chullachaqui. He's a trickster."

"What does that mean?"

"The trickster is a classic mythological figure. You find one in nearly every pantheon and folk tradition. It often takes the form of an animal. Br'er Rabbit in the Uncle Remus tales or the Raven in North American Indian lore. Loki in Norse mythology. The Greek god Hermes. They like to break the rules and often steal things from the gods and bring them to the mortal world."

"Such as?"

"Fire, or daylight. But mostly they spend their time playing pranks on people."

"You mean he's like a pixie or something?"

"Usually meaner. His pranks can be cruel, even deadly."

Nick leaned in. "Is that a picture of the guy? He's got a wooden leg."

"I found two tricksters in Amazonian folklore— one with a wooden leg and one with backward feet. Very interesting."

"Why backward?"

Emory stuck his head through the open door. "Hi, sorry to barge in, but I heard you talking about tricksters. Is that what you'd call the Chullachaqui?"

"Yes. You know anything about him?"

"Only that one or both of his feet face backward to make his victims follow his footprints in the wrong direction. Once they're lost in the jungle, he kills them." At her gesture, he came all the way into the room. "So you think Capac was right? Our Manuel was killed by a trickster?"

"Possibly."

He screwed his eyes shut. "Or someone pretending to be the Chullachaqui. Didn't Hector say there was bad blood between two of the villages downstream? I don't like this. We don't want to get in the middle of a feud. Not while we're—" He stopped and looked at Nick. "We're going to have to tell her."

"We'd better wait for Denys."

"Yes."

Petra bristled. "I'm sitting right here, guys."

Emory spun around and headed back out. "Oh, by the way, he was delayed. He won't arrive till tomorrow." He glanced back at Petra. "He can explain his theory better than I."

No amount of cajoling or threatening would shake Nick, and Petra eventually took herself off to swim in the river. Kicking her feet out, she felt something brush against her. She scrambled for the ladder and hauled herself up. When she turned around, a pink snout rose from the water, followed by a large, liquid eye. "A pink dolphin! Hey! Anybody? Lookee here!"

The animal breached, as if to give her a special show. She sat on the dock marveling at its grace and beauty. *This is an amazing place.* She looked across the river at the canopy alive with multicolored birds, and then over her shoulder at the monkeys playing in the dirt. In the kapok tree, scarlet macaws cracked nuts and bickered. Upriver a few yards, a gray-headed kite swooped close to the bank, snagged a frog, and flew off into the forest.

Such strange, exotic animals. She chuckled. *Not to mention the peculiar assortment of human beings living here.* And those were just the real creatures. There seemed to be a whole host of supernatural ones in the jungle as well. Bigfoot. The Trickster. The Amazonian equivalent of a siren. *What was her name? Iara.* A mermaid who lived in the black rivers and lured men into her bed. That is, unless she was hungry, in which case she ate them. *Wait—isn't there a mythical pink dolphin as well? What did I read?...A shapeshifter, that's it.* It transformed into human form, kidnapped young women, and had its way with them. *Hmm. Seems to be a lot of underwater sex going on.* She heard a shout from the house.

"Hey, Aguirre! Come look at this Amazon whip snake! What a beauty."

"Sure—as long as you have it in a cage."

"No—it's right up there in that palm tree...Oops."

She swung her legs in the water. It might be fun to link each of her fellow scientists to a particular folk character. *Let's see...Nick is of course Br'er Rabbit. Alex? With that fresh face, he must be Jack the Giant Killer. No, wait. Peter Pan. How about Aguirre? Something dark. Rumpelstiltskin? Or the Pied Piper—leading us into trouble? And John—definitely the White Rabbit. What about Emory?* She closed her eyes. *Paul Bunyan?*

****

October 8

To no one's surprise, Thursday turned out to be as

hot and humid as every other day. The institute director was due to arrive about midday. Petra wondered what he would be like. The others seemed to respect him. *What branch of science is he in? I think Nicky said biology.* That covered a lot.

She decided to go down to the dock in hopes of seeing the pink dolphin again. *Maybe he'll sweep me off my feet and down to his enchanted city beneath the waves.*

A horn bleated. The launch appeared around the bend in the river. She could make out a man standing in the stern next to Winston. His bristly sideburns reminded her of a Victorian gentleman. Adding to the effect were his plus fours and houndstooth coat. *He has to be sweltering in that outfit.*

The launch pulled alongside, and the man jumped out. Winston handed him his suitcase, an old-fashioned wooden box with leather straps. When he turned toward the lodge, Petra beheld a short man with a noticeable paunch, a luxuriant head of gray hair, and an equally luxuriant black mustache. *Dyed. Definitely.* He smiled at Petra, revealing a large gap between his front teeth. *My God, it's Terry Thomas.* Petra and Nick had grown up on the old British Ealing Studio comedies starring Thomas and Alec Guinness. It therefore came as a shock when the man opened his mouth and the drawn-out tones of South Boston issued forth.

"You must be Steele's sister. Petra, isn't it? How do you do? I'm Denys Ffoulkes, director of the Institute for Tropical Research." He put the suitcase down and took off his jacket. His shirt was soaked. "Bit warm here, what?"

She followed him up the steps. Emory stood at the

top. He towered over the shorter man. "Denys."

"Emory."

The man brushed past him and into the interior. Petra whispered to Emory, "What's with the English squire act?"

"Oh, he prides himself on his heritage. He claims to be a direct descendent of Charles Darwin." He gazed after the man. "Does a pretty good imitation, don't you think?"

When Ffoulkes appeared again, he was dressed in a bush jacket, khaki pants, and knee-high boots. Petra, seated at the bar nursing a beer, stifled a snicker. *Like something a British army officer would wear on the parade grounds of New Delhi. He only lacks a pipe.*

He called for a sherry and pulled a meerschaum pipe from his pocket, knocking the old tobacco out into an ashtray.

Never mind.

John came in and skipped toward Ffoulkes with his hand out, his face rosy with pleasure. "Professor Ffoulkes! Welcome to—" Just before he reached the director, he tripped over a shoelace and went down. He got up and dusted off his Bermuda shorts. "I'm okay, I'm okay."

Petra felt a twinge of sympathy. *Is he aware that no one was asking?*

Ffoulkes grunted. "Yes, well, hello, Dillinger. Call the rest of the team in, there's a good chap." He dug a leather pouch out from the folds of his jacket.

When they'd gathered, he took a pinch of tobacco from the pouch and tamped it into his pipe before clearing his throat. "I have heard the particulars of Dr. Lewis's death from John. I understand cause of death was accidental contact with a poisonous bush. Most unfortunate."

Petra had expected a long-winded eulogy—*I'll bet he's the kind who loves the sound of his own voice*—but Ffoulkes apparently thought he had adequately disposed of the recent demise of a colleague and could safely move on. *I guess Manuel isn't even worthy of mention.*

"I have deemed it necessary to set aside my substantial duties as Director of the Institute for Tropical Research—"

You can just hear the capital letters.

"—to come here to Pacaya myself in order to monitor your activities. John here"—he turned his head to where the rotund little man hovered—"cannot satisfactorily explain your lack of progress. Have you followed up on the sightings? Communicated with the natives? Where have you explored?" He glared at Nick. "Taken any photos?" When no one responded, he put down the unlit pipe. "May I remind you that a representative from Rook Enterprises is due here in a week with the prototype telescope. Have you put a plan in place to take it into the field? No?" He picked the pipe up again but still didn't put a match to it. Petra wondered if he ever did. "Yes. Well. In light of the lack of feedback, I have decided to lead our expedition myself. After all, we're working through grant money at a great clip, and John here has to justify our expenses to the board." He blinked and, pulling a box of matches from his pocket, spent several minutes trying to light the pipe before laying both pipe and matches down.

Petra watched him. *He's being awfully careful not to look at anyone. I wonder why?*

Alex began to talk, but John interrupted. "Never

mind that. We've found something else—something perhaps as significant, if not more, than the Mapinguari. Aguirre Tramposo—" He broke off and looked around. "Where is he, by the way?"

Alex responded. "He went to Nauta to pick up some supplies for the orchid specimens. He won't be back until tomorrow."

"But Mr. Ffoulkes has to see the fossil right away! Aguirre needs to describe…He needs to show…He—" In his agitation, the poor man actually began to hop.

The director brushed him off like so much dandruff. "That can wait. The Mapinguari is our main concern now."

Petra raised a hand. "Did you say 'Mapinguari'? Don César—the shaman—used that term. What is it?"

There was a short silence. Ffoulkes picked up his pipe again. "Haven't you told her?" When no one answered, he gave Petra a weary look. "The Mapinguari, young lady, is why we are here in this"— he wiped his upper lip—"godforsaken hellhole."

John chirped tentatively, "We thought you might explain it best."

"Ah, of course." He puffed out his chest.

Petra wondered if he'd packed a pith helmet. *Is he going to twirl that mustache?*

"Our original mission was to map this area for new species. However, the possibility of documenting something more…earth-shattering was brought to my attention, and I have decided to concentrate our energies on it."

Earth-shattering. Nick's very words.

"My dear Miss Steele"—he poured more sherry into his glass—"I have tasked this team of experts to search for the Mapinguari—a bloodthirsty creature of enormous size that, according to the locals, is believed to have survived for eons in these parts."

Petra looked at Nick. "A cryptid."

"What's that?"

Nick piped up. "Sasquatch. Mermaids. The Jersey Devil. A creature everyone believes in, but no one's definitively documented."

Denys regarded Petra disapprovingly. "That's not what we're talking about here."

"You're right. Nick's also right." Her voice rose over the ensuing babble. "A cryptid can be any number of fantastic beings—mythical or real. In some cases, what was believed to be a tall tale turned out to exist— for example, the Komodo dragon or the mountain gorilla. When that happens, it tends to bolster optimism that other creatures will be unearthed. Your Mapinguari fulfills several of the criteria. It is unusually large, and it is solitary." She nodded at her brother. "And very few people have glimpsed it."

The rest swarmed around Petra eagerly. "It would be one for the record books!"

"And make any other discoveries seem trivial by comparison."

"We'd be heroes!"

John muttered, "It wouldn't hurt our bottom line, either."

The only one apparently unmoved by the happy prospect was Emory. "Whoa, people. Let's not get ahead of ourselves. We have yet to corroborate any of the rumors."

Petra, caught up in the animated discussion, left him to his scruples and joined in. "When I was researching the Chullachaqui, I came across several other Amazonian cryptids—legendary beasts or paranormal entities. One was the shapeshifting pink dolphin. Another was the jungle equivalent of Bigfoot."

"That's the fellow." Nick's face flushed with excitement. "The natives describe him as very hairy, up to twenty feet tall, with only one eye, and a mouth in his stomach."

"Yes. He swallows people." Petra stared at Ffoulkes. "And you all think he is out there."

"There have been two sightings in the last three months by villagers. One who claims to have seen it is a relative of Hector's."

Petra noted Emory's obstinate expression before pivoting to see Nick's shining eyes. In her experience, when Nick was this enthusiastic it usually ended badly. *Okay, maybe Emory's right. Maybe we should rein this in a bit.* "Only seen? Hasn't he eaten anyone? Or are you thinking this jungle Sasquatch is what killed Dr. Lewis?"

"This is not a joke, Miss Steele. If we find him, it will be the greatest discovery in the history of exploration."

"Actually, I think the Loch Ness monster would beat him out."

Ffoulkes blew out his cheeks. "It would mean grant money and recognition for the institute."

"Or you could be drummed out of academia."

The director slapped his hand on the table, spilling the sherry. "Steele, either get your sister on board or get her out of here." He rose. "I'm going to take a nap."

"Wait! We haven't told you about Aguirre's discovery!" John ran after him. The others followed, leaving Petra and her brother alone. Nick rounded on his sister. She didn't give him a chance to start in on her. "This is one of your more ridiculous schemes, Nick. How did you get yourself sucked into this? It's got to be bunkum."

"Hey, I wouldn't be so quick to judge. Ffoulkes is a biologist. He thinks the Mapinguari may be a hitherto unrecorded species. Oh, not like the monster the natives depict, but something rare, if not unique."

"The man's a blowhard."

"He is also paying me a lot of money to record this expedition."

"Ah. Follow the money."

"Look, all we need you to do is check sources. Enjoy the trip. If we don't find our Yeti, what difference does it make?"

"Fine. I just don't want my name associated with it. The University of Chicago does not look kindly on quacks. I'd never get to go back."

Nick left, and Petra decided to rest a bit. She headed to the round room he had shown her that fronted on the river. Rows of hammocks were strung between bamboo columns. She climbed into one and began to swing. In the sweltering heat, the current of air caused by the movement cooled her down. She lay back and reviewed her situation. *Nick's right. It is a pretty neat place. The food is wonderful and so different. In the last few days, I've seen more wildlife than most people see in their lifetimes. I've swum in the Amazon, for heaven's sake! Plus, I have nothing else to do.* She thought of the tall, quiet man who watched her so much. *Emory is hard to fathom. I don't get the sense he's in it for fame or fortune. Then why? I wonder what*

73

he's searching for? She resolved to ask him the next time they were alone. *While I'm at it, I should ask the others as well.*

She awoke to a pair of green eyes inspecting her. "Mr. Andrews!"

"Emory. *Shh.* Come."

She rolled out of the hammock and followed him to the great bow window that looked out over the dock. On the grassy verge below them, a herd of strange yellow animals grazed. About three feet high at the shoulder, they looked like shaggy Highland cows. "What are they?" she whispered.

"Capybaras. Largest rodent on earth."

"Oh my. They would certainly put my pet guinea pig to shame."

Emory chuckled. "You know they eat guinea pigs here."

"Really? What do they taste like?"

"Chicken."

They watched the animals for a while as twilight fell. Petra relaxed for the first time since she had arrived. She was beginning to appreciate Emory's reticent manner. At first she suspected he wasn't very intelligent, but now she could see he simply didn't suffer fools gladly. *I like his gruffness. There are hidden depths in him.* She eyed his broad shoulders and flat stomach. *The outside ain't too shabby either.*

"Petra?"

"Yes?"

"I thought maybe I'd kiss you."

"Okay." She closed her eyes. He tilted her chin up with a finger. His lips grazed hers lightly. When she opened her eyes, he was gone. She didn't have time to examine her reaction to the kiss before John trotted in. "What are you looking at?"

What was I looking at? Oh, yes. "Capybaras."

He looked out the window. "Look like big hairy pigs. Dinner's ready." He left.

She was the last to arrive. Capac placed a bottle of beer in front of her without asking. Ffoulkes tipped his sherry down his throat.

"I have had an opportunity to study Mr. Tramposo's fossil."

"And?"

"It is not a fossil. It is a skeleton. Recent."

Emory nodded in satisfaction. "A chicken?"

"Possibly."

Nick leaned forward. "Could it be a hoatzin?"

"You mean that strange bird that lives in the swamps? I doubt it."

"But—"

He ignored Nick's protest. "I propose we set it aside for now. Meanwhile...Hector? Can you come in here?"

The ranger stood with his back to the wall, clearly ill at ease. "Yes, Dr. Ffoulkes?"

"Tell them."

Looking at the floor, Hector stuttered, "We found him."

Chapter Six
Ethnic Memories

October 8

Didn't we just hear that?
"Who did you find?"
Alex dropped his fork. "The Chullachaqui?"
"No." Ffoulkes beamed. "The Mapinguari."
"You're kidding."
"Did you capture him?"
"Um...."
"Where did you put him?" No one seemed to appreciate Petra's question, although she was actually serious. *The thing is supposed to be huge.*

Emory must have figured out where she was going. "She's right. How do you plan to hold a ferocious creature ten feet tall?"

Ffoulkes fidgeted. "We don't exactly have the creature in hand. We have his footprints."

"Ah."

"This afternoon I sent Hector back to the clearing where Manuel was killed. He was instructed to search for any other evidence that could point to a cause of death. He came across a clear footprint and took a picture of it with my phone."

The ranger held it up.

"So your phone's working?"

Denys looked puzzled. "Of course it is."

"Well, ours aren't."

"Yes, they are." Alex pressed an icon on his phone, and the screen lit up. "I used mine to call home right after the police left with Gordon's body. It must have been only a temporary glitch."

Hector shrugged. "Perhaps there was some weather interference. I had no problem using Mr. Ffoulkes's cell."

John agreed. "The service must be intermittent. We're deep in the jungle, after all."

The others gathered around and looked at the photo. Alex peered at it. "I don't see anything."

Hector almost rolled his eyes. "I covered it over with leaves to protect it."

"Then what the hell are we staring at?"

Petra had a better question. "Can you describe it, Hector?"

Ffoulkes didn't let him answer. "Never mind that. I intend to examine it in situ." He leaned back in his chair. "I propose we all go to the clearing, where Nick can take extensive photographs. I want a full record, with as many eyewitnesses as possible."

Alex muttered something.

"What was that?"

"All those heavy boots clumping around could obscure other evidence."

"True. Okay. How about if just the two guides, Emory, and I go?"

Emory reminded him, "We'll need Nick to take the pictures."

Petra cried, "What about me?"

"What about you?"

"I'm not going to sit here in the lodge. I only have two weeks here, and I want to get out and explore as much as I can."

Her brother added, "I'll keep an eye on her."

Denys said grudgingly, "All right. But keep in line, and don't touch anything. We head out at seven."

****

October 9

As the sun rose above the trees, five people gathered by the launch. Hector started the motor while Winston untied the lines. Ffoulkes was nowhere to be seen. Alex came down, shouldering a backpack. "I'm taking Denys's place. He says he needs to catch up on his sleep after the trip."

Nick raised an eyebrow. "Trip? He didn't come that far."

"Last I checked, Ocala is three thousand miles away. He's been traveling for three days."

"But…I saw him in Lima less than a week ago!"

Alex stared at him. "I don't see how. He sent me a text on Tuesday as he was boarding a flight in Orlando."

Nick opened his mouth, then shut it.

Petra whispered, "You may have been mistaken in Iquitos."

"I guess so."

John waved from the top of the steps. "Be careful!"

Nick called, "You don't want to come?"

"I'd just get in the way." Nobody argued with him. As the boat pulled away, Molly the toucan landed on a branch above him and pooped on his head. The last thing Petra saw was John staring up at the bird in disbelief.

A few minutes later, they pulled in at a bend in the river. Hector said, "This is it."

They moved single file through the forest. Strangler figs, their sinuous roots ready to trip up the unwary hiker at every step, snaked high up into their host trees. After five minutes' walking, Petra felt washed out and exhausted. The humidity bore down on her like a freshly skinned pelt. Capac had given her a cloth he'd chilled in the refrigerator, and she kept it pressed to the back of her neck. It didn't do much good, but at least it soaked up some of the sweat. Winston led the way, slicing through the lianas and underbrush with a razor-sharp machete. He seemed to know exactly where he was going, although to Petra it was only a blur of green and brown. Hector stepped off the path where a sapling grew. He smiled and tapped the wood gently. Three tiny brown bats flew out of a small hole in the trunk.

Alex ducked his head and batted at them. "Are those the bloodsucking kind?"

"You mean vampire bats? No. These little fellows eat insects. They won't hurt you." He caught one deftly and held it for them. Diaphanous, rubbery wings stood out in strange contrast to the furry brown body and puppy-like snout. Hector let it go, and they watched it glide off. He turned back to the path. After a few steps, he halted again. "Miss Petra, here's something you might appreciate." He held his hand up, and a huge butterfly the color of pure cobalt landed gently on his palm, covering it entirely. It flapped slowly, apparently unafraid. "It's a *Morpho menelaus* butterfly. Quite rare."

Nick took a close-up photograph. Winston shaded

his eyes and looked up. "It's getting late. We should continue." They hiked on.

What seemed like an age later, they arrived at a small opening in the trees. As Petra began to step into it, Hector threw an arm out to stall her. He bent down and picked up a leaf. Under it sat a tiny brown frog about five millimeters long. "You must be careful not to kill any animal in the forest. Their souls will haunt you." He set out slowly, skirting the edge of the clearing. "The Chullachaqui lies in wait near these spaces to lure unwary victims deeper into the forest until they are lost."

Petra was amused. *I guess a university education only goes so far to explain the Amazon.*

They came to a pile of leaves. "This is where I found the print." He carefully brushed the leaves aside to reveal the outline of a foot.

Nick whistled. "He must wear a size twenty shoe—that looks bigger than Michael Jordan's."

Emory pointed at the clear outline of toes. "Except this one's barefoot."

Winston bent down and traced dots about an inch from the tips of the toes. "Claws?"

"*Hmm.* Not human, then?"

"Or maybe he just doesn't trim his nails." When Emory sniffed, Petra feigned innocence. "What?"

He pointed at the track. "Let's get some photos of this. Then I want to do a quick sweep of the area." They spread out, checking for broken twigs or other prints. Nick, Alex, and Winston went around the clearing to the left, and Hector, Emory, and Petra to the right. When they met at the far side, Alex reported, "Nothing."

Emory said, "Nothing on our side either. Okay, the rest of you, wait here while we survey the clearing. I'll check the overhanging branches. You"—he indicated Petra—"you search the ground."

She crept along, knees bent. "I found another print!"

He stepped gingerly over to her. "Yup, that's the same foot."

Petra surveyed the surrounding soil. "Wait. What's that?"

Emory leaned down. "A snake hole? Some kind of burrow?"

Hector came over. "No...the edges are too smooth...Odd."

Petra remembered something. "El Chullachaqui... isn't he supposed to have a wooden leg?"

Emory's lips pressed together. "Do you think this belongs to the same creature who made the footprint?"

"No, couldn't be. The Mapinguari is huge and hairy, and the Chullachaqui is a tiny little man."

"Assuming we're dealing with fairy tale creatures." He chuckled. "I don't know...are two mythical creatures allowed to occupy the same territory?"

Petra started to say something and snapped her mouth shut. "You may think it's funny, but a man's dead."

"You're the one making jokes. And no, I don't think it's funny, but I *am* skeptical. It's all too artfully done."

She looked over at Nick. "Can you take pictures of this too?"

"Sure thing."

Two hours later, they trudged back into the lodge.

Petra went off to take a cold shower and change out of her sodden clothes. When she returned to the hammock room, she found everyone staring out at the river. "What's going on?"

Denys spoke haughtily, although Petra detected a tremor of uncertainty. "The local police."

"They've come back." Alex glanced at Petra with alarm.

"So has Aguirre. Won't he be pleased he didn't miss them." Emory's tone was dry.

The police boat followed the lodge launch to the dock and tied up next to it. Aguirre disembarked with a large sack and, ignoring the officers behind him, strode into the lodge and turned toward the lab.

No one spoke until the detective came in, followed by a sergeant. Ffoulkes took charge. "I'm Denys Ffoulkes, director of the Institute for Tropical Research in Ocala, Florida. I understand you took the body of our doctor, Lewis Gordon, back to Nauta."

"Detective Romeo Montoya at your service." He paused. Petra wondered if he expected someone to make a joke about his name. When no one said anything, he went on. "Yes, we took him from there to Iquitos. I have an autopsy report for you."

"What did he die of?"

"Paralysis due to absorption of curare, a lethal poison."

The shaman knows his stuff. "Absorption how? Could he have eaten it?"

"No. Ingesting curare won't kill you. It has to enter through the bloodstream. We found several small scratches on his forearm. If he had an open wound that came in contact with the sap of the *Chondrodendron* vine, it could have entered that way. The medical examiner said such accidents are very rare, since curare is usually made by boiling the stems down to a thick syrup. But it's not impossible."

Alex asked, "What about the...the missing parts?"

"Cheeks and arm presented ragged edges and were likely caused by piranhas after death. The missing internal organs...that's still under investigation."

"Not piranhas?"

"The stomach cavity was clean. Almost as though something had scooped it out." He shook his head. "Strangest thing the medical examiner had ever seen."

The Mapinguari?

Emory cleared his throat. "Could it have been cleaned out so you couldn't tell what killed him?"

The detective gazed at him. "Huh. An interesting thought." He jotted something down in a notebook. "Now, I would like to take statements from each of you. Please wait in the dining room until you are called."

Ffoulkes tried to demur. "We only have a limited time here. We do have research to do."

Petra knew no one wanted to mention the Mapinguari print or the skeleton. *But is anyone going to mention Manuel?*

As though he'd read her thoughts, Emory touched her arm and whispered, "Leave it alone."

The detective was firm. "This won't take long. Mr. Ffoulkes, will you come with me, please?"

The director followed him slowly. The rest sat quietly under the watchful eye of the sergeant.

When Montoya had finished with them all, he took his leave. Ffoulkes's attempts to elicit an opinion from him had met with an unresponsive stare. They gathered in the dining room for a late lunch. Capac for once did not complain, having spent the morning spying nervously on the police.

Ffoulkes started it off. "What did he ask you, Alex?"

"Where I was when Winston brought the body back. My impressions, that sort of thing." The young man scanned the others warily.

"Me too." Emory was calm. "The detective didn't seem too perturbed about the situation."

Aguirre spoke up. "He asked me how long Lewis had been gone."

The group was silent, mulling over the situation. No one seemed hungry except Nick, who ladled a generous second helping of stew into his bowl.

Ffoulkes summed up. "So…no leading questions. I think we can assume he's working on the theory that it was an accident."

"That's a relief."

Petra gave John a puzzled look. "Why do you say that?"

The little man hunched his shoulders. "I…uh…like Denys says, we have research to do and limited time. We don't need any messy investigations."

Denys nodded. "What about next of kin? John?"

"Yes, I gave him the particulars." He added, "And I sent a note to Gordon's brother."

"Oh, good." Denys harrumphed. "It had actually slipped my mind what with all the…the…"

"Yes." *No one is in much of a position to criticize.*

"Look," said Emory, "until further notice, we should consider it an accident as well. It's the only thing that makes sense." He scanned the jungle beyond the windows. "Pretty much everything here is hazardous to your health in some way. Remember that bush you touched, Alex?"

The herpetologist chuckled. "That was bizarre, wasn't it? Hector had just finished telling me not to touch anything when I passed this fuzzy little tree and rubbed a leaf."

"You would have been all right, but no…you had to go and touch that finger with your thumb."

Nick turned to Petra. "Turns out the tree has some kind of permanent glue that protects it from insects. His fingers stuck fast together. Winston had to cut them apart with the machete."

From the doorway, Winston sniggered. "Good thing I keep it so sharp."

Petra's jaw dropped. "Was there much blood?"

"Nah." Emory winked. "But it's a lucky thing his fingerprints are on file."

It took her a moment to figure out what he meant. "Oh." She avoided Emory's eyes but looked with renewed respect at Winston. She said brightly, "By the way, did anyone tell him about Manuel?"

No one answered. Hector said, "Just as well. It will be handled by his own people. We do not need the police involved."

"But…what if the deaths are related?"

In the uncomfortable silence that greeted this, Emory rose. "I've got work to do." He headed toward the lab.

Aguirre followed him. "I want to see that fossil under a microscope."

"Didn't Ffoulkes tell you? He's determined it's a skeleton, not a fossil. Only a few years old."

"Yeah, he told me. I want to see for myself."

Petra wondered if he was annoyed at the correction or simply didn't accept it. As she began to leave, Ffoulkes blocked her exit. "Miss Steele? May I have a word?"

"Certainly."

He led her outside. When they were out of earshot of the others, he took her elbow and swung her toward him. "Miss Steele—"

"Petra."

"Petra it is. What a lovely old-fashioned name." His eyes clouded over and a faint pink suffused his pale cheeks. "I want to thank you for being such a good sport under trying circumstances."

Huh?

"I…uh…have been so occupied with recent events that I haven't found the time to welcome you properly…that is, I would enjoy spending some time with you…" He straightened his cravat. "I find you very attractive, Miss Steele…Petra."

"Er…"

He leaned toward her, his breath smelling of sherry and tobacco. *And something else…sulfur?*

"I do hope we avail ourselves of this opportunity to become better acquainted." He straightened. "Please drop by whenever you're in the mood for a…cozy chat. I have"—he winked—"a small stash of cognac in my room."

"Thank you. I'll keep your kind offer in mind." *Not.*

Petra went to her room and booted up the laptop. She spent the rest of the day studying articles on the Mapinguari in the vain hope that a huge, hairy, ravenous beast would eclipse her recent encounter with a spindle-legged, bony-assed, hatchet-faced crank with leering eyes and a handsy attitude.

Emory knocked.

"Come in."

He looked over her shoulder at the screen. "What are you reading?"

"An article in the *Journal of Paleontology* about an ancient giant sloth. Its Latin name is *Megatherium americanum*. Flourished throughout South America during the Pliocene era." She read aloud. " 'Larger than an elephant, it weighed as much as four tons and stood up to twenty feet tall.' Bones indicate a vegetarian diet. Some researchers maintain it could stand upright."

"Big fella. With that bulk, you'd think it would be at least omnivorous."

"Maybe that's why it went extinct." She tapped the keyboard. "You know, I'm wondering if the Mapinguari is based on an ethnic memory."

"What's that?"

"Say a creature co-existed with humans sometime in the past, then disappeared. The memory of the beast eventually transforms in tribal lore into a monster or supernatural creature."

"So, as the stories are passed down generation to generation, the giant sloth slowly evolves into a man-eating Bigfoot?"

She nodded. "The land sloths overlapped humans for several thousand years. The last-known fossil was dated to 8500 BC, but there's one specimen in the Antilles that suggests it lived to 1550 BC. That's only thirty-five hundred years ago."

Emory tapped his chin. "An ethnic memory of an

extinct animal. Or...it could still exist. Ffoulkes certainly thinks so."

"Ffoulkes thinks he's Charles Darwin."

"Good point."

She looked at him curiously. "So what did you want?"

He backed toward the door hastily. "I came to tell you dinner's ready."

What the heck's bothering him? An unexpected new worry intruded. *Did he see me with Denys?* The idea left her slightly uneasy. *Come on, Petra. Why should you care?* "I just want to finish this article. Be there in a jiff."

After supper, she sought the hammock room, hoping to see the capybaras again, but the lawn was empty. For once, the sky was clear, and she wandered out and down to the dock to enjoy the stars. *Ah, there's Orion.* Usually people chose Venus or Polaris, but Petra always wished on Orion's left foot. Nick had once asked her why. "Because it's his foot that takes the first stride across space."

"So what does that have to do with your wishes?"

"Whenever I'm faced with a scary decision, Orion gives me the courage to take the first step."

Nick had laughed at her.

As she closed her eyes and pondered her request, a rustle sounded behind her.

"Don't fall in."

Chapter Seven
The Missing Link

October 9

Petra sprang forward and nearly did fall in, but a strong hand caught her around her waist and pulled her back. She felt warm breath in her ear. "Emory!"

He let go. "What are you doing anyway? You had one leg hovering over the water."

"I guess the stars distracted me." She glanced at him shyly. "I was wishing on Orion. Or rather, on his foot." She pointed at the star twinkling below the famous belt.

"Why Orion?"

No need to let on how weird I am just yet. "It's...uh...the only constellation I recognize?"

"It's probably the only constellation *most* people recognize." He looked down at her. "Okay, do you have a foot fetish, or what? Why wish on the foot?"

Just because Nick made fun of me doesn't mean Emory will. "It brings me luck."

"Like a rabbit's foot, only better?"

She didn't answer. The thing that had been simmering in the back of her mind for the last two days, obscured by the chaos of events, had made itself known. She knew what she wanted to wish for.

"Petra? Did you hear my question?"

Petra lowered her eyes to Emory. "I don't know about better—but it serves the same function. See, everyone zeroes in on Orion's belt, or his dog, or his manly physique, but his left foot—Rigel—is actually the brightest star in the constellation."

He inspected the night sky. "True. And?"

"Well, it reminds me that when you have to take that first step into the unknown you...um...put your best foot forward. I look at Orion striding across the cosmos, and he helps me believe I can meet any challenge."

Emory was silent for a minute. Petra was about to take her leave when he said, "Did you know that Orion claimed he was the greatest hunter of all time? Gaia sent a scorpion to kill him."

"Huh. Who is Gaia?"

"Gaia means Earth—she's the goddess the Greeks called the mother of all life—the primordial deity. The cool New Age kids all worship her. Don't tell me you aren't into crystals and yoga?"

"No. So why did Gaia want to kill Orion?"

"Because, to prove his prowess, he announced he was going to hunt down and kill all the animals in the world. Since Gaia is the guardian of every living thing, you might say his threat kinda ruffled her feathers."

"I'll bet. So she decided to kill him before he massacred her subjects. Did she succeed?"

"No. Another god—I forget his name—gave Orion the antidote. That's why you never see both Orion and Scorpio in the sky at the same time."

"*Hmm.*"

"So," he said softly, "Orion is hardly the hero you want to set your heart on. All the stories of him involve power, lust, and murder."

"Lust?" Without warning, her heart skipped a beat.

"Uh-huh. He pursued all of the Pleiades—the Seven Sisters." He pointed at a cluster of stars to the right of Orion. "Also Artemis, not to mention assorted demi-goddesses. Got himself in trouble a lot."

"Not unusual for a Greek hero, I guess." She gazed speculatively at Emory. "You also said 'power.' And 'murder.' "

"And murder." Emory growled, "Just what we don't need more of around here."

Maybe not murder, no. She eyed him. "Can I ask *you* a question?"

He stiffened, leery. "What?"

"Why do you watch me?"

He sat on the bench, avoiding her eyes. "You're the only female out here."

"Thanks a lot."

"Plus you happen to be very beautiful."

"I am?" *Oh, my God, Petra. Did you just simper?*

"Don't be arch. It's not in your nature." He swirled a stick in the water. "I actually meant beautiful inside. You have a generous soul."

"How do you know that?"

"I can see it in your eyes. You didn't know Lewis, but you looked more sad than frightened when you saw his body. You always make eye contact with everyone, even the skittish little Capac. The monkeys adore you almost as much as they do John."

At a loss for words, she studied him in the faint light from the lodge, noting with renewed approbation his high cheekbones, his tourmaline eyes glinting with amusement, and his strong chin, currently covered with a fine stubble.

He continued thoughtfully. "Of course, having chestnut hair cut in a fetching gamine style, not to mention eyes the color of the Hope diamond, doesn't detract from the generally pleasing impression." He stood up and touched her forehead. "The slender body—graceful but trim—the elfin little ears, and the perky butt, also contributed to my positive assessment."

"I see." She took his hand.

"Where are we going?"

"My room."

"I see."

****

October 10

Emory was gone when she woke up the next morning. Lost in visions of entwined limbs, of rich kisses, and whispered words of passion, she pulled the hard slab of foam that passed for a pillow over her face. "Wow." *That was incredible. I never thought I'd meet someone who made my heart go all nimbly-diddle like that.* She lapsed into happy thoughts of romantic boat rides and candlelit dinners.

Nick poked his head in. "Sis? Did you expect breakfast in bed? Don't."

"I'm coming."

Aguirre was missing from the breakfast table. Petra felt a warning buzz. *Not another one.*

Ffoulkes answered her unspoken question. "Tramposo returned to the spot where he found the stone slab. He said he'd be back by lunchtime."

Petra shot a self-conscious peek at Emory. He studiously avoided her gaze. She tried passing him the basket of fruit. He waved it away without looking at her. Her heart sank. *Maybe this wasn't what I thought. Maybe I've gone overboard...again. It wasn't a night of passion, after all, but of lust. Thanks a lot, Orion. What a fool I am!* She wiped her mouth and, when she was sure no one was looking, her eyes. *That's it. I'm not going to let it get to me.*

****

Petra and Nick were studying the photographs of the footprint when Aguirre came into the lounge.

"So you're back. Did you locate the place where you found the slab?"

His eyes alight, the botanist got a beer from the bar. "Oh, yes. Winston and I had marked the trail. But—"

"Did you find anything else?"

"Yes, if you'll let me speak."

His Spanish accent, tinged by the flat Midwest notes, grew broader with his heightened emotion. *I wonder where he comes from and who his family is?* She didn't recall the upper-tier states having much of a Hispanic population.

"All right, maybe the fossil isn't a fossil, but what I saw was..." He took a gulp of beer. "Something potentially even more significant." He gestured with the bottle at Emory. "I need you to come back with me."

"Why me?"

"You're the ornithologist."

"You've found a new bird?" Emory's eyes flashed, which Petra was beginning to understand signaled intense interest. *A dedicated scientist? Or a fanatic?* In keeping with her new determination to keep her distance, she came squarely down on the negative side. *Fanatic.*

93

"Better than that. An *old* bird."

"What the hell do you mean?"

"Proof of the survival of the creature whose fossil I found."

Emory snorted. "I reiterate: it's not a fossil. We've established that."

"Right. Okay. I have accepted your judgment." Aguirre brought his face closer to Emory. "But the skeleton is not that of a guan. Nor is it a chicken. I think it may belong to a still extant relative of the hoatzin. Or an evolutionary offshoot of it. At any rate, it's different from the bird we know."

"What makes you think so?"

"I may have stumbled onto evidence that it is still roaming the Amazon."

Denys huffed. "Out with it, Tramposo. What kind of evidence?"

He paused. "The bird itself." In the ensuing shocked silence, he hedged. "I only caught a glimpse of it. It was about the same size and shape as the hoatzin, but…*but* it's greenish rather than brown, and its face was red."

"Did it grunt?"

"Yes!" He seemed to notice the unsympathetic faces for the first time. "Really. Ask Winston."

Winston kept his head down and refused to confirm Aguirre's description. "I did not see it. Mr. Aguirre was behind me. When he shouted, I looked, but there was nothing there."

Emory sighed heavily. "I suppose we might as well try to flush it out."

Ffoulkes stood. "I want to come too. My expertise as a biologist is essential."

Aguirre hesitated. "A whole crew may spook the birds. Why don't Emory and I go first? If we discover a flock, we'll come back for reinforcements."

The director looked like he was going to insist but suddenly stopped. "As you wish, but take Winston with you for safety."

"All right."

The bell rang. Nick jumped up. "Lunch time!" He scampered to the dining room. The rest followed him more sedately but just as enthusiastically.

The cook came in with platters of food. Ffoulkes curled thumbs around his suspenders and brayed, "Ah, Capac, my good man. What toothsome dish have you prepared for us today?"

Capac stared at Ffoulkes blankly. Petra said kindly, "He wants to know what this is."

"*Inchicapi.*"

"Inchi—what? What's in it?" Denys shed a sliver of his heartiness.

Nick, who had immediately dug in, pronounced, "Chicken stew. I taste peanuts. Delicious." He nodded at Capac, who backed out of the room smiling.

When they had finished, Aguirre tapped Emory on the shoulder. "We'll go first thing tomorrow morning. Seven a.m. okay with you?"

Emory just nodded.

Later that night, Petra walked in on Emory playing solitaire in the dining room. She tried to turn around and leave, but he saw her. "Petra?"

She kept her expression bland. "I was looking for a little refreshment."

He turned a card over. "Beer's nice and warm." He smiled at her.

She drew strength from the smile and walked over. She gestured at the table. "Bored?"

"Just trying to relax. Something about this expedition bothers me."

"What do you mean?"

"Why won't Aguirre let Ffoulkes come with us?"

She leaned over him and put the black six on the red seven. "Maybe he doesn't want a bunch of loud humans lumbering around, should you actually come across a flock of ancient hoatzin."

"Yeah, but Ffoulkes is right—as a biologist, he is better versed in evolution than I am. And since his field is biogeography, he knows more about the rainforest."

She had a thought. "You don't suppose Aguirre thinks Denys is planning to kill one?"

Emory stopped with a card in midair. "No self-respecting scientist would do that."

"Darwin did."

"*Hmm.* You're suggesting that's why Aguirre doesn't want Ffoulkes along?"

"Who knows?" When he didn't answer, she said, "Well, I'm glad Winston will be with you, if only for protection."

"Don't be silly. What do we have to be afraid of? It'll be the middle of the day, on a clearly marked path."

"El Chullachaqui?"

Before she could stop him, he kissed her cheek.

"What was that for?"

"For worrying about me."

Her cheek burning, she gave in to utter confusion. *What the hell was that for? Does he like me? Doesn't he? How am I supposed to act? What am I supposed to feel? Should I be indifferent or friendly? Hostile or receptive?* She decided to ask the question that had been bugging her. *Not that it matters.* "No one...no one else worries about you?"

His eyes flickered. "No. No one."

Somehow I don't think that's the whole truth. She took a deep breath. "Emory? About last night—"

He gathered up all the cards and began to shuffle them. "Look, I'm sorry. I got carried away. It won't happen again."

I was right. "N...no. Of course not. It's just...I'm sure it was...well, like you said, I'm the only woman around, so—"

"What? What are you talking about?" He dropped the cards and stood up. "Petra, if you think I'm that kind of a man, then—" He snorted. "Do I have to explain? Yes, you are a beautiful woman, but you're also an interesting woman, an intriguing woman. You take up way too many of my waking thoughts. Not to mention my sleeping thoughts." He stopped. "Say, can you *have* sleeping thoughts?"

Petra, who had been staring at him, her mouth open in shock, giggled. "I think they're technically called dreams."

He sat down again. "Anyway, I'm sorry about last night. I am not in a position to commit to any emotional attachment right now." He regarded her solemnly, then blurted, "I don't think you are, either."

Oh, my God, he knows. Nicky must have told him about George. Well, I'm not going to give him the satisfaction of feeling sorry for me. Jackass. She straightened her shoulders and stuck out her chin. "You know nothing about me, sir. I suggest you mind your own business. Last night never happened."

This time it was his jaw's turn to drop.

She sailed out of the room, bottling up her tears.

****

October 11

The next morning Petra came out on the dock to see two canoes disappearing around the bend. From the kitchen she heard a cry, and Winston flew out, holding a boot in one hand and his shirt in the other. She turned. "Why didn't you go with them?"

"They left before I was ready." He dropped the boot and held up an empty hand. "And they took my machete."

Ffoulkes came out. "Winston? What are you raving about?" The little man yelled something in Spanish. "Damn it, man, I can't understand a word you say. I told you before: English only while you're working for me."

The man stopped. Petra could almost see him translating in his head. *I don't suppose it occurs to Denys to be impressed that Winston speaks at least three languages.*

She had just opened her mouth to tell him off when Denys remarked ruefully, "I just don't have the facility with languages other people do. Wish I did. Now, what's happened, Winston?"

"They left without me!"

Without another word, Denys went back inside and returned with his rifle. "Come on." He strode down to the launch. Winston pulled on his shirt, laced up his boots, and followed him.

Petra spent the day stewing. *Was I forceful enough with Emory? Did I make it clear I don't need his pity, and I sure don't need him? What did he say? He couldn't commit to anything emotional? What the hell does that mean? What's he hiding? And why am I still thinking about him?*

She tried to do some research, but her mind was on the absent men. *Focus on something else.* Like maybe figuring out what had cleaned out Dr. Gordon's stomach cavity. *Was it human? Animal? Vegetable? Mineral? Mythical?*

Nick came in carrying the photos of the clearing.

Petra glared at him. "You."

He drew back. "Me? What did I do this time?"

"You...you told Emory about...about...George."

Her brother's response was less than gratifying. He laughed. "Why on earth would I tell Andrews about your love life? Unless..." He searched her face. "What's going on between you two?"

"Nothing!" She tried to control her voice. "It's...it's that...something he said made me think he...knew."

"Wasn't me." Nick shrugged. "So..." He held up the photos. "I've been thinking. This so-called feud between the two villages Hector talked about. Stuff like that's gotta be frowned on by the local authorities."

"Well, sure. So what?"

"It could be as simple as an enemy killed Manuel, then doctored the site so the police would think the Chullachaqui got him."

"Chullachaqui, huh? You mean the print of the wooden leg? Wait—what about the enormous foot?" She mused, chin in palm. *Monsters.* "I wish we knew what—or who—gutted Dr. Gordon. Do you think someone tried to make it look like the Mapinguari attacked him as well?"

"But to what purpose?"

"Well, we seem like a rather gullible lot. Ffoulkes will believe anything. Maybe it's all a subterfuge set up by the natives to get rid of us."

"Yankee go home?"

"Something like that. I just hope they don't resort to violence."

"You mean, more violence."

Chapter Eight
Mating Rituals

October 11

She heard the *putt-putt* of the boat before anyone else did and ran down to the river. Winston stood at the stern, with Ffoulkes in the bow holding a rope. She couldn't see either Aguirre or Emory, but their canoes were laid athwart across the gunwales. Alex and Nick joined her. Alex pointed. "I wonder why they put the canoes in the launch?"

"Oh, dear, you don't think...?"

Winston steered into the dock, and Denys threw the line to Alex. Before he'd secured the bow, Aguirre came around the side and jumped off the boat. Nick tried to flag him down, but he ran past. "Take him to the kitchen!"

Denys turned to the darkened cabin and reached out a hand. Emory stumbled out, one sleeve red with blood. A handkerchief had been tied tightly around his biceps. His hand was wrapped in a T-shirt.

Petra stood rooted to the spot. She opened her mouth but nothing came out. Nick leapt to the gunwale and helped Emory over. He swayed on the dock, a pool of pink liquid spreading around him. Petra croaked, "Wha...what is that?"

Nick bent down and smelled it. "It's...bloody

water. He's soaking wet."

She found her voice. "What in God's name happened?"

Ffoulkes scrambled onto the dock, grabbed Emory's good arm, and together he and Nick half dragged him up the boardwalk. "Hurry. Let's get him inside."

They had reached the door when Hector came out, surveyed the scene, and headed toward a canoe. "I'll get the shaman."

No one objected.

Alex and Petra followed the trail of blood down the hall. Emory sat on the one stool in the kitchen. Aguirre hovered behind Capac while the cook fussed over the patient. "Where are you hurt?"

"My…my…it's my finger."

Capac tightened the tourniquet, then carefully unwound the T-shirt. Petra took one look and slapped a hand over her mouth to stop the scream. Where his right little finger should have been, there was only a bloody stump. Capac stanched the blood, then uncapped a plastic bottle and poured a clear liquid on the wound. Emory went white and promptly fell off the stool in a dead faint. Petra knelt by him, then looked up at the cook, fury distorting her features. "What the hell did you do to him?"

Denys picked up the bottle. "Rubbing alcohol."

Nick wiped Emory's forehead with a cold cloth. The injured man's eyes fluttered open, and he sat up. Alex helped him back to his seat. Capac danced around them, squawking, "I sorry, Mister Emory. I must clean out or bad things happen."

Alex checked out the cupboards. "That's the only

antiseptic we have. Capac is right—he had to act quickly to stave off any infection."

Emory barely nodded. The blood flow from his finger had slowed, and the cook removed the tourniquet and wrapped his hand tightly in a clean cloth. Aguirre took his good arm. "Come on, Nick. Let's take him to his room and get him out of these wet things."

Petra longed to come, but since it involved Emory being naked and since the others didn't know she'd already seen him that way, she stayed behind. With nothing to do, she paced. All her misgivings, all her resolutions, flew out the open window and she prayed. *Please, oh, please, make him be okay.*

Hector returned with Don César, and they disappeared into Emory's room. Half an hour later, Nick found her in the lounge. She rushed to him. "Is he...is he—?"

He gave her a hug and refilled her glass with rum. "He'll be all right. The shaman threw us out—said our 'vapors' were making the herbs less effective."

"When can I see him?"

"I suppose when Don César says you can. I'm willing to bet they have a rule about females provoking the spirits or something." Nick peered at her. "Say, wait a minute. Were you fibbing to your only brother? Do you in fact care for our resident ornithologist?"

"Me? Not at all. He's a...he's a pill." Her heart gave a little squeeze at the lie. "It's just...all that blood. Was it an accident? Did an animal attack him?"

"I haven't gotten the whole story yet. Aguirre says he'll tell us once he's sure Emory's out of danger."

Ffoulkes came in, dragged the bottle of single malt whiskey from behind the bar, and poured himself a tumblerful. As he raised the glass to his lips, the botanist appeared, went straight through to the kitchen, and grabbed three beers from the shelf before coming back to the lounge. Alex took one of the bottles from him. "All right, Aguirre. Spill."

Aguirre swallowed a mouthful and choked. When he'd recovered, he spluttered, "We took the canoes upriver to the spot I'd marked."

"Why didn't you wait for Winston and the launch?"

"Emory was in a hurry. Don't ask me why."

I'm betting that's not true. But why is he lying?

He gulped down the rest of the beer and uncapped a second. "Anyway, we landed and cut our way through the vines to the spot where I had tripped over the stone slab."

"Who had the machete?"

"I did. I remembered the path, so I went ahead." He stopped and wiped his forehead with his sleeve. "I had my arm up to cut a thick liana when this monkey came crashing down through the branches. I think it was squabbling with another one. Anyhow, it knocked me backward, and I heard a scream. I must have dropped the machete right on Emory's hand." He put his head in his hands. "It was a horrible accident. I am so sorry."

Nick asked, "Where's the machete now?"

Ffoulkes spoke. "Winston has it. We didn't catch up with them until they were in the canoes coming back down the river. When Aguirre yelled that Andrews was injured, we hauled them on board and came back as quickly as we could."

Petra had been listening with half an ear—waiting for the shaman to leave so she could see Emory—and almost missed Nick's question. "How come Emory was all wet?"

Aguirre mumbled. "Me again."

"On purpose?" *A misguided attempt to clean him up?*

"No, of course not. We got back to the riverbank, and I helped him into his canoe. I suppose I should have put him in mine, but I wasn't really thinking. He was losing a lot of blood, and I was scared. I pushed him out into the water. The canoe must have hit an underwater branch, because it flipped. I got him back in somehow, and we paddled out to midstream, where Denys and Winston found us."

Despite staring hard at the door, Petra didn't see the shaman until he stood beside her. He said softly, "Mr. Andrews will survive. La Sachamama will watch over him."

"Sachamama?"

"Mother of the forest."

Hector said aloud, "Don César will return tomorrow. He says Mr. Andrews should not be disturbed until he wakes."

The shaman paused, then spoke rapidly under his breath to the guide.

Petra felt alarm creeping back over her. "What did he say, Hector?"

"He said, the other man—the one who wielded the machete—should be very careful. He did not honor Sachamama. There will be consequences."

"You mean for Emory? Or for Aguirre?"

The shaman nodded at the name. Hector said, "Aguirre. Don César heard from the villagers that Mr. Tramposo left a swath of destruction in his wake when he was searching for the bird. There are many spirits in the interior—and they expect humans to respect their territory."

Nick asked curiously, "What kind of consequences are you talking about?"

But the shaman kept his mouth tightly closed, his lips in a thin line. His eyes darted from Aguirre to Ffoulkes, a spark of fear in them.

Hector hesitated. "Perhaps Mr. Tramposo should not venture into the jungle alone again."

The subject of the discussion retorted, "I sure as hell won't! I'm not a fool. But"—his eyes grew hooded—"we should organize another party to go back. Before I…slipped…we found something."

"What? Another 'fossil'?" Denys snorted.

"No. Spoor."

"You mean, of the hoatzin ancestor?"

He looked a little abashed. "We're not sure. We could hear the hoatzins around us—they don't cheep or trill, you know, but make these guttural barks and honks. Don't sound like birds at all. More like cows or pigs. We followed them and found tracks and feces, but mixed in with them were these pellets that looked more like rabbit dung. I was going to scoop some up and bring it back, but then…"

"Why couldn't they just be from a rabbit?"

"Or a deer?"

Hector shook his head. "No rabbits that I know of in this region. Deer only range up to southern Peru."

Ffoulkes knocked back his whiskey. "Too bad we don't have a mammalogist on the team."

As the men fell into a discussion of staffing needs, Petra meditated on Aguirre's news. *Spoor. Pellets.*

What animals have dung in the form of pellets? Rabbits were the obvious culprit, but Hector said there weren't any in the Amazon. *Maybe with all the exotic species here, there's no room for your run-of-the-mill fauna. Weird. No deer...no rabbits. Hmm.* Something else to research. As the men's voices rose, exhaustion hit her like a rubber hammer. *I need some rest before I tackle anything else.* "I'm going to take a nap."

Ffoulkes nodded absently and crooked a finger at Aguirre. "Let's have another look at the skeleton."

Petra went to her room, but when she lay down, her eyes refused to stay shut. She rose, booted up her laptop, and typed in "Deer-Peruvian-Amazon." *Well, lookee here, there are indeed two species of deer in the South American rainforest.* Could Hector have been wrong? She read on, but her initial enthusiasm waned. Both types were endangered, so first off, it would be very unusual to come across one of them. The marsh deer didn't live this far north—only reaching the southern portions of Peru. The brocket deer seemed more widespread, but not in this part of the country. *That'll teach me to question Hector's expertise.* "Okay, how about rabbits?"

It took her a while to find anything. There turned out to be a thousand species of rat in South America, but only one rabbit, called the tapeti. "One family, one genus, one species. How crazy is that?" The sole bunny was a small yellowish-brown cottontail that lived mainly in Brazil but ranged into the northeastern part of Peru now and then. "So the strangest creature on earth is more ubiquitous here than a rabbit." *Speaking of which, let's see what we can find on the hoatzin.*

It took no time at all to bring up reams of

information on the bird. Its behavior was just as remarkable as the physical features Emory had described. It couldn't fly very well and lived in shrubs, usually around oxbow lakes. Their nests were built on limbs overhanging water, presumably to protect the babies from predators. *I wonder how many fledglings drown learning to fly?*

The article went on to explain that, since the hoatzin's unvarying diet of leaves was broken down in the foregut rather than the hindgut, their digestive system more closely resembled that of a cow than a bird. And like a cow, it smelled awful, giving rise to its nickname of "stinkbird."

There was a section on evolution of the species. "Their strange appearance has led some paleontologists to postulate that it evolved from the pterodactyls, but no fossil record has ever been found linking them to earlier versions." *Right, that's why Emory got so exercised when I asked him if it was a living fossil.* Emory. She lapsed into worry mode again. *When can I see him? Do I want to see him? More crucial: does he want to see me?* She took a deep breath and went back to ruminating on Aguirre's story.

What about the skeleton he found? If he was right and a flock of ancient birds were still wandering around, it should surely trump their search for Bigfoot, shouldn't it?

Nick stuck his head in. "Emory's asking for you." He crooked an eyebrow.

She closed the laptop, got up, and, giving her hair a toss, sailed past him. *Nothing to see here, bro.*

Emory sat up in bed, his bandaged hand in his lap. A small incense burner sent whorls of fragrant smoke to the ceiling. Petra sniffed. "Smells like jasmine."

"My personal physician's own recipe." He gazed at her. "Petra?"

"Yes?"

"I've been thinking."

"Uh-oh."

"No, really. I suppose the sight of all that blood gave me a glimpse of my own mortality. I...I'd like to try again." When she took a step back, he said hurriedly, "Just to be friends." He cocked his head. "Maybe...spend a little time together. What do you say?"

Petra refused to acknowledge the rush of hope that coursed through her. She said slowly, "Maybe... Maybe."

He touched her hand. "Unless you're interested in someone else?" He grinned. "Denys, perhaps?"

"Pardon me?"

"I've seen the way he looks at you. A gorgeous woman like you attracts men like flies to a carcass."

"What a lovely image."

"In fact," he mused, "I'm surprised the shaman isn't planning to give you to his eldest son. Maybe I'll..."

"That's enough." She closed the door behind her and came to the bed. She traced a finger from his forehead to his chin. "When will you be—?"

"Available?" He smirked.

"No." She frowned. "Up and about."

"As soon as the witch doctor lets me. We have to be sure the spirits have been properly mollified."

"Are they upset?"

"According to him, yes. There's a disturbance in

the Force."

"The Mapinguari, maybe?"

"No idea."

"You know, I've been studying the hoatzin. If Aguirre really has found a living link—an earlier form of the bird—that would be even more important than discovering the Mapinguari, wouldn't it?"

Emory pursed his lips. "Perhaps. Nothing to stop us from multitasking, however. Say, how long can you stay?"

"Don César says I'm only allowed a few minutes."

"I mean in Peru."

A hand flew to her mouth. "Oh, my God, I forgot all about that. I have reservations to Chicago out of Lima in four days." His look of mingled hope and concern settled it for her. "I might be able to change them. After all, I still have five months on my sabbatical." *And a deadline in three weeks for my book, but what's the point in bringing that up now?* "I…I do want to see where this goes."

"The expedition? Or me?"

Something constricted her esophagus, and she could only gurgle.

"So…I'm guessing English is not your native language?" He chuckled.

"It's just…I…uh…"

"Spit it out."

"Look, Emory, you were right before. I'm not really available for…for…"

His eyes closed to slits, and his mouth hardened. "A relationship? You do have someone else, then?"

So he was guessing. He doesn't know about George. How do I explain without telling him my so-

pathetic story? She couldn't answer him. Her pride wouldn't let her. *Anyway, I'll be gone in a few days and he'll forget all about me.* What had he said? *You're the only female out here.* "No...but..." She turned toward the door.

"I see. Wait." She turned back to find him upright, although he leaned heavily on a chair. His hair was adorably tousled. "How about a fling, then?"

Her mouth opened and shut. She gazed into his eyes, lost in the emerald depths.

He straightened, his legs set slightly apart like the captain of a whaling ship. "Look, we're both adults. We've both been through the wars, I'll wager. We don't have to do more than dip our feet in a little romance. What do you say?"

Her heart went *clickety-clack. Why not?* "That would be acceptable."

They jumped apart at the knock.

Alex came in. "Do you want a tray, Emory, or are you up to coming to dinner?"

"I'll come."

"You might want to put on some pants."

Petra stared at Emory, and Alex stared at Petra. *I didn't even notice! What must Alex think?*

Alex's lips turned up, but he said merely, "You have a clean pair?"

"Sure." Emory gestured at the series of hooks that served as a closet. "Capac took the wet ones off to wash." He wrinkled his nose. "Smelled like a flatulent hoatzin."

"They're always flatulent." Petra handed Emory a pair of chinos. "You help him, Alex. I'll see you at dinner."

Dinner conversation centered around Aguirre's theory. "We have to get back there as soon as possible. Who knows how large their territory is?"

"Or if they migrate. They could be gone by now."

Emory said, "Hoatzin are found all across northern South America except for the coastal areas. As far as I know, they don't migrate."

"That doesn't mean an earlier species didn't."

Ffoulkes's voice cut through the babble. "It could explain why we haven't found a fossil record of them."

Emory said grumpily, "You know, not every species evolved from something in the Pleistocene."

Alex retorted, "Well, everything has to have evolved from something."

"Yes, but some species are older than others. Take the horseshoe crab, for instance. It has remained relatively unchanged for four hundred and fifty million years."

Petra had just been thinking this was a seriously unproductive line of debate when Nick said it out loud. "Look, why don't we all go with Aguirre tomorrow? We'll take the launch, and in case of accidents, one of the canoes."

"Agreed." Ffoulkes stood up and announced, "John, Alex, Nick, Aguirre, the staff, and I shall leave here at eight a.m. after tea." He reminded Petra of Charles de Gaulle, only without the epaulets. *The staff? Really?*

Emory raised a hand. "I'm coming too."

"Me too!"

The director looked from Emory to Petra. "You, Emory, are not in fit shape to go, and you, Miss Steele, are—"

"A woman?"

"Not a scientist."

"Oh, but I play one on TV." No one laughed. "Look, I think I've proved that I'm tough and fit. Another pair of eyes and binoculars couldn't hurt."

John added helpfully, "She can take my place, Denys."

After a minute, Emory said, "You should let her go, if only to keep you all on the straight and narrow."

****

October 12

As she passed Emory's room the next morning, he called her in. "Petra, did you mean what you said about staying longer?"

Petra couldn't tell from his impassive face whether he was asking if she wanted to stay because of him or because of the adventure. *I'd better play it cool.* "A little longer, maybe. I'm intrigued by your project."

"The prototype hoatzin?"

"No, the Mapinguari. Remember, I studied anthropology. I love myths and legends, particularly ones that are so universal."

"As in Sasquatch?"

"Uh-huh. Also the trickster. He turns up in German folklore, in Plains Indians tales, even in West Africa. He's a fascinating figure."

"They say all myths have a basis in fact."

"You know, I've never been sure about that. My theory is, myths arise due to the peculiar characteristics of human nature. Humans are rational beings—they want the world around them to be rational as well. So they attempt to classify nature."

"Classify it? Or tame it?"

She nodded. "Good point. Let's say both. In mythology, everything is animated by an intelligence that can be manipulated or reasoned with. This animal is malevolent; that tree is sympathetic."

"*Hmm.*"

Petra wasn't sure if he were interested or simply being polite, but she hadn't talked with a clever man in so long, she let herself enjoy it. "It's also as simple as the wish to make nature orderly—to define each element and put it in its proper place."

"I can see why you became a librarian."

"What's that supposed to mean?"

"You want to put everything into neat categories."

"And what's so wrong with that?"

He pulled her to him. "Because I don't fit in a neat category, and neither do you."

She grinned but pushed him off. "You're saying I'm *special*?"

"Yes. And so is every other creature on the planet." He kissed her hand. "However, if it will make you happy, I'll put you in the class Mammalia, order primates, family Hominidae, genus *Homo*, and species…let's call it *bibliothecarius.* And leave you there. Not very romantic, but rational."

Heaven forbid he should be romantic. She shrugged off the touch of melancholy. "They're waiting for me."

He grew serious. "Be very careful. Something out there is unhappy with us."

"I will."

The others waited in the boat. "Where have you been?"

"Getting last-minute instructions from Emory."

Denys's eyes narrowed. "Like what?"

Petra's hand went unconsciously to her top button. "Just to be careful." She held up Emory's phone. "And to record any bird sounds we hear."

Aguirre spat. "The hoatzin are easy—they sound like feral swine."

Nick tossed the line onto the dock. "I don't think we need to go by their calls—I hear you can smell 'em a mile away. It's like passing a dairy farm on a sultry summer afternoon."

"It's true. That's why we call them stinkbirds." Winston took the tiller, and they headed north. A few miles up, the Pacaya fed into the Amazon proper. As it had the first time Petra came down from Iquitos, the vastness of the channel awed her. The water—though not quite as silty as its tributary—still ran olive brown, giving the impression that the river carried a bit of everything in its currents: plants, animals, diseases and their cures, all the colors of the spectrum. Even the dreams of explorers were lifted and propelled ever deeper into the jungle on the mighty Amazon.

Explorers. That's *where I heard the name Aguirre! Let me see…a movie…that's right.* It was an old movie—black and white—about a Spanish explorer. *Aguirre—Wrath of God.* A conquistador named Aguirre had gone to Peru with a band of men to search for the lost cities of gold. Instead they dealt with hostile natives, swarms of mosquitoes, and carnivorous caimans. As his followers fell away—dead of fever, poisoned arrows, or predators—he soldiered on, clinging to a raft on the river and hurling invectives at his god.

She looked at the fellow's namesake. His sharp,

black eyes were riveted on the shoreline, his hawk-like nose raised as if waiting to catch the scent of his quarry. His body was taut, and his hands clenched the rail, the knuckles white. *He* is *driven. A true scholar? Or a madman?* She wondered if she could ever be so focused. A reference librarian touched on so many subjects—she'd never really buried herself in one discipline. *A dilettante. That's what Emory called me.* She sighed.

She was about to inquire how he came by the name when Alex shouted, "There's a flag!"

Chapter Nine
Living Fossil

October 12

Everyone moved to the starboard side. Petra could see a small red flag on the bank. Aguirre pointed a finger. "I planted that to mark the entrance to the path. Pull in here."

Winston said, "I'll anchor, and we can cross in the canoes." He idled the motor while Alex and Hector dropped the two canoes over the side. They clambered into them, Winston last, his machete in hand.

The humidity seemed to increase as they approached the shore and the breeze died down. Petra was soaked in sweat before they even landed. Mosquitoes descended on her like James Beard on foie gras. She slapped them away from her eyes, but they only moved as far as her neck. Soon a thin layer of insects coated the rest of her. "Help!"

"Hold on, Miss Petra." Hector turned off the path toward a large cacao tree. What looked like a huge gray football hung from it. He broke a branch off a nearby shrub and tapped. A cloud of winged insects flew out.

Petra swatted at them. "Are those wasps? Why did you do that, Hector? The mosquitoes are bad enough!"

"No, no. They're not wasps; they're termites." He caught a handful of the bugs, squashed them between his palms, and then rubbed them on his face. "See? It keeps the mosquitoes away."

"You're kidding." Petra wasn't sure which repelled her more, a face full of termites or a mouth full of mosquitoes, but she dutifully rubbed some on her cheeks. The mosquitoes backed off as though they'd been stung themselves. "It works!"

Hector gave her a look that reminded her she was on his home turf, and winked. "Old family recipe." He went around Aguirre to take the lead, and they stumbled on through the vines. "Remember not to touch anything."

"Like he has to remind us," grumbled Ffoulkes.

He walked a little too closely behind Petra. She could feel his fetid breath on her neck. When a drop of his perspiration landed on her shoulder, she turned. "Why don't you go ahead of me?"

"Yes, of course. Don't you worry, my dear. I shall be your knight in shining armor." He sashayed past her, his leg rubbing hers. *Ick. Ick. Ick.*

Aguirre stopped abruptly. "Hold up. I saw something—something colorful." He walked rapidly off the path into a thicket.

"Wait! Don't go alone."

"It's all right. I'll be right back." He reappeared, a feather in his hand. The others gathered around him to look at it. Horizontal stripes of black alternated with reddish-orange bands.

Hector took it. "It's a primary from a hoatzin. They must be roosting near here."

Aguirre shook his head. "No, no. Look again. It's not a primary. It's a different shape—see how asymmetrical it is? I think it's a tail feather."

"But hoatzin tails aren't red. They're black with one yellow band. And they're a uniform width."

Aguirre's smile widened. "That's right."

Hector scrutinized the feather, his face thoughtful. Petra, anxious to start walking, if only to generate some air movement, suggested, "Why don't we bring it back to Emory—see what he thinks? It could be a species he recognizes."

The guide's brow furrowed. "Trouble is, I can't think of any other bird around here with a tail feather patterned this way."

Nick offered, "A sunbittern? Isn't that reddish brown?"

"Only its wing bar." He rubbed his jaw.

Before he could continue, Aguirre said, "Let me see if there's anything else there." He spread the bushes where he'd found the feather and pointed. "What's that?"

Nick bent down and took a photo. "Looks like a bird track. But there's a weird little hole behind it. See there?"

Aguirre nodded in satisfaction. "A claw."

Hector said, "Hoatzin nestlings have claws on their wings."

"Yes, but look at the size of the print. This is an adult bird—maybe three or four feet long."

"So what are you getting at?"

"Better to show you when we return to the lodge."

Ffoulkes held out his hand for the feather. "I'll take it." Instead, Aguirre dropped it in a glassine envelope and placed it in his backpack. The director started to object but seemed to think better of it and merely said, "Let's keep moving. How far is it to the place where you found the stone slab?"

"Half a mile, I'd say."

They tramped along in silence for a while, the only sound that of hands slapping at insects. Finally, Petra made out another red flag up ahead. "Is that it?"

"Yes."

She looked to her left. "What's through there? Something's shimmering."

Hector answered. "It's an oxbow lake. Hoatzin usually congregate around them." As if to confirm, they heard a loud crashing and grunting. "That must be a flock of them now. They do not fly well, and so tend to thrash around on the ground when flushed."

Winston muttered, "Stupid birds."

That's what he said about Molly the toucan. Petra wondered if he thought all birds were stupid. Before she could ask, they broke out of the undergrowth onto the shore of a small body of black water. A kingfisher keened and swooped over the surface just as a fish jumped. The sun burned heavy. Petra shielded her eyes and surveyed the expanse of water. A flock of birds huddled in a clump on the far side. She took out her binoculars and trained them on one—a large, lumpy peacock-like bird. It was quite showy, with chestnut primaries and a square black-and-yellow tail. When it turned, she noted a bright blue face and a floppy reddish crest. Just then the breeze picked up from the west, rippling the water. Both Alex and Petra covered their mouths. "Oh, my God, what a stench."

"Like I said, they smell just like cattle."

Petra couldn't help it. "Some people claim cows cause global warming. Now we know the real culprit."

Nick guffawed.

Aguirre had been sweeping the opposite shore with his glasses when he stopped. "Look! There! To the right of the hoatzin!"

Everyone swung around, but only a wall of green met their eyes. "What?"

"It's…oh, damn. It's gone." His eyes lit up. "If it's what I think it is, we are in for a helluva ride."

"What did you see?"

"A living fossil."

****

Emory was sitting on the dock when the launch pulled in. Petra felt something lurch behind her rib cage when she saw him there, his hair fluffing in the breeze, his sparkling green eyes searching her out.

"Whoa! Did the boat just heel?" She caught the railing with both hands.

Nick glanced at her. "No, sis." He followed her gaze. "Could've been your heart."

"Don't be ridiculous."

"Is it? Have you packed for the trip home yet?"

"N…no. Listen, Nicky, I was thinking maybe I'd stay a little longer. After all, I'm still on sabbat—"

"Save your breath, hon." He winked. "You want to find Bigfoot, right? Or maybe whatever Aguirre's on to."

"I do." Her eyes strayed to the shore. "Absolutely."

"Okay, if that's your story, you stick with it."

Emory stood up and helped her out of the boat. "Success?"

Aguirre pumped his arms. "I need a cold shower and a colder drink."

Emory nudged Ffoulkes. "What's he in such a lather over?"

"He claims he sighted a living fossil. The rest of us only saw hoatzins, but his evidence bears discussion. Why don't we gather before dinner?" He took Petra's elbow. "Petra? May I escort you to your room?"

The nausea was barely controllable. "No, thank you, Denys. I'll be fine."

Emory glanced at her, then at Ffoulkes. He opened his mouth.

"Emory." She put a warning hand on his arm. "Hector, I have to make a phone call. Is there cell service here?"

"Did you buy a chip in Iquitos?"

"No. Should I have?"

"Sorry, my fault. Here, use mine." Nick handed her his phone. "I forgot to take care of that when we were in the city. You have to buy a prepaid chip to make calls in Peru."

"Thanks." She walked away from the others and punched in her mother's number.

"Is that you, Nicholas? Why are you calling now? I'm busy. I was going to ring you both later today."

Petra heard the clink of a glass. "It's me, Mom. Petra. I borrowed Nicky's phone. What are you having for lunch?"

"What am I having for lunch? You call from almost four thousand miles away and that's all you want to know?"

She knew her mother well. "Yes, Mother. That's why I called. Is Dad back yet?"

"No, and I've gained five pounds. You *know* when he's away I have no control. I've been through a whole bag of potato chips and a six-pack of beer."

"That doesn't sound too bad. He's been gone more

than three weeks."

"That's *today*."

"Oh."

She continued to grumble. "He has no sympathy—says I'm old enough to know better. Then, to salt the wound, he talks glowingly of his new press person—the one on the trip with him? Gail something. Apparently, she's gorgeous and brilliant and...and tall." Her mother refused to accept that she'd never see another growth spurt like the one at age eleven that got her to four feet ten.

"He's yanking your chain, Mother. You know you're the love of his life." The sound of a cap popping off came through the speaker. "I called to ask you to do me a favor."

"Anything, sweetie. What do you need?"

"I want you to cancel my plane reservation. Then call Phoebe Norton at the University of Chicago Press and tell her I've been delayed here. I probably won't have the second section of the book done by our deadline."

"Delayed! Why?"

Because I met this wonderful hunk of man flesh, and I want to spend every waking minute I can with him. Maybe every sleeping minute, too. "We've made some potentially bombshell discoveries here, and I want to follow through on them."

"But you're not a scientist."

"Nick says I'm more useful. I'm a librarian." She grinned, remembering Emory's rather mean-spirited comment. *Take that.* "We've come across some things that require expertise these guys don't have. They need my research skills. I can survey the literature while they

123

do the lab work."

"So what are these discoveries?"

A rough hand squeezed her upper arm painfully. She twisted around to see Aguirre, his black eyes glittering with rage. "Don't say a word," he hissed.

How long has he been eavesdropping? A peek at his stormy expression and she decided not to defy him. "I can't talk about it now, Mom. Look, please tell Phoebe I'll get in touch as soon as I can, but I'm extending my vacation another couple of weeks at least."

"What about the Galapagos trip? I thought you'd finally scraped together some courage and made the deposit."

"Uh, no. The brochure arrived the day Nick asked me to come down here. I'll…uh…go next year."

"That's what you said *last* year."

Ah, but this year I have a better excuse—I'm not avoiding adventure. I'm embracing it. She chuckled at the pun.

"What did you say?"

"I said, I'll text you Phoebe's number. Look, I have to go. This is a pre-paid phone, and I've already used five minutes. Love you."

"All right, but how is the boy child? Has he gotten himself in trouble yet?"

"He's fine. He's got a darkroom here and everything. Happy as a clam. I'll try to send you some photos."

"Do that. I need a distraction."

As Petra hung up, she heard the sound of another top popping.

Aguirre swung her around. "You didn't tell her

anything?"

She shook his hand off. "Nothing. Not that I have to answer to *you*." She knew he was right but wasn't about to be bullied.

"The bird is *my* discovery. You have no right to reveal it to anyone." His accent thickened the angry words.

Petra was about to retort when she saw her brother come up behind Aguirre. He tapped him on the shoulder. "I wouldn't take that tone of voice with my sister, Tramposo. It may not be healthy for you."

The transformation was instantaneous. He stepped back. "Ah...Steele. I beg your pardon." He made a little bow. "I suppose I am so overwhelmed by the potential of this find that I've become somewhat...er... hotheaded. It will not happen again."

Seeing no reason not to accept his apology, Petra nodded. She handed Nick the phone. "Mother says keep your nose clean."

He laughed. "Dad's not home yet, right?"

"Right."

"She's gained ten pounds and gone through the entire wine cellar."

"Five. Five pounds. And she's moved on to beer."

"Whatever. Dinner's ready. Ffoulkes wants to have a campfire sing-along after."

Petra had assumed her brother was joking, but it turned out the director was serious. After a few initial protests, the rest went along. Denys made sure Petra sat next to him and announced, "I shall start us off."

To her surprise, he had a rather pleasant voice, and true to form, sang several English ballads, including "Greensleeves." *He probably identifies with Henry VIII when he's not channeling Prince Bertie.*

Alex's turn came next. He started in on a squawling rendition of "Sweet Betsy from Pike," to which the squirrel monkeys strenuously objected. Since no one could hear him over their caterwauling, Petra stood. Denys jumped up, but she laid a hand on his shoulder. "I'm tired. I think I'll turn in."

She was undressing when someone tapped on the door. Emory slipped in. He drew her to him. "Do I take it I'm to have you for a little while longer?"

The thought came unbidden. *You can have me forever.* She cast it aside. Who knew what would happen when this idyll was over? She thought of the two dead men. Or before it was over?

Chapter Ten
Protective Coloration

October 13

Petra was passing the lab on her way to breakfast when she saw Aguirre sitting at the microscope. She stopped to watch him. He cut a bit of the feather and stuck it between two slides, carefully adjusting the microscope. He made a few notes on a pad of paper, then moved to the computer and tapped in some words. He clicked on a site, making more notes. She coughed.

He started and turned. "I didn't hear you come in."

"Have you identified the feather?"

"Not yet. I'm narrowing down the possibilities."

"It's not from a hoatzin?"

"No, but something very similar." He covered his notebooks with a casual hand. "I want to do a bit more research before I bring in the rest of the team. We should have irrefutable evidence before we take this public." He dismissed her with a nod.

"Okay…" She went on to the dining room.

"Where's Aguirre?"

"In the lab studying the feather. He really thinks he's on to something."

Denys huffed. "Well, as the leader of this expedition, I expect to be fully informed and included."

Emory raised his eyebrows. "As I recall, you're the

leader of an expedition looking for the *Mapinguari*, not for a bird."

Denys's concave chest ballooned with hot air. "I beg your pardon. This whole trip is funded by *my* grants and *my* applications. I expect due credit for underwriting this discovery." He sat down with a plop. "If in fact it *is* a discovery."

The rest began to eat. Nick took a huge bite of scrambled eggs. "Yum. Where'd you get the eggs, Capac? I haven't seen any hens around."

He pointed outside at the kapok tree. "Macaws."

"Excuse me?" Petra paused, her fork in midair.

Nick smacked his lips. "And the sausages are great too. What are they made of?"

"Agouti."

"Isn't that a kind of rodent?"

Emory smirked. "Yup."

Instead of being put off, Nick polished off three more links. "We used to hunt squirrel when I was a kid. That tastes like gamey chicken, but this has a spicy flavor. What's in it?"

The cook answered. "*Comino*—cumin. And *aji charapa*. A chile that grows wild here. Very hot."

"Love it. Thanks, Capac."

The cook bowed and went back to his kitchen. Noting the spring in his step, Petra had a feeling that dinner would be a triumph of local cuisine. "You did good, bro."

Nick forked another link from the platter. "Always flatter the cook, as Ma is fond of saying."

"So *that's* why Dad lets her have all the crispy turkey skin."

After breakfast, Alex and Hector left in a canoe.

"Hector's cousin Santiago swears he saw a pair of yacare caimans in a shallow backwater downriver."

Aguirre returned to the lab, and Denys announced with a pompous air that he had to take a conference call with two trustees. "No, I won't tell them anything... yet."

Petra went back to her room, intent on a short rest. Due to recent extracurricular activities, she hadn't gotten as much sleep as she was used to. When Emory knocked, she toyed briefly with the idea of telling him to go away. *Hello? It's been two years since you've been with a man, and who knows how long since you've been with a man who leaves you breathless. What are you thinking?* "Come in."

"You busy?"

"I thought I'd take a nap."

His lips turned up. "I'm not surprised. I'm a little stiff. I'm not used to such...er...athletic siestas."

She sat down on a chair. "Did you want something?"

"Always." When she pointed at the door, he said, "No, I wanted to talk. I'm a bit concerned about the expedition's sudden veering off into other arenas."

"Why? If Aguirre's found something new, shouldn't we pursue it?"

"Ye-esss. It's just that it seems too pat. We came down here to map this part of the Amazon basin, and within days switched to the search for the creature called a Mapinguari. And now, before we've even checked it out, we're off on some crazy fishing expedition for a new bird."

"Funny way to put it."

"What?" He seemed to realize what he'd just said.

"Well, you know what I mean."

"But Emory, you're an ornithologist. You should be more jazzed by a new bird species than by some big hairy mammal."

"You'd think so. It's just that…" His head went down, and so did his voice. "I don't want to make that mistake again."

Mistake? Does he mean me? "What are you talking about?"

He sat on the bed. "I might as well tell you. I've come to realize that Ffoulkes recruited me because he assumed I'd keep my mouth shut about our Sasquatch."

"Well, that's okay. You—"

"Because I was already persona non grata in the biological world."

"What?"

He rubbed his hands together, then suddenly blurted, "Three years ago, I was on the tenure track for a professorship at Cornell. Two years ago, they fired me. No one in the academic world will touch me. I've been reduced to finding spots at smaller institutions—obscure institutes like Ffoulkes's—as a visiting lecturer. I'll bite at anything that pays for room and board."

"You lost your job? How? Oh, you said 'make the same mistake again,' didn't you? What did you mean?"

He nodded, not looking at her. "I found a new species of hummingbird. Or thought I did."

"Ah." She sat up expectantly.

"It was spring break, and my research assistant and I were tramping the hills outside Tucson." He paused. "Did you know there's only one variety of hummingbird in the entire eastern United States?"

"The ruby-throated?"

He beamed. "Yes, well done. Most of the other species occur only in slivers of the far west. However, in the extreme southeast corner of Arizona up to fifteen types of hummingbird nest in an area only a few miles square. The region's been studied out the wazoo by ornithologists for decades." He stopped, a reminiscent smile on his lips. "Imagine my astonishment and elation when I caught sight of what I thought was an entirely new one. It was—get this—*yellow.*"

"Yellow. Aren't they generally iridescent greens and purples?"

"Yes. This one was a creamy color with white wings."

"Wow. Did you get a photo of it?"

"One shot from about fifty yards away. Grainy, although the coloring was clear enough. We spent another ten days in the desert trying to get a second, closer shot, but eventually my assistant Joel and I had to give up. We took the picture back to Cornell but couldn't hunt down any bird in the literature that matched the image we had. When we presented a paper on our findings, it created a sensation—we were interviewed on television and for the *Journal of Field Ornithology.* Brooks and Hudson offered me a book contract. The chairman of the department was making noises about expedited tenure hearings when the bottom fell out."

"It was a hoax?"

"No, worse. Sloppy research. Two months after we returned, Joel came across a 1926 journal from a Mexican birding club describing an identical bird."

"And what was it?"

"An immature Lucifer hummingbird. Exceedingly rare—hadn't been seen in northern Mexico for eighty years. But not new."

"I'm so sorry." Petra wasn't a scientist, but she had experienced the exhilaration that came with chance discovery. While in graduate school, she spent a summer working in the special collections at the library and came across a very rare first edition of Charles Kingsley's *The Water Babies* in the bottom of a box of old postcards. She remembered it had been signed on the flyleaf by Lady Darwin. *What Ffoulkes wouldn't do to get his hands on it. Ha.* "What happened then?"

"Oh, I reported it to my chairman, who took it to the dean, who took it to the tenure committee, who promptly denied my tenure application. The publishing house had no choice but to cancel my contract for the book." His grin was lopsided. "So now you see me in all my glory, in heroic pursuit of a mythical monster. By rights, I should be wearing a pith helmet and carrying a bullwhip. But no, we have Denys for that." He stopped. "What the hell's going on with him, anyway?"

"Never mind." She sat, chin in hand. "Did you come here to reveal past indiscretions? Is that why you aren't…er…ready for anything…" She petered out.

He jerked. "Why, no. I never intended to tell you all this." He gazed at her, his eyes questioning. "I wanted to…hoped to…talk you into going after the Mapinguari ourselves."

"Huh?" Now she was thoroughly muddled.

Before he could answer, the door flew open. Nick, out of breath, cried, "Aguirre has an announcement."

They followed him to the lab. Aguirre sat,

surrounded by the others, in front of the laptop. The screen displayed an artist's rendition of a strange bird-like creature. Petra bent closer. "Cary…*Caudipteryx*? What's that?"

"*Caudipteryx zoui*."

"I repeat, what is it?"

"Hang on." Aguirre opened another window. This one had a photograph of a hoatzin. "Notice the resemblance?"

Alex said, "They both look like turkeys."

"The bare face? The tail?"

"Yeah, what about them?" Nick looked puzzled.

"Well, I think they're related. I think—"

Ffoulkes held up a finger. "You're suggesting the *Caudipteryx* is the prehistoric ancestor of the stinkbird?"

"No, no. I—"

"Or are you suggesting the bird you saw is a living *Caudipteryx*?"

"No! Please, let me explain. Not exactly. There's another possibility. I'd better back up a little." They waited. Aguirre pointed. "You see, the *Caudipteryx* was a dinosaur."

"Go on." Emory beetled his brows.

"*Caudipteryx zoui* was a species of theropod that lived in the early Cretaceous period. It was about the size of a hoatzin. It had feathers and was once believed to be a potential evolutionary link between dinosaurs and birds."

"Isn't that a little late in the game?" Denys seemed skeptical. "Last I heard the *Archaeopteryx lithographica* was considered the link, and it lived some thirteen million years earlier."

Aguirre seemed annoyed. "Yes, I know, but that's not important."

"Important!" The biologist sat back on his heels. "Isn't it crucial?"

"I mean, it's not important in this case. What I'm saying is—"

Emory cut in. "Wait. Couldn't what you saw at the lake just be a species of carrion eater? Or a type of guan?"

"No. Neither of these animals are carrion eaters. They were—are—both vegetarian."

Alex seemed unconvinced. "Why the bald head, then? I thought vultures had no feathers on their heads to avoid infection when they're beak deep in a bloody carcass?"

Aguirre's voice simmered with impatience. "If you'll let me finish—"

Emory beat him to it. "You think it's still around."

Like the Mapinguari. "A cryptid."

"Yes." Aguirre picked up the feather. "This matches the fossilized tail feathers of the *Caudipteryx*. And it—like the hoatzin—had a claw. See—even its wings are similar to the hoatzin, so it probably doesn't fly very well."

"It doesn't have the hoatzin's crest."

"No, that must have developed separately. My point is, what I saw may be a new species—a direct descendent of the dinosaur."

"A divergent species? Like a cousin of the hoatzin?"

"Yes."

In the silence, a cell phone rang. Aguirre pulled one out of his pocket, checked the screen, and blanched.

"I have to take this." He ran out of the room.

Emory looked after him. "I wonder what that was all about?"

Denys smirked. "Probably his wife. According to him, she's one of those semi-invalid types who is constantly finding new diseases to be infected with and expects him to cater to her twenty-four seven. She's really irked that he's here."

Aguirre came back, clearly rattled.

Ffoulkes said loudly, "So how's your wife, Aguirre?"

"Who?" He peered at the director. "Oh, yeah. She's okay. Um...no feeling in her left side today." The two men laughed indulgently. Aguirre sat down before the computer. "I want to do some more research before we head out again."

"Head out?"

"Don't we all want to see if we can find the bird? I only caught a glimpse of it yesterday."

"That's right." Ffoulkes nodded sagely. "We must have solid proof—a live bird, or at least a better shot." He slapped his hands together. "That reminds me. I have to get in touch with Rook Enterprises about the scope."

Petra looked at the others. "Scope?"

Denys nodded at Nick. "Why don't you explain it to her? I'm going to put a call in to their headquarters." He left.

Nick paused by the door. "It's a new design for a long-range telescope, sis. This guy Rook invented it and wants to put it through its paces here in Pacaya. That's about all I know."

The others left. Petra repaired to the kitchen for a

bottle of water. Emory followed her, grousing under his breath. She stopped, letting him run into her. "What are you on about?"

"This pseudo-hoatzin fixation. I don't like it."

"Why not?"

"Number one, I'm not interested in flying dinosaurs. And number two, I think it's all nonsense."

"Isn't it a little early to be calling it nonsense? We only have bits of evidence."

"Maybe, but my primary goal at present is to find Bigfoot, and I aim to catch me one."

"I don't understand. Why are you so obsessed?"

He closed his eyes. "Twenty-five years ago, my father went on what birders call a 'big year'—a year-long bird-spotting contest. He traveled around the world seeking to rack up as many sightings for his life list as he could."

"Contest? Was he competing against other birders?"

"Not him. This was a personal challenge he took on. He'd lost his wife—my mother—and then was forced by company policy to retire. With nothing else to do, he picked himself up and took off." A spasm of pain crossed Emory's tan features. "In the final quarter of the year, he took a detour to South America and was lost in the Amazon. When they found his body, it had been ravaged by some large beast. The authorities said a jaguar had gotten to him, but his native guide insisted it was a Mapinguari."

"And you want to prove him right?"

"Or wrong."

Chapter Eleven
The Tree of Life

October 13

It took Petra three seconds to decide. "When do we go?"

"Tomorrow. We'll take Winston with us. The others can wallow in their bird dung."

The prospect of a jaunt into the rainforest with the man who turned her brain to mush swam before her like a shape-shifting pink dolphin. "What about Nick?"

"I don't want to attract attention to our little expedition. Tell him we're going on a romantic canoe ride."

"But then I'd have to tell him that we…we…"

He kissed her cheek. "You think he doesn't already know?"

"Did you tell him?"

"No, my dear. Your eyes did." He paused. "He's a good man."

****

October 14

Winston held the canoe for Petra. She still couldn't understand how the simple dugout could stay afloat—it was so shallow the water lapped over the sides, and it tipped badly. "All set?" He got in his own, and Emory dropped his gear in a third.

Nick stood on the dock. "You be careful, sis. This isn't Disney World, you know."

"What? You mean those monkeys are *real*?" Petra waved. "We have Winston. See you later!"

They floated down the river for a few miles, passing a couple of homesteads and a village. The houses stood on stilts, with hammocks strung along open galleries. Chickens picked in the mud, and little brown children played at the water's edge. She called to Winston. "Which tribe do those people belong to?"

He followed her pointing finger. "No tribe. *Ribereños*. Like me."

"*Ribereños*? I've heard that term before. What does it mean?"

Emory said, "It's used to describe the people who live along the banks of the rivers, especially here in northeast Peru. They're mestizos—mixed Spanish and detribalized folk."

"Detribalized? That sounds like ostracism. How did it happen?"

"No, not ostracism. Hector explained it to me. When the rubber boom started in the late nineteenth century, Indians from all over Peru were drawn to the area in hopes of employment. A few decades later, the boom collapsed, but many of them—cut off from family either by choice or happenstance—stayed, never returning to their tribes. They mixed with Europeans and members of other tribes and settled along the rivers. It's more or less a unique culture now."

A couple of men motored by in a slightly bigger boat, their hold full of fish. "Where are they going?"

Winston yelled something at them. They yelled back. "Taking their catch to Nauta. Most *ribereños* make their living fishing, but every family plants a garden. They also keep a few chickens and maybe a pig." He pointed at the shore, where Petra saw a man with a bundle over his shoulder and a rifle at his side. "Sometimes they hunt."

"Hunt?"

"Tapir. Agouti. Capybara." He drew back, caught off guard by her look of horror.

Emory sniggered. "Come on, Petra. You can't pretend you didn't enjoy Capac's agouti sausage."

"Oh, but those sweet tapirs. Charlie's a dear."

"Charlie?"

"The one who greets me every morning. He nudges me with his snout. It's like a kiss."

"Oh yeah, that one. Couldn't have anything to do with the fact that you give him a piece of fruit every day."

The jungle closed in again, although here and there they could see openings filled with the huge fronds of banana trees. It was hot. Winston called, "The villagers grow squashes and corn in their yards but plant bananas in the forest."

"How come?"

He pointed. "They get very large and spread quickly. No room for them in the settlements."

They pulled in at a small dock. "This is my brother's property. It was near here Hector's cousin Huayna says he saw the beast."

Emory turned to Petra. "Ffoulkes told me there were several reported sightings of the creature in the last few months."

"Yes. Do we have any more information on them?"

"Not much." He got out of the canoe. Winston

pulled it up on the bank. "This Huayna. He saw it clearly?"

Winston hesitated. "It was at twilight. He says he saw a shadow, but it was man-like and very tall. He says its head brushed a tall tree limb."

"And there was some hair stuck in the bark, right?"

"Yes. Dark brown, but wiry. Bristly. Not like native hair."

Petra noted his glossy black mane. *Smooth as satin.* "Show us."

"This way." They came upon a clearing. Banana plants rimmed the edges. A tall, smooth-barked palm tree with a noticeable middle bulge stood in the center. Petra pantomimed. "Looks like an old man's beer belly."

Winston's eyes crinkled. "Barrigona palm—it means 'potbellied.' "

Petra gazed about her but saw no signs of animal life. She could hear monkeys chattering but couldn't see them.

"It's just up here." Winston led them farther into the woods. He indicated a huge mahogany tree and, taking hold of a low branch, hitched himself up. He pointed at something stuck to the bark about two feet above Emory's head. "There."

They saw a tuft of brown hair. "Could it be from a monkey?"

He shook his head.

"A jaguar?"

"No. Only thing it is like is the...I don't know the English word. *Perezoso.*"

"What's that?"

Emory translated. "Sloth."

"Huh."

They heard a shout from the river and retraced their steps. A native in a dugout, obviously frantic, beckoned Winston.

The guide ran down and pushed off in his canoe. "Where are you going?" Petra tried not to panic.

"My village. My son was bitten by a snake. It's not far. I'll be back soon. Wait here. Do not stray into the forest." He went off, paddling hard.

Emory and Petra looked at each other. "Now what?"

He turned toward the bananas. "I say we explore a little."

"Okay, but you heard Winston."

"We'll go as far as that big tree and see if we can find any other evidence."

They went back down the path they'd come, surveying the ground and vegetation for any trace of a large animal. They had reached the mahogany tree when Petra checked her watch. "Winston's been gone half an hour. Maybe we should—" Her words were cut off by a low snarl. "Emory? Is that you?" She whirled around. "Where are you?"

For answer, the growl grew deeper and more menacing. *Sounds like a gorilla—but they don't live here, do they?* She whispered, "Emory?"

"*Shh.*" She looked up. Emory clung to a low branch of the mahogany tree. He held a hand out. "Quickly."

She grabbed a liana, hoping fervently it wasn't a curare vine, and scrambled up. The growl came again, closer. They climbed higher. Something crashed through the woods, puffing. Whatever it was entered the clearing, and the noise stopped. Petra held her breath and Emory's hand. *It must be looking for us.* After a lengthy pause that left her feeling chilled to the bone in the torrid heat, the puffing started again, gradually diminishing into the distance. She waited five more minutes to be sure it was gone before whispering, "Did you get a look at it?"

"No, the foliage was in the way, but it sounded awfully big. And grouchy. I'm going to—" As he started to climb down, a twig snapped below them. They froze.

Something's being dragged through the underbrush. They waited another five minutes. Finally, she ventured, "Do you think it's gone?"

"I don't know. Let me go first." He ducked and touched the top of his head. "Uh-oh. I hope that's not monkey scat."

She raised her face to the canopy. "It's rain."

"Just a drizzle. No problem. We...*shit*."

The downpour came suddenly, drenching them. They sat, huddled under the canopy of leaves, waiting it out. Petra tasted a drop on her forearm. "They don't have acid rain here, do they?"

"No—they have a lot of poisonous species here, but no industrial pollution that I know of." He shielded his face and looked up. "We can only hope manchineel trees don't grow here. We'll have to ask Aguirre when we get back."

"Manchineel?"

"Small trees of the swamp. Their sap is extremely toxic. If it drips on you, it burns and blisters the skin. Enough exposure can kill you."

"But if the poison is only in the sap, we're safe

unless we tap into the tree, right?"

"I wish. It's a particularly vicious plant—even runoff from the leaves in a rainstorm can sluice the poison onto your skin."

"Great." She began to shiver, mainly due to nerves. The rain stopped.

They heard a shout. Winston came tumbling into the clearing. "Up here!"

He looked up. "What are you doing up there?"

"We heard something."

"Never mind. I have news!" He panted. "My... my...son...he saw it."

"What?"

"The Mapinguari."

Emory started to climb down but paused. He stretched out an arm and grabbed at the hair, stuffing a hank in his pocket. "We should study it when we get back."

Petra followed him. When she reached the ground, she found Winston, his face aglow with feverish excitement. "Your son saw a Mapinguari? Is he sure?"

"It was running through the scrub. Acarapi followed it, but in his hurry he stepped on a snake. He pulled up and the Mapinguari got away, but he says it was very tall and hairy."

"Where was he when he saw it?"

"Only a few yards from here. He was picking herbs for the shaman. When the snake bit him, he went home for help."

They crossed the clearing on the way to the boats. Winston slipped but caught himself. "What's this? Were you people hungry? There is food in your backpacks." He picked up a peel. "You shouldn't have eaten Francisco's bananas. You will have to pay him."

A stalk of bananas had been stripped from the tree and dozens of empty peels lay about. Petra shook her head. "It wasn't us."

"Good. Stealing from other people's gardens is very bad. Like your cattle…is the word 'rustling'?" He mimicked riding a horse and throwing a lasso.

Petra guessed that Peruvian television ran to old westerns.

Emory pressed his lips together. "It might have been the creature. Maybe that's what it was hauling through the brush."

"Hopefully. Hopefully it wasn't a body." She turned to Winston. "Is your son going to be all right?"

"Oh, yes." He handed her into her canoe. "Would you like to talk to him?"

Emory glanced at Petra. "We could compare notes."

"Then yes, please."

The three canoes edged into the mainstream. A few minutes later, they beached near a family compound. A little girl ran down to them. "Papa! Acarapi *está despierto*."

Winston said something to her, then turned to Emory and Petra. "My son is awake. We can see him now."

A young boy of about fourteen lay in a hammock. A clean rag was tied around his raised leg. Winston kissed his forehead. "This is my eldest son, Acarapi. He is apprenticed to Don César."

The boy struggled to sit up. "You want to know about the Mapinguari." His English was surprisingly good.

"Yes."

He described it much as his father had.

"Did it make any sound?"

"Sort of *mahh, mahh*—like a goat, only louder."

Emory said, "We may have heard it too, but we couldn't see it clearly. Do you think you could draw a likeness for us?"

"Yes." On a piece of paper, he traced a crude image that looked exactly like all the other pictures of the creature Petra had found online.

She said gently, "Acarapi, did you actually see it?"

He hesitated, then shook his head. "I only saw a shadow. But it was big!" His eyes grew round. "And scary. I didn't want to get too close in case...in case he was hungry."

Emory grunted. "Not to worry. He filled up on bananas."

They took their leave and returned to the lodge. A babble of angry voices greeted them as they came up the steps. Petra was dying to get out of her wet clothes, but the hubbub aroused her curiosity. She and Emory marched into the lounge.

Alex, Denys, and Aguirre stood in a tight circle, arguing. Nick leaned against the bar, listening. Aguirre said vehemently, "We *have* to go back soon. We don't know how large their territory is. They could be long gone if we wait."

Ffoulkes said sharply, "We need that special scope, Aguirre. We haven't gotten close enough to the thing for a definite identification."

"Well, when is it going to get here?" Frustration sparked in Aguirre's eyes.

"I talked to Rook Enterprises yesterday. It's on its

way and should arrive tomorrow. A representative of the company is bringing it—fellow by the name of Kelly Chisholm."

Nick piped up. "Good. He'll help us set it up? I want to get some practice with it."

Ffoulkes raised a carefully trimmed brow. "You? What makes you think he'll allow *you* to handle the prototype? You're just a photographer."

Nick began to splutter, and Petra broke in. "What the hell do you mean, 'just a photographer'? He's at the top of his field. He's made prize-winning documentaries. His photographs hang in the gallery of the National Geographic building." She caught her breath. "*You* hired him, after all."

Her rant didn't seem to affect him. "Maybe so, but is he experienced with an image-erecting prism system?"

"Of course." She didn't look at Nick.

Ffoulkes turned red. "He's not a scientist."

"And you're not a photographer."

Petra and Denys faced off. Emory started to snicker. "What is this, extreme cage fighting? Really, children. Back off."

It broke the tension, and Alex pushed the adversaries apart. Denys hissed, "Rook himself emailed me and made it clear that his employee is authorized to grant me total control of the instrument."

Petra glanced at Nick. He shrugged. "No reason to get riled up. I'll talk to the guy when he gets here."

She didn't feel as sanguine. In fact, she was getting dreadfully sick of Denys and his arrogance. "So will I."

Her look of challenge made Denys bristle. "We wait until the scope gets here. That's final."

"But…the birds!" Aguirre sounded increasingly close to hysteria.

"I said, it's final."

Aguirre cast a look full of hatred at him. "We'll see." He stalked out of the room.

"Whew." Alex picked up a half-empty beer bottle and took a swig. "What's gotten into him?"

Nick watched Aguirre's retreating figure. "It's his baby. I'd be pretty anxious to confirm it too."

Petra's soaked clothes clung to her. She plucked at them. "I'm going to my room."

Emory caught up with her in the corridor. "Don't you want to tell the others about our brush with Sasquatch?"

"Not now." She shot him a tired look. "We should discuss it first." He started to follow her, but she spun around. "Later, okay? I want to dry off and just veg for a bit."

His face hardened, but he let her go.

As she lay on her bunk after a—for once, welcome—cold shower, she thought about their day. *We didn't actually see anything. Nor did Acarapi. Wait—we do have the hair. What did Emory do with it?*

Someone knocked. *Emory.* "Go away." When she heard footsteps start to recede, she got up. "Wait!" She opened the door.

Aguirre was passing, a phone in his hand. He stopped. "Miss Steele? Did you need something?"

"Oh…it's you. No, nothing. Never mind." She turned back to her room to find Emory standing by the railing.

"Were you looking for me?"

"Yes." The blush rose despite her best efforts.

"I…uh…was wondering if you still had the hair?"

He pulled it out of his pocket.

"Let me hang on to it."

He gave it to her and left, his face expressionless.

I can't help it if he's miffed. She just needed a break from the emotional roller coaster she'd been on for too many days.

She slipped the hair into a small plastic bag. After a moment's thought, she took a pen and marked the date on the corner. *Now, where to hide it?* She looked around the room, finally settling on her desk drawer. She slid the bag under a wad of tissues. *It should be safe there until we get a chance to study it.*

****

She must have been asleep for several hours, for when she woke darkness had fallen. She found her way to the kitchen. "Capac, did I miss dinner?"

Luckily, the cook was in a good mood and willing to forgive her. "I make you a sandwich."

"Thanks." She batted her eyelashes. "I promise not to ask again."

The cook winked.

She took her beer and the food to the hammock room. The sky was an inky black. Only a few stars poked through. She searched. *Ah, there he is.* Orion hovered overhead. She could see his bow arm stretched, the arrow pointing across the galaxy. A frisson of apprehension tickled the back of her neck. *What is he aiming at? Power? Sex? What does he hunt?* She shivered. *The Mapinguari?*

****

October 15

Morning arrived with the customary shout. *Who*

needs an alarm clock in this place?

"He's gone! Dammit."

She threw on a robe and went out into the corridor. Before she could take a step, she heard a large *craack*. In the palm tree across from her door, a brown bird clutched a tarantula the size of an octopus in his beak. He crunched down. The spider struggled and managed to free itself, landing on Petra's foot. She jumped back and squealed. In response, it dug into her slipper and held on for dear life. Petra danced around the hall, shaking her leg madly, but couldn't loosen its grip. Out of nowhere, Hector appeared, Winston's machete in his hand.

"No! Don't cut my foot off!"

"Hold still." Hector slipped the tip of the sword between her foot and the giant spider, flipping it off into the yard. Then he knelt down. "Did it sting you?"

"I...I don't think so."

He examined the skin. "Doesn't look like it. Tarantulas move very slowly. He was probably more scared than you were. How did it happen?"

She pointed at the bird, still perched on the palm. If she didn't know better, Petra would have sworn it was pissed.

Hector cackled. "I don't think that spider's day is going to get any better." He stood and held a hand out. "Are you all right?"

The tremors had by now diminished. "Yes...I guess so. I came out to see what the commotion was about. Who's gone?"

The man looked distressed. "Mr. Tramposo."

"Where did he go?"

Emory and Nick came around the corner. Nick

answered, "The little bastard took my Nikon and my best wide-angle lens."

"We think he went up to the oxbow lake on his own."

Petra turned to her brother. "Why wide angle? He won't get a detailed enough shot with that, will he?"

"Not of the bird, no, but he has a better chance of picking it up if he covers more ground."

Ffoulkes appeared holding a piece of paper. "He left a note." He read it aloud. " 'Went back to the lake.' Damned fool."

"Should we go after him?"

"No. I understand the Rook telescope will be delivered today. I want to be here for it. If he hasn't returned by the time we get it set up, we can send Winston after him."

"Let's get some breakfast, then."

They walked down to the dining room. Petra dressed and followed them. Capac silently placed plates of bread and watermelon before them.

Petra gulped down her mango juice. "Where's John?"

A low titter went around the table. Nick answered. "Winston's fixing him up."

"What? With a date?"

"No. A date would have been safer. With a Band-Aid."

"Huh?"

Alex's lip twitched. "He went outside to eat a banana. Said he wanted to enjoy a water view with his breakfast. Unfortunately, he sat down next to Molly."

"Molly? The toucan?" Petra was having trouble following the narrative.

Ffoulkes answered. "Yes. Molly—who loves bananas."

Nick added helpfully, "And thought it was a gift."

"Which she accepted with alacrity?"

"Or relish. Take your pick."

Alex took up the tale again. "John tried to explain that she had misinterpreted his intentions—"

"He tried to bat her away." Nick grinned.

"But she was not disposed to accept his declaration and bit his hand."

"Almost took a finger off."

Emory shook his head. "John seems to have a knack for riling up the local citizenry."

"Oh, I don't know. The monkeys love him."

Nick raised his eyes to the ceiling. "I wonder why that is?"

"His aura?" Alex giggled.

Petra thought they'd had enough fun at John's expense and changed the subject. "Who did you say was bringing the scope?"

Denys answered, "Kelly Chisholm. A marketing manager from Rook Enterprises. He'll put it together and train us on it."

"What's so special about it?"

"It's a prototype. Victor Rook is trying to sell it to the Pentagon. I believe it's a shoulder-mounted spotting scope with night-vision capabilities and a built-in camera."

Nick gasped. "The camera is built into the machine? Wow. Right now you can only buy kits where you attach a regular digital camera to the scope. Compatibility is a bitch. Plus the output is lousy." He sighed. "What I wouldn't do for an instrument like that."

Petra poked him and whispered, "Play your cards right, and maybe Chisholm will let you have a go at it when Denys isn't looking."

After breakfast, the team scattered. Nick asked his sister how she planned to spend the morning.

"I think I'll do a little more research on the ancient sloth."

"What was it called?"

"The *Megatherium*."

She was making some notes when Emory knocked. She let him in. "What are you working on?"

"Sloths." She pointed at the screen. "There are two distinct types—the ground sloth and the tree dwellers. They think all ground sloths are extinct now, but like I told you, the *Megatherium* was still wandering the forests up to a few thousand years ago. We should really take a look at that hair we brought back."

"That's why I came by, Petra. I've been thinking. You're right—I don't think we should mention our little escapade just yet."

"Why not?"

"I don't want to be accused of announcing some great find and have it turn out to be a fake again. After all, we didn't see the beast."

"But isn't the Mapinguari the reason we're all here?"

"Not precisely. Remember, this was billed to us as a simple expedition to catalogue the Pacaya region. When the natives brought the stories of the Mapinguari sightings to Denys, he went off the deep end. Until this *Caudipteryx* cousin turned up, the idea of a new mammalian species consumed him."

"What about you?"

He raised his hands and let them fall. "If I could prove or disprove its existence, I'd still be no closer to finding out what happened to my father. At this point, what difference would it make?"

"I...see." *Emory sure is complicated. But since this is just—in his words—a fling, it's probably wise not to try to figure him out.* Nevertheless, she was tempted to know more—in fact, to find out all about him. His sea-green eyes lured her into their pelagic depths. His full lips drew hers toward them. *A fling. Remember that.* "Well, maybe Denys will change his mind and set the hoatzin aside for the Mapinguari."

"And how would that help?"

Honest to God, he's impossible.

Chapter Twelve
Camouflage

October 15

It was late afternoon before they heard the horn announcing the arrival of a water taxi. "That must be Chisholm." Denys trotted down to the dock. Petra suspected he was trying hard not to break into a run. John had no such compunction and skipped ahead of him.

The boat pulled in. A man jumped off and turned to the operator, who helped him with a large cardboard box. They lowered it to the dock. When the passenger turned, Petra noted a gaunt, almost skeletal body and a seriously receding hairline. His massive hook nose reminded her of a raptor's beak. John almost saluted. "Mr. Chisholm?"

The man skimmed the faces of the two men on the dock, his steel gray eyes cold. "Chisholm couldn't make it. I'm Victor…Gardener. Who are you?"

The little man backed up a foot. "I…uh…I am John Dillinger, public relations for the Institute for Tropical Research in Florida. May I present Denys Ffoulkes, the director?" He stepped aside like a magician displaying the miraculously empty coffin.

"At your service." Denys bowed. "Let us help you with that." He pointed at the box but made no move toward it.

Petra watched, amused, as Gardener waited, then bent down to lift the box. When it became clear that he couldn't manage it on his own, he straightened and strode up the steps toward the lodge. Denys followed him, leaving John standing alone on the dock.

As he neared the front steps, he looked past Petra to Emory. "And you are?"

"Emory Andrews. Ornithologist."

"Huh." He swiveled his head to the right, where Alex stood. "You?"

"Alex Bönickhausen, herpetologist." He held his hand out, but Gardener ignored it. He still hadn't acknowledged Petra. "Where's the lab?"

Alex pointed down the hall.

He nodded and focused on Emory. "I want to wash up."

"Bathroom's next to the kitchen."

He was back almost instantly. "There's no hot water."

"No. We use only solar power in the lodge." Winston proudly pointed to a small panel about six feet square installed in the courtyard. "It serves our needs well and is good for nature."

Gardener reddened. "Well, it doesn't serve *my* needs. I have to wash my hands. *Now*. Boil me some water." He waited while the cook set a kettle on the stove, then took the hot water to the sink and poured it into a shallow basin. "Soap." Capac handed it to him. Petra watched, fascinated, as he scrubbed his hands for a full five minutes. He dried them carefully. "I'll need water on the heat all day." He walked out of the kitchen and down the hall. Over his shoulder he commanded,

"Meet me in the lab, and bring the box."

Denys hesitated, then plodded after him.

Emory whispered, "Quite the little martinet, isn't he? I thought he was just a salesman."

Alex chuckled. "I guess one who's used to having his orders followed."

"Or," put in Nick, "one who got Denys's number in less time than it took to wash his hands. I'll go help John."

Petra watched the little man bluster before grudgingly taking one end of the box. Nick picked up the other end. She preceded them down the hall to the lab. They found Gardener sitting before a keyboard. Up close, he displayed a weathered face, a sandy, untrimmed beard, and tropic-weight clothes which, while obviously expensive, were well-worn. *A seasoned traveler?* That would explain how thin he was—*too many bouts of Montezuma's revenge.*

"Put it down over there. You—" He snapped a finger at Emory. "Unpack it."

Emory squinted at him, then held up his bandaged hand. "Sorry, no can do."

The man didn't blink. "Well, someone better. I don't have time. I have to check in at the company." He tapped some keys on his phone. A tinny voice came on. Gardener increased the volume.

"Chisholm?"

"No. It's Victor Gardener."

"Gardener? But how—?"

"Never mind. Patch me through to Havel Air Freight Service in Lima. I want to talk to Igor Havel."

"But—"

"Now." He turned around to the others. "Get out."

Ffoulkes and John said in unison, "Pardon me?"

Gardener blew out a long breath. "Sorry. I have to pass on some proprietary information. Can't have it fall into the wrong hands. Company policy. Understand?"

Emory pulled at Ffoulkes's elbow. "Sure, sure." They shuffled out.

Nick followed with Petra. "A trifle abrupt, isn't he?"

"Maybe he's used to working alone."

"Well, he better make nice—at least with Capac— or he won't get any dinner."

Gardener yelled from behind them. "What's the passkey for Wi-Fi on this computer?"

Nick started to backtrack, but Petra stopped him. "I'll go. I want to see if he actually acknowledges my presence before I help him." She went back to the lab.

"Who are you?"

"Petra Steele."

"*Hmmph.*"

Sheesh. For all he cares, I could be the backer of this expedition. Or the queen. "You wanted the passcode?"

"Write it down."

"No. I'll key it in. Would you mind moving over?"

He started and gave her a second look. Something in her manner must have registered, for he moved over without another word.

They were still in the lab when the next outburst occurred.

****

"Help! Help! *Ayuda*! *Ayuda*!"

Again?

Gardener didn't look up. "Go see what it is," he

barked.

Petra paused. After she'd counted to ten, she said evenly, "I'm going to go see what's going on. You stay where you are." Before he could reply, she marched out.

John was running full tilt down the boardwalk and tripped over Molly. He went sprawling. Two spider monkeys leapt to his aid, scrambling over his back and swishing their tails in his face. He got up slowly, brushing the animals off like pesky flies. The man who had been yelling—a short dark *ribereño*—halted in front of him, his mouth opened wide. "*Ayuda!*"

John said angrily, "I heard you the first time. What is it?"

The man gawked at him. "I see…you know…I—" He stuttered to a stop. John stared hard at him, then turned away.

By this time, most of the camp had gathered. Hector came around the corner of the lodge. "It's Huayna, my cousin. He's the one who saw the Mapinguari." He spoke to the man. "He says he's found the tracks of a human and el Chullachaqui together."

"A native?"

"No. A European. Wearing hiking boots."

"Could it be Aguirre?"

Gardener had strolled down and heard the last sentence. "You mean Aguirre Tramposo? I was told he's the botanist on your team. Where is he?"

"We don't know." Ffoulkes grabbed Huayna's arm. "Where is he? Where are the prints?"

Hector gestured north. "Near where the hoatzin are nesting."

"So it could be Aguirre."

Hector said, "Huayna can take us to them." He broke off as the man gabbled a few more words. He replied heatedly before explaining in English. "He wants money."

"Money! What for?"

"He says he can track the man—if the Chullachaqui hasn't killed him—but he wants one hundred soles to do it."

"How much is that in American currency?"

Hector did a quick calculation. "About thirty dollars."

The group was silent. Finally Emory said, "Do you trust him, Hector?"

"He's my third cousin on my mother's side, so…no."

"What should we do?"

Ffoulkes spoke firmly. "I say we go. Aguirre could be in trouble. At best, we'll run into him returning."

Gardener growled, "What the hell do you think you're doing? I need help with the machine assembly. Now."

The director answered quickly, "Nick can help you. Nick Steele is our staff photographer."

The man looked Nick up and down. "Know anything about lenses?"

"Some. I'd be happy to learn from a master." Petra recognized the tick of humor in Nick's eyes. She knew from experience that he rarely let boors like Gardener get under his skin, preferring to treat them with lightly disguised contempt. If the victim suspected he was being ridiculed, he wouldn't want to admit it. *One of Nick's best talents.*

Gardener looked at him carefully. "Ah, well…"

159

Denys had continued without noticing the exchange. "Hector, you go with Huayna and Emory and Alex." With a small smile, he said, "Petra and I will hold the fort."

Emory took a step toward him. Petra gave him a warning look. *Don't blow our cover.*

He blew out his cheeks but stepped back. "All right, on one condition. We're not paying Huayna until we see the prints." The man started to argue, but at a word from Hector, subsided.

Denys peered at the sky. "It'll be dark soon. If you can't find him in an hour, come back."

"That man is more trouble…" Emory pounded his fist into his injured hand, breaking off with a curse when he realized what he was doing.

Alex agreed. "He should at least have taken a phone."

Nick blinked. "So his works here?"

"They all do now. Signal must be intermittent."

The four men got in the launch and started upriver. Petra walked back to the lodge, Denys beside her. He wheezed, "My dear Petra, you look a little peaked. Why don't you let me get you a sherry? It will tide you over till dinner is ready."

He led her to the dining room and poured her a glass. "Alone at last." His Cary Grant impression fell flat. She remained silent, sipping the drink. Denys's face worked as though he were desperately trying to find a topic of conversation. Capac brought in a tray with cancha and fruit. "Did you take something to Nick and Mr. Gardener?"

"No want food."

Twilight was closing in, and Petra began to feel

restless. "They should have been back before dark. Where are they?"

Just then they heard the launch chugging toward the dock, but when she ran down to the river, she saw only one man in the boat. Aguirre got out, his face alight. "Hello, Petra. Fantastic news. You won't believe this!"

"Where are the others?"

"What others? I went alone. That moron Ffoulkes would have made us miss the flock. As it was, they did move another mile. If I hadn't gone after them today, we would have lost them forever."

"But a native said he'd found your footprints. Emory, Alex, and Hector went after you. You didn't see them?"

He shook his head. "They must have just missed me. I anchored in a small cove out of sight of the river and hiked to the lake." He shoved past her. "Is Ffoulkes here?"

"Yes. Oh, and that man from Rook Enterprises has arrived. A Mr. Gardener."

"Gardener? Who's he? Wasn't Chisholm supposed to come with the scope?"

"He couldn't make it. Gardener seems to know what he's doing. He and Nick have been working all afternoon."

He strode into the lodge. At that moment, Gardener and Nick came out of the lab. Aguirre stopped midstride. "Mister—"

The man interrupted him. "You must be Tramposo. I'm Victor Gardener. I'm replacing Chisholm. He's...uh...busy on another project."

Aguirre's jaw dropped, but he recovered quickly.

"Gardener. Pleased to meet you. Have you put the scope together yet?"

"Except for some tweaking, it should be ready by tomorrow." Gardener elbowed him aside. "I need to make a phone call." He walked down the side stairs and vanished into the undergrowth.

Nick watched him go. "Nice old fart, isn't he? So, where are the others?"

Petra's voice trembled. "We don't know. They—"

Nick pointed over her shoulder. "Don't worry, sis. Lassie's come home."

Sure enough, the second launch had just pulled up. Emory got out and turned back to the boat. Huayna didn't move. Emory grabbed something from him and started toward Petra while Hector tied up the boat.

She called, "What's that you have?"

When he reached her, he held up a long stick. A leather strap hung from it. In his other hand he held a man's boot. "Our Chullachaqui…and his 'victim.' "

The native slunk over to his canoe and paddled furtively away.

"Let me guess: Huayna is a flim-flam man?"

"Uh-huh. Hector immediately saw through it. Locals do it to tourists all the time. He'd heard about Manuel's death and our suspicions and thought he could make a quick buck. You've got to admire his initiative."

Hector spat. "It gives my family a bad name."

Petra gestured at the items in Emory's hands. "How did he do it?"

"He strapped this to one leg to make the pegleg prints, and put the shoe on his other foot."

"Do you think he's responsible for the other

prints—the ones near Manuel's body?"

Alex shook his head. "The other ones were different—for one thing, they were huge."

"And bare."

Nick added, "And had claws."

Emory snorted. "Apparently, little Huayna can be flexible. 'You looking for the Mapinguari? Sure, I can do him! El Chullachaqui? No problem!' "

Petra giggled. "You didn't pay him, did you?"

"No." He watched the retreating form of the native. "He confessed as soon as he realized we were onto him."

Hector was grim, but a touch of mirth danced in his eyes. "I'll have a word with his mother."

Aguirre appeared momentarily, then disappeared.

Emory raised his head. "So he's back?"

"Just arrived. It seems he has news."

"Let's get cleaned up, and we can hear all about it over a drink."

Petra was on her way to her room when she saw Gardener coming out from the trees in the back of the compound. The weak light from the corridor shone on his face. Aguirre was with him. They seemed to be arguing.

Aguirre said, his voice imploring, "I just want to show them—"

Gardener cut him off. "Most idiotic idea I've ever heard. You have one job and one job only. Now, did you get the bag?"

Aguirre muttered, "Not yet, but I—" He broke off when he saw Petra. "Later." He took off toward the main building. Gardener caught sight of her and turned back to the woods, his phone at his ear.

Petra opened the door to her room and nearly ran smack into Emory, who stood inside. "Emory! Why are you skulking in here? Go away before someone sees you."

He took a step toward her. "Petra, I have to talk to you."

"What is it?"

"I…my wife…" He stuttered to a stop.

"Your *what?*" *Oh my God, that's why he was so reluctant to commit. It had nothing to do with that stupid hummingbird. A wife!* She scrambled to pull up her defenses, but before she could slap him and flounce out of the room, he started in again, his voice tentative.

"My wife. Or rather, ex-wife. We've been divorced for over a year. But we're still colleagues." He went on quickly before Petra could interrupt. "She's a paleontologist specializing in bird fossils. I wrote asking her opinion of Aguirre's theory. She was very intrigued. She asked if she could come see the evidence for herself."

"I…see."

"I just thought you ought to know." He gave her a lopsided smile.

She gazed at him sadly. *Of course. I should have known.* She shrugged, pretending to an indifference she didn't feel. *It's not like I own him. It's not like this relationship is going anywhere. It's just a fling, right?* "Why?"

He seemed uncertain. "Well, because…"

Petra opened the door and indicated the hall. "I look forward to meeting her. Now, if you'll excuse me."

Emory stiffened. "You're being unfair."

All the years of loving and losing crashed in on her. *I'm not going to do it again. My heart can't take it.* "Maybe. Goodbye."

He walked out.

She changed into a light shift and headed to the lounge. Capac brought her a cocktail. Nick and Alex rocked in the rattan chairs, chatting quietly. Emory drifted in and tried to sit next to Petra, but she moved away. Gardener tapped a spoon on his glass, drawing their attention. "My boss—Mr. Rook—has instructed me to stay a few days. He wants to make sure the scope is working properly. I will put it through its paces before I begin training you on it."

Ffoulkes frowned. "I thought it was in the ready-to-manufacture phase?"

"It is, but the company has to jump through a lot more hoops before the Pentagon will consider buying it. Mr. Rook wants that defense contract badly."

Ffoulkes had been fidgeting while Gardener talked. "Well, that's all well and good, but we don't have a place for you to stay." He looked around the room. "I don't see why you can't just leave it with us. That was the original deal. My assistant John arranged it with your CFO. I—"

"I have direct orders from Rook himself. If you have a problem with that, I can always take my business elsewhere."

Somebody's used to playing hardball.

Alex remarked, "I suppose you can bunk with me."

Gardener gave the young herpetologist a look brimming with scorn. "Not acceptable. I need my own room and sufficient workspace." He rubbed his hands together. "Oh, and of course, a separate bathroom."

Aguirre spoke in a high, nervous voice. "Mr. Gardener may have my room. I have a full bath and a hotplate. I…um…I can sleep in the hammock room."

Petra noticed a tiny upturn of Gardener's lips. *This seems to be going his way. But in what direction are we being herded?*

Alex patted Aguirre on the back. "Come on, man. I'll put you up. I managed with Lewis, after all. Let's go get your swag."

Dinner was quiet, and soon after, the party broke up. Emory tried to block Petra, but she sidestepped him and went along down the corridor. *A wife, no less. That's it. We're done here.* Actually, it came as a relief. She'd spent a lifetime throwing herself into every relationship that came along, pouring her heart into each one, only to have it mutilated beyond recognition. The last straw was George. *Three years.* Three years in which her career stalled while she followed him around the world. She made every sacrifice required, tolerated his workaholic habits, kept any disagreement to herself to avoid his explosive temper, saw any chance of children slip away. *And for what?* She remembered vividly the upturned faces of her family sitting in the front pew, still heard the music start up for the fifth time. Suffered again through the sympathetic expression on Reverend Drudge's face as he handed her the note. *Never again.*

She uncapped the small bottle of Jack Daniels she kept as a soporific and poured a tot. As she pulled off her dress, she considered the newcomer. *There's something shady about him.* Aguirre had pretended not to know him, but…*What were they talking about in the forest?* What had Gardener said? "You have one job."

Could Aguirre be working for Rook Enterprises? Could Gardener have been sent to goose him? What for?

She turned on the laptop and searched on Rook Enterprises. *Ah, here it is.* A billion-dollar research and development company producing innovative optical and scientific equipment, they specialized in portable units that could be used in the field. Most of their contracts were with the defense department. *Who did Denys say was the CEO? Victor Rook. Wait...Victor?*

She looked the name up.

A *People* magazine profile stated, "Trained as a mechanical engineer, Victor Rook parlayed his invention of a critical component for a hydraulic crane into a global corporation, which now boasts over three hundred thousand employees and business interests in ten countries. Up until five years ago, Rook operated in Spain, but when the new US president cut corporate taxes, he moved the headquarters back to Kansas City. Rook is well known in elite social circles and likes to spend lavishly on vintage cars and rare wines. It is rumored that he has a private zoo. He owns a Monster Energy Nascar cup team as well as the Honolulu Hoopsters. He is unmarried."

Hmm. One of those jet-setting entrepreneurs. I wonder if there's a picture of him? She scrolled down. At the bottom of the page was a black-and-white photo of a man in black tie, an anorexic woman arrayed in silk and diamonds dangling from his left arm. He was snarling at a paparazzo. *Looks like he wants to smash the man's camera.* She zoomed in on his face. *He also looks exactly like Victor Gardener.*

She closed the laptop. *That at least explains why he struts around like some tin-pot dictator.* It didn't explain what the head of a mammoth company might be doing at a research station in the Amazon. And why he was traveling incognito.

Her ruminations were cut short by a pounding on the door. "Petra!" She caught her breath. *Emory.*

"What?"

"Let me in."

"No."

"We have to talk."

"I'm tired. Go away." *Real smooth, Petra.* He made no response. *But effective.* After a minute, she looked out. The aisle was empty. This did not make her feel better.

Chapter Thirteen
Apex Predator

October 16

She didn't have much time to brood. The next morning at breakfast, several things happened. Aguirre announced that he had managed to snap several photos of the birds with Nick's camera. "You should be able to blow them up."

Nick took it from him. "Next time, ask me."

"Next time we won't need it." Denys faced Gardener. "Is the machine assembled?"

"Almost. Steele and I will put the finishing touches on it after breakfast. Then we can test it."

Nick shook his head. "Can't today. I'll be busy in the darkroom."

Aguirre put down his coffee cup. "I can help."

Gardener looked him up and down and finally said reluctantly, "All right."

Emory asked curiously, "What does the scope do?"

For the first time, Gardener grew animated. "This incredible little piece of machinery melds three operations in one lightweight, portable telescope. It's a spotting scope, with the largest eyepiece and highest magnification you can get without losing resolution—a hundred-millimeter radius and apochromatic capability for fantastic color imaging. You should be able to see

Orion's Horsehead Nebula through this baby."

"Orion?"

"Yes. Even though this scope is designed for spotting objects on the ground rather than in the sky, it is powerful enough to pick up celestial bodies, and Orion is one of the brightest." He stroked his chin. "My favorite constellation—the hunter." His eyes gleamed. "That's why I named my baby the Orion X."

Orion—what did Emory say he represented? Lust—yes. But also murder and power. Orion, the hunter. The killer. Petra felt a chill. *Rook wants to sell this to the military. Could Orion X be more than just a telescope?*

Gardener had resumed. "The second feature is the camera."

Nick interrupted. "It's incorporated into the design so it can conform to the exact specs of the scope."

"Right. A real breakthrough. None of the extra cost and effort that goes into attaching a camera manually."

Nick leaned forward, his head bobbing with anticipation. "And no constant mucking with adjustments to synchronize the telephoto lens with the camera lens."

The two men faced each other, the onlookers clearly forgotten. "Exactly. Not only that, but it comes with Wi-Fi, 5K video recording, and a 20x zoom lens, giving the user the ability to take clear photos up to fifteen kilometers away."

Nick sat back on his heels and whistled. "You didn't mention that. Boy, I could sure have used that when I was filming in Botswana. Had to get way too close for comfort to the lions."

Emory tapped the table. "Denys says Rook

Enterprises is selling this to the Pentagon. Why would they want a scope with a camera? What military use does it have?"

"Ah, that's the third element." He held up a schematic drawing. "See there, underneath the barrel?"

"The thing that looks like a second scope?"

Gardener cocked an eyebrow. "Yeah, that's what you're supposed to think. It's actually a gun barrel that can be configured either for tranquilizer darts or as a flame-thrower."

Emory said through rigid lips, "So you thought you'd come here, to a station dedicated to research, and test a weapon."

"Wait a minute, Andrews." Ffoulkes held up a hand in protest. "Mr. Gardener says the gun can be loaded with tranquilizer darts. This could be a boon for wildlife researchers."

"And zoos," added John helpfully. "It'll be so much easier to capture specimens, and—"

"Yes, thank you, John," interrupted Ffoulkes hastily. "What I'm saying is, Orion X is not primarily a weapon. Right, Gardener?"

Gardener didn't answer him. While Emory continued to fume, the others fiddled with their silverware or played with their napkins. Nick took a third helping of eggs.

When the silence had grown deafening, Petra coughed. "Perhaps you could clear up one mystery for me." She looked straight at Gardener. "Why is the head of Rook Enterprises traveling under an assumed name, and why is he busying himself with a technician's job? *Mr. Rook?*"

No one breathed. Gardener's face tightened. His

eyes flashed with adamantine fury. He stood up, towering over Petra. The others half rose, ready to defend her. "How do you know who I am?"

"It's not rocket science. You're all over the internet, not to mention your company's website." She put down her napkin. "You had to expect that one of us would figure out who you are pretty quickly. Especially considering your, shall we say, imperious attitude."

His hands rolled into fists, then relaxed. Petra sensed that he was more annoyed she had preempted him than by the unmasking itself. "You are correct—perhaps my penchant for ordering people around gave me away." He gave her a cold smile. "Yes, I am Victor Rook, at your service."

"And?"

He sat down again. So did the others. "As you probably read on the website, I am a mechanical engineer by trade. I invented a rotating gear for the hydraulic crane and on the strength of the patent founded my company. Miss Steele will no doubt tell you that it's now a multimillion-dollar, multinational corporation. Great, huh? Unfortunately, that means I spend most of my time in Kansas City behind an empty desk." He eyed Aguirre. "I freely admit I still like to get my hands dirty once in a while."

An odd metaphor for a man who washes those hands ten times a day.

He continued. "When we decided to test the new machine in the Amazon, it got my juices flowing. I've been to every continent except South America, and virtually every ecosystem except the tropical rainforest." He grinned and fluttered a gracious hand at the room. "This place is fabulous. I just might buy it as a retreat for my staff."

This last did not go over well with the scientists. Emory's yell drowned Ffoulkes out. "You can't close this station off to research. That would be outrageous!"

Finally Ffoulkes called for quiet and said, his tone conciliatory, "I'm sure Mr. Rook—with his background in the sciences—would never cut us off from these wonderful facilities. Would you?" He gave the entrepreneur an unctuous smile.

Rook laughed, a sound that struck Petra as both artificial and mean. "Relax. I was just joking. Please...consider me part of the team."

Petra had one more question. "What's your relationship to Aguirre? I heard you two talking."

He gave the man a sidelong glance. "Tramposo? We met in the States. He told me about this expedition and agreed to scout out the territory before I arrived."

"But why did you pretend you didn't know him?" She watched him. *He hasn't figured the whole story out yet, has he?*

"I...uh...thought that would blow my cover. Besides"—he seemed to gain assurance—*working out the kinks?*—"I wanted to make sure you people were legitimate scientists."

"Well, of course we are. What would make you suspect otherwise?"

He pursed his lips. "In my line of business—defense contracting—we can't be too careful. There are industrial spies everywhere. I didn't want to risk having the technology stolen before I patent it."

That made sense, and Alex and Ffoulkes rose to leave. Rook smiled at Petra, but his eyes were hard. "Have I answered your questions?"

"For now."

John puffed out his chest. "I assume you prefer to continue under your alias, Mr. Rook? I can arrange that."

He rolled his eyes. "Don't be ridiculous. I have nothing to hide."

"Certainly, certainly. As the public relations man for this expedition, I am at your disposal. I can draft press releases, deal with reporters, anything." His sallow, fleshy face turned pink, and his bovine eyes pleaded. *He probably thinks he's adorable.*

"I have my own publicity department, Dillinger. Just stay out of my way."

A surge of malevolence flooded John's wishy-washy features before the bland expression of a media person settled back over his face. It caught Petra off guard. *Rook's dismissal was unnecessarily rude, but...* She sized up the little man. Perhaps the palpable disdain the others felt for him affected John more than he let on. She resolved to be nicer to him. On the other hand, Rook seemed to want to keep everyone at a distance. *You'd think a high roller like him would be more sociable.* The man's stiff back disappeared down the hall. *Either he's a skunk or he's got a secret agenda. Or both.*

She left. Emory was in the hallway. He saw her and turned aside into the lounge. Her chest contracted, but she kept walking. *So now* I'm *the one getting the cold shoulder.* She squared said shoulders. *I'll be fine.*

At lunch, Nick announced that he would spend the afternoon developing Aguirre's pictures.

Ever pompous, Ffoulkes brayed, "Be careful, Steele. They may be the only record we have."

Nick said, "What do you mean? Now that the machine's put together, we can go back and try for some better shots."

Aguirre's eyes went wide. "Oh...er...no. That is..."

Rook rumbled, "I ain't wasting a two-million-dollar product on some dimwitted notion that there's a dinosaur running around in the jungle." He glared at Aguirre.

"Before you make an ass of yourself, Rook, I suggest we see what Aguirre's captured on film." Nick took his leave, unaware of the bullets shooting from the gunmetal eyes of an infuriated Rook.

A few hours later, Petra, working in her room, heard a tapping sound. She looked up and noticed for the first time a loudspeaker attached to the wall. A throat cleared. "This is Director Ffoulkes. Will everyone please gather in the lounge? Nick has something to show us."

As Petra headed down the corridor, she caught up with her brother. "What is it?"

He grinned. "Wanna see a dinosaur in the flesh?"

****

Alex, Emory, Ffoulkes, and John were already there. Only Rook was absent. On the table were spread several eight-by-ten glossy photos. Petra drew closer. One showed a hoatzin, its blue face, lumpy body, and long tail distinctive. Another one was also familiar—a sketch of a feathered creature with short forearms and a long tail. It was labeled *Caudipteryx zoui*. Next to it lay the skeleton, the bag of droppings, and Aguirre's feather. Denys spread his arms. "See?"

"See what? Aguirre showed us this drawing before.

We all agree they look alike."

Ffoulkes cleared his throat. "They do more than look alike. I have determined they are likely linked." He pointed dramatically at the other items.

I guess he's moved from skeptic to cheerleader in one fluid motion. "What about the *Archaeopteryx*?"

He dispatched the question with an airy flick of the hand. "We're talking apples and oranges. Before feathered theropods were discovered, scientists believed that birds were descended from arboreal reptiles— reptiles that lived in trees and developed wings. That hypothesis has been laid to rest. The *Archaeopteryx* is now thought to be the link between dinosaurs and birds. He pointed at the photo. "As I said, *Caudipteryx* lived in the Cretaceous period, several million years after the *Archaeopteryx*. This oviraptor was flightless, but it had feathers—"

"What did it need them for?"

"Probably to control body temperature. Maybe for protection."

"Oh." John seemed to lose interest.

"It also had a gizzard filled with pebbles to help digest its food—much like modern birds."

Alex looked at Emory for confirmation.

"He means the crop. As far as I know, dinosaurs didn't have them. I have a colleague who is an expert. She's—"

"So you're hypothesizing that Aguirre's found a link between *Archaeopteryx* and the hoatzin? That's not what he—"

"No…no!" Ffoulkes had grown increasingly flustered. "If you'll be quiet, I can explain." He waited until everyone was paying attention. "Now, you all know there is no fossil record for the hoatzin—"

"So we don't know how long it's been around."

"Precisely. If we found fossil evidence, we could trace its lineage—discover the origin of its singular features."

Petra was getting impatient. "Get on with it, Denys. I thought this was about Aguirre's trek back to the lake and his photographs. Does he think he's found an extinct bird or a living fossil?"

Aguirre walked in. "Neither. I now have proof of an evolutionary twist in the path between the *Caudipteryx* and the hoatzin." He held up another photo. "This one is finally dry." He handed it to Nick. The others gathered around.

"Whatever it is, it's hidden behind all that high grass."

"Is it a bird or what?"

Aguirre snatched the photograph back. "Of course it's a bird. See? There." He pointed. "It's the size of a turkey. There's the crest and there's the tail."

Petra saw a strange whirl of feathers at the end of a bulky body covered in very dark feathers. "It's a bit grainy."

"I only had the twenty-millimeter wide angle, and it was probably sixty yards away."

Nick mumbled something. Petra nudged him. "What did you say?"

"You were right, Petra. If Aguirre had taken the telephoto, he'd have gotten a much clearer image of the bird." He gazed speculatively at Tramposo.

Emory looked up from the photo. "Couldn't you get any closer?"

He shook his head. "Too marshy. Crocodiles

everywhere."

"Not crocodiles." Alex was stern. "Caimans."

"Whatever. Predators with big teeth. I tried to walk around the perimeter of the lake, staying on solid ground, but I hit a grove of thorny trees and couldn't get through."

Ffoulkes began to pace. "This could be the find of the century. Imagine! A new species—a link to the dinosaurs—tracked down by a member of the team from the Institute for Tropical Research. It will make our name preeminent in the scientific community."

John, who had been dozing in a corner, a glass of vodka at his elbow, woke up and cheeped, "Think of the grant money that would flow in!"

His boss, floating on a cloud of self-delusion, ignored him. "I'd be invited to the Peabody, to the British Museum, even to the White House!"

"Cornell might donate this station to us for further research!" John's eyes glowed.

"You forget, John." Nick seemed to delight in pricking the poor man's bubble. "Cornell doesn't actually own it. Some millionaire in South Africa owns it. You'd have to get him to give it up, and from what I understand, renting it to research groups is very lucrative."

Emory held up a hand. "Before we get ahead of ourselves, we should at least get an outside opinion— from a disinterested source—that this is what we think it is. My wife…" He stopped and glared at Petra. "My *ex-wife*, Felicity Lintu, is a paleontologist. She specializes in the connection between birds and dinosaurs. I've been in touch with her. She'd like to take a look at your photos."

Ffoulkes bristled. "Are you saying I'm not qualified to authenticate this discovery?"

"No, no." He said it mildly. "I told her about it, and she would very much like to come and confer with you. She spoke highly of your work and would be honored to provide a second opinion."

The director rather ungraciously acknowledged the compliment. "I suppose. When is she coming?"

"I wanted to confirm the invitation with you before she made reservations. She can be on a flight from Ithaca Saturday."

"Ithaca! She's at Cornell?"

"Yes."

Petra noticed his eyes clouded. *Was she there when he went up in flames? Is that why they divorced?*

Denys started to say something, but Aguirre interrupted. "I'm not sure we want any outsider looking at this until we have more evidence, do we?"

"I…uh…"

Poor Ffoulkes. I don't think he does well with choices.

Aguirre continued eagerly. "Perhaps you should go up to the site and check it out for yourself."

Petra started. *This was the guy who wanted to do it all alone. What's changed?* She heard a sound and swiveled to the door. Rook stood on the threshold, eyes glittering. Aguirre glanced quickly at him. Petra caught an almost imperceptible nod.

"I don't know…" Ffoulkes hesitated.

Aguirre said, "I propose we put off Ms. Lintu's arrival until we've had a chance to take the new scope up there."

"No!" Everyone turned to Rook. He strode into the

middle of the room. "I don't want amateurs touching my machine."

"Then why don't you come?"

"Can't. I have a conference call tomorrow. After that, I intend to check it out myself. Besides, I don't want to risk the lens getting scratched on those spiny trees you were talking about." He spoke to Emory. "If you take the canoes, you can likely get closer. Nick is a good cameraman—he'll get better shots than Aguirre did." When no one answered, he said heartily, "All right, then. When the scope is ready, I'll take it out for a spin. Meanwhile, you all go upriver with Hector tomorrow."

Emory, who had been on a slow boil, burst out, "Look, if we find more evidence tomorrow, I still want Felicity to come down and examine it. I'll tell her to get here by Monday."

A gnarly fist squeezed Petra's heart. *He seems awfully keen to have her come. Maybe he's hoping for a reconciliation. Why call her otherwise?* "She'll stay with you, I suppose."

His eyebrows went up. "I certainly hope not. She snores."

I guess that's the only reason. And since— according to Nicky—I do too, it doesn't give me any advantage. She sighed.

Ffoulkes had recovered enough to reclaim the floor. "Then it's agreed"—he ignored the slight snuffle from Alex—"we'll head north tomorrow, crack of dawn."

"Or even later." This time no one missed the snuffle.

Ffoulkes glared at him. "After breakfast. We'll take

the launch and three canoes." He headed toward the dining room. "Anyone care to join me for a sherry?"

Later that night, Petra sat back from the laptop. She had to admit there were definite similarities between the hoatzin and the *Caudipteryx*. Aguirre had kept the grainy shot of the unidentified bird, so she couldn't compare it to the ones Nick had developed. "It's all I have," he said as he tucked it into a manila envelope. "I'm not letting this photo out of my sight."

She was a little concerned about Ffoulkes's obsession—*he wants this so badly I wonder if his judgement is impaired? Perhaps it's a good thing a paleontologist is coming. Even if it is Emory's ex.* Her mood dipped.

****

October 17

They had gathered by the boats when Aguirre sauntered out. "Come on, we're ready."

Rook appeared behind him. "I need him here. You don't have room anyway."

"But how will we find the spot?"

Aguirre shrugged. "You've been there. Just pull in at the same bend in the river and follow the path to the lake, about a mile farther than where we stopped last time. I saw them on the northeast corner."

"You didn't leave a flag?"

He shook his head.

Hector spoke diffidently. "I know the way."

Emory patted him on the back. "Of course you do—what were we thinking? You know this whole area like the back of your hand." He stopped and spoke low. "Did Winston tell you what we heard? Do you think it was a Mapinguari?"

Noting his doubtful expression, Petra guessed Hector was torn. On the one hand, he wanted to be the worldly, sophisticated guide, but on the other, he still believed in many of the legends of his home. "I don't know."

Ffoulkes opened his mouth, probably intending to argue with Rook, but before he could object, the two men turned and went back into the building. With an irritated frown, he said, "We'd best get going."

Petra recognized the spot where they'd landed before. Winston headed in to the bank and anchored the launch. "We'll have to portage the canoes across this spit of land." Hector led the way through the brush to the shore of the oxbow lake.

Ffoulkes took charge. "All right, I'll go in the first canoe with Nick. I want him in the lead to take pictures. Then Alex, you and Hector. Petra"—he winked—"I wish you could accompany me, but you'll have to make do with Emory."

Shoot. Emory held the canoe for her, and she got in the bow. The lake was fairly large for an oxbow. They could just make out the far bank, with trees growing right to the edge. "I wonder if the dinosaur birds roost with the hoatzin."

"I doubt it, or they'd have been discovered before this."

They paddled quietly for a while. Emory muttered something.

"What did you say?"

"Me? Oh I was just wondering—to myself of course—whether you were universally close-minded or just when it came to men."

"Huh?"

"You heard me."

She knocked the canoe away from a rock with her paddle. "Let me get this straight. You want me to welcome your wife with open arms, a wife you never mentioned while we were...we were..."

"Making love?"

She banged at another rock and almost lost her balance. "Look, we agreed it was just a one-off, a flirtation. Let's leave it at that."

"It's not."

"Not what?"

"Not a fling. You know that, Petra. Maybe it started that way, but, well, it's changed. For me, at least. And Felicity's my ex-wife."

"Because of the snoring?"

He snorted. "For God's sake, because she's an officious perfectionist, that's why."

Tell me more. "And you aren't?"

"Not me. You must be thinking of your boyfriend, Denys." He pretended to throw a ball in her direction.

"Well, why *did* you get divorced?"

"Finally, a reasonable question."

"Well?"

"I'm thinking..."

"Let me guess. She's hideous? Stupid? Philandering?"

"N...no. She's actually quite pretty and brilliant. And never even looked at another man. At least, while we were married. But she is wholly absorbed in her career—as you'll see. Plus..." He stopped paddling.

"Plus?"

"She didn't love me."

Petra twisted around, but she couldn't see his face.

"Emory—"
  "Watch out!"

Chapter Fourteen
Dominant Species

October 17

She heard Nick's shout, but it was too late. The other canoe hit them broadside, and they flipped. Emory's head disappeared under the water. As she began to swim toward him, Nick shouted again. "Sis! Behind you!" She rolled and found herself eye to cold, empty eye with a large caiman that had surfaced two inches from her. Going entirely on instinct, she smacked him across his snout with the flat of her hand. "Ouch!"

Evidently, the caiman considered her response to his friendly little overture rather uncivil, for he sank beneath the water. To Petra's consternation, he immediately resurfaced and started moving in Emory's direction. Just then, the latter burst out of the water, lips spewing black mud. "Help! I can't…can't swim!"

"Emory!" She ducked under the water and extended her legs until she touched the squishy lake bottom. Ignoring the sickening sensation, she pushed off and launched herself at him.

At the same time, Hector's canoe came alongside. He raised his paddle and whapped the caiman, then righted their canoe with his paddle. "Catch hold of the boat." He towed them toward the land until they could both touch bottom. "Now, walk it to shore. Be careful of underwater branches. I'll watch your backs."

Petra took one step and tripped on something in the swirling depths, sprawling face first. Emory yanked her up with his free arm. They hauled the boat the last few feet and fell on the bank.

When Emory had caught his breath, he began to titter. "If it isn't one thing, it's another."

"I can't believe you never learned to swim."

"What can I say? I had a deprived childhood. We lived in the city, and my mother wouldn't let me go to public pools—she was terrified that I'd catch typhus or cooties or something."

She sighed. "There was a time when every American child was taught how to swim. Now, the only muscles they use are the ones in their thumbs."

"You mean to text on their phones?"

"Yeah."

The other two canoes pulled up. "You two okay?"

Alex pointed out rather unnecessarily, "You're both covered in mud."

Petra touched her chin. "It's my new look. Thanks for noticing."

Hector took his canteen from his knapsack. "Here." He poured a tot of water over Petra's and then Emory's heads and handed her a rag. "Can't waste any more water, but at least you'll be able to see."

Ffoulkes made no move to get out of his canoe. His nose wrinkled in distaste. "My God, you stink."

Hector laughed. "The good news is, mud works almost as well as termites to ward off mosquitoes."

Nick joined him. "And the smell can be used as camouflage. The stinkbirds won't know we're anywhere near them. You guys take the lead."

"Can't we just go home?"

Ffoulkes looked shocked. "When we're so close? I want to explore the area a bit before we head back."

Nick agreed. "I'm surprised at you, Petra."

Hector picked up the machete. "I had better go ahead. Miss Petra, take care around the silk floss trees." He nodded behind her.

"Silk floss? What a pretty name." She looked over her shoulder. A grove of small trees covered in beautiful red foamy flowers stood a few feet away. When she drew nearer she noticed that they were covered with huge conical spikes. "These must be the trees Aguirre was talking about. Look at the prickers on those babies! They're as big as my hand."

"They store water for the tree, like a cactus."

Emory said, "I'm guessing they protect the trees from predators as well."

"I'll bet they do." She held out a hand to touch one of the spikes.

"Don't touch it!" Hector shoved her hand away. "It can take a finger off."

"Another friendly denizen of the Amazon." She knocked a chunk of mud off her foot. "I think if it's all the same to you, I'd really prefer to head back."

"Oh, come on, Petra." Nick pouted. "We're already here. Let's at least paddle around the perimeter of the lake. I can take pictures from the boat."

It made some sense. She turned back to the canoe. "Okay, but—" A wave of dizziness hit her suddenly, and she started to stumble. Emory tried to grab her, but it was too late. She fell backward onto the silk floss tree. A thorn penetrated the thick canvas of her pants and plunged into her thigh. She let out a scream. Blood spread across the fabric and pooled in her boot. Hector pulled the muddy rag from his pocket and pressed it hard into her leg. Alex tossed him his bandanna, and he cinched it just above the tear. The bleeding slowed to a trickle.

He tore the hole a little wider and checked the wound. "It's not too bad." Holding up the dangling end of her binocular strap, he said, "I think this broke the tip of the spine off. Still—we should get you home."

Emory helped her into their canoe, and the flotilla set out across the lake in the direction of the river. Petra's leg ached, but that wasn't what was bothering her the most. She watched Emory's shoulders as he propelled the canoe through the water with strong strokes. *Why does he have to be so handsome?* Despite the Sturm und Drang surrounding this expedition, it was her personal issue that consumed her. *I can't give in to the attraction.* She felt drained—not just physically but emotionally. *What does Emory want of me? How do I tell him I have nothing left to give?* She peered at the back of his head. *He claims Felicity doesn't love him...but does he still love her?* She angrily set the thought aside. *I'm not going down that path again. Strangers passing in the night. Nothing more.*

Nick and Emory helped her onto the launch, and they motored back down the river. As they approached the station, Denys shaded his eyes. "There's a canoe missing. Who left without my permission?"

Hector was unconcerned. "Perhaps Capac went shopping."

"Oh, really? Well, if he did, he'd better have

188

remembered my tea." Grumbling, Denys stumped to the kitchen.

Poor little Napoleon. It must be tough when no one follows orders.

Emory watched him go. "I guess Capac didn't read the memo."

Petra giggled.

He escorted her to her room. When she had showered and changed into a robe, he came back with Hector, who cleaned and bandaged the cut. "You'll be fine by tomorrow. Luckily, this tree doesn't have poisonous sap." He grinned at her gasp. "You barely missed the one that does."

Hector left, and Emory fussed around her bed. "You comfortable? Can I get you anything? Anything else I can do for you?" He patted her cheek, leaving a swath of black slime.

"You could wash."

"Oh! Okay. Yes. I'll do that." He turned back at the door. "Petra…"

He probably wants to apologize. "Later, okay?"

"Okay."

She was almost asleep when she heard pounding feet outside and Denys's shrill voice. "Where the hell have they been?"

She got up and went out to the corridor. The missing canoe had been pulled up on the bank. She could make out Rook and Aguirre manhandling something large and apparently heavy out of the boat. It slipped out of their grasp and dropped with a crash on the ground. Now she knew something was wrong. *That must be Orion X—Rook's pride and joy.*

She limped down after the others. Both Rook and

Aguirre looked as if they'd seen a ghost. *Or maybe a Chullachaqui? A Mapinguari?* It struck her that there were way too many hazardous things in this here jungle.

When she got closer, she could see their eyes were bloodshot and their clothes torn. Rook let out a string of curses. "Blasted thing didn't work."

With Alex's help, Aguirre picked the scope up and carried it up the steps. Ffoulkes paced on the top step, his chest puffed out and jabbing his pipe at them. He reminded Petra of an agitated rooster. "Where did you go? Why didn't you tell anyone? I didn't give permission to take the boat. You—"

They ignored him and went on inside.

Emory came around Denys and called to Rook. "What happened?"

"I'll tell you later." He pushed past the two men and stalked off after Aguirre. His hands were clenched. Petra wondered if he was aching to wash them.

An hour later, he came into the lounge, went to the bar, and took down a highball glass and the single malt whiskey.

Ffoulkes eyed the glass. He opened his mouth, but Nick spoke first. "So what went wrong?"

Rook took a deep swallow of the scotch. "The telescope worked fine. We went down the river a few miles. Viewed a crested caracara from three hundred yards away, clear as a bell. I swear, it's powerful enough to pick out the navel on a native kid. But then when we saw...I mean, when I tried the camera, the lens locked." He slammed his drink down, spilling the rest of the whiskey.

Aguirre sidled in. He poured himself a brandy,

knocked it off, and poured another. Rook glared at him. Aguirre turned a shoulder to him and burst out, his words tumbling over each other, "The viewfinder was fantastic. Did he tell you about the caracara? Once we get the camera fixed, we'll be able to capture the new bird on film, I'm sure. And then—"

Rook made a sound deep in his throat.

Aguirre raised his voice. "And after that we can go back downriver. I know this time we'll get closer and maybe—"

"Shut up, Aguirre."

But the man was clearly a little drunk and wanted to talk.

"What? Did you see something?" Alex sounded bored.

John burst out, irritated. "Oh, for heaven's sake, tell us. Did you find another dinosaur?"

"No. No."

"Then what?"

Aguirre raised his glass, triumph in his eyes. "A Mapinguari."

After that, everyone took him seriously.

****

Everyone, that is, except for Rook. He sneered, "What rot. We saw no such thing. You're a fool, Aguirre."

"Am not." He was beginning to slur his words. He gave Emory a sly look. "He knows what I'm talking about, don't you, Andrews? I know about the hair."

Rook looked like he wanted to spit. "Rubbish. Probably planted there by that fellow who tried to swindle you people with that pixie or whatever it was."

Denys's eyes widened in alarm. "The faked

191

Chullachaqui? *Hmm.*"

"See? Don't listen to this moron." He took Aguirre by the arm and marched him out of the room.

Emory watched them go. "Methinks the Rook protests too much."

Ffoulkes declared, "Rook is right. Aguirre is a fool. Why doesn't he just stick to his botany? I think he's dying to find some fantastical creature and doesn't care whether or not he can back it up."

Emory caught Petra's glance. *Like a certain biologist we know?*

Denys continued to ruminate. "The more I think about it, the more I'm convinced we should drop this ludicrous chase after a bird. A bird that's likely just a figment of Tramposo's imagination anyway. Let us resume our search for the Mapinguari." He nodded his head vigorously. "Yes, indeed."

Gee, it couldn't have anything to do with Aguirre taking the credit, could it?

Nick burst out, "But Denys, what made you pivot? This morning it was the bird and nothing but the bird, and now…"

"Now, I have come to my senses. Tomorrow, we set off after our primary target."

Emory snapped, "No. We wait for my…ex-wife. When she comes, we can set priorities."

Ffoulkes opened his mouth but apparently thought better of it. "I'd forgotten about Professor Lintu. After I confer with her, we shall decide our course of action."

By mutual consent, the others let him have his little victory.

They saw no more of either Rook or Aguirre that day, but the door to the lab was locked. Petra took herself to the hammock room and dozed until dinner. The overhead light clicked on, and Nick slammed into the room. "You awake, Petra?"

"I am now." She rolled out of the hammock and wiped her eyes. "What's wrong?"

"Goddamn bastard won't let me look at it," he fumed.

Emory came in, John at his heels. "What is 'it'?"

"The camera. I know I can fix it. That's *my* area of expertise—not his. Fathead. Engineers—they always think they know everything. What a prick." He subsided, grumbling to himself.

Petra said mildly, "Well, it's his invention."

"Yeah, but if he doesn't get it working, he'll lose the contract."

Emory patted Nick's shoulder. "I'm sure every bell and whistle is proprietary. Until he gets the patent, he's not going to let anyone else work on it."

"Yeah," John jeered. "You could be a Chinese spy."

No one else thought this was humorous.

After dinner, Petra walked down to the dock to think. The capybaras grazed in the grass by the water's edge, their soft munching adding a bass element to the trilling of an antbird. A hawk swooped low over the river and back up to a tall tree, its talons holding a wiggling fish. Without wanting to, her thoughts drifted to Emory and his wife. *What's her name? Something cheerful…Felicity, that's right.* They must be close or he wouldn't have invited her. *They're probably in constant contact.* She supposed it was worthwhile to maintain good relations with an ex-spouse. She wouldn't know. The last communication she'd had from George was through the UPS guy who came to pick up his stuff. That was how she learned he was living in San Francisco with her predecessor at the University of Chicago library. *At least* someone *appreciates librarians. Not like Emory…and…we're back.*

Think, Petra. The Mapinguari. Was Aguirre being honest? Aguirre—like Denys—had a tendency to jump the gun. So then was Rook right to dismiss his claims as the ravings of a lunatic? *Let's play devil's advocate.* Rook is trying to keep the discovery to himself, and Aguirre spilled the beans. Or…Rook was quite sensibly withholding judgment. *Just like Emory and me. Face it: there are altogether too many unknown species and mythical boogeymen cropping up to be credible. On the other hand, this* is *the rainforest.* Suddenly, the capybaras beside her began to bark and whinny. Pushing and jostling each other, they cantered into the woods. A minute later, two *ribereños* floated past, shotguns at the ready. *You just missed 'em, fellas.* She snickered. *Somebody's having yuca and plaintains for dinner again.*

She sighed. *Okay, forget Aguirre and Rook and the Mapinguari for now. I'm going to go wash my hair.* She stood up. *Wait a minute…hair. Didn't Aguirre mention he knew about the hair? That must mean he knows we went looking for Bigfoot. Hmm.* Maybe it *was* time they told the others. There didn't seem much point in keeping it a secret any longer.

She saw Emory loitering in the hallway. A sudden shyness overcame her, and she ducked into the kitchen. After a minute, he slapped his hands together with a loud clap and strode away. She zipped down the corridor and into her room. When she was sure she was alone, she unlocked the drawer of her desk. Pens, paper clips, a half-used tissue, a screwdriver, and the cap to a travel bottle of bourbon met her eye. No plastic bag. She scrabbled around in the drawer. Nothing. *Where the hell did it go? Did Emory take it?* Had he been hanging around near her room to steal it and not, as she assumed, to talk to her? He had argued for keeping their little exploit under wraps, after all. Did he go so far as to remove their only bit of evidence? To find out, she'd have to talk to him. And she wasn't quite ready to do that. *Not until the eminent Felicity arrives and I see the lay of the land.*

Chapter Fifteen
Recessive Genes

October 19

Petra only managed to avoid being alone with Emory over the next two days with some difficulty. He kept casting eloquent looks her way and following her around. If he tried to talk to her, she said only, "Later." And once, "When does Felicity arrive?"

Early Tuesday morning, he took the launch with Winston to Iquitos to pick up his ex-wife. Despite her best intentions, Petra was apprehensive. What did he call her? *Officious. Immersed in her career.* Made him sound rather selfish—why shouldn't she have a career? *It's not all about* you, *Emory.* He probably kept whining that she didn't pay enough attention to him until she threw him out. *Yeah, that's it.*

She got a beer from the pantry.

Capac eyed her. "Lunch no ready yet."

"It's okay. I'm over twenty-one." She patted his shoulder. "I need it, Capac."

He shook his head and went back to slicing fish.

She heard Winston's halloo before anyone else. She'd already decided to stay in her room until the lunch bell rang, then nonchalantly stroll to the dining hall. *I'll be fashionably late.* Instead she ran to the hammock room so she could see the arriving passengers without being seen. Emory's dark head towered over someone who handed him a suitcase. Petra couldn't get a good look until they reached the stairs. Emory stepped aside to let his companion pass, giving Petra a full bead on the new guest. *Damn damn damn damn.*

Emory had said she was pretty. He should have used the words "drop-dead gorgeous." If Petra believed in reincarnation, she would have sworn Felicity had been a wood nymph in a former life. Tiny, delicate, she stood maybe five feet tall. Masses of straight, white-blonde hair fell down her back. Her alabaster skin almost matched her hair. As she approached the lodge, moving with the grace of a prima ballerina, Petra noted ice-blue eyes and a delicate, arrow-shaped chin. *Maybe not a dryad, but one of those Viking goddesses who decides who lives and who dies. A Valkyrie. Yeah. Or the bride of Dracula.* She hunched her shoulders, her limbs heavy. *Why do I suddenly feel as though I've put on ten pounds?* Molly the toucan took one look at the ethereal Felicity and flew off with a squawk.

Ffoulkes came out, both hands extended. From the way his mouth wobbled, she guessed he was gushing platitudes. He took Felicity's arm and led her into the building. Petra noted with amusement her slight recoil at his touch. Nick stuck his head in. "Doctor Lintu is here, sis. Aren't you coming to meet her?"

Sigh. She plodded after him. Emory and Felicity stood in the lounge like a newlywed couple in a receiving line. First Alex, then Nick solemnly shook her hand. Aguirre appeared and did the same. Emory excused himself. As he passed Petra, she noted an unhappy look in his eyes.

Rook came in, and Aguirre introduced him to

Felicity. Her eyes widened. "Mr. Rook? Mr. Victor Rook?"

He drew back. "Yes."

"My fiancé, Kelly Chisholm, works for you. He's supposed to meet me here in a few days. He didn't mention you were coming too."

Rook went to the bar and poured himself a whiskey before answering. "I decided to take his place. Wanted to test the invention myself."

She stared at him. "When Emory first told me about the fossil, I asked to come see it for myself. Kelly found out at the same time that you were sending him to Pacaya, so we thought we could combine business with pleasure—make it a mini vacation. I haven't heard from him since I left Ithaca. Is he back in Kansas City?"

"No. I sent him on another errand. He's in Turkmenistan."

"Turkmenistan!" Her eyebrows went up.

Rook rattled the ice in his glass. "It's a secret trip—business. Corporate deal. I ordered him to remain incommunicado for the time being. You understand."

Felicity looked about to protest, but Hector and Capac came forward, and Rook retreated to the bar. She shook their hands solemnly. "I've already had the pleasure of meeting Winston." She smiled at the guide, who fidgeted by the door. "I have offered to write a recommendation to the University of Lima for his middle son. He wants to go to medical school. You must be so proud of all ten children, Winston."

My God—how did she find all that out so quickly? Winston hasn't said more than two words to me or anyone else since I got here.

Ffoulkes opened his mouth to speak, but Felicity

laid a gentle hand on Nick's arm. "Could you show me to my room, Mr. Steele? I'd like to freshen up. Then perhaps I can have a look at those photos."

"Certainly, but please call me Nick."

Emory poked his head in and said stiffly, "I have vacated my room for you, Felicity."

"Oh? Where will you sleep?"

"There's a guest room in the staff quarters. Hector has had it made up for me."

"Shall we?" As Nick held his arm out for Felicity, the lunch bell rang. "Oops. We'll have to eat first, though."

"Why?"

"Our cook, Capac, runs a tight ship."

"I see." She swept past Petra, giving her only a passing glance. Petra felt another chill.

The newcomer spent the meal in close conversation with Ffoulkes. As they finished their coffee, she announced, "Denys has kindly consented to show me the evidence. If we are able to corroborate it, it has great potential for expansion of our knowledge of evolution." She rose and walked out of the dining room. The director dropped the forkful of fish that hovered halfway to his lips and ran after her. The men at the table sat as though they'd been stunned by a poison dart. Nick gazed toward the lab. "I wonder how long they'll be?"

Emory growled, "As long as it takes. You'll just have to wait, kid." He stalked out.

"Kid! I—"

"Never mind, Nicky." Petra kept her voice firm, although a slight crack was audible on the last word. "He obviously doesn't appreciate other men admiring his wife."

Her brother blew out a long breath. He patted her hand. "Ex-wife, Petra. Remember that. But you made your point—I'm off to drown my sorrows in the darkroom."

Petra, at loose ends, decided to take a swim. She found Emory on the dock. She dove in past him, but when she rose to the surface he caught her arm. "What do you think?"

"What do you mean?"

He said impatiently, "You know…Felicity."

"Emory, I haven't spoken a word to her yet—or rather, she hasn't spoken to me. Does she dislike women?"

"No, no. She's just wrapped up in the task ahead."

Petra had a frightening thought. "Did you say something to her about me? About us?"

He was silent.

"You did. Why?"

"Because I wanted her to know I was okay. She worries about me."

"Huh?" There were so many parts of that sentence that bewildered her. *Why is he okay?*

He bent down so his face was inches from hers. "I'm okay because I've found you. Petra, you can't fight this. This isn't some passing fancy. There's something between us—something deep, which will grow even deeper in time. You have to feel it."

Now was not the time to get into an argument. For one thing, she'd just seen a caiman slide into the water. For another, something with sharp teeth was nipping at her toes. She climbed out. "Take me to meet her."

"Not now. Later."

"Damn it, Emory! This is ridiculous. We're only, what, ten people stuck in a tiny lodge in an utterly remote part of the jungle. We can't avoid each other forever."

He patted her wet head. "You're right. That's why she asked me to invite you to her room for a cocktail before dinner."

Ack. "Um."

"She won't bite you. I'll come with you if you like."

Petra wasn't sure if that would help or hurt. "We'll see. Tell her I accept."

Two hours later, she made her way along the corridor, feeling ugly. She'd washed her hair and put a little mascara on, which the heat had quickly melted. She had little hope that Felicity would look as bedraggled as she did, and sure enough, the woman came to her door in a ravishing blue linen jumpsuit. *My God, it isn't even wrinkled!* Her hand was cool to the touch.

"Miss Steele?"

Petra managed to gurgle, "Please, call me Petra," before her throat closed up entirely.

"Petra, then. And I am Felicity. Won't you sit down?" Emory knocked and stuck his head around the door. She dismissed him with a flick of her dainty hand. "Emory, dear, do you mind? Girl talk." Somehow the words didn't ring false.

"Fine, fine." He backed out.

Felicity closed the door. "I'd like for us to have a little time to get acquainted." She held up a bottle. "May I offer you a glass of wine? It's a lovely Pinot Gris. Capac was so kind as to chill it for me."

"Thank you." *Although I could really use a slug of whiskey.*

Felicity poured two glasses and handed one to Petra. "I apologize for not greeting you properly when I arrived. I was exhausted. Plus, I wanted to get an idea of what we were dealing with. I knew the men wouldn't let me have a minute to myself, but I thought you would understand."

What can I say?

They sat for a minute, sipping. Felicity abruptly broke the silence. "You're perfect for him, you know."

Is it painted on my face? "Who?"

"Emory, of course. I freely admit that that's one of the reasons I wanted to come. Not the official one, nor even the most important, but still." She contemplated Petra. "He tells me you are keeping him at arm's length. Why?"

Faced with such a direct question, Petra was tempted to confess all. In the semi-darkness, Felicity's eyes were much warmer. The seemingly shatterproof face was relaxed now, her lips curved in a welcoming smile. "I…uh…haven't had much luck with men."

Felicity let a small sigh escape. "I know what you mean."

Does she mean Emory? A little click of hope stirred. "All my life I've gone for the wrong guy—womanizers, scoundrels, pathological liars, even a crook or two. Before I knew it, I'd hit thirty-five and the pickings were slim. I met George when I was working in the library at the University of Chicago."

"You were ready to settle for him?"

"No, no." *Or was I?* "I loved him. I thought I was the luckiest person in the world." *How many times did I tell myself that? So why the sudden doubt now?* She considered her new acquaintance. *Either she's remarkably perceptive, or Emory has yakked way too much about me.*

"But you weren't. The luckiest person in the world."

"No."

"He left you at the altar?"

Lucky guess—or is it? "Yes."

She refilled their glasses. "It is never too late."

Okay...so now we're moving into the cliché portion of the evening?

Before Petra could make the caustic remark buzzing in her head, Felicity whispered, "Do you know how old I am?"

The question caught her off guard. She took a second, closer look at her companion's face. On first sight, she'd assumed her to be no more than forty, but now she could see the fine lines at her eyes and mouth, etched into the clear white skin. Her eyes were a bit less luminous here in the gloom, and her hair was not in fact blonde but white. "I don't know."

"I'm fifty-two. Emory's age. We parted a year ago. I assumed I would never find romance again. That I was too old." She held out her hand. A beautiful sapphire sparkled on her left ring finger. "Eight months ago, I met Kelly Chisholm. We became engaged last month."

"Oh, that's right. You mentioned that to Rook." Petra observed Felicity's radiant face. "Does Emory know?"

"I haven't had time to tell him." She flushed pink, endearing her even more to Petra. "It's still so new to me."

"How do you think he'll react?"

"I don't think he'll care one way or another. He only has eyes for you."

"He does?" *Oh shoot, I didn't mean to say that out loud. Is my cover blown? Time to change the subject.* She sipped her wine. "Um…how was your trip?"

Felicity went on as though she hadn't heard the question. "He says he tried to explain about our relationship to you, but you brushed him off."

Oh my God, the man's the biggest blabbermouth on the planet. "Not true. We did discuss it. He says you don't love him."

"He's right."

Petra didn't know what to say.

Felicity stood up and paced. "I wanted to…so badly. He's a wonderful man, a fantastic lover, a brilliant ornithologist. He's kind, patient, and generous—especially to a fault. And I'm afraid I'm riddled with faults." She looked at Petra. "I would have stayed with him forever, even though I couldn't love him."

"What happened?"

"Did he tell you about the hummingbird?"

"Yes."

"We were colleagues at the university. It was such a horrible mess. The faculty met to decide what to do. They were already disposed against him after the West Overbrook affair. I stood up for him, but no one listened. After all, I was his wife—hardly an unprejudiced witness. They voted to deny him tenure." She put the glass down. "His contract wasn't renewed, so in essence he was fired. It broke his heart."

"If you were on his side, what made you divorce him?"

"That came later. No one trusted him anymore. He couldn't find a steady academic job and roamed the country accepting work as a guest lecturer here and there. At first, he kept in touch, but we drifted apart and eventually separated." She slammed a tiny fist down. "He couldn't handle the shame. Still, I know he could have weathered it if it hadn't been for the blackballing."

"Blackballing? Wait a minute, you said something about West Overbrook. The name sounds familiar. What happened?"

"That was really the beginning of the end, only we didn't know it. Emory had been invited to teach a semester at the University of West Overbrook in England. When he got there, he discovered it was a hotbed of the global warming movement. They wanted him to invent a link between Euro-Asian migratory bird patterns and climate change. You know that's his specialty—migration routes?"

Petra nodded.

"Well, anyway, Emory discovered they were systematically suppressing the work of scientists skeptical of the so-called hockey stick—a graph that depicts the earth dramatically warming in the last hundred years. Anyone who dared question their theory was denied publication in peer-reviewed journals."

"Sounds like something out of the Dark Ages."

"Too much." Felicity poured more wine. "When no dissenting opinions saw the light of day, they could claim there was consensus, that it was settled science."

"I've read a bit about it. Haven't they recently found that the hockey-stick graph was based on incorrect mathematics?"

"Yes. And to top it off, when the conspirators were confronted with the fact that in the last twenty years the world hasn't warmed at all—"

"The so-called hiatus?"

"No so-called—real. Even the UN has had to acknowledge it, but that didn't stop the bureaucrats at NOAA from manipulating the temperature numbers so they could pretend to correct the results."

"That's terrible. How did their machinations come to light?"

"One of their top scientists went public and charged that they ignored satellite data and relied on notoriously inaccurate readings from sea-going ships' bilge water." She stopped. "I'm not a climate scientist, but I understand they used other discredited methods as well—tree rings and land-based readings."

"That seems a little farfetched. Why would a government science agency want to fudge its statistics?"

She threw up her hands. "I don't know! To pad their budget appropriations? There's a huge amount of money to be made in solving a crisis. The whole issue has become so politicized that it's hard to separate real science from propaganda."

"Huh. So what does this have to do with Emory?"

"Well, he refused to go along with their schemes. He didn't threaten to expose them, but I think they saw him as untrustworthy—a potential whistleblower. They blackballed him."

"Did they have that much power?"

"Yes."

"Oh, now I remember. They uncovered a bunch of

emails between the West Overbrook faculty proving they colluded to stifle debate." She thought back. "That uncomfortable fact never reached the ears of the politicians, did it?"

"Or it was ignored. Doomsday scenarios create juicy opportunities for power. Anyway, Emory barely survived their attempt to sabotage him, mainly because his reputation was made in ornithology, not climate science. Cornell needed someone with his expertise, and they hired him. That's where we met."

"And then came the hummingbird incident…"

"It was the last straw for him. After the tenure denial, he went off for days at a time. He felt if he could find an authentic new species, he could redeem himself, but every potential candidate proved a dead end. He became more and more haunted…and unreachable." Felicity blinked back a tear. "He left me in spirit long before the divorce." She patted Petra's hand. "But I think he's found that spirit again."

"How could you possibly tell in these few hours?"

She smiled, looking more than ever like a Norse goddess—wise and good. "Because I know him."

Petra began to wonder if the frozen tundra bit was only an act. Here was a woman of considerable depth. *And really rather nice.*

The dinner bell sounded.

"Shall we?"

When they entered the dining room, the men stood as one. Denys held Felicity's chair out for her. She gazed up at him with sympathy. "Have you heard from your sister? I do hope the prognosis is good."

Ffoulkes surveyed the faces at the table. "We'll talk later." His eyes filled with tears.

"Oh, oh. Certainly." She touched his cheek. "I'm sorry."

Denys must have told her something in confidence. She contemplated the woman. *Really rather nice after all.*

Capac brought Felicity a plate and laid it reverently before her. "*Seco de cabrito.*"

Alex translated. "Kid stew."

"As in goat?"

"Yes, flavored with *aji amarillo* and cilantro."

She took a taste. "Delicious."

Capac nodded happily and swaggered back to the kitchen, passing a young boy. The child skipped to the head of the table and tapped his chest. "I Esteban. I help."

Winston came in behind him and said proudly, "He's my youngest. He'll take care of Manuel's garden until Capac's cousin gets here from Puerto Maldonado. He knows English."

Well, some.

The boy interrupted, piping, "I help Capac here too. Capac say he need me to bring plates." To prove it, he took two plates from his father and set them before Denys and Alex.

Emory didn't say a word to Petra during the meal, nor did he make eye contact. She didn't mind. *I need some time to think over Felicity's revelations.*

The latter put down her glass, rose, and took Ffoulkes's arm. "I don't believe we completed our examination of Mr. Tramposo's evidence. Shall we?"

The man flushed, his full lips caught in a simper. "Certainly, my dear. It's in my room for safekeeping." As they left, Petra caught the words, "Would you care for a snifter of cognac?"

She swiveled to see Aguirre, his mouth hanging open as he watched them go. Rook, pouring himself a large whiskey from the bottle at the bar, sported a vengeful little smirk.

Searching for a glass of water, she stepped into the kitchen. Esteban stood by a screened hutch she hadn't noticed before. "What does he have there?"

Capac glanced at the boy. "His *cuy*."

"*Cuy?*

In response, he said something to Esteban. The boy opened the hutch and brought out a small calico rodent.

"Oh, it's a guinea pig!"

Esteban stroked the creature's fur. "My pet. Topo." He offered it to her.

She scratched its ears. "I had a pet guinea pig once too. They're sweet animals."

He put the guinea pig back in the hutch, and she continued her meandering. She didn't see anyone else that night, even though she spent a longer time than usual in the hammock room watching the monkeys play in the moonlight. Finally, she went to bed.

****

October 21

The next morning she found Felicity alone eating breakfast. "Did you sleep well?"

"Oh, yes, I always sleep like a baby when I'm traveling."

"The heat doesn't get to you?"

She pulled the light sweater closer. "On the contrary—I'm always cold."

The ice queen—but now I know she has a liquid heart.

Hector looked in. "Miss Felicity, may I have a word?"

She dropped her napkin on the table and glided out to the corridor. When she returned, Petra asked curiously, "What was that all about?"

Felicity raised her eyebrows. "Poor Hector—henpecked by all his female relatives. He wants advice on how to put them off."

"What are they pestering him about? Oh wait…it's about getting married, isn't it? He mentioned how hard it was to stay single with such a large family."

"Right. I gave him a sure-fire method for distracting them."

"And what's that?"

"Sic them on his little brother."

"Ha-ha."

Felicity put down her coffee cup. "Perhaps you can help me. I have to find a way to announce my conclusion without ruffling too many feathers." Her eyes crinkled as if at some private joke.

"Your conclusion?"

"Yes. The skeleton is indeed modern, but it's not a chicken. Nor is it a hoatzin. I need more time to examine it, but it may be a new species—or possibly a very old one."

Chapter Sixteen
Origin of the Species

October 21

"Oh, my God, could Aguirre be right, then? That he saw a living fossil? Does Ffoulkes know?"

"I haven't told him yet. Still..." She put her chin in her hand.

Petra was about to ask what concerned her when the director arrived. "Good morning. I understand you have an announcement to make."

"We. We have an announcement to make." She beamed at Ffoulkes.

He took the bait. "Of course. Shall I muster the troops?"

Felicity bowed her head but winked at Petra. "Yes, please do. I'm so glad I came. Now we can begin to tackle the additional research."

He raised a dyed eyebrow. " 'Research'? Of what?"

"*Shh.* Let's announce it to the whole group, shall we?" She fluttered her lashes at him, which had the effect both women expected. When the others had gathered, Felicity told them of her hypothesis.

Ffoulkes, whose expression during the recitation had changed from complacency to panic to calculation, took over and pronounced in ringing tones, "Now that

Miss Lintu and I have cleared up that little mystery, we can resume our primary mission."

Felicity stared at him. "Did you not hear me? We may be looking at a hitherto undocumented species."

Ffoulkes looked down his nose at her. He whispered, "My dear Ms. Lintu, you don't think I would have recognized it myself?" He shook his head before raising his voice. "No, I'm convinced Aguirre saw a hoatzin. Perhaps a juvenile. Nothing more."

"I see." Icy silver shafts streaked through Felicity's blue eyes.

Denys went on hurriedly. "Therefore, we return to our search for the Mapinguari."

"The what?"

"The Mapinguari. It's a—"

Aguirre cried out, "Wait! Ffoulkes could be wrong. One person's opinion shouldn't decide our course of action. I may be a botanist, but if there's a new species of bird out there, we should at least attempt to find it."

Rook pursed his lips. "Tramposo, for once, is right. We shouldn't be diverted quite so easily. The skeleton is the only real evidence we have, since he failed to obtain adequate photographic evidence."

The object of his criticism shot him a venomous look. "What about the feather?"

Felicity opened her eyes wide. "Feather?"

He turned to her. "I found a tail feather that doesn't match any known bird. And I do have a photograph."

"I'd like to see them."

Aguirre stood up, but Rook pushed him back down. "Before we get to that, what else can you tell us about the skeleton, Miss Lintu?"

Ffoulkes started to remonstrate, but Felicity put a

small hand on his chest. He sat down abruptly. "Certain features are very distinctive. Since Mr. Tramposo appears to have further evidence"—she ignored Denys's snort—"evidence of which I was unaware, that is even more reason not to set the bird aside too precipitously."

The director's face flushed with anger. "Really, Miss Lintu, we're wasting precious time. I have to explain our expenses to the board. I—"

"Please...call me Felicity. Is the slab still in your room?" She gazed at him warmly.

"Yes, of course. It..." He stopped as the implication of her question dawned. "Well, perhaps one more day wouldn't hurt."

"An excellent plan, Denys." She turned to Aguirre. "Can you bring the feather and photograph to his room?"

Aguirre, with a side glance at Rook, nodded.

Felicity accepted more coffee from Capac. "I understand Dr. Lewis Gordon is a member of your team. I worked with him once before, on a project in South Africa. There were traces of some kind of fern on the slab that might help us. Did he get a look at the stone?"

Silence. Finally, Aguirre stammered, "I'm afraid there was an accident."

"Accident?"

Emory didn't look at her. "Lewis is dead. He...uh...came in contact with a *Chondrodendron tomentosum* vine."

Petra explained. "The curare vine."

"You mean the plant the natives use to make the arrow poison?"

"The very one. We think he may have cut himself and the open wound was infected with sap from the stem. He was dead when we found him." Emory didn't mention the piranhas, and neither did anyone else.

Felicity frowned. "But Lewis is an expert in rainforest plants. I understand he's been working off and on in the Amazon basin for years. How could he make such a mistake?"

No one had an answer. Felicity looked at the men, eyes narrowed, but she said nothing. She finished her coffee and the last bite of papaya. "Denys, shall I meet you in your room in two hours?"

"Yes, yes. We'll have a spot of tea." He went into the kitchen. The others could hear him giving orders to the cook. Felicity took Petra aside. "Petra, how well do you know these people?"

"Nick is my brother."

"Alex? Aguirre? Denys?"

She shook her head. "I only met them a couple of weeks ago."

"I want to talk to Emory. There's something not quite kosher going on."

This did not comfort Petra.

****

When Petra walked past Ffoulkes's room later that day, she heard Felicity's tinkling laughter and Denys's pompous voice. *They must be getting along famously. I'm glad* someone *likes him.*

Emory came up behind her. "The great director seems to have transferred his affections without so much as a 'kiss my foot or have an apple.' "

"Love the one you're with, I suppose." *Shall I? Maybe it's time to bury the hatchet.* A funny feeling

214

came over her. *It's like I can breathe freely again.* She turned to Emory. "Did Felicity tell you she'd like us to meet in her room before dinner?"

He nodded. "Wonder what she wants?" He gave her a speculative glance. "How did your cocktail hour go yesterday?"

She didn't tell him? "Very pleasant. Your wife—"

"Ex-wife."

"Your ex-wife is really very sweet."

"Despite the frigid façade?"

She checked his face for signs of emotion. "She is so pale—almost porcelain, isn't she? Is she of Scandinavian descent?"

"Her family's originally from Finland, but they settled in Greenland a few generations ago. I don't think they intermarried with the locals."

"Is that a joke?"

"Well, look at her. She sure wouldn't need makeup to play the part of Frigga, Queen of Asgard."

"You sound bitter."

"Me? Not at all. As I'm sure she told you, we parted amicably. She was a model of grace and strength. I was a louse."

Petra wanted to kiss him so badly, she was afraid if she didn't her heart would start to leak. "She told me about West Overbrook."

He slammed a fist into the wall. Luckily, it was made of bamboo paneling, and he only scraped his knuckles. He sucked on them. "Why do the bad guys always get away with it?"

"They don't. Eventually it will catch up with them. And you—you've survived and prospered despite them." *And you have me.* She gulped at the thought.

"Hardly prospered. And this expedition is turning out to be a bust. What are we doing here anyway? Hoping to discover a new species of stinkbird?"

"I thought we were looking for the Mapinguari."

He grunted. "I've given up on that. Face it—it's a myth. What we heard was probably a tapir or a howler monkey. We let our imaginations run away with us." He started to turn away.

"So you want to give up just like that? What about your father?" *Wait. The hair.* "Did you by any chance take the hair specimen from my desk? Emory? Emory?"

A crash came from the end of the covered walkway. Emory strode a few steps toward the sound. A wastebasket lay on its side on the floor, its contents strewn over the planks. A broom lay across it. She called, "It's nothing. The broom must have knocked the basket over."

"Maybe...but I thought I heard—oh, there he is." He pointed. Dillinger sat in a mud puddle out in the courtyard, holding his hands over his head while a pair of blue-and-yellow macaws pecked at them. Emory turned back to Petra. "And anyway, what would we do with Bigfoot if we found him?"

She had no answer for that. "We still have the mystery of the skeleton. Felicity thought it was unique. It could be the find of the century, as Denys is so fond of saying." She hoped that would cheer him up. *Unless it reminds him of the hummingbird fiasco.*

"We'll see." He paused. "Hey, look at us...we're talking."

Thank you, Felicity. "Yes." She smiled at him. He leaned toward her. Just before their lips met, Ffoulkes's door opened, and Felicity came out. She didn't say a word, but stepped between them and kept walking. Petra thought she heard a slight titter, but couldn't be sure.

At six, she made her way to Felicity's room. She had raised a hand to knock when Emory's angry voice clanged, "No! I won't be a party to it, Fel. I've had enough."

Felicity murmured something indistinguishable.

"I don't care. I won't do it again. You're not the one who got tripped up the last time. The money isn't worth it."

Petra listened wide-eyed. *Not worth the money?* Could she have been that naïve? *Are they all in it together?* Was Aguirre's skeleton part of an elaborate plot to deceive the academic world? For that matter, were all Emory's stories—from West Overbrook to the hummingbird—mere fabrications? *Or worse, failed scams?*

How could she have been so wrong about a person? Why, she'd almost fallen in love with him! She couldn't bear to think where that would have led her. *To jail? To the witness stand?*

She spun around and went in search of her brother. *He may be the only one I can trust.* She found him in the darkroom. "May I come in?"

"Hang on a sec…okay." He turned on the light.

A drawer jutted slightly ajar. "What's that?"

He closed it quickly. "Nothing."

She backed out. *Oh my God, Nicky's involved too.*

"Sis? What did you want?"

"Nothing." She fled outside. She saw Emory emerge from Felicity's room and stomp down the hall. *Who do I turn to? Who is on the level?* She caught sight of Rook. *He's a swine, but he doesn't seem to have any secrets. At least anymore.* "Mr. Rook!"

The man turned at her call. He had a machete in one hand and a monkey in the other. His telescope lay at his feet. "Miss Steele?"

She caught up with him and panted, "What are you doing? You're not going to kill it, are you?"

He looked down. "Don't be ridiculous. I was trying to split a Brazil nut with Winston's machete, and this stupid monkey decided it would be fun to use me as a jungle gym." He shook the creature off. "Did you want something?"

All of a sudden, Petra's suspicions seemed overblown. She stammered, "Do you know if Miss Lintu and Denys figured out what the fossil is?"

"You mean the skeleton?" He shook his head. "Even if it's a new species, it's still a distraction from my real purpose."

"Testing your product?"

"That's why I'm here, isn't it? And once I heard about this Mapinguari, I jumped at the chance to catch it and photograph it. Some hoatzin doppelgänger is not going to be as impressive as a huge hairy monster."

"I thought you were in favor of examining the skeleton!"

"At first. I didn't think they'd devote all the lab resources to it. Waste of time and money."

Petra remembered Rook was a businessman, not a scientist. *He doesn't want anything interfering with his project.* The thought made her feel better. *No conniving, no conspiracies, no lies. Just clear-eyed capitalism.* "Mr. Rook? I think this whole thing is an elaborate fiction."

He stopped short, his face suffused with anger. "What the hell are you talking about?"

"I think all of them"—she waved a hand at the lodge—"they're all in it. They're pretending they've found a new bird species."

"You mean they're making it all up? What for?"

Er... "For the money?"

He scoffed. "You don't make money finding new species." He hefted the machine. "You make money developing one of these."

"I see. Then why are you so set on finding the Mapinguari?"

He hesitated. "If I can capture a monster on film, I can prove that this scope has multiple uses—not just military, but law enforcement, exploration, maybe crowd control. I'll make a fortune."

"Okay, fine, but what should we do about the plot?"

He stared at her. " 'We'? Why should *we* do anything? If they want to dupe the scientific world, it won't be the first time. It doesn't make any difference to nature." He spat. "Humans and their petty little schemes. They're like gnats to Gaia."

"Huh?"

"Gaia. Mother Earth."

"Yes...but...gnats?"

"Useless, pesky insects—only serve to annoy." He swept his arm out. "One day, they'll be gone, and she can go back to her peaceable kingdom."

Don't you mean movable feast? "Humans are a part of nature too."

"An aberration." He knit his brows. "They're like a virus that ultimately destroys an otherwise healthy host.

They insinuate themselves into the natural order and infect it. Once it's ravaged by disease, they claim they can fix it, but the more they manipulate nature, the more screwed up she gets. A pox on them. Unclean filth."

Petra had no idea how to respond to this diatribe. *Just another eccentric billionaire, I guess.* "So…you won't help me?"

"I've got my own problems, lady. Where the hell is Aguirre? He was supposed to meet me an hour ago."

Just then a boyish voice cried out in Spanish.

"I think that's Winston's son, Esteban. He sounds upset. Come on."

She followed the keening to the kitchen, Rook reluctantly trailing her. Esteban knelt on the floor, cradling a small furry object. Tears splattered on it, mixing with the blood. Petra looked closer. "Isn't that his pet guinea pig?"

Capac bent down to the child and patted his head awkwardly. Winston rushed in. "Esteban! What is wrong? What happened?"

"Oh, Papi." His voice broke. "A big bird killed my Topo."

"A bird! What bird?"

"Dunno. Found feather." He held one up.

Just then Emory and Denys appeared. Ffoulkes took the feather from Esteban. "It looks identical to the one Aguirre found."

Emory said, "Why would a hoatzin kill a guinea pig? Their diet consists entirely of leaves. In fact, I'm unaware of any birds of the Amazon that eat meat other than carrion."

Ffoulkes blew out his cheeks. "Your wife says

otherwise."

"What are you talking about?"

"She says the *Caudipteryx* was an omnivore."

"*Caudipteryx*?"

"You remember, the dinosaur that's a possible link to the hoatzin?"

Before Emory could answer, Rook slammed a fist on the counter. "Oh, for heaven's sake. When will this ridiculous sensationalism stop?" He stalked out.

Emory stared after him, then turned to Denys. "What are you saying?"

"Just ask her."

The two men shoved each other in a battle to get through the door. Ffoulkes finally won the day. Emory sprinted after him.

Capac gently pried the dead guinea pig loose from Esteban's fingers. Winston pulled the boy to his feet and hugged him, making sympathetic noises. Father and son shambled out the back door to their quarters. Capac took the animal over to the sink.

"Where will you bury it?"

He goggled at Petra. "Bury it? Why would I do that?"

"In my country, we bury our pets. We sometimes perform a little memorial service. Pets are part of the family."

He continued to stare. "Not so much here. Topo is dinner." He picked up a butcher knife and, in one quick motion, split the guinea pig in half.

Petra gulped. *I forgot. Emory told me they raised guinea pigs here for food.* She backed out of the kitchen. Emory, Alex, and Denys sat in the lounge. "I thought you two were going to talk to Felicity?"

Denys seemed embarrassed. "She's…uh…She was indisposed."

Emory gave Petra a penetrating look. "You didn't show up at her room earlier. Any reason?"

Petra didn't reply. *I want to think this through. Were they really talking about defrauding the public? Am I jumping to conclusions? What about the others? Are they all in it?*

Ffoulkes held up the feather. "I repeat, it looks exactly like the tail feather Aguirre found."

Felicity appeared. "Sorry I couldn't talk earlier. What did you want?"

Nick, coming in on her heels, chimed in, "And what was all the fuss about? I heard Esteban wailing."

Alex rubbed his stomach. "I hear we're having *cuy* for supper." Petra told the two newcomers what happened to Esteban's pet. Denys handed Felicity the feather.

"It certainly does look similar." She tapped her chin. "You say you thought at first that the stone was a fossil *Caudipteryx*, right?"

"Yes."

"We're agreed it's not a fossil but the skeleton of a hitherto unknown bird, right?"

Everyone but Petra nodded. *Here goes.*

Felicity continued. "One of the big differences between the hoatzin—as well as other birds—and the *Caudipteryx zoui*, is that the theropod was a carnivore."

Denys whispered loudly, "I told you so."

Emory ignored him. "And the hoatzin's diet is vegetarian—almost exclusively leaves. So what's your point?"

"So…if this bird killed the guinea pig, then it's a

predator, and may be a direct descendent of the *Caudipteryx*. One that still walks the earth." She looked around. "We need Aguirre on this. Has anyone seen him?"

Alex said, "He and Winston took the canoe downriver. One of Hector's cousins thinks he caught a glimpse of Aguirre's bird."

"Great! Let's hope they come back with news."

I was right! Aguirre, Felicity, Emory, Nick—maybe even Alex. They're all in on it. Petra ran out of the room. *What am I going to do? I have to get out of here. I can't be involved in this. Rook will have to deal with it.* She looked for her phone before realizing it didn't work without the chip. Frustrated, she started to pack.

She heard a tentative knock on the door. "Sis? Are you coming to dinner?"

No! "I don't feel very well, Nick. You go on."

When his footsteps had faded, she snuck out and took the back stairs to the staff quarters. Hector sat at a table eating his meal. "Hector? Can I ask you a big favor?"

He stood up quickly. "Of course."

"Could you take me to Iquitos in the launch tonight?"

"Certainly. But if I may ask, why?"

"I…uh…my mother called. My father is away, and she's alone, and…um…she needs me."

"Is something wrong?"

"No. No, yes. She's…broken her ankle."

"Oh, dear. Yes, certainly I'll take you. Shall I arrange a hotel in Iquitos and a flight to Lima?"

"Yes, please. You're very good."

"All right, that's two rooms and two tickets. When

will you be returning?"

"Two? Why?"

"Will not your brother accompany you?"

"No, he's staying here. He's under contract. I'm on vacation, so I can leave if I want to."

He blinked. *He doesn't believe me.* "I'll be in my room. Come and get me when you're ready. And please, don't tell anyone else. My brother will feel guilty that he can't come with me." Hector said nothing. *Now I'm sure he doesn't believe me. Probably thinking how weird these Americans are.*

An hour later, she watched the sun set on the vast Amazon River as the launch moved swiftly through the brown waters toward Iquitos and home.

Chapter Seventeen
Dispersion

October 24

"So, the Amazon didn't agree with you?"

"The Amazon is fantastic, Dad, but very hot." She wrapped her arms around her chest. "Not like here. *Brr.*"

"Is it hotter than Phoenix?"

"It's not the heat, it's the...you know the rest. You're used to the arid West."

Petra's father sighed. "Still, I would love to explore the rainforest someday. That, and the Galapagos." He peered at her. "Seems to me you were heading there. How did you end up in Peru anyway?"

"Didn't Mother tell you?"

"Hasn't had time. I just got back from Colorado yesterday." They crossed the bridge at Hunting Creek and entered the park that extended all the way to Mount Vernon. "We've another five miles to go. So?"

Petra decided the best policy was to change the subject. "You want to go gallivanting around the world now? Are you tired of dams?"

"Never. They're the perfect union of natural beauty and human ingenuity. Take a dam like Glen Canyon—it fits like a pocket, smoothing out the rough edges of the cliffs. You can almost believe it's always been there."

Petra didn't respond, and her father didn't press until they turned onto their street. "Now, if you won't tell me why you went to Peru, at least tell me why you came back. I know it's not to keep your mother company. With me home, she's back on the wagon."

"No more beer?"

"Strictly white wine. And salad." He smiled fondly. "Eloise is fine too, by the way."

"Thanks for taking care of her."

"It may have been a mistake. Your mother is quite attached to the little thing."

"Well, Eloise originally belonged to her, after all." Considering the exotic creatures she'd been living with, a cat suddenly seemed awfully tame. "Maybe she'll want to keep her for a while longer."

Her father shot her a sharp look. "You haven't answered either of my questions, so I must resort to guessing. Has Nick been treating you badly? I believe that is to be expected in a younger brother."

"He's fine." Petra had already resolved not to tell her parents of her suspicions. She didn't know if she should tell anyone at all yet. *After all, I have no real proof—snippets of conversation, and a certain sneaky air.* Even if the bunch of them were conspiring to unveil a fictitious species, it was hardly up to her to expose them. The scientific world—as it had with the hummingbird—would surely take care of it. *What about West Overbrook, then?* As far as she knew, the people involved in that skulduggery were still in their jobs. *And what about Nick? How did he get roped into it?* Until she had the answers, their parents should be kept in the dark.

Her mother stood on the front step, Eloise

slithering like Salome between her legs. "Why are you here?"

"Glad to see you too, Mother."

Her mother held her arms out, but her eyes flashed with both curiosity and annoyance. "Call Nick."

"Why?"

"He phoned yesterday from Peru. You didn't tell him you were skipping out."

Damn. I hadn't thought of that. Maybe it's out of my hands. Still, after two days of travel, she wasn't quite ready. "It's a long story. Can I just go unpack?"

Her father carried her suitcase up the stairs. "Leave her alone, Naomi. There'll be plenty of time for the third degree at dinner."

"You keep an eye on her, then, Oliver. She's a proven flight risk."

Petra had the bite of swordfish halfway to her mouth when Naomi launched into the interrogation. "I thought you were staying another two weeks. You asked me to explain to Phoebe. Which I did—after several days of phone tag." Left unspoken were the words "and at great inconvenience."

"I have to get back to work on the book."

"I understand there was a budding romance."

"Not true. Nick doesn't know what he's talking about."

"How did you know I heard it from your brother?"

"Who else would you get it from?"

Naomi was unwilling to concede the point. "I have my sources."

Oliver grunted. "For heaven's sake, Naomi."

"All right, I'll ask again. Why are you here?"

Stall. Stall. What's my story anyway? "This is my

home."

"No, it's not. You live on Blackstone Avenue. Last I checked, that was in Chicago, not Alexandria, Virginia." Naomi tapped her fingers. "Petra…"

I've got it. "It is true—I met a man there. We enjoyed each other's company."

"I see." Her mother folded her arms. "I sense a 'but monkey' coming."

"His ex-wife showed up. She's beautiful."

"So are you."

"Not like her. Felicity's…well, picture Botticelli's Aphrodite, only more striking. I…I could tell Emory was still…in love with her." Petra knew her mother couldn't resist a love triangle. *Let her chew on that. It won't occur to her there's another, less romantic reason for bolting.*

Sure enough, Naomi spent the rest of the meal mulling over possible outcomes. Petra's dad watched them spar, making no effort to join the conversation. Despite the smile on his lips, his eyes were watchful. When Naomi left to make coffee, he said, "Come with me, Petra."

She counted herself lucky it had taken as long as it did. "Yes, Dad."

He turned on her when they reached his study. "Now, what's the real reason you ran away?"

"Me? Run away? I…yes, I did." *Bite the bullet. Gird your loins. Squeal.* "Dad, I think the scientists are conspiring to pretend to find a new species. Even Nick."

He sat at his desk. "Tell me."

She related the conversation she'd overheard, Aguirre's odd behavior, Nick hiding something in a drawer. "The only person who seems uninvolved is Victor Rook."

"Victor Rook! The billionaire? What's he doing there?"

She told him.

He mulled it over. "He does have a reputation for being hands-on, but why the alias? And why come alone?"

"I think Aguirre—the botanist—works for him." She considered. "Maybe he just wanted to keep the machine a secret until he'd tested it."

"And what better place than deep in the jungle, I guess. Still—"

Naomi called from the dining room. "Coffee's getting cold, you two."

"Coming." Oliver looked at his daughter. "We'll just keep this to ourselves for now. Your mother doesn't need to get all in a tizzy about your brother. Not until we have proof."

"Agreed."

****

October 25

As it happened, Petra didn't have to keep anything from her mother for very long. The next morning she awoke to a shriek. *Will I ever get to wake up in peace?* She threw on a robe and ran downstairs. "Mother?"

Her mother had collapsed on the sofa, the cell phone dangling from her fingers. Oliver rushed in barefoot. He took the phone from Naomi and listened. "Yes? This is Mr. Steele. Yes. Where is he now? And the diagnosis?...All right, thank you." He hung up. "That was the American embassy in Lima. The Peruvian police contacted them. Nick has had an accident. They're transporting him to the regional hospital in Iquitos. He'll be evaluated there and, if necessary, they'll airlift him to Lima."

"But what happened to him?"

"An accident in the darkroom. The consular officer on the phone said he was told Nick has severe burns to his eyes."

****

October 27

Emory met her at the airport in Iquitos and led her to a waiting taxi. "I'll take you to the hospital."

"I got your message that he's still here. Why didn't they take him to Lima?"

"Turns out they have a burn unit here, and the doctor said the damage isn't as serious as they initially thought."

"Oh, Emory." Petra tried to compose herself. She wanted his arms around her, comforting her, telling her everything would be okay. She didn't have the strength to distrust him right now. *I'll deal with conspiracies later.*

He seemed to sense her need and tentatively patted her arm. "He'll be fine. When you work with those kinds of chemicals, there's always a risk."

"Yes, but Nick has been developing photographs since he was seven. He's never had an accident before. He's extremely careful." She crabbed her fingers under his large hand. He squeezed them without looking at her. "Do you know how it happened?"

"Not exactly. I was down by the dock when all hell broke loose. By the time I got to the lodge, Nick had made it to the kitchen and Capac was rinsing his eyes out."

"And no one else saw anything?"

"No. As far as I know, he was alone. If he's awake, we can ask him."

The small hospital was located on the outskirts of Iquitos. The receptionist directed them to a room on the second floor. Nick lay in the bed, eyes bandaged. The nurse whispered in halting English, "I have administered his pain medication. He'll be asleep in a few minutes."

"Can I talk to him? I'm his sister."

"I doubt if he'll make much sense, but I'm sure he'll be reassured by your presence."

Petra approached the bed. "Nicky? It's me, Petra."

He lifted a hand. "Oh, sis, is that you? How did you get here so fast?"

"As soon as we heard, I hopped a plane. Mom and Dad are very concerned. Mom is frantic—she demanded to come with me. Dad talked her out of it."

"Oh, thank God." He held out a hand blindly. She grasped it in both her own. "I'll be okay, Petra. The doctor said the corneas should heal in a few days. Let them know, would you?" He yawned. "Now, the question is: why did you leave without telling me?"

She glanced at Emory. He didn't hide his interest. "That's for another time. How did the accident occur?"

"Really strange...developer bath...something pushed..." His chest began to rise and fall.

The nurse stepped forward. "You'll have to come back tomorrow."

Emory took Petra's arm and led her out. "I've booked a hotel room for you."

In a sudden panic, she cried, "You have to go back to Pacaya? You can't stay?" *I don't want to be here alone.*

He paused. "I can stay if you want me to."

In her relief, she didn't consider the implications. "I…thank you."

He tipped an invisible cap. "I'll see if I can get a second room."

"Oh. Oh!" Petra felt her face burn. "Yes, please do."

Unfortunately, the hotel was sold out. "It is high season, señor. Many tourists." He pointed at a passing bus. "Amazon tours very popular. Iquitos is the gateway to the Amazon."

Where have I heard that before?

He winked. "Lots of American dollars."

Emory frowned. "Is there another hotel you can recommend? We only need one night." The desk clerk surveyed the couple. "The lady's room has a sofa. We can provide bed linens. Perhaps that will be satisfactory?"

Petra gulped. Emory remained stone-faced. *He's not going to help, is he?* Finally she muttered, "That will be fine." The bellhop took her suitcase up. She was about to step on the elevator when she realized Emory wasn't behind her. "Aren't you coming?"

His mouth twisted in a wry grin. "I didn't expect to be staying over. I have to go buy a toothbrush. And tell Winston to go home."

He returned as the sun set. "I called the lodge. They'll send the launch back tomorrow. Will you be coming with me?"

Until now, distraught over her brother, Petra hadn't thought beyond the next few hours. *Do I want to go back there? No!* "We'll…we'll see."

He drew back. "Are you planning to return to DC then?"

"When Nick is better, I'll probably take him home, yes."

Emory turned away. He said quietly, "Okay." He looked out the window at the lights winking on in the city. "How about some dinner? We can go to the corniche."

"Oh, yes, I'd like that. Nick and I went there when I first arrived. It's lovely."

"Good. There's a restaurant I think you'll enjoy. Shall we?"

They walked down Jirón Putumayo toward the river. As they passed a big square, busy with evening revelers, Petra halted. "What's that?"

"Plaza de Armas—Arms Square. It's the main square in Iquitos."

She pointed at a strange building on the corner. "And what do you suppose that is?"

"Let's go see." As they got closer to the two-story building, lights blazed on in the upper level, revealing a restaurant. An iron filigree balcony held tables filled with chattering customers. "Shall we eat here?"

"No. I have another place in mind—a bit more beguiling." He turned away so she couldn't see his face.

"Wait, there's an historical marker." She stopped to read. "Casa de Fierro—The Iron House. Oh right, I read about this. It's built entirely of iron."

"Hence the name." He said it without irony.

Petra read on. "A rubber baron named Toots—"

"You're kidding."

"That what it says. He bought it in France in 1889 and shipped it here in pieces. Says it was one of the world's first prefab buildings."

"Eighteen eighty-nine? That's the same year the Paris Exposition opened, with Gustave Eiffel's tower at its entrance. As I recall, Eiffel was already famous for his ironworks." He scanned the house. "I wonder if he had a hand in this one as well."

A man who had been lounging by the door straightened and tipped his cap. "Excuse me, I couldn't help overhearing." He spoke with a strong Irish brogue. "It is generally believed that Eiffel designed it, but there's no actual proof." He gestured at the far end of the building. "It was supposed to be twice this size, but once they shipped it here, they decided to break it up into two sections."

"What happened to the second section?"

He shrugged. "Dunno. It's rumored that Fitzcarrald bought it and took it to Madre de Dios."

"Fitzcarrald?"

Emory took her arm. "Come on, I'll show you."

She took a last look at the iron palace. "Fascinating. Thanks." The Irishman saluted smartly.

They walked another block to a small restaurant on the corner of Napo and Malecón Tarapata, the avenue that ran along the river. Bay windows opened onto the promenade. Inside, movie posters covered the walls and giant ferns in pots were scattered among the tables. They chose a spot overlooking the river. Pedestrians strolled along under the gas lamps—families with children, businessmen on their cell phones, boys trundling dollies filled with crates of plantains. A white man in shorts and a khaki shirt passed, his face in a book. He bumped into a baby carriage and raised his head, revealing a familiar shock of red hair and a face full of freckles. "Oh, look, isn't that Alex?"

Emery followed her pointing finger. "It is indeed. Funny, he told me he'd found a nest of yacare caimans and would be camping out for a few days to study them. I wonder why he lied?"

Chapter Eighteen
Natural Selection

October 27

"Hey, Alex!"

The man jumped. He closed the book but kept his thumb between the pages and walked over to the window. "Hi, Emory." He swiveled to Petra. "I see you've come back. Have you been to visit your brother?"

"Yes. They're keeping him in the hospital a few days, but he's been told he'll recover his eyesight."

"Good news! Are you staying in Iquitos?"

"For the night at least."

Emory glanced at the book, still in Alex's hand. "I thought you were checking out the caimans down near Tamshiyacu. What are you doing in Iquitos?"

His eyes fixed on something over their heads, Alex stammered, "Um, we'd…uh…kind of put work on hold while you and Nick are unavailable. I decided to do a little sightseeing. I'm going up to see the Iron House."

"Oh? We were just there. Evidently, it's one of two."

Alex's eyes narrowed. "Who told you that?"

"A man standing there."

"Did he have an Irish accent?"

Petra felt a warning nibble but wasn't sure why.

Something fey gleamed in the normally sweet Alex's eyes. "Yes, why?"

Alex relaxed. "I'm supposed to meet him there."

"Is he a scientist?"

"No." He looked away down the street. "A tour guide. Well, I'll see you two later. When are you coming back to the lodge?"

Her mistrust reignited. "I don't know. We have to talk to the doctors tomorrow."

"Okay. Gotta go." He loped off.

Emory watched him until he melted into the crowds. "*Hmm*. Interesting."

"What? That a scientist would want to take in some of the sights now and then?"

"Yes."

"Oh, for heaven's sake." She looked over at the bar. "They have wine? How wonderful. I can't tell you how sick I was getting of warm beer."

"Let's order some, then."

A waiter in black pants and a crisp white shirt came over. "*Buenas tardes*. I am Felipe. Would you like something to drink?"

"A carafe of white wine, please." She perused the menu while he went to get it. As he set down the jug and poured wine in her glass, she asked, "This *sarapatera*—what is it, Felipe?"

"*Sopa de motelo*. Turtle soup."

"Really? I've always heard that turtle soup is tasty...but is it legal to offer it on the menu? Aren't turtles endangered?"

Emory answered. "Only the sea turtles. This must be from a river turtle. I believe there's a giant Amazon river turtle, isn't there?" He appealed to Felipe.

"Yes, but *our* soup is made from the yellow-footed tortoise. It lives in the dry forest—what we call *terra firme*. The *sopa*, it is quite spicy." He draped a concerned look over his dark features.

She twinkled at him. "Don't worry. I love spicy food." She put the menu down. "I'll try that, and a hearts of palm salad."

"Make that two of each."

When the waiter had gone, she surveyed the walls. "What great posters." She pointed. "Fitzcarraldo? Where did I hear that name before?"

"The Irishman mentioned him. His real name was Carlos Fermin Fitzgerald. The natives couldn't pronounce the Irish name, so they called him Fitzcarrald. He was half Peruvian and half Irish, although the rumor persists that his father was American."

"But who was he? And where does the 'o' come in?"

"Have you heard of Werner Herzog, the German moviemaker?"

"Sure. He was famous for his cult films."

"Uh-huh. He made several movies right here in Iquitos. *Fitzcarraldo* was one of them. It's based on Fitzgerald's life. He was a rubber baron who hauled a steamboat over a mountain in southern Peru. He discovered an isthmus between tributaries of the Urubamba and the Madre de Dios rivers, opening up a route to ship rubber down the Amazon. In the movie, Herzog makes him out to be a raving maniac who builds an opera house in the middle of the jungle. You remember that rusting old paddle boat at the confluence of the Amazon and the Pacaya? That was used in the movie."

Petra put her wine glass down. "He must have filmed *Aguirre* here then as well. Too funny."

"Huh?"

"*Aguirre*. It's the only one of Herzog's movies I've seen. It was playing at the Commons at U of C— University of Chicago—one night, and a bunch of us grad students went." She giggled, then—in a fairly good imitation of James Earl Jones—intoned, " 'Aguirre: Wrath of God!' " She poured more wine into her glass. "One of the silliest movies I've ever seen."

"I don't recall that Werner Herzog made any comedies."

"No, no, it was because the premise was so outlandish. See, Aguirre is this conquistador who comes to South America looking for gold. One by one his entire posse gets killed or eaten or something. In the last scene, he's all alone. He's lost all his supplies, his weapons…even his clothes. The finale swells as you watch him float downstream on a raft, pounding his naked chest and cursing his fate." She tittered. "For weeks after that we'd all shout 'Aguirre, Wrath of God!' whenever it rained."

Emory straightened his shoulders, his tone one of cold disapproval. "As I recall, the German actor Klaus Kinski took on the role of Fitzcarraldo when Jason Robards dropped out due to the heat. Kinski not only didn't mind it; he thrived in it. Truly gifted, if slightly mad."

Petra wasn't listening. She mused, "I never got a chance to ask him how he came by the name. It's not exactly common. He's American, though, isn't he?"

"Kinski? I told you, he was German." Emory was still annoyed. "Didn't you hear me?"

"No. I meant Aguirre."

"But…Oh, you mean, *our* Aguirre?" He shrugged. "No idea. I assume he's Hispanic, but he never talks about his family or background. Let's get some more wine." He raised a finger.

The evening slanted toward night, and Petra began to relax. She gazed out the open windows at the passing couples. The sun set behind them, sending dueling lances of deep red and blue over their heads to splash down into the ferruginous Amazon. "It's so beautiful here."

Emory started out of his reverie, and she realized he hadn't been staring at the river, but at her. "It is indeed. Shall we go?"

When she stood up, her head began to spin. He took her arm. "You must be exhausted. You need to get to bed."

She didn't argue, and by the time they reached the hotel, she could barely keep her eyes open. He gently laid her on the bed. "I'll go make up the sofa." She didn't answer.

It was pitch black when she woke up. "Where am I?" She looked around. A light shone under a door. *The hotel. Iquitos. Nicky.* She swung her legs off the bed and headed toward the door. It opened into another dark room, but across the way a nightlight indicated the bathroom. *Since I'm up, I might as well brush my teeth.* She managed to make it there without incident, but on the return trip she ran smack into something hard. She felt with her hands. *Must be the couch.* Her hand encountered a face. "Oops, sorry!"

Emory caught her hand and pulled her to him. He kissed her fiercely.

"Stop it." She pulled away.

He turned on a lamp and raised up on one elbow. "Well, you were pawing me. What did you expect me to do?"

"I...uh...I just tripped over you in the dark."

"I see." He watched her. For some reason she couldn't move. "Shall I try it again?"

She looked down into that handsome face. A lock of hair had fallen over his brow. His face was flushed with sleep. *So what if he's a crook?* "Uh-huh."

Two minutes later, they landed on the bed.

****

October 28

As dawn rose, Petra woke. Emory lay next to her, snoring. She poked him. He rolled over. "Wha—"

"How did you end up here?"

"You don't remember? Thanks a lot."

She threw off the covers and realized she was naked. "Emory!"

In response, he pulled her to him and rubbed her nose with his. "Morning, sunshine."

"But...but...you were...I was...what the hell?"

He sat up. "All right. I put you to bed and made up the sofa. All was peaceful until, sometime in the middle of the night, this ravenous creature attacked me, pulled my clothes off, and dragged me off to her lair."

Petra couldn't stop the giggle. "That would be me?"

He brought his face close to hers. "*Hmm*...Why, yes. Come to think of it, it *was* you." He felt her legs. "As I suspected, a fish tail."

"Fish tail?"

"You haven't heard the myth of Iara, the river mermaid?"

She consulted her memory banks. "Ah, yes. She who lures unsuspecting men into her bed."

"When she doesn't eat them."

"I promise not to eat you." When he didn't reply, she ventured, "Should I apologize?"

"There's only one way to fully apologize for your atrocious behavior last night."

"Let me guess."

The rest played out satisfactorily for both predator and prey.

As they lay panting, Emory's cell phone rang. Before he picked it up, he said, "Remind me to get you a prepaid phone while we're in Iquitos."

"Is that all you need to get me?"

He grinned and clicked Talk. "Andrews here." He listened. "Okay, thank you."

"Who was that?"

"The hospital. Nick is doing much better today. They will perform another examination later, but the doctor is ninety percent sure he'll keep his eyesight. Nick wants us to come over."

"Right now?" She jumped out of bed.

He caught her elbow. "Visiting hours aren't until ten."

"Oh."

He smiled at her crestfallen face. "It's nine now. Let's get some food and then head over."

"Okay." Her belly grumbled. "I'm starved."

"I wonder why."

The restaurant offered a heartier breakfast than the

bread and fruit they were used to. Emory ordered a tamale and chicken soup. Petra asked about the *pastel de choclo*.

"It's a sweet corn and beef pie. Traditional Peruvian breakfast."

Emory leaned over. "Like shepherd's pie."

"I'll have that—haven't had beef since that yummy *lomo saltado* in Lima...my God, that was more than three weeks ago!"

Nick was sitting up when they arrived. His eyes were bandaged, but he had the TV on anyway. "Don't turn it off—it keeps me company."

"But it's in Spanish!"

"Music to my ears." He beckoned them to come closer. "So the doctors say I will definitely get my sight back. I have Capac to thank for his quick action."

Petra sat on a chair by the bed. "Tell us what happened."

His head swiveled to where Emory stood. "Don't you know?"

"No one was nearby. We heard a lot of noise. You were already in the kitchen when I reached you."

"Oh? But...Well, let's see...I was in the darkroom getting ready to develop the film Aguirre and Rook shot...what's so funny?"

Wrath of God! "Never mind. Go on."

"I'd filled the basin with the developer solution and was reaching for my goggles, when the door opened behind me. It knocked me forward, and the goggles fell in the basin. Fluid splashed back up into my face."

"Oh, dear! What did you do?"

"I screamed bloody murder. Tried to get out and down to the lab to rinse my eyes, but something was in

243

the way."

Petra leaned forward. "A person?"

"I don't think so. I knocked it aside and stumbled out into the corridor."

"Did you hear anyone else?"

"No...Wait." He scratched at the bandage. "A woman's voice."

"Felicity?"

"No. Whoever it was, she was yelling for help in Spanish."

Petra's lips turned up despite her anxiety. "*Ayuda*, right? One of the few words I know now."

Emory leaned on the edge of the windowsill. "It must have been Capac's wife, Luz. She was in the kitchen with Winston and Capac when we arrived." He rubbed his chin. "Maybe she was mopping the hall and left her bucket in the way."

"Did you hear any sloshing when you pushed the thing aside?"

Nick hunched his shoulders. "I wasn't thinking about anything but getting to the lab at that point. Although..." He thought a minute. "I do remember my feet feeling wet. Of course that could have been because Capac was pouring water over my head."

Petra frowned. "She must have been what blocked you, since you heard her yelling."

"But why did she try to come into the darkroom?"

"Why wouldn't she? She has to clean."

Nick shook his head. "I made it clear to the staff from the beginning that I didn't want anyone in there."

Petra thought. "It could have been one of the team...say, Aguirre coming to check on your progress. But surely you have one of those little red warning lights outside the room?"

"Not here. Didn't seem necessary." He chuckled. "Wastes too much electricity. I do have a blackout curtain that draws across the door on the inside. No one uses the darkroom except me anyway."

Emory stood. "We're back to the only likely scenario being that Luz tried to go into the darkroom."

Nick nodded. "And when she heard me cry out, she ran to get help, leaving her bucket at the door. She and Winston helped me to the kitchen." He broke off. "Her Spanish is pretty colloquial, but in all the gibberish, I picked out *hombre*—a man."

"*Hombre*? She must have meant you."

Petra patted the bed and rose. "Capac should be able to give us more details."

"Yes. Are you going back to Pacaya today?"

Petra looked at Emory. "Emory is. I'm going to stay here for a few days. I don't want to leave you."

"No! Petra, I want you to go back with him." He waved in the direction of the door. "Emory, would you mind leaving us alone for a minute?"

Emory hesitated but left.

Nick crooked a finger at Petra. She came nearer. He whispered, "Sis, there's something fishy going on at the lodge. The photos—well, there were certain anomalies. I hadn't developed enough to really review them, but I'm not sure the negatives weren't altered."

The fraudulent species? Oh, dear, do I want to go back there if they're all in it? I've got to be sure—at least of Nick. "Nick? When I came into the darkroom the day I left, you hid something in a drawer. What was it?"

"You saw that? Yes, it was one of the photos. I was

afraid Aguirre would ask for all of them, and I wanted to keep one safe, in case."

Thank God. She didn't think she could handle this alone. At least her brother was on her side. "Who do you think is involved?"

"Aguirre definitely. Maybe Ffoulkes. I don't see any of the others as either that fanatical or that unethical. Your Emory is obviously in the clear—you wouldn't love a phony—"

"Love!"

"Yes, yes, but that's beside the point. Also among the innocent is the beauteous Felicity. She arrived too late."

"Ah, but she immediately closeted herself with Denys. And she's the one who first suggested it was a new species."

"Wasn't that Aguirre?"

"Oh. Well. She's the expert who confirmed his hypothesis."

"Not exactly. As I recall, she was only open to the idea." He touched her hand. "I can't see your face, but I'm hearing a touch of jealousy in your voice. Am I right?"

Petra thought of her conversation with Emory's ex-wife. "No, I'm not. I just want to be cautious."

"Let's bring Emory in, then."

"No!" Suddenly Nick's calm assumptions about her feelings for Emory frightened her. *I don't want to have to rely on his integrity...not yet anyway.* She wasn't ready to be that vulnerable. *What if Nick is wrong, and he* is *dishonest?*

Emory poked his head around the door. "All set?"

"Yes." Petra gathered her purse.

Emory went to Nick's bed. "I'll keep an eye on your sister, but Nick, we need to get to the bottom of all these accidents. Lewis, me, Manuel, John…and now you. Do you think somebody has it in for us?"

Nick shrugged. "Could be just coincidence. Or"— he grinned—"it could be el Chullachaqui playing tricks."

"Dangerous tricks. Come on, Petra, let's go."

Nick grabbed her sleeve. "Be careful, sis. I know we absolved the others, but, to be safe, don't confide in anyone except me and Emory."

She cast a glance at her lover. *I don't think I can make an exception for him.* Nick may trust her instincts, but she hardly had a good track record in that regard. Still, for now it seemed unwise to let him know she had doubts. "All right. I'm going to get a cell phone chip so you can call me."

"Great. I hope the phones are still working. You never know."

They stopped at the local version of a Radio Shack. "Señorita, may I suggest a disposable phone? Cheaper, and you don't have to depend on a service contract."

"Fine."

They checked out of the hotel and made their way to the dock. On the way, Emory mumbled something.

"What did you say?"

"I said, thanks for trusting me."

She didn't reply.

The launch was tied up to a pier. Winston lounged on the deck. Emory saluted. "We're ready to go when you are." The guide sprang into action, and soon they were motoring down the broad brown river toward Pacaya. Emory stood in the bow. Petra came up to him.

He put an arm around her. "Nick will be all right."

"I hope so. I'm glad I could be here."

"Me too." He touched her hair lightly. "I missed you. Why did you leave so suddenly anyway?"

Just enough information. "I thought there was something fishy going on too, but I didn't know who was in on it."

His arm tightened. "And you thought it could be me."

"Or even Nick."

"I see." Emory knit his brows. "I've been thinking about the accident. Question: if Luz's bucket was in the way, how did she open the door?"

Chapter Nineteen
Arrested Development

October 28

Felicity waited for them on the dock. "How is he?"

"The doctor says he'll be all right, but the corneas will take time to heal."

"Will he come back here?"

Petra realized they hadn't asked that particular question. "I don't know. He'll have to get his stuff eventually, but if it takes weeks…"

Felicity frowned. "He's your only photographer, right? I mean, the only one with the expertise to develop the film." She looked at Emory. "So you're off the hook. If we can't prove it…"

Off the hook? For whatever they were planning? Aha. I was right to have reservations. Petra's mind whirled.

Emory glared at Felicity. "We've been over that."

Petra picked up her bag. Felicity called after her, "Could we meet in my room after dinner?"

Do they want to reel me in too? No way, folks. About to refuse, she felt again Emory's warm hands on her breasts. Nick believed he was honorable—"You wouldn't love a phony, sis." She sighed. *Might as well hear them out.*

At dinner, they had to describe in detail Nick's

medical treatment, frame of mind, and plans, such as they were. By tacit consent, neither she nor Emory mentioned the bucket. After coffee, they walked down to Felicity's room. As they neared it, Petra whispered, "Go ask Capac what his wife said."

"Will do."

She knocked on the door.

Felicity opened it and looked over Petra's shoulder. "Where's Emory?"

"He had a question for…uh…Winston." She stepped into the room. "And I have a question for you."

"We all have a lot of questions. That's why I wanted us to talk. Since I've been here, I've sensed a tension in the air. I think someone has an agenda that is not the official one."

"Me too." Petra stared hard at Felicity. Emory came in.

"What did Capac say?"

"He said Luz was extremely upset after the accident and kept babbling about a man in the corridor."

"A man." Petra frowned. "Could someone have opened the darkroom door on purpose?" It scared her to say it, but she had to. "To injure Nick?"

Emory shook his head. "Couldn't be. How would anyone know he'd be handling the developer fluid?"

"What else would he be doing?" Petra looked at Felicity. "When the incident occurred, who arrived first on the scene?"

She pursed her lips. "It was midafternoon. Most of us were in the hammock room napping. When we heard the maid screech, we all headed toward the sound."

"Most of you? Who wasn't in the hammock

room?"

"Well, Capac was in the kitchen. Denys must have been in his room, since he came from the opposite direction."

Emory added, "I'd gone down to the dock."

"That's right." Felicity nodded. "And Winston was out back sharpening his machete. Not sure where Hector was."

"Luz was by the darkroom when you got there?"

"No, she was running toward the back stairs to fetch Winston."

"That's probably all it is, then." Emory planted his hands on his knees. "She put the bucket down and tried the door. After all, like Nick said, there's no indicator light, so no one would know he was in there."

"That's right." Felicity tapped her fingers on the table. "In fact, I remember he announced at lunch that some of the photos were developed, and he was going to let them dry before starting on the rest."

"So everyone would assume the darkroom would be empty."

"Yes."

Someone knocked. Denys stood on the threshold, pipe in hand. "Oh, Felicity. I didn't know you had company. I had hoped to lure you to my quarters for a glass of sherry." He leered at her.

Wait a minute...Denys. She grabbed the director and pulled him inside. "Hold on. Felicity, didn't you say Denys came from his room? It's at the far end of the walkway, isn't it?"

Before the other woman could answer, Emory broke in. "The same one as the darkroom, yes. Are you suggesting..."

251

Petra kept her eyes glued to Denys. "Denys, were you in the corridor when Nick had his accident?"

"How did you—" The pompous demeanor cracked like a rotten walnut. "I...I didn't mean to. I expected the room to be unoccupied." His lower lip quivered.

Felicity led him to a chair. "Tell us all about it."

He put his head in his hands. "It's this new bird. If we're right and it's a totally new creature—a link to the dinosaurs..."

"Yes, we're all agreed it would be a bombshell."

"I...I..."

Petra had a flash of intuition. "You were going to steal the photographs, weren't you?"

He nodded, his face covered.

Emory said slowly, "Nick told everyone that he'd left Aguirre's photos to dry. You sneaked along the corridor when you thought we'd all be in the hammock room."

Felicity chimed in. "You pushed the door open and heard the crash and Nick's scream. As you backed out, you almost ran into Luz. She was coming down the hall pushing her mop and bucket. You ran away, but she saw you—"

"Or at least your back. She only knew it was an *hombre*, a *científico*."

Denys hadn't moved. Petra stood before him. "Why? It makes no sense. Why would you steal photos you have a proprietary right to? The pictures and any research data belong to the Institute for Tropical Research."

Ffoulkes said nothing for a full minute. The others waited him out. Finally he spoke, his voice muffled. "I wanted—needed—sole credit." He raised his head.

"Look, I've had nothing for the last twenty years—no discoveries, no breakthroughs in my work, no new ideas. I established the institute when it became clear that no university was ever going to offer me tenure. And now, what little standing I have left is beginning to erode. I'm no longer invited to speak at conferences. And my articles are all rehashes or critiques of the work of others. I was at the end of my rope."

"What made you think you could get away with it? You wouldn't be able to silence every member of the team."

"I have a colleague—a close friend I collaborated with on my landmark study of microclimates in rainforest ecosystems in 1991." He paused, perhaps reliving the glory days. "He said he'd take them and get them published in my name. The inevitable publicity would revive my career, and I would finally be treated with the respect I deserve."

Petra was indignant. "Without crediting the others? You would do that?"

Ffoulkes was undeterred. "It was my project. It's my institute. Why shouldn't I get the prestige? As to the rest of you"—his gaze swept quickly over Emory— "your careers wouldn't suffer one way or another. Why, I might even mention your contributions in the acknowledgements."

Emory thundered, "Why, you self-aggrandizing clown! What sort of idiots do you take us for? We—"

Felicity laid a hand on his raised arm. "You were responsible for almost maiming Nick for life. That alone would have destroyed his career."

Denys averted his gaze, his face suffused with guilt. "I didn't mean to hurt Nick. I didn't know he was in there. I—"

Felicity patted his head. "Luckily, he'll be okay. But Denys, what an...an *addlepated* plan. There are enough of us here who can debunk your claims. Instead of burnishing it, it would decimate your reputation."

"I know!" he wailed. "I wasn't thinking. After Rook made that comment..."

"What comment?"

"Oh, something about how he wished he'd discovered the bird on his own, and that if he had, he'd make damn sure he'd be the first to publish. Of course he was joking. He's not even a scientist. What does he know about scientific integrity?"

No one felt like pointing out that Denys was hardly in a position to explain it to him. *The man's absolutely bonkers.*

Finally Felicity said gently, "You need to apologize to Nick."

"I will. And I'll pay his medical expenses. I don't know how I went so far off the rails. Forgive me?"

There was a pause. Finally Emory said, "We'll have to think about it." He opened the door, and Denys shuffled out.

Petra began to follow him.

"Where are you going? We haven't even touched on the main topic."

I'm not going to get sucked into your crooked plan. "Look, at least Denys really believes we've found a new species. But you...well, if you want to put one over on the academic world"—she glared at Emory—"*again*, I want no part of it."

Felicity raised her eyebrows. "Excuse me?"

"I heard you two talking right before I left. You"—

254

she turned to Felicity—"were begging Emory to go in on it with you. I'm guessing you intend to falsely claim you found a new bird." She pointed an accusatory finger at Emory. "He said, and I quote, there wasn't enough money in it."

The object of her charge straightened. His voice low and ominous, he hissed, "What the hell are you talking about?"

Felicity put her hands together in a time-out signal. "You misunderstood, Petra. I want to expose the fraud. I was trying to talk Emory into helping me. Cornell didn't in fact *let* me come down—they sent me down. They had given Denys a partial grant to catalogue the species in the Pacaya region and asked me to investigate reports that he had deviated from that mission. If true, they didn't want to be caught up in another..." She glanced quickly at Emory and away. "In any attempted chicanery. I was given a stipend for the trip." She nodded at Emory. "I wanted to share it with him."

He spat out, "She thought it would help repair my soiled record. Yeah, right. When pigs fly."

Petra, caught off guard, could only stare.

Felicity continued. "When I first got here, I was struck by how overwrought Aguirre was—to the point of near-mania. His desire to convince everybody of the legitimacy of his find went far beyond normal scientific fervor. Then Emory mentioned that he always seemed to come across the evidence—a blurry photo, a feather, a fossil—when he was alone. I began to wonder. It seemed very odd—especially because no non-native with any sense would be wandering around the rainforest alone."

Petra thought back. "We were with him when he found the feather."

"Were you? As I understand it, he went off the path and picked it up."

Petra reluctantly acknowledged her point, and then remembered something else. "He'd been along that path before—he could have planted the feather so he could find it when we were with him."

"True. You may be on to something." Felicity jumped up. "He bears watching."

Emory didn't appear ecstatic at the prospect.

Petra touched his hand. "What's wrong?"

"Felicity sees a spider's web of conspiracy under every bush." He stared down at his ex-wife. "You always assume the worst about people. Why couldn't it be true—that Aguirre has in fact found a new species?"

"That's not fair. I stood up for you during the hummingbird mess...I mean affair."

"You didn't believe me, though, did you? At best, you thought I was incompetent. At worst..."

The two faced each other. Petra felt helpless before such entrenched mistrust. Finally, Felicity said in a soft voice, "You know that's not true, Emory. You blamed yourself. You called yourself all those names...not me. I would have defended you to the death, if you'd let me." Her eyes glistened.

Emory stood rigid. Suddenly, he picked up a book and threw it across the room. "Damn it, Fel. I know that. I just couldn't live with myself. I did shut you out. You never wavered in your loyalty, but I knew it was that of a friend." He held a hand out to her, palm up. "A good friend." He pulled the hand back. "Not a lover. And I think the only one who could have saved me from the despair was a lover. I'm sorry."

Felicity stroked his cheek with a pale hand. "And now you've found one." She pointed at Petra and smiled through her tears.

Emory shook himself. "All right. Let's forget about the past for now. Maybe you're right and my lust to find a new species has clouded my judgment."

Petra realized she'd been holding her breath during the whole exchange and let the air out of her lungs. *Emory loves me? Emory...but...no. I can't afford to dwell on this new revelation now. Have to focus.* She took another, deeper, breath. "Tell me how you came to your conclusion, Felicity."

"When the fossil turned out to be a skeleton, I began to wonder if it was all a hoax."

"But to what purpose?"

"I have no idea. Wasn't the original mission to find the Mapinguari?"

Emory answered. "Not the original mission, no. Once we got down here, John announced the news of the sightings, and Ffoulkes took it into his head to concentrate on them. Then Aguirre discovered the skeleton, and in less than a New York minute, we'd moved on to the next amusement ride." His eyes lit up. "After all, to discover a living link between dinosaurs and birds!" He paced from one side to the other of the little room. Petra began to understand the source of his reluctance to accept Felicity's theory. *The lure of the chase.* The full-bore pursuit of science, of answers, was capable of overwhelming even the most negative headwind. Petra took a moment to appreciate Emory in a different light. Then common sense settled in. *He may be a true scientist, but he's also naïve. Just like Denys.*

Petra studied Felicity. *Now me, I'm a mere "dilettante"—a librarian. And I'm going with Felicity's assessment.*

The other woman continued to press her argument, the logic inexorable. "So his clues distracted you from your primary purpose."

"Ye-ess…but that doesn't mean it isn't real. After all, this is the rainforest. New species show up every day."

Emory was wavering but not fast enough for Petra. She stepped in. "Come on, Emory. Let's just say, for the sake of argument, that Felicity's right. But even if she's wrong, why not help her find the truth?"

Felicity answered for him. "It's all right. I can't really blame him. He was burned by the other episodes. He doesn't want to stick his neck out again."

"But you—you think it's true? That Aguirre is manipulating the evidence?"

"I'm not sure, but it's suspicious enough to warrant investigation."

Emory sat down. "We should be careful not to get ahead of ourselves. The skeleton does have some unusual features. I think we should examine it more carefully before we start indicting people."

They both looked at Petra. "On this point, I agree with Emory. There's no real hurry, is there? And he and I have already collected some evidence of the Mapinguari. Did you tell Felicity about our little adventure?"

"No. With everything else, I forgot all about it." He related their close encounter with the monster.

"Not much to go on there. I say we concentrate on the authenticity of the bird for now. When we've solved that mystery, we can move on to the Mapinguari. We really need your expertise as an ornithologist, Emory."

Emory seemed inclined to argue, but Petra cut him off. "It's a plan." She thought of something. "You know, like I said, Denys at least doesn't seem to have any doubt that it's a new species. Why else would he try to steal the photos?"

"True. Okay, it's settled then? The idea for now is to continue our research."

Petra's cell phone went off. "Hello, Doctor. I understand. Yes. Thank you." She hung up. "The doctor says Nick should be released tomorrow."

"Has his eyesight returned?"

"Partially. He'll have to wear dark glasses for another week or so."

Emory frowned. "Perhaps we should just put him on a plane home."

The phone rang again. "Hello? Nick? The doctor just called. What—I see…Okay. We'll pick you up at ten tomorrow."

"What did he want?"

"He wants to come back here."

"How come?"

"He says he got a message from Rook."

Chapter Twenty
Spontaneous Reproduction

October 29

"Okay, you have to take a little hop off the boat. I've got you. That's it. Okay, now the steps."

"I'm fine, Petra. I can see a little. And I have this nifty cane." Nick tapped out a tune with the white walking stick.

"The doctor said not to strain your eyes." She fumbled in her purse. "He gave me some medication for you. You're to take it twice a day with water."

"Or vodka. I explicitly asked Maria—she's the nurse—and she gave me permission." Nick chortled. "You just gotta know who to talk to."

Ffoulkes was waiting for him in the lounge. "Nick."

"Denys."

"I…I…know Petra told you what I did. I can only apologize. I have no excuse other than an overzealous interest in scientific discovery."

Yeah, right. More like an overzealous interest in promoting yourself.

Nick said, "Apology accepted. It was an accident. Now, where's that vodka?"

Denys's vapid face reddened with uncertain hope. "I'll get you some. I think John has it out. He's at the bar."

Petra felt she should put a damper on the festivities before they got too boisterous. "A little early for him, isn't it?"

"Not for me." Nick started toward the bar, tapping his cane.

Alex passed them in the hall. "Hey, welcome back, Nick. If you're looking for John, he's self-administering a bit of medicinal brandy."

"We know. He beat me to it. How come?"

"He's had another little mishap." He snickered.

"What was it this time?"

"A snake fell on him."

Emory's lip jiggled. "Venomous?"

"No. An emerald boa. Lovely creature. About eight feet long and this beautiful chartreuse color."

"That doesn't sound so bad."

"It wouldn't be, but instead of springing away, John managed to get himself caught in the coils. She knocked him over into the mud and was proceeding to have her way with him when we rescued him."

"Any the worse for wear?"

"Bruises on his legs and his new safari pants ruined."

"What happened to the snake?"

Before Alex could answer, Capac rang the lunch bell. Esteban announced, "Lunch served."

"What's on the menu today, Esteban?"

He grinned. "Snake fritters."

"Ah." Nick knocked his vodka back. "If John does nothing else, he provides us with locally sourced victuals." He followed Petra and Emory into the dining room. Rook and Aguirre were already seated.

They were having coffee when Petra decided to broach the subject on her mind. "So, Mr. Rook, Nick tells me you sent him a message."

Rook picked up his napkin and began to wipe his hands. Petra counted. *Ten times. Always ten times. Must be the magic number, otherwise he's not clean enough.* "That was in confidence, Steele."

"I didn't say what it was, just that it was momentous." Nick gulped his beer. "I think you should tell everyone."

Rook folded the napkin, meticulously pressing the creases with his thumb. "All right. Aguirre and I took the boat back up the river while you were all gone. I've been tinkering with the mechanism on the built-in camera. Aguirre went on ahead to see if he could flush the birds. He did."

"Really?"

"Did you get a good look?"

"Good enough."

"Were they hoatzin?"

"Neither of us are ornithologists. They seemed different, but a similar size and shape."

Aguirre, who had been staring open-mouthed at him, said, "Um…yeah. Could be the same bird I saw…I'm not sure…"

Rook said to his plate, "I think I got some shots of one, though."

Aguirre half rose. "You did?" He seemed to choke on the word.

"As I said, it was a large bird, with what looked like a rooster's comb on its head." Rook ignored Aguirre's intake of breath. "I was panning the underbrush and, when I saw movement, snapped as many pictures as I could." He glanced at Nick. "Too bad you're not in any condition to develop the film." He produced a ponderous sigh. "I guess it'll have to wait."

Aguirre sat back down.

"Not necessarily." Nick nodded at Petra. "My sister is an accomplished production assistant."

Aguirre's fork clattered to the table. Alex said, "Well, isn't that great!" Rook shot Petra a look that mixed surprise and suspicion.

Something tickled the back of her neck. *What is Nick playing at?*

Denys frowned. "But the camera is experimental. You don't want to damage it."

"True. Perhaps Mr. Rook can remove the film. It's just ordinary thirty-five-millimeter, isn't it?"

Rook made no attempt to hide the derisive smile. "Actually, it's one-twenty medium format. Only pros have experience with it."

Nick wouldn't be deterred. "I can walk her through it. No problem...We do want to develop the photos quickly. As I recall, that type of film degrades pretty rapidly."

Rook reared back like a cornered wild boar. His nostrils flared, and his eyes pinged angrily from face to face. "I will not have some amateur handling my equipment!"

Nick pressed him. "You don't risk losing any technical secrets, Rook, if that's what you're worried about. I can't see, and Petra will only work with the film."

He considered this. Petra watched Aguirre, who sat stiffly, his hand clenched on his napkin. Finally, Rook said, "All right, then. Go ahead."

Aguirre's mouth opened and shut. "But—"

Rook smiled at him, but his eyes threatened. "Let's see what we get."

After lunch, Petra helped Nick to his room. "You think you can manage the developing, sis?'

"I don't know why you said I could—I haven't been in a darkroom in years."

"It's not rocket science. This type of film needs delicate handling, but the technique isn't that different."

"Okay. I'm going to go lie down for a bit. I suggest you get some rest as well."

"See you in an hour."

She ran into Emory in the hall. "How's he doing?"

"Fine. A little tired."

"When are you going to work on Rook's film? I want to stand guard outside the darkroom." He did not smile.

"In an hour or so. Emory? What did you think of that little scene?"

"You mean Victor? He's a piece of work, isn't he? I can't tell if he's an ornery genius or just a bastard."

"There's something between him and Aguirre. A connection."

"Don't you remember? Rook asked him to check us out. As I recall, he said they'd met when Aguirre was on his way here."

"Yes, I know that was his story, but I'm not sure he didn't make it up. How long has Aguirre worked at the ITR?"

"I've no idea. We could ask John."

"Ask me what?" The public relations man stood directly behind Petra. She jumped forward, barely avoiding Emory's arms.

Emory skipped aside. "Aguirre Tramposo. How long has he been with the institute?"

"He's not with the institute."

"Really? How did he get in on this expedition, then?"

John looked over his shoulder, then ducked his head and whispered, "We have an anonymous donor. He represents him."

"Who is it?"

"Hello? I said he was anonymous."

"But you know who it is, right? Who signs the checks?"

His gaze slipped past her. "It's in the name of a shell company. Something called the Castle Group. Address in the Caymans. Look, I don't want to rock the boat, okay? He's provided transportation, equipment, and staff. The agreement was very clear. Don't ask questions."

He sprinted away before Petra could stop him.

Emory watched him go. "Donor has to be Rook."

"Has to be. *The Castle Group*? Really? Did he think no one would figure that out?"

"So Aguirre is his agent. There's nothing wrong with that."

"Then why lie about it?" Petra scratched her head. "And what made him think he had to use an alias?"

Emory shrugged. "No idea. He's got a perfectly legitimate reason to be here."

"You mean the scope? I don't know. He could test it anywhere. Why choose the jungle?"

"Away from prying eyes?"

"I'm sure there are isolated places closer to home."

Emory threw up his hands. "Oh, well, as always, with the rich and famous…"

****

"All right, now, count to ten and remove it."

"Okay."

"Quickly!"

"I'm dancing as fast as I can, Nick."

"I know, I'm sorry. It's hard not being able to see."

"I'm sorry too, hon." She hung the last wet sheet on the line. "That's it."

"Okay. We can let them dry and check 'em out tomorrow." He chuckled. "I may even be able to see them by then."

"Now, you know the doctor said no straining, and no bright light."

She pulled the curtain aside and opened the door carefully. Emory stood outside. "All clear?"

"Yup." He took Nick's arm and turned to Petra. "See you at dinner?"

"Uh-huh." After a second's thought, she locked the door and pocketed the key.

Dinner was quiet. Alex ate fast and left. Felicity and Denys went off for a game of cards. "Would you prefer cribbage or whist?"

Whist?

As she passed the darkroom door on her way to bed, she gave the knob a quick twist. "Good. Still locked."

****

October 30

"They're sure gone." Petra scoured the darkroom. "Where the hell are the photographs?" She ran out into the corridor. "Denys! Denys Ffoulkes! Show yourself!"

266

The director appeared at the end of the hallway, a piece of toast in his hand. "I'm eating my breakfast. What do you want?"

She marched toward him, hands rolled into balls. "What did you do with them?"

"With what?"

"The photographs, you big jerk. Did you think I wouldn't notice?"

He dropped his toast. A monkey zipped between his legs, picked it up, and ran off with it. "Gone? Did you look in the darkroom?"

"You mean where I left them? Duh."

"Well, it wasn't me." He ducked back into the dining room. She followed him. Alex, Rook, and Aguirre sat at the table. "Did any of you take the photographs?"

"Nope."

"Not me."

Rook craned his neck around Petra. "I saw Andrews going into the lab. Maybe he picked them up and took them there."

Petra spun around and strode down the hall. Felicity squatted next to Emory. They were studying something on the computer monitor. Nick sat in a chair to one side. "Oh, hi, Petra. Sleep well?"

She didn't stop for pleasantries. "Do any of you know anything about the theft of the photos?"

"You mean these?" Felicity pointed at a pile on the table.

Petra stared at it. "But...but...how did you get them out of the darkroom? I locked the door." To prove it, she held up the key.

Emory produced his own key. "There was a spare

in the kitchen."

"Oh." Her cheeks burning, she backed up a step and landed right on Denys.

"Ooph."

"Sorry." She frowned at him. "What are you doing here?"

Denys said resolutely, "I wanted to make sure no one stole the photos." The irony seemed to be lost on him.

Petra caught Felicity's eye. "Have you examined them yet? Any theories?"

"Most of them weren't exposed. Not sure if it was the camera or the developing fluid." Emory held a sheet of shiny paper up. "This is the only one that came out. Give us a few minutes, and we'll come report to the gang."

"I'll let the others know." Denys led Petra back to the dining room.

They were gathered in the lounge when Felicity, Emory, and Nick arrived half an hour later. "Well, it's official. The photo is fake."

"Fake? How?" Petra felt she should defend herself. "We watched Mr. Rook remove the film from the camera, and Nick and I were the only ones in the darkroom."

Emory waggled a finger. "You misunderstand me. The photo is real. The thing in it is not."

Aguirre tried to grab the sheet out of his hands. "That's impossible. I saw the bird with my own eyes."

"Ah, but what did you see?"

He pointed. "That. I saw that. So did Mr. Rook."

Rook took the photo. He studied it, then looked up. "What makes you think the bird isn't real?"

Felicity pointed. "Both the hoatzin fledgling and the *Caudipteryx zoui* have claws on their wings. The hoatzin uses them to cling to overhanging branches to avoid falling into the water. This bird's claws are on its legs."

Emory added, "Plus, its wings are too short, and its head is too big. It would literally tip over, even on flat ground."

"So you see"—Felicity took up the narrative—"such a bird could never have *existed*, let alone *persisted* into the modern era. It looks like something a child would put together with Legos or play-dough. Someone's trying to put one over on us."

"Could Huayna be playing his tricks again?" Alex appeared hopeful.

If Huayna were behind all this, it would certainly simplify things.

Denys shook his head. "Hector told me he's off on a hunting trip downstream."

Rook suddenly tore the picture in half. He stood up and pointed a trembling finger at Aguirre. "You! You deliberately led me on this wild goose chase—"

Or wild hoatzin chase. I wonder—was Rook trying to call Aguirre out by insisting we develop the photos? Then why claim he saw it too? Or—alternatively—was he duped too? Petra weighed what she knew of the man. *He's not the type to take that lightly.*

Aguirre had jumped up to face Rook. "Me! It's your fault. You gave me no guidance. I had to distract the team until you arrived. I had to improvise. If the team found it before you did…" He seemed to suddenly realize what he was saying and sat down abruptly.

Rook's face had gone from red to purple. "What

the hell are you talking about? I gave you one job—to assist me in the testing. You go off on some wild tangent. You're a liar and a cheat, Tramposo." He pounded his fist on the table. "You're fired."

Wait, that's what they were arguing about the day Rook arrived. Petra tried to remember the conversation she'd overheard between Rook and Tramposo. *Something else...*

"Bullshit. I quit. You can find the damned Mapinguari on your own." Aguirre whirled and left.

The room was silent. Finally, Denys asked, "You want the Mapinguari too? You didn't come here just to test your prototype?"

"Don't be absurd."

Waiting for further elucidation proved fruitless. Petra felt she had to step in. *He really has to improve his people skills.* "He's telling the truth. He came to test the scope, but when he heard of the Mapinguari, he figured a valid photo taken of the animal with his prototype would open up more market opportunities."

Rook seemed pleased. "Well said, young lady. If you're interested in a position with my company, I have an opening." His nostrils curled in disgust at the chair Aguirre had just vacated.

He really is a jackass. "Thank you for the offer, but no."

This had no effect on him. "So I say we disregard the sham bird and resume our search for the Mapinguari." He stepped to the door and called Hector in. "Hector, we'll be heading out first thing tomorrow to go after the beast."

Hector blanched. "Are you sure? The only evidence we have is Huayna's statement."

"No. There have been two more recent sightings."

When Hector continued dubious, Petra glanced at Emory and Felicity, searching for an answer to the obvious question. *Should we tell them our story?* He slowly shook his head. Felicity folded her hands.

Alex asked Denys, "Didn't Huayna claim the monster left some hair on a tree? Did he retrieve any of it?"

"No, but I did ask Winston to go back and try to find it."

We've got to say something.

Petra opened her mouth, but Alex interrupted her. "Ask him if he was successful. We could test it. If it's just a monkey, we can stop this charade and get back to real research."

Petra glanced at Emory. His face remained closed.

Nick said, "Too bad we don't have a primate specialist on the team."

"I can do it." Denys said it firmly, but his nose twitched. "I'll be able to identify the species."

Emory said slowly, catching Petra off guard, "Winston said the hair could have come from a tree sloth." He watched Denys carefully. "Can you tell the difference between a primate and…Wait, is a sloth a primate?"

"No, although early researchers thought it might be. Current opinion is they're most closely related to anteaters."

Nick scoffed. "That's a stretch. Have you ever seen a sloth? I wouldn't even call it a poor third cousin twice removed of an anteater. Do anteaters even *live* around here?"

"The giant anteater does—he eats primarily

termites."

"Giant, huh. Could the hair have come from one of those?"

Denys held up a hand. "Perhaps I should explain. The term 'giant' is a relative term. They only grow to about four feet long. And they can't stand upright. The hair Huayna saw was way up in the tree—at least ten feet."

In the thoughtful silence, Alex's voice rang loud. "So what makes you think you could identify it, Denys?"

Ffoulkes ignored the question and instead asked, "Has anyone seen Winston? Did he bring the hair back?"

The room fell silent.

Petra spoke quickly before Emory could stop her. "I don't know, but we did."

Emory mumbled to Petra, "I give up." He raised his voice. "Petra's correct." He told them about climbing the tree, hearing the grunts of a large animal, and Winston rescuing them.

"So it couldn't be an anteater, then."

"No." Emory added, "Like Petra said, we got a sample of the hair."

"Oh?" Denys leaned forward. "Let's see it."

He looked expectantly at Petra. She said miserably, "I don't have it."

Rook rounded on her. "What do you mean, you don't have it?"

"It's disappeared."

Emory gawked at Petra. "Disappeared?"

Everyone began to talk at once. Petra whispered to Emory, "I hid it in my desk. When I looked for it the

Sunday before Felicity arrived, it was gone."

"Did you lock the drawer?"

She shook her head. "I didn't see the need."

"Did you mention it to anyone when you discovered it missing?"

"No, I swear. Except for you."

"Me? I think I'd remember if you told me you couldn't find it."

"You were…um…distracted."

Emory blew air out of his nostrils like a maddened stallion and raised his voice. "We only took a swatch. A remnant could still be stuck on the tree."

"Time to ask Winston." Alex went in search of the guide. They returned a minute later.

Winston remained standing just inside the room, staring at his bare toes. Petra could tell he was nervous in the presence of so many serious faces. "You remember when you took us to the place where Huayna said he saw a Mapinguari?"

He nodded.

"You showed us the hair on the tree."

"Yes. Huayna left it there. He didn't want to touch it."

"Did you go back to fetch it when Mr. Ffoulkes asked you to?"

"No." He shivered. "Only evil comes from touching the fur of the beast."

"So there may be some left." Emory started toward the door.

Alex stopped him. "Don't forget, we also have the sightings."

"Yes. Tell us about them, Winston." Rook was suspiciously cordial.

"The first was Huayna."

Denys snorted. "Well, that doesn't do us much good."

"He was correct about the hair."

"Which we don't have." Emory didn't look at Petra.

Rook prompted, "And the second?"

"One of Manuel's children said they saw tracks after his father was killed."

"But he didn't see the animal."

"N…no."

"Wasn't there a third sighting?"

"My son Acarapi." Winston gazed defiantly at the director.

Denys had better not belittle his son. Winston is very handy with that machete. Plus the child may have learned some bewitching spells from Don César. She thought of something. "Wait! I think I have the drawing Acarapi made of what he'd seen." She started to go get it, but Emory coughed.

"Remember? He admitted he hadn't actually seen the beast either."

Rook stood up. "This is getting us nowhere. I propose we go back to the spot and collect the hair ourselves. Winston, can you bring your son?"

The man shook his head. "I'm afraid he's still recovering from the snake bite."

"How about Huayna?"

Hector said, "I can ask him, but…"

John said, "Just because he tried to trick us with the Chullachaqui doesn't mean he deceived us about the Mapinguari."

Denys agreed.

Rook gestured at Petra and Emory. "You two better come along. You may have something to contribute as well."

Petra bit her tongue. Emory said acidly, "Refresh my memory, Rook. What, if anything, have *you* done for the cause?"

"Which reminds me..." John's question was tentative. "Did you have a chance to look at the press release I gave you, Mr. Rook?"

"Press release?"

"You know, announcing that you are devoting your personal attention to our expedition. Your presence will provide extra stature to our endeavor." He wiped a streaming forehead.

"Sure, sure." Rook waved him away. "I'm going to go put some supplies together."

After he left, Alex announced, "I can't go with you tomorrow."

Denys huffed. "Why not? You're part of this team, Alex. You've been gone more than you've been here. When did you last check the caiman eggs?"

"They have a couple more days to go." His glance shifted to the window. "I have to see someone in Nauta."

"Nauta! What about?"

"I...uh...Hector said he'd heard a man killed a rare species of pit viper there. I asked him not to destroy it until I can examine it."

Denys sighed. "All right. There probably isn't enough room in the launch for all of us anyway."

Alex is not very good at lying. I wonder what he's up to? Petra caught up with the herpetologist by the kitchen. She opted for a casual yet friendly tone. "We haven't had much chance to talk, with all that's been going on, have we? I understand you're hoping to document a yacare caiman."

He grew eager. "Yes, yes, it's also known as the piranha caiman. It's never been found this far north in the Amazon basin. I'd like to map its entire range."

"What about the snake?"

"Snake? Oh, well, I'm interested in anything that might be uncommon." He pretended to laugh. "That's why we're here, isn't it?" The blush covered his freckles. He loped down the hall.

Is it just me, or does everyone seem to have something to hide?

Chapter Twenty-One
Genetic Drift

October 31

"Hurry! Hurry! Breakfast ready!" Esteban herded the group to the dining room. "Boat go one hour."

They sat down to parrot eggs and tapir bacon. Rook griped, "I specifically told that cook of yours—what's his name? Chappaquiddick?—that I expect only vegan food at this table. Is that too much to ask? Why does he continue to serve this disgusting flesh?"

"You're vegan? Huh." No one seemed surprised.

Anything to make life harder for everyone else. I was so right.

Next to her, Nick murmured, "Typical."

Alex, his mouth full of egg, said, "Sorry, fella. Your alternative is corn or…corn."

"Wait—you can eat potatoes, can't you? Capac makes the best fries…Oh darn, that's because they're cooked in lard." Emory made a sad face at Rook.

"What about quinoa?"

Nick had the answer. "Can't get it here. It's grown in the Andes. Considered an import item. Very expensive." He pressed his lips together.

Felicity said, "We've got plenty of fruit. Oh, and I saw a couple of cans of baked beans on the shelf. B&M. Best brand in the US."

"Are you kidding? You know what they put in that garbage?"

"Caramel coloring? MSG?" She smiled sweetly at him.

Petra was surprised to see how long it took for Rook to recognize he was being razzed, but then it likely didn't happen often. He rose. "I have some nutrition bars in my room." He stalked off.

Emory watched him go. "Whew, what a prick."

Felicity said, "While I think a vegan diet is basically unhealthy—"

"Or at least unnatural."

"I respect those who follow it because they don't believe in exploiting animals. There's an argument to be made for that."

Alex huffed. "Tell that to a dairy cow with an udder about to burst. Not pretty."

Felicity went on dreamily, "I once asked this nice young vegan woman how she felt about breastfeeding. She didn't have an answer."

Apparently, neither did anyone else.

An air horn blew outside.

"Is that the signal for all aboard?"

"No, it's my water taxi." Alex picked up a knapsack. "I'll see you guys tonight."

"Good luck with the snake."

"The snake? Oh, yeah." He left.

Nick watched him go. "He sure doesn't seem all that interested in our project, does he?"

"Why did he sign on, then?"

"Wasn't it for the caimans?"

Denys brushed that aside. "A true scientist would be willing to pursue any new avenues of exploration."

John cleared his throat. "You know, I'd forgotten until now. After you invited him to join us, he dropped by to sign the contract papers. He asked me if I had any information on Iquitos. I gave him some brochures and websites, but then as he was leaving he said something odd."

"Odd?"

"Yeah. Something about tracing his roots."

Nick knit his brows. "Roots, huh? What's his last name again? Something long and German-sounding."

Denys answered. "Bönickhausen."

"Did any Germans immigrate to Peru? Lots of Japanese and Chinese settled here, but I thought all the Nazis fled to Argentina."

Emory tapped his chin. "Only German I can think of is Werner Herzog. He made a couple of movies here."

Petra pictured the young herpetologist. "He looks more British to me anyway—all those freckles."

"Definitely Irish. Wait…a lot of Irishmen did turn up in Iquitos during the rubber boom."

Emory mused, "Fitzcarrald was Irish. His real name was Fitzgerald."

"But Alex told me he grew up in France." Felicity put down her napkin.

"He did?" Petra stared at her. *She knew about Denys's sister and Winston's children. Even about Hector's tribulations with his family. How does she manage to wheedle so much information out of people?*

"Maybe he's just a mutt."

Nick chuckled. "With a *lot* of roots."

Winston hallooed from outside.

Nick stood up, stuffing the last bite of bacon into

his mouth. "That's our ride."

John said something about work and made himself scarce. Felicity stood. "I'll see you off."

Emory, Denys, Petra, and Nick boarded the boat. Hector stood at the bow and Winston in the stern, his son Esteban hanging onto the hand that wasn't holding the wheel. Just before they cast off, Rook came running down, shouldering a large duffel bag. He sat down amidships and began to fuss with the contents. Everyone avoided him.

Hector steered them out into midstream. They floated down the river, the only sounds the *tick-tick* of the motor and the scree of a hunting raptor. A couple of pink dolphins kept them company. Esteban sat in the stern trawling with a fishing pole. "*Oye! Oye!*"

"He's caught something!"

The boy reeled in a small, red-bellied piranha. Hector took it off the hook for him and carried it over to Petra. "Want to see him smile?" He squeezed the fish's jaws. Its mouth opened, revealing rows of jagged teeth.

She pushed it away. "It could take a toe off, Hector." Hiding her qualms as best she could, she squinted down into the swirling depths. *Maybe I should avoid swimming for a while.*

Winston was surveying the topmost branches of the tall trees on the far bank. He took the fish from Hector. With a grin, he chirped, "Watch this." He hooked the piranha onto the end of a short stick, held it high above his head, and whistled.

As Petra watched, a great black hawk swooped down, tore the fish from its post, then sailed back up into the trees. "Amazing!"

"Is he a pet?" Denys stared up at the bird, who was

tearing the fish to pieces with its talons and swallowing the bits.

Hector laughed. "No, just an opportunity feeder."

Winston said cheerfully, "Very smart."

At least there's one bird Winston doesn't think is stupid.

They tied up at Winston's brother's dock near the spot where Emory and Petra had been treed. Hector let Winston go ahead to cut through the vines and open up the path, then signaled the others to follow him.

As Petra batted back a spiderweb, she wondered if they would find the tree again. "The place has become overgrown awfully quickly, hasn't it?"

Denys huffed. "Doesn't take the jungle long to take back its own."

"Do you know where we're going?"

Hector nodded. "The big mahogany tree you climbed, right?"

"Uh-huh." *Mahogany. Not manchineel. Good.*

"It's just up here."

They came to a small clearing. Winston's gaze darted around.

"Nervous about the Chullachaqui, Winston?" Emory said it with a straight face, but Denys snickered.

"Not funny, Mr. Ffoulkes. Remember Manuel."

"He didn't die here, though, did he?"

"No. He was killed on his banana plot—not far from the lodge."

Emory spread his hands out. "Who does this land belong to?"

"It is tended by the del Rio—my family."

Petra nudged Emory and whispered, "Nick told me Hector talked about a feud between villages. Could such disputes turn violent?"

He swung on Hector. "Huayna is your cousin, right? Was he involved in a quarrel with Manuel's family?"

"Y…yes."

"Do you think he…?"

"Killed him? No, my cousin is a con artist, not a murderer." Still, Hector looked uncomfortable.

They reached the tree. Winston pointed. "The hair was caught on that branch." He climbed up nimbly. After a minute, he called, "It's not here."

"How could it be gone?"

He scrambled back down. "No *ribereño* would take it. Maybe it just fell off."

Denys took charge. "Okay, let's spread out and look for it."

Half an hour later, they had to give up. "It's no use. We need something to go on. Let's find Huayna. He's all we've got left."

They took the launch upriver and docked next to a family compound. Hector got out and trudged toward a big house set on stilts. Chickens flushed, and pigs went squealing off into the jungle. A knot of young children approached and stood shyly, rocking on their heels. Petra saw a man come around the corner holding a machete and a bunch of bananas. "Hector. There!"

Heads down, the two men spoke. Hector came back. "Huayna's gone to town to sell his fish. My cousin Luis will ask him to come to the lodge when he gets back. But…"

"But what?"

"He may refuse. He may think you want to punish him for his attempt to cheat us."

"Tell him all is forgiven, but we expect him to tell the truth about the Mapinguari."

Hector relayed the message to his cousin. They got in the boat and returned to the lodge.

That evening, Luis poled up in his dugout and spoke to Hector, who brought the news that Huayna didn't believe them. He wouldn't come.

Nick put down the camera he was fiddling with. "Well, that sucks. Can you talk to him? Maybe record his story?"

"I can try, but I'm afraid he may have been lying about the Mapinguari as well."

"What about the hair?" Petra's voice rose. *We can't give up yet.* "We did find it, after all."

"Who knows?" Hector shrugged. "Maybe that's all he saw. Could have belonged to a tree sloth."

Denys slapped a fist into his palm. "Then we've hit a dead end."

Emory stirred. "But what did Petra and I hear, then? It was definitely something large."

"Most likely a jaguar." Hector gave Petra a sympathetic look. "Maybe a capybara."

Denys pursed his lips. "Let's face it, we've got no real proof it was a Mapinguari."

Rook turned away. "That's it. I'm packing. Wasted enough of my time." He headed to his room.

Petra watched him go. She tugged at Emory's sleeve. "I don't think either of those eat bananas."

****

At dinner, Emory asked Rook, "So you're determined to leave?"

John squeaked, "He's leaving? Mr. Rook, why are you leaving? You can't leave!"

"Why not?"

The little man stopped, his face puckering.

Rook's tone was menacing. "Why not, Dillinger?"

"I…I arranged a press conference for you. To announce the successful testing of the scope."

"Here?"

"No, in Iquitos. November tenth."

Rook seemed to reconsider. "I might be persuaded to stay, but I'm on a plane to Lima November eleventh."

This calmed John, and the evening played out quietly. That is, until Denys's phone went off.

"Ffoulkes…Oh, for God's sake." He listened. "We'll be there tomorrow morning. Thanks." He heaved a deep sigh.

"Who was that?"

"The police."

"Oh, no! Not another murder?"

"No. It's Alex. He's been arrested."

"What for?"

"The officer said bribery." Denys scratched his head. "Do you suppose he wanted to buy a hot snake?"

Emory rolled his eyes. "Please. It's not like the Victorian era when gentlemen trekkers purchased trophies for their country houses."

Rook dropped his book and hissed, "No, it certainly isn't."

Petra asked, "Did the policeman say anything else?"

"No. We'll have to find out when we get there. All right, who wants to come with me to spring the jailbird?" When no one answered, Denys harrumphed. "Hector and I will go, then. We'll take the launch to

Nauta, then drive up to Iquitos."

Felicity dropped her napkin. "Oh, he's in Iquitos? Why didn't you say so? I thought he was going to Nauta."

Ffoulkes's tone was dry. "Evidently, he lied."

Emory was firm. "Well, if you're going to Iquitos, I want to come along."

"Me too." Felicity's blue eyes sparkled.

Petra figured if Felicity got to go she should too. "Me too."

Denys put down the pipe. "Okay, Felicity and Petra can come. Emory should stay here. We need someone in charge. Besides, any car we rent is unlikely to hold more than four."

****

November 1

The next day saw Denys, Felicity, Petra, and Hector steaming toward the small town that lay near the confluence of the Marañón and Ucayali rivers. Once there, they rented a tiny Kia. Denys asked Hector to take the wheel. "You know the way." He accepted with what Petra considered altogether too big a grin and drove at top speed the entire seventy miles to the big city, weaving among ancient Schwinn bicycles, even more ancient Fiats, gangs of chickens, and peasant families walking down the middle of the road. Felicity squeezed Petra's hand tightly as they roared through tiny villages consisting only of a couple of rickety houses, a vegetable stand, and a dusty chichi bar.

At the outskirts of Iquitos, Denys pulled out a map. "The police station is here, on Calle Morona."

"I know it." Hector swung the wheel. They drove through the center of the city and down toward the waterfront.

Petra gazed around at the neighborhood. "This is close to the hotel Emory and I stayed in."

Felicity let go of her hand. "Hotel?" She winked at Petra.

"It was when Nick was in the hospital. We had to stay overnight and…uh…we couldn't find two rooms because it's high season. We—"

"So…no room at the inn?" Laughter burbled in the other woman's voice.

Denys turned his head. "What are you two canoodling about?"

"Nothing!" they said simultaneously.

They parked in a lot by a building marked Policia Nacional. Hector said, "It's probably better that the ladies stay in the car."

Felicity seemed inclined to protest, but the guide made a face. "I'm afraid it would not be helpful. We do not want the police distracted."

He and Denys went in. After a minute, Denys returned to the car. "The desk sergeant informed us that Bönickhausen is charged with trying to bribe a city official. We can see him now, but they're waiting for the chief to come before he can be released."

"What do they need the chief for?"

"According to Hector, they want to up the price for his get-out-of-jail-free card, since Alex refused to bribe the first policeman."

"Is that normal?"

"Hector says it is."

"Hold on a sec," said Felicity. "He was arrested for trying to bribe one official, but they'll let him go if he bribes another one?"

"Welcome to Peru."

Petra was curious. "So who did he supposedly bribe?"

"An agent of the property registry."

"What on earth for?"

"I have no clue. We'll have to ask Alex. Come on."

They waited in a small room until the prisoner was brought in. He wore a jumpsuit but no handcuffs. His hair was messy, and his face dirty. A policeman in a black uniform lounged on the wall. Denys shook Alex's hand. "So what's this all about?"

"Stupid, stupid." Alex blinked several times rapidly. Petra suspected he was exhausted. "I figured everyone in this damned country took bribes. I guess I found the one man who doesn't."

Hector muttered, "Or maybe it wasn't enough."

"But you did try to bribe someone?"

"Yes."

Felicity leaned forward. "Tell us."

"I want to get the title to my house."

Chapter Twenty-Two
Common Ancestor

November 1

"Your house?"

"The Iron House."

Petra sat up. "The Casa de Fierro?" At her words the guard straightened and stared at her, his brows lowered. "But isn't that a historic monument?"

"Yes, but it's administered by the privately funded Club Social de Iquitos. They're renovating it."

Denys seemed mystified. "What makes you think it belongs to you?"

"I think my great-great-grandfather designed it."

Felicity started and leaned forward. "Designing is different from owning."

His chin wobbled. "I know. That's why I wanted to purchase it. They'd never let me tear it down unless it belongs to me."

"Tear it down! That would be awful. Why on earth would you do that?"

"To get at the back of the iron panels. I believe there's an inscription on one of them that credits Gustave Eiffel with the design."

"Eiffel...of Eiffel Tower fame?"

"The very one."

Hector had been watching the policeman but turned

his attention to Alex. "But, Mr. Alex, if you tore the building down, it would be worthless to you, wouldn't it?"

"It's not the building that's valuable, it's the inscription."

"Why?" Petra was confused. "What does that have to do with you?"

"I am Gustave Eiffel's great-great-grandson."

Denys seemed even more confused than Petra. "Eiffel? But that's not your name...unless...what *is* your real name?"

Felicity said softly, "This has to do with looking for your roots, doesn't it?"

Alex shot her a look. "Who told you that?"

"John mentioned it."

"Oh. Well." He sat down heavily. "It's true. The man who built the Eiffel Tower was born Alexandre-Gustave Bönickhausen in 1837. His family originally came from Germany but settled in France. He changed his name legally to Eiffel in the 1850s, but before he did so he had a son out of wedlock. The child was christened Jean-Claude Bönickhausen. It was never officially acknowledged or recorded, but Eiffel made sure his alternate family was well taken care of. I am the descendent of that son."

"If the child's parentage wasn't registered, how do you know about it?"

"The fact was known to the relatives who stayed in Germany. Plus it was written down in the family Bible."

Everyone began to speak at once. A second uniformed officer came in. He barked an order. Hector translated. "The magistrate is here. They have to take

Mr. Alex to him now."

Petra tamped down her frustration. "Can we wait?"

Hector asked the guard. "He says no decision will be handed down until tomorrow."

"Tomorrow!"

Denys took out his phone. "We'd better let Emory know." He surveyed the group. "Looks like we have to get a hotel room." He ogled Felicity.

Both women started to protest, but since they only had the one car, they didn't have much choice. *It's not like we can walk home.*

Denys checked his watch. "It's too late to head back now anyway."

Hector found them two rooms at the Emperador Terraza Hotel on Fitzcarrald Street. Felicity pointed at the stores fronting the sidewalk. "Is *everything* here named after Fitzcarrald?"

Denys laughed. "Considering his exploits occurred in Puerto Maldonado and he was only born here, it *is* odd."

Hector remarked, "I think they're referring to Werner Herzog's film, not to the actual historical figure."

"Ah, yes. *Fitzcarraldo.*" Denys smiled, revealing the large gap in his front teeth. "A classic."

Huh. I'll bet you'd prefer a Terry Thomas comedy.

Hector left them in the lobby. "I have family nearby I can stay with. I shall meet you at the police station tomorrow at nine."

The hotel was basic, the rooms reached by a winding stair—not as romantic as the one Petra and Emory had stayed in, but clean and modern. *It's not the ambiance, it's the company anyway.* They stopped at a general store and bought toothbrushes and underwear. "What shall we do now?"

Felicity said, "I want to go down to the Iron House. Even if they don't offer tours, we can at least see what all the fuss is about."

They took a taxi to the plaza. Petra showed Felicity the plaque, but everything seemed shut up tight. A security guard opened to their knock.

"Are we allowed inside?"

He shook his head. "Not now. The building is closed. Tours are conducted on Monday and Thursday mornings. They are free, but you must reserve a spot."

Petra looked up to the second floor. "Even the restaurant is closed?"

"I am afraid so."

"Damn." Denys smacked his lips. "I'm hungry."

The man pointed down the street. "Try Long Fung. Good Chifa restaurant. It's not far."

"Chifa?"

Petra explained. "It's the word they use for Chinese food."

Felicity stared at the guard. "Huh. Who would expect to find a Chinese restaurant in the middle of the Peruvian Amazon?"

"Didn't Nick mention Japanese and Chinese immigration to Peru?" Petra pulled out her guidebook and thumbed through it. "Yeah, here it is. They began arriving in the late nineteenth century and heavily influenced the local cuisine."

Felicity was amused. "It's said that the first thing every Asian immigrant does in America is open a noodle restaurant. Why not here too?"

"I guess." Petra turned a page. "Evidently, it's

easier to get Chifa food in Lima than local Peruvian specialties. Sweet and sour chicken and fried rice are more popular than *anticuchos* and *aji de gallina*." She looked up. "I'd forgotten. Nick told me the *lomo saltado* I ate the night I arrived is basically a Chinese dish."

Denys hesitated. "Um...what were those other dishes—anti...anti what-what?"

The guard patted his chest and grinned. "*Anticuchos*—grilled cow heart. Delicious."

Denys gave him a horrified look and grabbed Felicity's arm. "Noodles it is, then."

They followed the fellow's directions. A couple of turns took them to Avenida Mariscal Caceres. "There it is. Long Fung."

The restaurant proved to be a small place with Formica-topped tables, heavy white crockery, and—to Petra's delight—delicate English teacups. The menu was written in both Chinese and Spanish. "Shall we order a selection?"

"Sounds good." They shared plates of *arroz chaufa*—the Peruvian version of fried rice—wontons, and shrimp dumplings, washed down with beer.

Back at the hotel, Petra asked the manager if they had Wi-Fi. "We certainly do, señorita. It was installed last month." He beamed. "You can access it in our business office."

"Thank you." She was making her way there when Felicity stopped her. "Are you going to do some research on Alex's story?"

"Yes. I don't know anything about Eiffel or his work, other than the Tower."

"Okay." She turned to Denys. "Fancy a pisco sour?

There's a bar here."

He wrinkled his nose. "I don't suppose they have a Pimm's cup."

She took his arm. "We'll see." She shot a conspiratorial look at Petra.

Petra settled down at the computer. An hour later, she had enough. As expected, she couldn't confirm Alex's story about his heritage but did learn more about Gustave Eiffel's career. He was a very successful engineer, winning commissions for several major works—most notably for the casting of the Statue of Liberty. *Interesting how global his business was. Not to mention varied.*

"I wonder if there are any buildings in Peru that are certified as his work?" She tapped a few words in. "Ha..." She counted. "Wow! Eight buildings." A gasworks, a fountain, a cathedral, a theater, and even a market. She drummed her fingers on the table. "How about Casa de Fierro?" She found a website devoted to its history. There was much debate about its origins. It was likely the product of the Société Eiffel de Paris— from a line of pre-fab buildings designed for use in the African colonies. *But that doesn't prove Eiffel himself had a hand in the design of Alex's house.*

She also learned that what the Irish tour guide told them was true—the house had been broken up into two parts. However, a man named Diego Aquilino bought it, not Fitzcarrald himself. An associate of the famous entrepreneur, he planned to relocate it to Madre de Dios for Fitzcarrald, but failed due to unknown reasons—*lost in the woods?* As a result, bits of it were scattered over the countryside, eventually incorporated into people's houses. She tapped her lip with a pencil. *Maybe Alex should try to find all the pieces of the second section rather than destroy this one. It would at least keep him out of jail.*

Felicity and Denys came in. "We're ready for bed. Are you still working?"

"No." She yawned. "I'll come with you."

They said good night to Ffoulkes and settled in. "Did you find anything on the computer?"

Petra told her of Eiffel's ironworks and Fitzcarrald. "His real name was Fitzgerald, but the story is the natives couldn't pronounce that and dubbed him Fitzcarrald."

"The bartender told us about Werner Herzog's movie. A truly unique fellow, this Fitzcarraldo."

"Unique? I don't know about that. I'd say he belongs to the brotherhood of those intrepid heroes who explored Africa and the Americas. Remarkable men."

"You seem to admire them. Why?"

"Why? Without them we wouldn't have a transcontinental railroad, or a Panama Canal. Fitzcarrald found an overland route to the Madre de Dios River by hauling a ship over a mountain. That route made it possible to transport the rubber and other products all the way to the Atlantic."

Felicity fluffed her pillow. "A lot of people died at the hands of those explorers. A lot of people died building those railroads. And I'll bet our intrepid Mr. Fitzcarrald didn't carry the ship on his own skinny shoulders."

"Likely not, but didn't a lot of people die before life-saving medicines could find their way to isolated areas? How many people's lives were transformed with the invention of rubber tires? When the telegraph lines were strung across Brazil? That little enterprise took thirty years and countless lives. Without those improvements, wouldn't we all still be living out our nasty, brutish lives in darkness?"

"They treated the natives like animals!"

"At first, but every time they came in contact with a new culture, understanding and eventually tolerance would seep into their consciousness. Yes, it's taken centuries, but I believe humans are gradually becoming less parochial."

"You're such an optimist." Felicity turned out the light. In the dark she said, "Do you suppose they'll let Alex out tomorrow?"

Petra giggled. "Maybe we should try a bribe?"

****

November 2

It turned out they did have to pay a massive fine— *aka a bribe*—to secure Alex's release.

They returned to the lodge, Denys fuming. "The institute is not going to cover these costs, Bönickhausen. I expect to be reimbursed by the end of the month."

Alex—wedged between the two women in the tiny car—was subdued. "Will do, but I still want to get a look at those panels."

"Do it on your own dime, then."

Emory met them on the dock. "Dinner will be ready in an hour. You can tell us what happened then."

Fifteen minutes later, he tapped on Petra's door. When she opened it, clad only in her underwear, he put a hand on her chest and drove her backward into the room. "What are—" She couldn't finish the sentence because his mouth had clamped down on hers. She stumbled, landing on the bed. "Emory!"

He fumbled with her bra. "It's been two days, Petra. I haven't been able to work or read or even think. Well, amend that last bit. Think about anything but you."

A sudden rush of joy coursed through her. She had been so focused on the events of the past few weeks that she hadn't recognized her growing dependence on this large man. His presence gave her unexpected strength. His need comforted her. Impossible as it seemed in such a short time, she couldn't conceive of him not being at her side. *Emory? Could it be? Nah.* She pushed him away. "Emory, I need to think."

"Sure. Go ahead. I have other things to do." He continued his slow march down her body. When he got to her toes, he started back up again. About halfway up, he rested. "This seems as good a place as any to dig in."

She arched her back and rubbed her body against his lips. All rational thought dissolved with the wail as she rolled into her climax.

"*Shh.* I'm not finished yet." He proceeded to bring her to a second orgasm, but this time they came in unison. He lay back, puffing. "Okay, now you may return to your regular programming."

She smiled timidly. "I still have to think about this, Emory. I…I'm not sure. I—"

He kissed her. "Just so long as I can have you in my arms while you work things out."

He was tickling the palm of her hand when heavy feet pounded down the corridor outside. They heard Winston yelling. Petra jumped up, searching madly for her clothes. Emory threw on his pants and ran out.

When she got to the steps leading to the rear

entrance, a group was gathered around someone lying on the grass. It parted, revealing a dirty, bedraggled man, his black hair matted, his shirt in tatters. She came down the stairs. He looked up at her, bleary-eyed. *Aguirre.*

Chapter Twenty-Three
Adaptation

November 2

Hector and Winston half carried Aguirre into the lodge. Alex and Emory trailed after him. Felicity came up beside Petra. "What's going on?"

"I don't know. He looks like he's been through hell." Her brother appeared. "Nick, when Aguirre stormed out, did he take a boat?"

"No idea. It would have been a canoe anyway. Both launches are here."

"We'll just have to wait till he's coherent." The two women went to the bar.

Capac came out of the kitchen. "Cocktail, ladies?"

"Vodka gimlet?"

"Certainly. And for you, Miss Lintu?"

"I think a pisco sour." She licked her lips. "I'm developing a taste for them." They watched the cook expertly mix the drinks. "In some ways, this place is quite civilized," she said cheerfully. "I could stay here for a while."

Petra, mesmerized by a troop of blue-and-yellow macaws squabbling with each other in the trees, agreed.

Presently, Emory and Denys came in. "We got him patched up and washed. Alex is sitting with him."

Rook sidled around the group and leaned on the

bar. "I hear my former employee has returned." His voice was flat, his face expressionless. "Is he all right?"

"Looks like mainly cuts and bruises. Nothing serious."

Denys added, "He must have gotten lost."

"Didn't he take a boat?"

Emory shook his head. "We're not sure. A canoe is missing, but Aguirre came through the woods at the back of the compound."

"I see." Rook raised a finger. "Beer." When Capac had uncapped a bottle and handed to him, he said morosely, "I suppose he has to stay."

Denys said firmly, "He's in no shape to move right now. It's not clear if he was attacked by an animal or just hurt himself floundering around. He's gabbling on about killing 'it.' "

Rook flushed. " 'Killing it'? Do you suppose he murdered some defenseless animal? And lurching through the rainforest like a fool. I wonder how much devastation he left in his wake."

You really do hate humans. "I'm sure he was only trying to survive."

Felicity leaned forward. "About this 'it.' Did he give a description? Animal? Human?"

Denys replied, "No. It's probably just the dehydration talking. We'll have to wait until he's more himself."

Hector volunteered, "If he's not better by the morning, I will send for the shaman."

"You do that," sneered Rook. "That's about the level of professional medical expertise he deserves."

No one answered him.

Esteban announced dinner. The meal crawled

along, with the bare minimum of conversation. Rook had managed to depress or annoy every member of the team except John, who chattered excitedly about the upcoming press conference. Eventually, even he petered out. Petra wasn't sure anyone else noticed. Outside, monkeys howled and yammered. Parrots screeched. Trees creaked in the breeze. Everyone took to their rooms early. When he was sure no one was looking, Emory kissed Petra. "I shall dream of capybaras frolicking in the moonlight. And you?"

She didn't trust herself to tell him what she intended to dream about.

****

November 3

Winston came in while they were eating breakfast. "Hector has sent for the shaman."

"For Aguirre? Is he conscious?"

"Yes, but he has a fever."

A few minutes later, Don César nodded to the group as he passed them before ducking into Aguirre's room. Everyone waited impatiently, unable to work. Rook shut himself up in the lab.

Petra was coming up from a swim to change before lunch when she found the shaman blocking the doorway. He was speaking to Denys, who stood just inside. "He will be all right. I gave him a potion, and I shall leave a gift for La Sachamama tonight."

Petra approached. "Sachamama?" She looked at Denys. "Don César mentioned her before. What—or who—is she?"

The shaman answered. "She is the mother of the forest. A boa so big she cannot move. Though this man has angered her and endangered her children, she protected him from serious harm. We must offer our thanks for her mercy."

Petra knew enough not to say out loud what she was thinking. *I wonder what shape he'd be in if she* hadn't *protected him?*

Don César passed Hector on his way to the dock. "Do not disturb him for six hours." He got into the dugout Winston held.

Petra and Denys returned to the lounge, where he told the group what the shaman had said. Emory slammed a fist on the table. "Damn it, what are we supposed to do now? When are we going to get some answers from him? Where was he? How did he lose his canoe? Was he attacked?"

Petra's own frustration was nearing the tipping point. She picked up her towel. "I'm going to my room."

"*Now*?"

She plucked at her bathing suit. "I hardly want to stay in this, do I?" She had changed into a light shift and was heading back to the dining room when she saw Rook, his hand up in front of Aguirre's room. *He's not going to chew him out* now*, is he? Or worse, would he dare assault him?* "Mr. Rook!"

He turned around. "What?"

"You didn't hear Denys? Aguirre must be left alone." She shot daggers at him, hoping one would hit him squarely between the eyes.

He turned away.

"What the hell are you playing at, Rook?" Petra jumped at Emory's voice behind her.

The man slowed. In a testy voice, he snapped, "Not that it's any of your business, but I was going to offer him his job back. Apologize for beating up on him." He spun on his heel and marched away.

Emory raised his eyebrows. "Oops."

Petra tugged his sleeve. "He couldn't really be a good guy…could he? Maybe just cantankerous?"

"No friggin' idea."

Petra sighed. "You know what? I'm tired of second-guessing and, to be honest, tired of disliking people. There's the bell. Let's go eat."

****

The afternoon dragged on, and it wasn't until they were finishing dinner that Aguirre showed up. He was shaved and his hair combed back. He wore a clean shirt and jeans. The only evidence of his ordeal was a large bandage across his nose.

Alex greeted him cheerfully. "Welcome back." No one laughed.

Capac placed a beer in front of him. He slurped it down and gestured for another. "That goo the shaman gave me to drink was disgusting. Some kind of diuretic. I'm dying of thirst."

"Did it help though?"

"Slept like a log."

Petra couldn't wait any longer. "Can you tell us what happened to you?"

He gave her a lopsided smile. "According to the shaman, I must thank La Sachamama for my deliverance."

"But how did you lose your canoe?"

"Maybe I'd better start at the beginning."

"Wait, let me get Hector and Winston." Emory left and came back with the two guides in tow. "Now, you were saying?"

"When I left"—Aguirre glanced at Rook, his expression unreadable—"I started north, thinking I'd head to Nauta. About a mile up, I noticed an unfamiliar orchid on the bank and paddled toward it. I didn't see the whirlpool until it was too late. It spun me around and almost sank me. Then it spit me out, and before I knew it, the current had carried me several miles downstream. I passed the lodge. No one answered my cries, and by the time I could get control of the canoe, I had no idea where I was. I pulled in at one of those native compounds, but it was deserted. I spent a few minutes searching the place—"

"Searching? What for?"

"For someone to help me." He hesitated, then went on, his embarrassment palpable. "All right, I was hungry. I hoped I'd find a banana or something. When I went back to the river, the boat was gone."

"Stolen?"

"No idea. I didn't tie it up very securely. The rope might have loosened and the current carried it away. I don't know."

Winston asked, "Did you see any blankets? Hammocks?"

"Huh? Why?" He rubbed his forehead. "Let me see…Yes. I saw a blanket hung over the railing."

"What color was it?"

"Green and yellow. Why?"

Winston and Hector exchanged looks. "You stumbled across the home of one of the feuding families. The house wouldn't have been empty unless they were either on a raiding party or hiding from one."

Aguirre's eyes opened wide. "Would they have shot at me?"

"No, no. It's just between them. It's like...who are the famous American families—the Hatracks and the Mickeys?"

Felicity took a minute before sputtering, "Oh, you mean the Hatfields and McCoys." Then she sobered. "But their feud resulted in many casualties. Why—"

Petra, unwilling to let the conversation veer off topic, intervened. "What did you do when you found the canoe gone?"

"Well, I had no sense of how far I'd floated, but I knew I was on the lodge side of the river, so I decided to strike back along the shore. I ran into those trees with the big spines—"

"Silk floss trees?"

"Yes." He shivered. "At some spots, the creepy things came all the way to the waterline, and I had to make my way inland. I was tearing through some heavy underbrush when I heard a noise."

This caught everyone's attention. Even Rook leaned forward. "A noise?"

"Yes. A really deep grunting, like from some large animal. I scrunched down in the thicket, hoping whatever it was wouldn't see me. It passed me by, but I still waited a few minutes before moving again."

"And now you were lost?"

"No, not yet. I could see the glint of water through the trees, so I knew the river was close. But the minute I resumed walking, I heard it again. This time it was behind me."

Emory said, "It had circled around?"

Aguirre nodded, his eyes wild at the memory. "It was stalking me! I started to run."

"And that's when you got lost." Denys leaned

back, satisfied.

"Yes. I ran until I couldn't run any more, then found a log to sit on and catch my breath. I figured I'd thrown him off the scent."

"You hadn't?"

"I don't know for sure. As I was sitting there, I heard this whoosh right in my ear—like a moo or a neigh. I rolled out of sight behind the log, but it was only a tapir wandering through the brush. He looked at me and plodded on. I was about to start on again when I heard a crash and a lot of squealing. A few feet away, a tree had fallen on the tapir. He was thrashing around under it, but he didn't sound like he was in pain. More like he was terrified."

"Scared? Of what?"

Aguirre's eyes went white with remembered horror. "An enormous animal covered in dark hair. He strode out of the jungle and stood over it, his back to me."

"Oh God, was it going to eat the tapir?"

"I don't know. He pawed at it, but then he sniffed the air and suddenly took off in the opposite direction. I ventured out to look at the tapir. It was dead. But—this is the important part. On the bark of the tree, I found a hank of brown hair." He looked straight at Rook.

"From the tapir?"

"No." He looked from face to face. "From the Mapinguari."

****

Rook burst out, "What a load of hogwash."

Denys stared at him. "I thought you wanted to find it."

Rook growled, "I do, but why should we trust

Tramposo, considering his history? Besides, if it's out there, you think it would show itself to this bozo? And it sure wouldn't let some human scare it off. You probably saw one of those big monkeys—howlers."

Aguirre said sullenly, "I saw what I saw. It was huge—maybe ten feet tall."

"You didn't see it from the front?"

"No. But it wasn't a monkey. It wasn't like anything I've ever seen before. For one thing, it was upright."

Alex rubbed his jaw. "Do you think it would have eaten the tapir if it hadn't detected your scent?"

Aguirre thought hard. "I don't know, but why would it touch a dead animal if it didn't intend to?"

"And you say it fled when it heard you?"

"Yes."

Emory said, "A carnivore would have fought off any intruder to protect its meal."

Nick spoke up. "Yes, but a carrion eater wouldn't. Hyenas and vultures snatch bits of the kill when the lions are distracted."

Petra said deliberately, "From my research, I concluded that the Mapinguari may in fact be an ethnic memory of the *Megatherium*, the giant land sloth. The *Megatherium* was a vegetarian."

Emory interrupted. "Yes, but you told me it died out ten thousand years ago."

"Or not." She gazed around at the anxious faces. "It could have survived, adapted."

Felicity sucked in her breath. "And in an increasingly harsh environment, it could have converted to a diet that included meat."

Emory looked at Aguirre. "You say you brought

back some more hair?"

"Yes. It's in my room. I'll go get it."

They waited what seemed an inordinately long time. Petra finally said, "I wonder what's keeping him?"

Rook poured himself a cup of coffee. "Probably cutting off a hunk of his hair and doctoring it to look bestial."

Nick scoffed. "Why tell us he had it, then? I mean, what's in it for him?"

Emory considered. "Maybe he thought he could get his job back?"

Rook glared at him. "I've changed my mind. The guy's a charlatan. I can't have a man like that on my team."

Denys stood up. "I'm going to go check on him. He may not have recovered as much as he thought. Perhaps he collapsed."

Petra said, "I'll go with you."

The door to Aguirre's room stood open. He slumped on the cot, his head in his hands.

"Are you okay?"

He raised a stricken face. "It's not here."

"What's not here?"

Petra understood. "The hair?"

For answer he shrugged. "Gone."

Chapter Twenty-Four
Symbiotic Relationships

November 3

Petra sat down next to him. "Aguirre, were you telling the truth?"

Aguirre's voice was tired. "If you mean, did I see the creature? Yes, I saw the creature."

"And the hair?"

He didn't answer. *Wait. The hair. Could he be…* Before she could accuse him, Aguirre leapt up.

"The hair too. Yes! I know you don't believe me because of the fake bird, but that was all part of his plan."

"Whose plan?"

"Rook's."

"Rook's!"

"What about me?" The man stood in the doorway.

Aguirre rose and pointed a shaking finger at him. "It was all his idea. He sent me here to scout out how far along the project had progressed. When it looked like you were getting close to finding the Mapinguari, I was supposed to call Victor. He ordered me to distract you from your quest long enough for me to capture the beast."

Does this whole kerfuffle go back to Rook? "So the ersatz fossil thing was *his* idea?"

308

"No!" Rook's voice rang out. "Aguirre's an idiot. I never told him to concoct such an utterly implausible story."

"And you never told me you were coming yourself."

The two faced off. There was a strange moment of anticipation. Petra watched them. *Will they come to blows?* When neither moved, she began to wonder, to look back at their earlier engagements. *There's a queer kind of bond between them. More than employer-employee, I think.* Love-hate? Codependency? *What in fact are they to each other?* She tried to remember what she'd read about Rook. *That's right—he never married. Could they be lovers?* She contemplated the expression on Aguirre's face, then moved on to Rook and found herself still at a loss. Both were indecipherable.

Emory and Alex appeared, looming over Rook, the afternoon sun glinting off their heads. "What's going on?"

"Aguirre's confessing."

They crowded into the room, prodding Rook farther to the center. He tried to push back through them, only to come up against John. "Oh, oh, sorry, Mr. Rook. Is Tramposo okay?"

"Get out of my way, Dillinger."

For once, the PR man stood his ground.

Alex shouted, "Don't let him go, John!"

This had the effect of terrifying the little man. He started to step aside, but Emory grabbed Rook's elbow and propelled him to the only chair. "I don't think you're going anywhere just yet."

"Don't touch me!" Rook rubbed his elbow with frenzied urgency. "This is ridiculous. That man's a

lunatic. I'll sue your asses for everything you've got."
But he sat down.

Aguirre resumed. "He told me to do whatever it
took to get you off the track. I admit the fossil was my
idea—but it was the only thing I could think of that
would hold the attention of you scientists long enough."

John seemed bewildered. "I thought Tramposo was
confessing?"

"He is." Petra held a finger to her lips. "Go on."

"I knew about Andrews's history and figured he'd
do anything to get his professional standing back. The
day I went upriver by myself, I laid down the string of
clues. I wanted Emory to come back with me because
he'd be easier to fool alone."

Emory stiffened. Petra took his hand and squeezed
it. "Let him finish," she whispered.

"Also, if he got on board, my story would be taken
seriously and we'd have a full-fledged undertaking. The
Mapinguari would be forgotten in the general hysteria."
He looked directly at Denys, who fidgeted. Aguirre
went on. "But Andrews wouldn't bite." He sneered.
"Maybe because he's been burned too often."

Emory broke away from Petra and lunged at him.
Felicity jumped between them, but Emory's momentum
carried him right into her, bowling her backward onto
Aguirre. In the ensuing melee, Rook slipped out.

Emory raced out after him. Petra helped Felicity
up. As Aguirre brushed himself off, Petra turned a
wrathful eye on him. "And when Emory didn't bite,
you decided to kill him."

Aguirre went pale. "Never! That was truly an
accident. The machete slipped." He looked at his hands.

"You're lying."

"No!" He peered up at her through his dark eyelashes. "Although I admit, with him out of the way, it was easier to sway the others."

Petra felt her fingers curl and wished she had them around Aguirre's throat. *I'm just as bad as Emory.* Felicity must have sensed her fury and intervened. "Nonetheless, you injured him badly."

John pointed a plump finger at Tramposo. "Why, I'll bet you even killed little Esteban's guinea pig, didn't you? I'll bet you told him it was attacked by a bird and handed him the feather yourself." He stopped in the sudden silence. "To keep the story line going."

Aguirre was staring at him blankly. "Guinea pig?"

Nick startled them all by asking calmly, "More to the point, why does Rook want to capture the Mapinguari? Doesn't seem quite his shtick."

Aguirre's eyes grew shifty. "I don't know. He's a very wealthy man. Perhaps he wanted a pet."

Petra was beginning to wonder if Rook were right—Aguirre seemed incapable of giving a straight answer. "Why doesn't he just get a dog?"

"He's also very eccentric. He read about the beast and learned of your expedition. He sent me here, but then he must have decided to come down and see for himself."

Alex declared, "But we didn't know we were going after it until we got here. This was supposed to be a general exploratory expedition."

Petra eyed him. "You mean you weren't planning all along to take the Iron House apart?"

"No, no." He shook his head vigorously. His rufous hair flopped into his eyes. He flung it back impatiently. "I knew nothing about that when I signed on for the

Pacaya expedition. The itinerary Denys sent included Iquitos. It rang a bell—see, the Iron House and my great-great-grandfather's connection to it had been a story in my family for generations. I did a little research and learned that only one of the original two parts was in Iquitos. The second was carted off by a friend of Fitzcarrald."

"That's right. It's never been found."

Aguirre had been listening to this exchange with interest. "Fitzcarrald you say? Iron House? You mean the Casa de Fierro? Do you remember the name of this friend?"

Alex's forehead creased. "Not off hand."

"Was it by chance Diego Aquilino?"

"That sounds about right. How did you know?"

Aguirre clapped Alex on the back, his face wreathed in smiles. "Diego Aquilino was my great-great-uncle and Fitzcarrald's bosom buddy. He helped him find the isthmus to Puerto Maldonado and open the route to Brazil."

"How do you know this?"

"When my mother died, I found her diary. In it, she told the story of how the two of them moved not just the steamboat but a building over the mountain." A shadow passed over his face. "It's all I know of my family—at least, that is good."

Alex seemed to have trouble taking this in. "You mean, your ancestor and—?"

"Yes! And Fitzcarrald were the ones who took the second Eiffel house away. Isn't it grand?"

From the expression on Alex's face, Petra wasn't sure he concurred. "I…I don't know what to say…Wait a minute. Did she say specifically it was the Eiffel house?"

Aguirre was growing impatient. "Yes, yes. My mother wrote that Fitzcarrald and his friend Diego Aquilino dragged an iron building from Iquitos over the mountain."

Alex dropped into the chair Rook had occupied. "Did she say what happened to it?"

He shook his head. "Only that Aquilino was last seen in Puerto Maldonado."

Felicity interrupted. "This is all fascinating, but can we get back to the topic at hand? Emory also thought this was just an exploratory mission. So most of the crew was misled—but one of you must have known all along. Denys?"

"I…uh…"

"It was all his idea." John's voice throbbed like a plucked E string. "We had received grant money for the expedition, but then he got this bee in his bonnet about the monster. Catching one would bring renewed celebrity. He made me bring the sightings to everyone's attention and drum up interest for it."

Denys harrumphed. "It's not as though everyone was disappointed that we might find a new species."

Nick asked curiously, "So why did you lose interest in it so quickly when Aguirre turned up with the skeleton?"

John spoke for him. "I don't think he cares what he finds, so long as it's momentous."

Petra's original assessment of Ffoulkes now seemed prescient. *In it for the glory. Not a serious scientist.*

Denys demurred. "Not true. We only had native tales of the Mapinguari to go on, but when Aguirre found the slab we had something tangible in our hands."

"What about the footprint?"

Before he could answer, Winston knocked. "Mr. Andrews and Mr. Rook would like you all to come to the kitchen."

They filed out of the room and down the hall. Petra was beginning to feel a bit like the Keystone Kops. Emory, Rook, and Capac stood by the big butcher block table. A slight, shy woman, her hair in a kerchief, hovered near the back door. Denys had recovered some of his swagger. "What's all this, my good man?"

Capac gestured at the woman. "My wife, Luz. She does the cleaning and the laundry."

Ffoulkes shrank back. "Oh...I...uh..."

He's afraid she's going to publicly denounce him for injuring Nick.

Instead, Rook stepped forward. "She had Aguirre's clothes and was about to wash them. I stopped her and checked his trousers. This was in a pocket." He held up a wad of coarse black hair in a plastic bag. "Aguirre was in terrible physical and mental shape when we found him. We'd stripped him of his clothes and left him with the shaman. He had no clear recollection of his rescue. So this evening, when he couldn't find the hair, I thought, what could have happened to it? Could he have dropped it before he found his way back? Maybe. After all, he was running for his life, crashing through the jungle..." He paused. Petra saw a spark of repugnance flit across his features. "Destroying the fragile ecosystem with no regard to its pristine nature. People like that..." He shook himself. "At any rate, he'd need both hands to protect himself as he tore through the brush. What would he do with his trophy?"

"Stuff it in his pocket."

"Yes."

Emory spoke, his chagrin clear. "I was about to collar Rook when he showed me the bag."

"Let me see it." Petra held it up. "Just as I thought. You didn't find this in the forest. You stole it from my room. *Didn't you, Aguirre?*"

Aguirre stared at Petra. "No! I told you. Like I said, a wad of hair was stuck to a vine near the dead tapir." But for the first time he seemed a little uncertain.

Emory asked Petra, "Can you prove it's the hair we found?"

She pointed at a small mark. "I wrote the date in red on the corner of the bag."

"So his entire account is yet another work of fiction?" Rook's voice rose.

For the first time, Aguirre looked at the object in Petra's hand. He seemed puzzled. "Wait a minute. I didn't put the hair in a plastic bag. I didn't *have* a plastic bag."

Denys pinched it from Petra. "Nevertheless, this sample is from the monster. I'm taking it to the lab."

Emory and Rook spoke together. "We'll go with you."

Petra had had enough for one night. "Go ahead. It's almost midnight. I'm going to bed."

Felicity followed. "Me too."

Nick saluted. "Me three."

She was awakened by the sound of jubilant male voices. "Oh, for God's sake, what *now*?"

She threw on a robe and walked down to a lab blazing with light. Three men were huddled around a laptop. In the middle sat the slight figure of Denys. He was singing. When Petra drew nearer, she recognized it. The "Hallelujah Chorus."

"Hello?"

The rest of the crew stood behind her.

Denys crowed, "We've found it!"

Petra sighed. "Let me guess. The Mapinguari."

****

"Well, not exactly."

"Then what?"

Emory said, "We think it's the giant ground sloth. Remember? The *Megatherium* you told me about. It may not have gone extinct after all."

Didn't I just say that? "How will you know for sure?"

"I'll send the hair off to Ocala for further analysis—"

Rook interrupted Denys. "Don't tell them what we think it is," he warned.

"It would be rather hard to avoid."

"Okay—just tell them it's an unidentified sample and we want a general description—order, genus, gender, age…that kind of thing." The entrepreneur went to the door. "We should get an early start in the morning."

"For what?"

"What else?"

Petra's heart sank.

Alex burst out, "Does anyone else here think we've gotten off track? I came to study yacare caimans, after all. If we're going to spend all our time chasing extinct animals, I might as well go look for the second iron house."

Petra agreed wholeheartedly with him but knew any protest would be a waste of breath. "You'd better tell Hector."

And with that she went back to bed. She fell asleep to the sound of heated argument.

Chapter Twenty-Five
Intelligent Design

November 4

"Where's Aguirre?"

"He's not coming."

"*What*? How are we going to find the sloth without him?"

John handed Denys a paper. "He's in no shape to travel. Unless you want to wait till he's fully recovered, you'll have to go by this rough map he drew."

Emory took it and studied it. "He doesn't think he strayed too far from the water. He remembers passing two native compounds. Plus we know where Petra and I heard it before. It's enough to start with."

Alex pointed north. "Didn't he say he first headed toward Nauta?"

"Yes, but the whirlpool turned him around and shot him south for a few miles."

Denys nodded to Hector. "South it is."

Alex picked up a paddle and dropped it in one of the canoes. Denys glanced at him. "What are you doing?"

"I'm not coming either." Denys began to argue, but Alex was adamant. "Like I said, the distractions are interfering with my work. I intend to spend some time on the river."

Purple outrage tinged Denys's face. "I'm the director of this expedition, and I say all able-bodied team members have to follow my orders."

"Bullshit. Who do you think you are? General Patton? My university gave me leave to come after you invited me."

"You signed an agreement!"

"An agreement to study reptiles in the Pacaya River basin—not to go haring off after mythical beasts. Or fossil birds."

Petra began to worry that Denys would actually explode and wondered if she should seek cover from the incoming shrapnel. She looked to Felicity for guidance. The other woman's eyes bulged. She took a step back. *Academia—an extreme sport.*

The two men stood a few feet apart, steaming in the muggy atmosphere. Emory and John had retreated to the steps. Rook appeared to be enjoying the battle. Finally Denys, who must have realized his attempt at intimidation wasn't working, muttered, "Fine. Have it your way."

Alex turned on his heel and pushed the dugout into the water. Denys looked at the others. "Nick? Think you're up to it?"

Petra's brother took the dark glasses off, blinked, and put them back on. "Sorry. I think it'll be a couple more days at least."

Denys counted heads. "All right, it's me, Emory, Rook, and the staff. That makes five. We could use another hand. Anyone else game?"

Why not? Petra stepped forward.

Denys hesitated. He looked over her head toward the lodge. "John?"

John didn't bother to answer. Felicity shook her head. Denys sighed. "All right, Petra, but you'd better be able to keep up."

"Excuse me?"

Emory rasped, "Easy, Denys. She's been a trouper so far. Which is more than I can say for some of the *men*."

A few minutes later, Rook, Emory, Denys, and Petra, along with Winston and Hector, took off in the launch. John and Felicity waved them off.

The air shimmered with moisture as they floated downstream. Petra was by now used to the heat and the constant chittering of monkeys. They passed a small herd of tapirs grazing on the bank. Hector whistled and pointed at the top of a tall tree. "Sloth."

Everyone jumped. "Oh, it's a *tree* sloth. Don't scare us like that."

He hid the smile.

Emory came up to stand beside Petra in the bow. "I'm wondering about the hair."

"Me too."

"I mean, we now know Aguirre invented the fictional bird, but this time he seems to sincerely believe he saw the animal. So why lie about the hair?"

"And so obviously. He must have known I'd recognize the plastic bag."

"Maybe…" Emory rubbed the rail thoughtfully. "Maybe he did find some. Maybe Rook pulled a switcheroo."

"You mean put our hair in Aguirre's pocket?"

"Uh-huh."

"But that would mean…"

"Yes, that it was Rook who stole the plastic bag

from your desk."

"In order to discredit Aguirre? But why?"

He shook his head. "I have no idea. We all want the Mapinguari. The more help we have, the better. Unless…"

"Unless Aguirre has information Rook doesn't want shared." Petra mused. "They were working together until that spat over the defective camera. I had the distinct feeling then that Rook wanted Aguirre to shut up."

"Me too. And again the night he left. Along with his other faults, Aguirre just might suffer from a loose tongue."

"The night he left…wait a minute! I just remembered something."

"What?"

"Rook fired Aguirre on the same night that you announced the bird in the photograph was fake."

"Pretended to fire Aguirre. I think that may be part of the scheme." Emory was warming to his theory.

Better cool him down a bit. "Yes, well. Both of them have been playing a complex game."

"It would be nice to know what Rook really wants." Emory began to stroll toward the stern.

Petra pinched him. "Don't walk away. I haven't finished."

"Ouch." Emory pinched her back, then caught her fingers. He looked over his shoulder at the others, held her hand up, and kissed each finger in turn. His mouth was about to land on hers when she pulled away.

"Emory!"

"No one's looking."

"It's not that. Will you listen to me?"

He pulled back, his eyes vague. "I've forgotten what we were talking about."

Petra counted to ten. "Aguirre acknowledged yesterday that he'd cooked up the fake hoatzin to distract us from the search for the Mapinguari. Rook was furious—"

"Or was he?"

"Will you please keep quiet?"

"Yes, ma'am." Emory pointed at a large caiman sunning himself on the bank.

She watched it slither into the water just as a duck and four ducklings paddled by. A second later, there were three ducklings. The survivors paddled a little faster. "As I was saying, Rook was peeved. He told Aguirre that he'd given him one job—to test the instrument—"

"Which we now know was also a lie."

"Yes, but what you don't know is that I heard Rook say the same thing to Aguirre once before."

"When?"

"It was the day Rook arrived. I overheard them arguing. Rook told Aguirre he'd been given one job."

"So?"

"So…then he asked him if he'd gotten the 'bag.' "

"Bag."

"Our plastic bag." She forced herself to be patient. "I'd forgotten that bit until yesterday. Aguirre must have told him about our little escapade and that we'd brought the hair back. Rook ordered him to steal it."

"How would he know about it? We didn't tell anyone until four days ago. And Aguirre wasn't in the room then."

Petra thought hard. "I've got it. When we returned

from our scrape with Bigfoot, I asked you to give me the hair to keep."

"Right."

"We were standing in the corridor. Aguirre had just passed me. He must have overheard our conversation."

"So Aguirre did take it? Then why be so ecstatic that he'd found his own sample?"

"No, no, he didn't steal it. Rook did."

"Aha. Didn't I say that? Yes, I did."

If he waited for acknowledgement, he waited in vain. Petra's mind was on something else. "But then why didn't he tell Aguirre?"

"Back to square one." They stared at each other.

Hector called from the stern. "This is where you pulled off, and where Winston's son saw the creature." He motored toward the shore and dropped anchor.

Rook picked up a large knapsack and shrugged it on. It clanked.

Emory, one leg over the gunwale, asked, "What's in there?"

"You'll see."

They disembarked and hiked through the underbrush. As they followed the flash of Winston's machete, Petra panted, "Has anyone considered what we do with the sloth if we find it?"

Denys halted. "Um. Take photos, I suppose. See if there's any scat to take back to the lab."

Rook rumbled, "And capture it."

"Capture it!" Emory snorted. "If, as advertised, it's ten feet high and weighs two tons, just exactly how do you propose we manage that?"

"And where will we put him if we do catch him?"

Rook said shortly, "Unlike you lightweights, I have

it all mapped out."

He really needs to learn to play with others.

They reached the clearing where Petra and Emory had been treed. "Okay, let's go north. Spread out."

After a few minutes, Winston called. "I think I found something."

They gathered around. On the ground was a pile of dung. Denys checked it out. "It could be sloth…or giant anteater." He shoveled some into a plastic bag.

"Over here." Hector pointed at another bit of hair. A patch of bark had been shorn away. "Scratching his back?"

"Or marking his territory."

Rook dropped his knapsack. "Okay, this looks like a good place to set up."

"Set what up?"

He opened the bag. "The trap." He pulled out a roll of brown netting tied with four thick ropes. "This is polypropylene fiber—strong enough to hold an elephant."

"And hopefully something even bigger." Emory watched Rook, his expression skeptical.

Rook laid a motor with a spool attachment and a steel pulley on the ground beside the net. *That's what was clanking.*

He ran one end of each rope through the pulley, around the spool, and attached the other ends to the motor. "Hector, would you mind pounding this stake into the tree?" Hector obliged. Rook fiddled with the motor, then hooked it onto the stake. He tossed the other end of the ropes over a high branch and laid the net on the ground. "Help me." Winston and Hector snapped the ropes into grommets at each corner of the net before kicking leaves and dirt on top of it.

Denys surveyed the set. "So the plan is, he walks onto the net and gets hoisted into the tree."

Rook didn't bother to respond.

"What if he sees the ropes?"

Hector grabbed one. "They should look like lianas to him."

Emory gestured at the canopy. "How do we ensure it's the sloth that's trapped and not some other animal?"

"Excellent question." Rook pointed. "See that? It's a pressure-sensitive sensor. It won't activate the motor unless an animal the size of the sloth steps on it. The motor winds the rope. The net goes up, carrying Big Boy Bob with it."

"You're assuming the net will hold."

Rook shook the ropes. "Tested and retested."

Emory frowned. "The lodge is five miles away. How will we know when he's caught?"

"Yes, it could be days before the fellow comes this way again. I for one do not intend to camp out here." Petra guessed Denys was thinking of his nightly sherry.

"You won't have to." He held up a transmitter. "When the net rises, it sets off a radio signal which can be picked up with this."

Hector scratched his head. "How far does the signal travel?"

"Audible for up to two miles."

"Not far enough, then." Emory rubbed his chin. "So what do we do now?"

Rook tugged at a rope. "You all go back to the lodge and wait till the morning."

"Us! What about you?"

"Someone's got to be close enough to hear the

transmitter when it goes off." Rook squinted up at the sun filtering through the trees. "I don't mind staying here overnight. I'll call you if anything happens."

Emory overrode Denys's gasp of fury. "That's not a good idea. You shouldn't be alone in the jungle. Boy Scout rules."

Rook pulled one last object out of his knapsack and held it up. "I'll be perfectly safe."

Oh God. He brought Orion X.

Denys sucked in his breath. "You're not intending to kill it, are you? You said…you promised…"

Rook shot him a look filled with scorn. "Maybe you weren't listening when I described the elements of the scope." He adjusted a knob under the barrel. "This is loaded with tranquilizer darts."

Emory actually seemed relieved. "Makes sense. You can zap it while it's still hanging in the net."

Rook set the scope down. "So I'll stay here and keep watch."

"No. We all go back. If you like, we can return at twilight. That's when he probably comes out to feed."

Denys nodded. "Good point. All the sightings have been near dusk."

Rook looked unhappy but acquiesced.

****

John greeted them at the lodge. Petra told him what the plan was. He announced, "Aguirre is feeling better. He might be able to come with you tonight."

"No." Rook spoke quickly. "I have another task for him. Is he in his room?"

"Yes."

He took himself off.

Emory gathered a rucksack and his binoculars.

"Well, then, I'm going out to do what I actually came here for."

Felicity laughed. "Fall in love?"

He gave her an odd look. "No, look for birds. I think I saw jacanas on the giant lily pads over on the oxbow lake, and Hector told me a black skimmer had been sighted a week ago. It shouldn't be here this time of year. If it's solitary, it may only have been separated from the flock, but if there are more than one, it could be changing its migratory patterns."

As he walked down to the dugout, Felicity jiggled Petra's elbow. "Go with him."

"Huh?"

She stuck out her chin. "I said, go with him, if only to please an ex-wife."

Petra realized she hadn't been alone with Emory for days. *So that's what those pangs are.* "I believe I will." She grabbed her binoculars and bag and ran after him. "Can I come with you?"

He hesitated. Dismay pinched her heart. *He doesn't want me with him.*

"Did Felicity tell you to come?"

I think...yes, I think a fib is in order. "No. I just...would like to. Is it okay?"

"You have to be very quiet. I'm serious—I want to get some real work done if I can. Hop in." She got in the bow, and they paddled across the river. They had to portage the canoe over a wedge of land to get to the lake. When they broke through the trees, a broad expanse of water teeming with wildlife opened before them. Caimans basked on the shore and long-toed jacanas stepped daintily from one six-foot-wide lily pad to the next, jabbing at insects with their long yellow bills. A large, silvery bird soared overhead. As it passed, she glimpsed a black cap like a burger's hat and a bright blue bill. "Capped heron. Must be breeding."

"How do you know?"

"Yellow breast and head plumes." Petra felt suddenly very shy. Emory seemed lost in thought or distracted by the sights. He kept his eyes on the understory line, raising his binoculars now and then. "See, on that branch there? Isn't it beautiful!" He pointed. Petra saw a small bird sitting motionlessly a few feet above the water. Its royal blue head and striking red breast stood out from the mass of green shrubbery. "Blue-headed trogon. Uncommon."

Searching desperately for something to contribute, Petra pointed at a dark, undistinguished little bird pecking on the ground. "How about that one?"

"Ooh, maybe...Let me check." He flipped rapidly through a thick book, his eyes jumping from the page to the bird and back. "Yes...yes...yes! It could be an Allpahuayo antbird. It was only recently discovered. Wow, are we lucky!" His zeal was contagious, and Petra found herself watching him rather than the birds. He read farther, his face darkening. He turned some pages. "No, I'm wrong. The Allpahuayo species only occurs in the white sand forests. This must be the spot-winged antbird." He closed the book and dropped it into the bottom of the dugout.

"Did you say sand forest? Bit of an oxymoron, eh?"

"Sort of. They're a very distinctive formation. Found only in northeastern Peru, geologists think they're the remnants of coastal dunes. The soil is pure sand, so the trees are quite stunted and the canopy is very low. On the bright side, they're home to some twenty-five species of bird found nowhere else in the world. The Allpahuayo antbird is endemic to that ecosystem." He tapped his lip. "What I wouldn't give to see one."

Petra recognized the signs. Whenever Emory was reminded of the hummingbird affair, he grew despondent. *Quick, quick, change the subject.* "Um...Felicity really is very nice." *Sooo smart—draw his attention to his beautiful ex-wife. Idiot. Maybe he won't respond.*

"Yup." He pointed at a tall tree. "Emperor tamarin."

"The little monkey?"

"Uh-huh." A black-haired animal about ten inches tall with a flowing white mustache scampered down a limb and leapt ten feet to another one. Petra began to think she was in the clear when he barked abruptly, "What about Felicity?"

"She and I had a good talk. Did she tell you she's engaged?"

He dropped the glasses. "Engaged? No. When did that happen?"

"Just before she came down here."

He scowled. "Didn't think she was capable of that much affection."

"His name is Kelly Chisholm. He works for Rook."

"Chisholm! Wasn't he the one who was supposed to bring the scope?"

"I think so. Rook came in his place. He told Felicity he'd sent him somewhere else, somewhere exotic. Now where was it?" She frowned in thought.

"Chisholm probably jumped at the chance to put

some miles between himself and Felicity."

"Spiteful doesn't become you. You should have seen her face when she told me of the engagement. She's very happy." She paused. "I wonder if she's heard from him?"

"Don't ask me." His face closed down again.

Petra sucked in a breath. *Is he angry with me? Or…is he jealous?*

After a minute, he said, "Look, do me a favor, get my notebook out and record the species we see here."

"Okay." She was rooting around in his knapsack when he mumbled something. "Excuse me?"

"Can we not talk about Felicity?"

Annoyed, she snapped, "You're being childish. She's here at your request, after all. You can't ignore her. If you have a problem, you should tell her." *And me.*

He put down the glasses. "It's not that. It's…well—" He scooched forward and, turning her shoulders to face him, delivered a hard kiss. "I'd rather be doing that." He moved back to the stern.

Petra waited for the boat and her heart to stop bobbing so she could come up with an answer—*any answer…I mean, what do I want to tell him?*

He checked his watch. "We'd better be getting back. We want to get down to the site before twilight."

"Do we? Maybe we should wait until the beast is actually caught."

"And how will we know that unless we go?"

"What about the radio transmitter?"

"Won't work. Too far away."

"But—"

Emory interrupted. " 'Caught.' That reminds me. I

knew there was something missing in Rook's plan but couldn't put my finger on it."

"Well?"

"What do we do with a four-ton creature that's going berserk while hanging in a net ten feet above us?"

"Wing it?"

Chapter Twenty-Six
Divergent Species

November 4

"Well, Rook was awfully confident. He did say he had it all worked out."

"I guess we'll find out."

As they paddled up to the dock, they heard a whirring overhead. A seaplane buzzed the lodge before making a pinpoint landing at a wide spot in the river. It taxied over to them. A man in flight overalls cut the engine, jumped out, and tied it up. He spied Emory and called, "You Victor Rook?"

"No, I am." Rook came down the steps.

The man stuck his hand out. Rook ignored it. "You have the shipment?"

"Yup. Some guy named Gardener wired me in Lima to bring a box out here. Name's Igor Havel, Havel Air Freight Service. I've got some paperwork for you."

"Let's go inside."

Emory and Petra pulled the canoe up on the bank and walked over to the plane. Emory inspected it. "Looks like it's designed for cargo. I wonder…Come on."

They entered the lounge just behind Denys. Aguirre and Alex sat at the bar, in deep conversation.

"Where's Nick?"

Alex looked up. "In his room resting his eyes."

Ffoulkes peered outside. "What's that plane doing here?"

Emory cocked his head at Rook's retreating back. "I think it's phase two of his plan."

"What? For the sloth?" Petra could almost see Denys's brain fermenting as he weighed his options. He settled on outrage. "Where does it say Rook gets to plan *anything*? This is *my* project, not his. *I* applied for and received the grants. *I* recruited the team. *I* arranged for the research station and equipment. I—am—in—charge. Who the hell does he think he is?"

Did he just whinny?

John had been standing just inside the door. He said something under his breath. Denys rounded on him. "What was that, Dillinger?"

He came all the way in. "Um…actually, it was me who applied for the grants…and reserved the facilities…and besides—"

"Your point being?"

Petra reflected that the director's high dudgeon would have been more effective if he were taller than five feet six and his nose didn't drip.

Before John could answer, Victor and the pilot entered. "Greetings, all. This is Igor Havel. You were wondering what we'd do when we caught the creature. Mr. Havel here has brought us a crate."

Denys deflated, but only slightly. He marched up to the pilot. "I am Dr. Denys Ffoulkes, head of this expedition. You may deal directly with me."

"Oh? No problem. Here's the invoice."

Denys snatched it out of his hand and skimmed it. Fingers went to his throat, and his eyes turned back in his head. He staggered back, the paper floating gently to the floor.

Rook, not even trying to hide his malicious glee, picked it up. "Tell you what—I'll cover the cost of the plane and crate…if that's all right with you, *Doctor* Ffoulkes."

Denys recovered nicely. "Very gracious of you. May I see the crate?"

Havel went to the door. "It's in the plane. You'll have to unload it."

"Sure." Emory pried John from the bar, and they all trudged down to the dock. Havel opened a large hatch. The men pulled out a shrink-wrapped package tied to a pallet.

Rook removed some papers that had been taped to the outside and read them. "It comes as a kit, but the sections simply snap-lock into each other."

They leaned the pallet against the pylons. Alex surveyed it dubiously. "So how do you propose to get the sloth into it?"

Aguirre scratched his head. "Some kind of bait?"

John chirped, "When we had unwanted critters in the basement, my mom put out tuna fish. Possums and raccoons love it."

"Tuna."

"For an animal the size of an elephant."

"And possibly a vegetarian."

Alex snickered. "So…John. How much tuna ya think we need?"

The fat man glared at him. "I don't hear *you* coming up with a solution."

Emory intervened. "That's great, but let's say we actually capture the Mapinguari—or rather, the sloth—

and manage to stuff it into the crate. How do we get it from there to here?"

Hector stepped forward. "We can lash two or three canoes together and tow them behind the launch."

"Like a raft. Good idea."

"So…" Rook picked at the ropes tying the package. "Shall we assemble it and head downriver?"

Alex answered. "It'll be easier to assemble once we get there." Everyone nodded in agreement.

Petra gazed inquiringly at Rook. "Why are you in such a hurry? Did you get a ping? Has the creature been trapped?"

"N…no."

Aguirre—to Rook's obvious displeasure—observed, "We wouldn't hear it here anyway. We're five miles from the site."

"We still might be able to catch a faint signal." John looked hopeful. "We should give it a little more time."

Rook wasn't the type to yield easily. "It wouldn't hurt to be set up and ready before the sloth appears."

Denys peered at the sky. "I think we should wait until morning. By the time we get the crate assembled and find a way to get the animal inside, night will have fallen. If the Mapinguari is indeed in the net, it'll keep overnight."

Rook began to complain, but the others were too much for him, and they repaired to the bar. Nick met them. "Doctor says I can keep the glasses off now, but I have to be careful to shield my eyes from bright light for a bit longer."

Igor proved to be a gregarious fellow and over dinner told a stream of stories of near collisions and other mishaps he'd had over the course of a colorful career. "Finally decided to settle in Lima—for the women." He winked at Felicity, who sat on the divan with Emory. "And the pisco." He held up his glass for a refill. "I usually contract with museums and archaeological expeditions. Haven't had much truck with scientific types. What do you all need the crate for?"

Rook hastily rose. "I forgot. You have to sign a waiver for me. It's down in the lab. Come on."

Havel put down his glass reluctantly. "Save that for me, guys." They left.

Nick looked after them. "I'm guessing our fearless leader doesn't want the help to be privy to too much information."

Aguirre said, "I don't blame him. If we can bring a new species back—"

Denys interrupted him. "Not a new species—a long-lost mammal, thought to have gone extinct thousands of years ago." He turned to Petra. "What did you call it?"

"A cryptid."

"Right. Not a new species. An *old* one." Felicity patted Emory's hand. "And this time a real one." He jerked and threw her a furious look. "No, no, dear. I was only talking about Aguirre's bird."

Denys jumped up, spilling his drink. "Yes, indeed. Like the sturgeon—enormous, magnificent creatures that have lived virtually unchanged for sixty-five million years. What a trophy this could be!" His eyes shone.

Emory tossed him a napkin. "If it exists. We haven't caught it yet, after all." He glared at his ex-wife, who sat rigidly, her eyes reproachful.

Denys tut-tutted. "We found its scat—"

"Could be an anteater's."

"And the hair."

"Could belong to a tree sloth."

Petra cried, "But Emory, we heard it!"

"We didn't see it, though." His face was a mask of stubborn defiance.

"Aguirre saw it."

"So he says."

Nick peered at Emory. "Why are you suddenly so negative? I thought you were as gung ho as the rest of us."

Felicity murmured, eyes cast down, "Emory's right. I believe we should maintain an agnostic attitude, at least until we have the animal in hand." She smiled a bit mistily at her ex-husband.

Petra stared at her. *Why is she taking his side? To make up for angering him?* She noticed for the first time how close Felicity sat to Emory, their thighs nearly touching. *Is she…is she flirting with him?* An icy cold laser burned a hole through her heart. *She's been warming up to him for the last few days—that wintry shell is melting. Could she want him back?* She wondered at herself. *What's the matter with you, Petra? If I didn't know better, I'd say you were jealous.* She looked up to see Nick grinning at her. *Could he be right? Could I be?…No.*

Havel came back in. "So where can I flop for the night?"

Nick raised a hand. "You can bunk with me."

In the general movement toward the corridor, Denys cleared his throat. "I have decided that tomorrow's team will consist of all the men. Nick, are you up to it?" Nick nodded. "The ladies should stay here."

Petra and Felicity spoke sharply and simultaneously. "Why?"

"Because…in case…that is…"

Rook took charge. "I agree. Someone should man the fort in case we need reinforcements—or medical assistance."

John raised a hand. "I should probably stay with the women—they'll need some male protection."

"Uh…sure." Even Denys had trouble keeping a straight face.

As the others went their separate ways, Petra put a hand on Felicity's arm. "Can I talk to you?"

"Sure."

"I have a question."

"Fire away."

"Emory asked you to come and take a look at the fossil hoatzin. We've now determined it was a fake."

"Correct."

"So…why are you still here?"

She expected Felicity to be surprised or annoyed. She didn't expect her to giggle. "Are you worried that I want to take Emory back?" The giggle turned into a belly laugh. Petra had no choice but to wait for her to calm down. "Oh, my dear, too funny. You should see the look on your face." She caught her breath. "I couldn't take Emory from you even if I wanted to. Haven't you seen the way he looks at you? He adores you." Her blue eyes snapped with mirth.

All of a sudden, Petra felt like a five-year-old who'd been upstaged before she could drill really deep into the tantrum. "I…uh…Well, why *are* you still here, then?"

Felicity checked that the room was empty, then lowered her voice. "I'm waiting for my fiancé, for Kelly. I received a message from him. Remember, Rook told us he'd sent him to Turkmenistan? Well, when he got to Ashgabat—that's the capital city—he met with the man Rook had contacted. The whole thing was a bust. The guy claimed he'd fabricated a micro-bomb, but it turned out to be a bit of plastic explosive on a safety pin. Kelly's on his way back to Kansas City now, but he's still hoping to get down here so we can have that vacation."

"What about Rook?"

"I suppose he'll report to him here."

"He knows Rook is here?"

"Oh, yes, but Rook doesn't know he's coming. He told me to keep it under my hat."

"I wonder why."

"Maybe he's afraid Rook will send him haring off somewhere else. Kelly says he's a holy terror to work for. One of those hypocrites who fly around the world in a gas-guzzling corporate jet while spouting off about the desolation caused by human consumption."

"Yeah, he said something along those lines to me…" *What did that magazine article say about him?* "He's not married, is he?"

"Not that I know of. Not gay either." She lowered her voice again. "I've heard stories about…animals."

Petra felt sick. "Gross."

"Eh." She leaned closer. "I'll tell you what's weirder. He's been linked to a group called the Voluntary Human Extinction project."

"Doesn't sound very appetizing."

"They want people to opt out of reproducing, for the good of the planet."

"Didn't the Shakers try that?"

"Yes, but they believed God wanted them to act that way, not some bully who raves about Gaia." She tapped her fingers on the table. "You suppose he thinks doing it with animals is more environmentally friendly?"

"Felicity, you have a very warped imagination."

She smirked and rose. "Well, you have your answer at least. I'm waiting for the love of my life to arrive. And please don't tell anyone—not even the love of *your* life."

Before Petra could respond, she was gone. Petra waited a minute, then rose, walked down the corridor, and knocked on Emory's door. He opened it. "Why, hello. What can I do for you?"

She pushed him back into the room and spent quite a few hours making it very clear what he could do for her.

****

November 5

Alex appeared while they were at breakfast, holding a sheet of paper. He walked over to Denys. "I've had the most productive conversation with Mr. Tramposo. He has proposed—and I have accepted—that we pool our resources and go find the second iron house."

Aguirre limped into the room. "We leave this morning."

"What!" Rook and Denys were equally furious. Rook spat out, "You leave now, you're fired."

Aguirre shrugged. "I thought you already fired me."

Petra's mouth had dropped open. "But, Aguirre, what about your wife?"

He started and goggled at her. "My wife? I don't have a wife."

"But...Denys..."

Ffoulkes nodded vigorously. "Your wife—the invalid? You told me...you told me..." He wound down, at the last only his jaw flapping in the slight breeze.

Petra thought she understood. Aguirre had forgotten all about his ruse. "That was a lie to cover up your communications with Rook, wasn't it?" *Oh, what a tangled web we weave, when first we practice to deceive. I know that's not Shakespeare...but who?* Distracted, Petra missed Aguirre's feeble response. "Wasn't it?"

"Um..."

Rook jeered. "Denys, I swear to God, you're the biggest boob on the planet."

Denys chose to ignore the jab and spluttered, "And you, Bönickhausen. I'll see to it your reputation is besmirched, destroyed, dragged through the mud!" His voice pulsed with several more exclamation points.

Alex burst into laughter. "You're kidding, right? I'm a tenured professor at the University of Miami. You, on the other hand, are the director"—he crooked fingers in the air to indicate quotation marks—"of a dinky nonprofit, hanging onto your last grant by a thread. I'm betting the place won't survive after this little debacle goes public."

John gasped. No one spoke. Aguirre touched

Alex's elbow. "Let's go."

Before he turned, Alex held up the sheet. "Oh, I almost forgot. Here's the contract." He ripped it into two pieces and laid them before Denys the way a cat lays a dead mouse at his master's feet.

Petra wasn't sure if Denys would recover, but the Victorian wannabe apparently had some spine. "Let them go. If we find the sloth, they'll have to eat their words."

If the Mapinguari doesn't eat us first.

****

Denys counted heads. "Nick, Emory, Winston, Rook, Hector. Are we all ready to go?" Petra supposed he was using his most officious voice in order to lend added gravitas to his taupe-colored, tropic-weight, moisture-wicking, instant-dry shirt made of fairly traded, non-GMO bamboo…and matching pants. He was already soaked through with sweat.

Nick pointed at the crate. "What about that?"

"We'll assemble it on site. No reason to set it up until we've captured Mappie."

"Mappie?"

Ffoulkes's accent took on a British twinge. "I thought it would be amusing to give him a nickname."

Havel appeared and boarded his seaplane.

"Where are you going?"

"Another delivery. Toodle-oo." He flew off without further explanation.

The two women waved the company off, then went back inside to finish their breakfast. Felicity, buttering a piece of cornbread, remarked, "I hope they find it."

"You do?"

"Sure. What a discovery!"

John, his mouth full of bread, said, "Yeah, I suppose it would be a coup for the institute."

"All of a sudden you don't sound very enthusiastic."

"Oh, I am. It's just…"

"Just what?"

"Denys tends to get all hopped up in these affairs—to the point that, instead of being enhanced—the reputation of the institute suffers. He's totally obsessed with making his name. Sometimes, I think he'd do anything to get noticed."

Felicity eyed him doubtfully. "Denys? I don't see it. He's too pompous to be a fanatic…unless it's about Darwin."

Petra, having seen Denys in action, sided with John. "Well, that's his trouble, isn't it? He wants so badly to make some kind of scientific breakthrough. Sometimes, I wonder if he cares whether it's real or not."

The other woman remained unconvinced. "He didn't jump onto the hoatzin hoax immediately."

"No, but it didn't take much to set him off, did it?"

Felicity was silent a minute, then responded, "Well, scientists do tend to be obsessive-compulsive. We wouldn't have any innovations unless they were, would we?"

After breakfast, Petra decided to take a much-needed nap. Felicity watched her go, a thin smile on her lips. "A trifle tired today?"

Ordinarily Petra would have been embarrassed, but she was beginning to enjoy having a female companion to confide in. *I could never have told Nick about Emory.* "A little." She smiled at her friend. "But it was worth it."

****

She must have slept for hours. A yell woke her. She dragged herself from the pillow, threw on a robe, and went out to the corridor. Capac stood in the courtyard. "They got it! They got it!"

She said sleepily, "Let me guess: the Mapinguari."

Chapter Twenty-Seven
Migratory Species

November 5

Since Capac's English did not extend to sarcasm, he cried in delight, "Why, yes, it is the Mapinguari. You are very clever. Come quickly!"

Back in her room, she pulled on a shirt and shorts and headed to the river. The men were lifting a large crate from the nested canoes and yelling at each other. "Careful!"

"Whoops, there it goes!"

"I can't hold on!"

"I've got it."

Using the gangplank as a ramp, they manhandled the crate onto the dock and stood around it, panting. From the interior came growls and grunts. Whatever was inside banged noisily on the crate wall. Nick scratched his head. "Sounds like the tranquilizer's wearing off."

Petra came closer. "Is it the—"

"Well, it's not the Chullachaqui."

Felicity appeared at the lodge door, tying a blue satin peignoir around her waist, her long hair in a messy bun. "Is it the—"

Petra called to her. "Nick says yes."

She ran down to the dock and stood next to Petra.

"Can it breathe in there?"

"Oh, yeah, there are several air holes."

"What does it look like?"

Emory raised his eyebrows. "Big and hairy."

Nick relented. "We couldn't get a good view through the netting, and then we funneled him right into the crate. We'll have to wait for—" He stopped abruptly and gulped.

Emory had the same thought. "How are we going to study it if we can't see it?"

Rook, who had been standing to the side, not helping, grunted. "I swear, you guys couldn't find your own ass without me. I have a cage coming."

"Is that what Havel went to get?"

"Yes. It's the same setup zoos use to move dangerous animals from one area to another. You lock the doors of the crate and cage together, then pull up the crate door and prod him into the cage."

Hector, hands on hips, surveyed the box. "When will Mr. Havel get here? It's not right to leave the animal cooped up like that."

"It's got plenty of air. Plane should arrive this evening." Rook knocked on the box. "Might as well leave it here for now."

At that moment, the beast banged hard against the crate, which shifted slightly. Nick paced off the distance between the box and the water. "Is he strong enough to knock himself over?"

Rook rolled his eyes. "Sheesh. Bunch of gutless ninnies. I'll zap him again, okay? This time I'll use a double dose. Not to worry. He'll sleep till morning."

They trooped into the lodge and separated to clean up before meeting for a late lunch. Hector and Winston repaired to the staff quarters. Capac, his eyes straying to the box on the dock, was too flustered to complain about their tardiness. Ever hungry, Nick asked, "What's on the menu?"

"*Chancho con tamarindo.*"

Esteban translated. "Pork with tamarind sauce. Is chifa dish."

John stepped back from the table warily. "Chifa?"

"Chinese," Petra explained. "Very popular in Peru. We had dinner in a Chifa restaurant in Iquitos while we waited to spring Alex from the hoosegow."

Felicity sniggered. "Ha ha. I'm guessing that's *Chifa* for jail?"

Petra opened her mouth, but John interrupted. "Actually, it's from the Spanish word *juzgado*, meaning court of justice. One of over two hundred slang words for jail." The others stared at him. "What?"

Emory dragged his eyes from the little man. "Petra's guidebook says there's more Chinese food in Peru than Peruvian food. Sort of like New York."

Felicity scooped up a bite while John watched her, his lips curled in distaste. "Whatever."

Nick refilled his plate. "Well, I think it's delicious."

Petra smiled at her brother. "Everything is delicious to you as long as it's hot and plentiful."

When they'd eaten, Denys and Rook went to check on the crate. The others gathered in the lounge. Felicity set her coffee cup down. "So tell us everything. You start, Nick."

"Okay. When we reached the clearing, we could see the trap had been sprung, but all was quiet."

Emory added, "We were afraid he'd escaped, or

another animal had walked into the net."

"But when we approached, the thing started thrashing around and barking."

"Like a dog?" John seemed nervous at the idea.

Emory shook his head. "More like a seal. Shrieks and squeals."

Nick resumed. "So while Denys surveyed the site, we dragged the kit from the boat and put the crate together."

Felicity asked, "Was there any evidence as to why he frequents that area?"

John clicked his tongue. "What she means is…er…was the tapir gone?"

Nick took the question. Petra could have sworn he licked his lips. "That was the interesting part. It was still there, but it looked like something had been snacking on it. Could've been Bigfoot. Could've been a jaguar or vultures."

Emory cut in. "In that case, the carcass would have been either carried away or picked clean by now. There were still bits of flesh scattered around the tree and close to the clearing. It's quite likely the sloth ate some of it."

"But"—Petra was thoughtful—"sloths are herbivores. Even the *Megatherium* is believed to have been primarily vegetarian. He had a very long tongue and flat molars."

John pounced on her statement. "Aha. You said 'primarily.' Perhaps you should recheck your sources."

"Not a bad idea. I'll go see what else I can find out."

As she rose, Felicity cried, "What if the animal does turn out to be a meat eater?" Her voice crackled with concern. "What if he's strong enough to break out of the crate?"

Emory said deliberately, "The slats are four inches thick. He's not going anywhere."

She hunched her shoulders. "I do hope the plane gets here soon."

Petra passed Denys on the way to her room. He said, "Our 'guest' seems to be quiet for now. Rook gave him another shot just in case."

"Oh, good. Tell Felicity—she doesn't like the idea of it waking up before Havel gets here."

She pulled up her research folder and read through the various articles on the giant land sloth. Emory came in. She pointed at the screen. "John was right." She read, " 'Recent studies have postulated that the sloth was exclusively vegetarian, but there are some who feel the monster may have been omnivorous. Being related to the anteaters, it would have consumed insects, grubs, fruits, and even birds' eggs.' "

"*Hmm*. A tapir is a lot bigger than a grub."

"Yes, but the Megatherium was a lot bigger than an anteater."

"True. Plus, Aguirre said the tree had fallen on the tapir, killing it."

She smiled. "Free food?"

"Uh-huh. There were scraps of meat scattered around, almost as though he were grazing rather than wolfing it down. He may have been hungry enough to try something he wouldn't normally consume."

"A body that bulky must require a lot of fuel."

Emory paused. "Unless of course the rumors are true."

"You mean, of the Mapinguari eating stray

villagers?"

"Yup. You know"—he rubbed a temple—"if this thing has survived ten thousand years, it must have evolved at least somewhat. Maybe, as its habitat shrank, it developed a taste for meat. Maybe…."

"Maybe what?"

"Maybe the stories are true. Maybe my father's guide was right, and Dad was in fact killed by a giant sloth."

Petra, unsure whether finding answers to his father's death would satisfy Emory or make it worse, said merely, "We'll see."

Havel didn't appear by dinner time, nor did he show up that evening. Denys asked Rook if he'd heard from him. "No. He may have hit some rough weather. He'll come tomorrow."

"Are you sure?" Felicity seemed increasingly apprehensive. "I don't like the thing crammed into that flimsy wooden box. It could wake up and break out at any moment."

"Havel will be here. For the kind of money I paid him? Yes, I'm sure he'll come."

By ten o'clock the men were yawning. Petra watched Emory go. At the doorway, he turned. "Uh, Petra?"

She rose and strolled toward him. When she got close, he whispered, "You coming?"

She did not look back.

****

November 6

Petra was getting used to being awakened by cries and shouts, and this morning did not disappoint. She rose and pulled on a robe, ready for the next crisis.

Someone knocked. "It's me, Nicky." She checked to make sure Emory hadn't left any traces of his visit before opening the door. "Guess what?"

"Well, whatever it is, it's got something to do with the Mapinguari." She sighed.

"Huh?"

"Never mind. What's happened?"

"The crate is gone."

"Is the Mapinguari?"

"Well, of course it is. Oh, you're joking." Nick clearly was not in the mood.

"Did Havel come back with the plane?"

"I don't know. The other night when he stayed here, he crashed on the extra cot in my room. If he'd come back last night, I figure he would have woken me up. At any rate, he's not here now."

"Let me get dressed."

The others were milling around on the dock. Denys, in a silk brocade dressing gown, searched the other bank with a pair of opera glasses.

"It's just...vanished." John seemed completely befuddled.

"Where's Rook?"

Nobody seemed to know.

"Did anyone hear the plane land?"

"Not me."

"Nor me." Nick added for the benefit of the others, "I think I'd have heard Havel come into my room."

Winston spoke. "Capac says the squirrel monkeys went crazy in the middle of the night. He assumed it was a harpy eagle hunting them and went back to sleep."

"Do you suppose the sloth could have knocked

351

himself into the water?"

"What, and floated away? Wouldn't he just sink?"

"Hang on." John went over to the water and looked down. "Nothing here." As he turned around, his foot slipped off the platform. Nick caught him before he could tumble in.

"Well, just in case, we should take some canoes and check out the riverbanks." Emory shaded his eyes and gazed downriver.

"Right." Denys took charge. "Nick, you and Hector take one boat north. Emory and Winston can go south. If you see the box, come back here and we'll take the launch. Don't go much more than a couple of miles. If we don't find it by then, it's long gone."

When the men had paddled off, Denys went to his room. "I shall dress, then seek out the elusive Mr. Rook." Petra led the way to the dining room. Capac stuck his head out of the kitchen. Fastening his eyes on John, he said, "You ladies want breakfast?"

Both Petra and Felicity shook their heads. "Might as well wait for the others."

"But—" John started to protest but subsided after Felicity directed at him the kind of look a mother superior might give a naughty third-grader.

Ffoulkes returned, encased in seersucker. "Rook is nowhere to be found."

An hour later, both boats came back. Denys, presiding at the dining hall table, demanded news.

"No sign of the crate. All we can figure is that Havel flew in and then back out in the middle of the night."

"Taking the Mapinguari—"

"And Victor Rook—"

"With him."

All eyes turned to Denys. "Rook?"

"Yes, he's disappeared. He's cleared out his things as well."

Petra mused, chin in hand. "It must have been his plan all along."

"To steal the creature?"

"Uh-huh. First he wanted to stay at the trap by himself, and when that didn't work, he arranged with Havel to fetch him and his booty after we went to bed."

"So there never was any cage." It seemed to upset Felicity.

Petra patted her hand. "I'm sure the crate is sturdy enough. Rook would never endanger himself unnecessarily."

Everyone had a question. "Do you suppose all the rest—"

"The scope?"

"The camera—"

"Was only a cover?"

"Do we know for sure that the man is really Victor Rook?"

Petra nodded. "I am. I saw his picture in a magazine article."

Nick chimed in. "And he definitely knew what he was doing with the instrument."

"Then what the hell does he want with a giant sloth?" Emory's eyes flashed.

John was thoughtful. "Maybe when he got here and learned about our quarry, he decided he wanted it for himself."

"No." Denys was firm. "Rook planted Aguirre at the station. Why else would he do that except to preempt us? Aguirre himself admitted that he'd been charged with catching the creature." He gazed down the table. "I wish Tramposo were still here. He might have some answers for us."

Felicity put her coffee cup down. "Are we sure he went to Puerto Maldonado with Alex? Could he have gone ahead to Lima to arrange transport for the sloth?"

In the midst of the hubbub, John cried plaintively, "Could we possibly have our breakfast now?" Capac brought in platters of fruit and corn tamales. John piled his plate high before passing the platters on. His mouth full of papaya, he lisped, "I'll call Alex after breakfast and ask if Aguirre is with him."

"You have a phone number for him?"

"He gave it to me before he left."

Emory picked up a slice of mango. "Well, if he and Aguirre are together, see if he can wring the information out of him."

"You mean, about Rook's original purpose?"

"Right."

Denys blurted out, "What about the rest of you? What are *your* motives? Who can distinguish what's planned and what's spontaneous in all this?" His glare rocketed from one face to the next. "You all have your own agendas, after all—"

"Hey!"

He must have realized from their rebellious expressions that he'd gone too far, and said more calmly, "I mean, each of you has a different specialty, and you each came with a different goal. How can we possibly determine who has a trick up his sleeve and who doesn't?"

Emory growled, "What are you accusing us of?"

"Nothing. I don't know." He ran a shaking palm over his forehead. "I'm sorry. I'm just frustrated."

Felicity wiped her mouth with a napkin. "Denys has a point, though. Each of you had your own goal when you joined the team, and it didn't include the Mapinguari. So what has Rook done wrong? He'll ensure its existence is made public, which is all that's important, right? You"—she looked pointedly at Denys—"may want to take the credit, but after all, it wasn't your original objective either, was it?"

Before he could answer, Emory said haltingly, "Are you saying we shouldn't be bothered?"

"Yes. Why not let Rook claim the prize? If you're honest, you have to admit we couldn't have captured it without him."

"But…but…" Denys could do no more than splutter.

Petra interrupted him. "I have to disagree, Felicity. Rook waltzed in here, set up an elaborate hoax to distract us from the sloth, then proceeded to steal it. Not only do we have a legitimate stake in the discovery—we don't even know what he intends to do with it. He may keep it a secret."

That was enough for the rest. Nick volunteered, "Okay, what do we do now?"

Petra considered. "We know one thing for certain—that Rook was lying from the beginning. Aguirre told us that much. I think Aguirre's doubts about Rook started growing right from the get-go."

"When he showed up with that ridiculous alias." John scowled.

"That's right. And after that, Rook tried to sell Aguirre out several times—with the doctored photo and then with the hair. After his encounter with the Mapinguari, Aguirre just wanted out and decided to go with Alex."

Denys, apparently tired of being upstaged, held up a hand. "Thank you, Petra. If John gets hold of those two, we'll know one way or the other. Aguirre may be willing to divulge the whole scheme."

Emory said, "We also need to call the police."

"Why?"

"If Rook intends to take the sloth out of the country, he'll have to obtain permits. They can check with the airport in Iquitos."

Nick tittered. "Lieutenant Montoya is going to start wondering about us."

****

Two hours later, Hector found the remaining team members assembled in the lounge and announced that he'd heard back from the police. "The airport reported to Lieutenant Montoya that the Havel cargo plane landed in Iquitos about one a.m. and took off for Lima at four a.m."

"Was anyone able to inspect it?"

"They had no reason to."

"Can Montoya contact the Lima police?"

"I'm not sure what they can do either. Unless Rook was delayed in Lima, he should be on his way to the States by now."

"No." Emory spoke decisively. "First, he'd have to find some kind of conveyance for the crate—that can't be easy. And I doubt if he had that arranged before he left, because he didn't know he'd have the animal."

Petra stirred. "Remember, before you guys went to set up the trap, he said he had one more job for Aguirre to do."

"To reserve another cargo plane. *Aha*. But did he come through? Aguirre was pretty sore at Rook."

Nick scratched his head. "Only way to find out is to have Montoya get hold of his counterparts—see if the plane has left Lima yet."

Emory added, "While they're at it, they should check warehouses or buildings near the airport as well."

"What for?"

"A large animal in an even larger crate."

Nick chuckled. "Who's probably *really* pissed about now."

Hector went off to radio. With so much speculation running around in Petra's head, it was hard to get a word in edgewise. She sensed the same thing happening in the others' heads, resulting in a rather restful period of complete silence. *At least no one's yelling about the Mapinguari.*

They received no word from Montoya that morning. Hector volunteered to wait by the station two-way radio in case he called. Winston took Petra and Nick fishing in the afternoon. They came back with a long string of piranha and a gorgeous yellow-and-red fish. Emory was swimming by the dock. "Whew, where'd you catch those?"

Petra pointed a short way upstream. Emory scrambled out of the water. "Winston caught the yellow one. It's a royal peacock bass. Isn't it beautiful? He says it's excellent fried."

John wandered down, a banana in his hand. Petra wondered if he realized that the little monkey attached to his shoulder had already bitten off half of it. He gestured with the other half. "Well, no one can say we don't eat well here."

You do, for sure. In fact, that's about all you do *do, isn't it, John?* But Petra no longer expected the fat fellow to offer anything beyond platitudes...*and a little refreshing slapstick.*

After dinner, she and Emory chose adjoining hammocks. As they swung slowly in the slight breeze, his hand sought hers. "This place would be so inviting if it weren't for all the monsters running around."

Petra mumbled drowsily, "Felicity and her fiancé planned to stay a few days and relax. I wonder if he'll make it?"

He rolled toward her. "Who cares?" He traced a finger down her face. "If I were rich, I'd rent the lodge for just the two of us."

"Well, you'd better keep Hector and Capac on."

"What for? In the immortal words of Greta Garbo, I *vant* to be alone." His eyes crinkled.

"Hector for protection and Capac to cook."

"All right, I'll indulge you."

The ranger came in. "I heard from the detective. Havel's plane is still at Lima airport in the general aviation terminal. They questioned the pilot. He told them once the crate was unloaded, Rook said he didn't need him any more. The police are canvassing the area."

"Someone had to have helped Rook. They couldn't just leave the sloth on the tarmac."

"He didn't say anything about that." Hector headed toward the door but stopped and turned around. "Oh, by the way, he told them he had another passenger for Pacaya. They'll be flying in tomorrow."

"Did he say who?"

"A Mr. Kelly Chisholm."

Chapter Twenty-Eight
Endangered Species

November 7

Felicity stood on the dock watching the plane land gently on the water and taxi over to her. Petra had kept the others inside—"Let her have a minute alone with him." When they weren't looking, she peeked out the hammock room window. *After all, who wants to miss a classic reunion scene?*

Havel jumped out and opened the rear door. A man stepped over the sill and turned around to pick up a duffel. When he turned back, Petra saw a shock of shaggy brown hair, twinkly brown eyes in a darkly tanned face, and a wiry, lean body. He walked with a slight limp as well as a certain grace. Felicity ran to him, her white-blonde hair flowing out behind her, and stood on tiptoe to kiss him. *By rights, there should be music—Mendelssohn, I think. Or Liszt.*

Felicity took Chisholm's hand and brought him into the lodge. She smiled at Petra. "This is my friend Petra Steele." The men stood to welcome him. Felicity surveyed them with approval. "John Dillinger, Denys Ffoulkes—" When she came to Emory, she hesitated a mere second. "—Emory Andrews, and Nick Steele. I'd like to introduce Kelly Chisholm, my fiancé."

Nick shook his hand. "Glad you could make it. I've

heard so much about you."

Chisholm replied, humor illuminating his dark features, "Felicity talks too much." He turned to his fiancée. "Rook didn't call here?"

"Did you expect him to?" Felicity looked alarmed. "Do you have to report to him? Does it mean you can't stay?"

He patted her arm affectionately. "It depends on whether they catch him before he leaves the country."

Emory started. "What do you know about that?"

John squealed, "You know about the sloth? That he took it?"

He looked grim. "Yes. I'll explain everything, but first, I'd like to freshen up." He took Felicity's hand and said with a mischievous smile, "It might take a while."

Havel sauntered in. "Where does a fellow have to go to get a drink around here?" Nick handed him a beer. He popped the top. "That was easy."

Emory pointed at a chair. "Tell us what happened, Havel."

"Huh?"

"How much did he compensate you to steal the sloth?"

"Steal? I don't know what you're talking about." He did seem surprised.

Either he wasn't in the loop, or he's a very good liar.

Denys's voice rose. "You're telling us you found nothing suspicious in Rook asking you to take him to Iquitos in the middle of the night? With a huge crate? By himself?"

"Look, I just get paid to fly. I don't ask questions.

Especially not in South America." He downed his beer and looked around for another.

Emory sat across from him. "So Rook called you and asked you to pick him up here at midnight and fly him to Iquitos."

"Right."

"How did he explain the crate? You must have helped him load it."

"Not me." He held up his hands. "And risk injuring these babies? A couple of natives helped him."

Hector had been listening at the door and came in. "It wasn't me. Winston was with his family."

"Ask around, would you?" He left. Emory turned back to Havel. "And when you got to Iquitos?"

"Some guys arrived in a truck and unloaded the crate. Rook paid me twice as much as we'd agreed on, which I thought was real big of him."

Denys bellowed, "And *that* didn't set off any alarm bells? Did he ask you not to mention the flight too?"

Petra tried to temper what was rapidly becoming an explosive atmosphere. "Did he tell you what was in the crate?"

"No, and I didn't ask."

Emory huffed. "Well, did you hear any strange noises? Grunts or growls?"

Havel's jaw dropped. "Grunts? Growls? What are you talking about?"

"Rook stole an animal of potentially monumental importance. A giant land sloth thought to have been extinct for thousands of years."

For some reason, this didn't faze Havel. "Oh, is that all? God, for a minute there I thought you meant he was in the slave trade or something."

Denys muttered, "Nothing so mundane."

"He potentially broke the law by removing an endangered species from its habitat." Petra didn't look for or expect a reaction from the pilot.

Havel shrugged. "Not my problem."

Emory shot him a look. "So the sloth was quiet?"

Havel swigged his beer. "Yeah. Rook was puttering around the box before we took off. He must have shot him with a tranquilizer dart."

The room fell silent. Finally, the pilot rose. "I've got to get back to Iquitos. Another client. Sorry I couldn't be more help."

Denys sneered, "Maybe if we crossed your palm with silver—"

"Hey! I told the police everything I know, and now I've told you. I'm just a businessman. If I went around broadcasting what people shipped on my plane, I wouldn't stay in business very long."

Emory said, "That may happen sooner than you think. The police are alerted to you—we can assume they'll keep close tabs on you."

Havel blanched. "Shit. This is what I get for opening my fat trap. I'm off. Thanks for the beer." He plunked down the bottle and strode down to the plane. A few minutes later, it took off.

"Piece of work, isn't he?" said Nick.

John shrugged. "It's tough making a living in a place like this. I'd cut him some slack."

"What, at least he doesn't smuggle drugs?"

"Or children?"

"Uh...yeah."

****

Hector showed up an hour later with two terrified

363

ribereños in tow. "Rook paid each of them two hundred soles. For that kind of money, they'd feed their prize pig to the caimans." He slapped one of them, who shrieked and was only prevented from falling down and groveling at Emory's feet by the grip Hector had on his shoulder. "They also knew they were going to get in trouble."

"Who are these guys?"

"My cousins."

Petra nudged Emory. "How many cousins does Hector have, anyway?"

Emory chuckled. "You'd think he'd have some marriageable female ones at least. Felicity told me he says if he doesn't get hitched soon, his family will disown him."

"Yes, he told me too, but he wants a girl with some higher education." She sighed. "Not much chance of that when he's tucked away out here."

Emory stepped in front of the first trembling man and glared. Then he moved to the second. Out of the corner of his mouth, he told Hector, "When you think we've frightened them sufficiently, you may let them go."

"But Mr. Emory—"

"We can't hold the fact that they accepted work from Rook against them. Our issue is with Rook, not your cousins."

Hector reluctantly nodded and dragged the men back to the canoe. He gave each of them a good shake before seeing them off.

Felicity and Kelly showed up for dinner but spent no time eating and even less time participating in the conversation. Petra, sitting next to Emory, wished she could be that obvious. *Of course, they don't have to hide their relationship.* She straightened. *Wait a minute—why exactly are we hiding ours?* Glancing at Emory, she realized he was watching Felicity intently. Her old fears came tumbling back. *Is that jealousy in his eyes? Does he still care for her? Oh, God, what am I going to do?* A tiny bit of her crumbled. *I need to be alone.* She rose. "I think I'll turn in early."

Emory started to say something, but she cut him off with a yawn. "So tired. Night, all."

Unfortunately, she wasn't tired at all. It only took her ten minutes to realize she'd get no sleep that night. She rose and went to stand by the window. As the hours grudgingly passed, she listened to the macaws and monkeys and whatever little lizards came out to play at night in the palms. The clock didn't have to tell her how late it was. She sighed. *Where are we going with this? First he says it's a fling, then he says it's not. What's in his mind? What happens after we leave here? Has it crossed his mind that our time is limited? That we* do *have to part? He—*

There was a tap on the door. She knew it was Emory. *Do I let him in?* She shut her eyes and opened the door.

"Petra? Why are your eyes closed?" She opened them wide. Emory's bulk filled the space. "What's wrong?"

She stared at him, at his wavy hair—a little mussed now—at his deep green eyes glinting like Columbian emeralds, at his Arnold Schwarzenegger chin. Her heart took a flying leap. *Damn it. I'm going to have to tell him.* She opened her mouth.

He said, "Petra? I have something to confess."

Her mouth snapped shut. *He's going to say he's still in love with Felicity. And me? If I'd told him…if I'd said it out loud, I'd be standing here with my heart hanging between us like a pair of wet underpants pinned to a clothesline.* "Do you have to?"

"I think so."

Get it over with then. Or just shoot me.

"Well…" He hesitated. "It's really two things, but I have to explain the first before we move on to the second. In case it matters." He peered at her.

Baffled, she sat down. "All right."

"May I?" She nodded, and he sat next to her.

He did not try to take her hand, for which she was grateful. "It's about the hummingbird flap."

Well, that's encouraging. He wants to let me down easy. "Okay."

"I told you I'd misidentified a hummingbird and the publicity cost me my job."

"Yes."

"Well, I wasn't the one who made the original identification. It was my research assistant."

"Wait a minute—wasn't he the one who found the article?"

"Yes. And no." At her mystified expression, he pursed his lips. "Let me back up a little. I did make one very big mistake, so in a sense it was my responsibility. I relied on Joel's photograph. See, I saw the bird from a greater distance than he did. He was the one who took the shot." He stood and paced. "He came across the journal article during his research. Once he developed the photograph, he realized his initial determination that it was a new species was wrong, but instead of telling me, he…uh…he doctored the photo."

"Doctored it? Why?"

"Joel was desperate. He had gotten married three months before our trip. His wife had just informed him she was pregnant. His fellowship was running out, and the foundation wasn't going to renew it. They couldn't survive on his piddling research assistant's salary alone. He had to do something fast. A sensational find like a new hummingbird would ensure grant money and maybe a chance at a permanent position at the university when he finished his doctorate."

"So he airbrushed the photograph." *Like Aguirre's fake dinosaur bird.*

"Yes. Just enough to add features that were slightly different from the Lucifer."

"And you were so excited about a new species you didn't think twice."

"Or check his work too closely."

"And you saw the article?"

He nodded. "Found it tucked under a pile of other journals. The resemblance was too close for comfort, so I reexamined the photograph and discovered the discrepancies. I told Joel we'd have to make a public statement. He begged me not to." He sucked in a deep breath. "I couldn't as a scientist let the charade continue. So I took the fall."

"Oh, Emory." She longed to hold him, comfort him, but knew he had to finish his story. "Why? Why did you have to? You must have known the damage it would do to your career."

"Yes, but how does that compare to the well-being of a young family? I had no children, no parents—no dependents. Felicity already had tenure, so we were on solid ground financially. Joel and I agreed that I would only report the error. The alteration of the photo would remain a secret. With my reputation, I figured I could weather the storm a lot better than Joel." He put his head in his hands. "Turns out a reputation is only as good as your last paper."

Petra touched his shoulder. "I'm so sorry."

"Felicity went to bat for me but without success. I couldn't tell her the truth. It wasn't her fault that I couldn't handle the vitriol. She's a marvelous person. Which brings me to my second confession."

She steeled herself. "You...still love her."

"What? No...I mean, yes, I love her, but as one of my best friends."

Yeah, right. I saw your eyes tear up just looking at her.

"It was at dinner."

"You were watching her." *Wishing you could have her back.*

"I was watching *them*." He blinked. "She and Kelly are so blissful, aren't they? She has finally found her soul mate."

Is he going to cry? Am I? I was right all along—he still loves her. That's it. I can't take another heartbreak. It's too much. I have to get out of here.

She started to get up, but he put a hand on her arm. "Where are you going?"

"I...I..." She closed her eyes, unable to come up with any words that would allow her to escape before she broke down completely.

"Seeing their happiness...It made me realize just how much...how much...Felicity's right—"

She broke away and made for the door.

He called after her. "That I'm in love with you,

Petra."

She stood stock still. "I'm sorry, could you repeat that?"

He laughed delightedly. "I...am...in...love... with...you...Petra. How's that?"

She didn't really feel the need to answer. *As the good book—by which I mean Strunk and White—says, show, don't tell.*

****

November 8

The two couples met in the hall as the sun rose. The monkeys and toucans were already up and making a fuss. Charlie the tapir lumbered up to the kitchen door to accept a banana from Esteban. Felicity peered at Emory. "Well, it's about time."

He just smiled.

The breakfast table offered up a bounty of fried plantains, juicy slices of papaya, and *pan chapla*— sweet yeast rolls flavored with anise. Kelly had two platefuls, then asked if he could have something more substantial. Capac brought him an omelet, bacon, and half a pineapple, which he ate, washing it all down with three cups of coffee. He patted his stomach. "Haven't eaten anything but airplane food in days."

"Really? Why not?"

"Took me about twenty-eight hours to get back to DC from Turkmenistan. Then I had to turn right around and fly down here."

"DC? I thought you were going to Rook's head office in Kansas City." Felicity was surprised.

Kelly sat back. "It's time I told you all why I'm here."

John muttered, "*What's My Line* on location in

Pacaya?" He lobbed guarded glances from under his brows at each in turn.

"You weren't fired, were you?" Felicity's voice trembled. "Victor Rook is a horrible man. I knew he was lying about why he sent you to Turkmenistan. You should quit before he fires you. Why—"

"Indeed he is horrible, but he is not in a position to fire me."

"Why not?"

"Because I don't work for him. I work for the United States Fish and Wildlife Service. For the American government."

Nick burst out, "I *knew* I'd seen you somewhere before. You were in a photograph in the latest *Smithsonian* magazine. It was about agents who hunt animal traffickers."

Kelly grimaced. "Yes, I was. That was a terrible blunder. We allowed a Smithsonian photographer to accompany us on a mission on the assurance that he would take shots solely of the animals we rescued. He turned out to have his own agenda—an environmental crazy who was somehow under the impression that we were the problem, not the smugglers. He thought he was saving the world by outing us."

"You're kidding."

"I wish I was."

"What will happen to you? Will you be taken off the covert...what do they call it? Branch?" Petra worried for her friend. *To have this happen right before they get married...*

"That's why I was in DC. We were going over options. My superiors have decided to reassign me to a desk job."

Felicity rubbed his arm. "Oh, my dear. That's awful."

He winced. "It's certainly not what I signed up for."

Petra poured more coffee into her cup. "Can you tell us anything about your investigations?"

He held out his mug, and she refilled it. "My unit monitors several criminal operations across the globe which smuggle endangered and threatened species. You've no doubt heard of the Chinese appetite for rhino horn and fish bladders. There's also high demand from at least fifteen other countries for illegal animal parts. I'm on a team that goes undercover and gathers evidence to arrest the ring leaders. I'd had some success—"

"Yes, the article talked about the turtles…"

"The Kemp's ridley turtles, yes."

"You closed down the syndicate that trapped and sold them to Mexican enterprises."

"Let me guess," said Emory. "They use them to make an aphrodisiac."

The men grinned at each other. "Nah, just a heavenly soup."

Petra stifled the giggle. *I guess I can't fault him for having sex on his mind.* She remembered a very passionate set of lips and a very active set of fingers.

"Anyway, the photographer wrote an article that disclosed our sources and methods. He even published pictures of us. We tried to stop publication, but they refused. Something about wanting revenge on the president because he doesn't have a dog in the White House." He shook his head. "These people are as irrational as they are immoral. They don't know what real environmentalism is. It's all political with them. They want total power over human activity, not stewardship of nature."

"So the article was published. Then what happened?"

"As it turns out, it was the beginning of the end of my covert career."

"Why? After all, how many people would see it and recognize you?"

"It only took one—Rook. I had been working for him for two years, trying to discover what, if any, connections he had with the Martel gang."

"Martel?"

"Bolivian bunch—traffic in exotic birds—hyacinth macaws, Amazon parrots, cotingas. They had a trade route set up that took the birds by boat to Brazil where they sold them to private collectors. Anyway, Rook seemed to be clean. I'd about decided it was a dead end when I came across some information—potentially sensational information—about him. The *Smithsonian* article came out at the same time." He patted Felicity's hand. "My bosses at Fish and Wildlife were so disturbed by the publicity that they ignored my pleas to continue the Rook investigation and sent me out of the country."

"To Turkmenistan?"

"No, no. I was assigned to come down here and check out rumors that several carcasses of an endangered guan—that's a bird—had been seen in a butcher shop in Nauta. Rook was looking for a remote area to test his new scope, and I thought I'd persuaded him to let me scout it out first. It must have been about that time he saw the article and recognized me.

Abruptly, he sent me off to Turkmenistan. I didn't think much about it, until I heard he'd gone to Peru in my stead. Alone."

"I don't understand." A tiny monkey hand appeared at John's side and stole a plantain from his plate. "If Rook wasn't involved with the gang, why did you continue to investigate him?"

"For his zoo."

"Zoo!"

Petra and Felicity exchanged glances. "We'd heard he had a reputation among the...er...high flyers that he...er...had a thing for animals."

Emory squinted at Petra. "I didn't take you for the type to subscribe to *Jetset* magazine."

Kelly interrupted before Petra could retort. "He has a thing for animals, all right. We think he's procuring endangered species. Which is just as illegal as what you and your warped little minds"—he winked—"were imagining."

"You mean, for his own personal menagerie?"

Denys seemed intrigued. "Wow. To have a backyard full of rare animals. It must be fabulous to have that kind of money."

Kelly stared at him. "I repeat: it is illegal. Very. The Convention on International Trade in Endangered Species of Wild Fauna and Flora of 1975 makes it a crime to catch, sell, possess, or consume animals that are designated endangered or threatened. If we obtained evidence that Rook was harboring anything of the sort, he could spend the rest of his life in prison."

Denys said nothing. Petra watched him. *I think John is right—he's really obsessive about this. I wonder to what lengths he'd go to get his own zoo?*

Hector came in. "Is everyone sitting down?"

"Why? Is it someone's birthday?"

"No. It's bad news. Detective Montoya just called. Victor Rook is dead."

Chapter Twenty-Nine
Extinction

November 8

Pandemonium would sound like doves cooing by a tranquil pond compared to the response to this announcement. When Emory had succeeded in calming the waters, Hector continued. "Lieutenant Montoya has no details as yet. When he gets more information, he'll come out here and report to us."

"What about the sloth?"

Hector shook his head. "No idea. If they find it, they'll confiscate it."

"And then what happens?"

"I do not know." He backed out of the room.

That's smart—bail out before Denys takes it into his head to punish the messenger.

Kelly said, "Hopefully, they'll let experts examine it and return it to the wild."

"At least they know where it came from." Felicity tried to be optimistic.

Denys cried, "We must get it back! I want to be the one to study it. We found it—not Rook. It's ours." His voice cracked. Petra feared he was closing in on hysteria. He jumped up and paced. "Chisholm—you must force them to return it to us."

"Me! I have no jurisdiction here."

Emory said soothingly, "Like Felicity said, they know Rook captured the sloth in the Pacaya region. It's a good thing we called the police, or we'd have no chance to retrieve it. Let's sit tight and wait to hear from the detective. It will have to be returned to its territory eventually."

Denys stopped in the middle of the room and said defiantly, "I can't wait that long. I'm going to Lima."

"What happens if you pass them on the way?"

"Impossible. This is a third-world country, Andrews. Depend upon it—unless someone takes charge, the wheels of justice will grind to a halt."

Petra thought of Alex and the bribe. *Not if they're well-greased.*

"I doubt whether ordering the police around will do any good, Ffoulkes."

Nick added, "Especially by a foreigner. I'm with Emory. I advocate patience."

Denys's voice had risen an octave. "The beast will be there for months, mark my words. They could kill it. Or let it die. Or"—the whites of his eyes showed—"they'll give someone else—a *Peruvian*—access before me." He edged away from the others.

John caught his arm. "You can't just walk out and leave us here."

Denys shook him off. His eyes shot around the room. Then he abruptly spun around and made for the door. Unfortunately for him, Hector blocked it. "Get out of my way!"

He let him past. Denys sped down the hall, his arms flailing.

Hector stepped back into the room and stood by the table.

"You have news?"

"Montoya radioed again. He asked that we all remain in the lodge until he can break away. He wants to question us and search the area."

"Well, then you might want to stop Mr. Ffoulkes. He's headed to Lima to get his pet back."

At that moment, they heard a crash. Denys stood on the front steps, the contents of his briefcase strewn across the boardwalk. Before they could reach him, he'd gathered it up and galloped to the launch. Winston stood on the dock, a fishing pole in his hand. He turned at Denys's cry. "Start it up, Winston. Look sharp! I have to get to Iquitos *now*."

Emory waved furiously over his head. "Don't move! The police ordered him to stay here!"

Winston hesitated only a moment. Petra wondered if he'd caught the wild look in Ffoulkes's eyes. He dropped the rod and lifted his arm. His machete sprouted from his hand, gleaming evilly in the sun. Denys didn't slow. Winston brought the machete down so fast, all Petra saw was a blur. She prayed as hard as she could. *Don't kill him. Oh, please. Don't kill him.*

Denys stopped short. His briefcase dropped from his hand. The machete vibrated, stuck in the wood decking a centimeter from the tip of his shoe. When he tried to step around it, the two halves of his belt—cut clean through—split, and his pants fell off. His shoulders sagged, reminding Petra of a member of the audience who's brought up to the stage only to be humiliated. The others ran down. "Thank you, Winston!"

"Nice work."

Winston retrieved his machete, and Felicity gently

took Ffoulkes's elbow. "Come on, Denys, let's go back. The lieutenant ordered us to stay here. You can make your case to him tomorrow."

"But…but my sloth."

"If you left the station, he would have had you arrested, and you'd never be allowed to study the creature."

"Yes," put in Nick. "We still have a good chance of convincing the authorities that we're the best qualified and the best situated to do the work."

Denys pulled up his trousers and, holding them closed with one hand, consented to be helped back to the lodge. He went to his room mumbling.

The day passed quietly despite an undercurrent of apprehension bubbling beneath the surface. Nick and Emory played checkers while Petra tried to read. After fifteen minutes, she threw the book down. "I just wish we knew how he died. Was it in a shootout with police? An accident? Where's the crate? Do they have the sloth, or did it escape?"

"Here—maybe this will take your mind off useless speculation." Her brother handed her a well-thumbed copy of *Jetset* magazine. "I found it in Rook's room. There's an article on the exotic pets of the royal family of Bhutan."

"Very funny."

****

November 9

The police didn't arrive until they had finished breakfast the next day. Montoya brought two uniformed officers with him into the lodge. "Greetings. This is Sergeant Vasquez, and this is Sergeant Garcia." He turned to Vasquez. "Sergeant, please fetch the two guides." When Vasquez had gone, Montoya leaned forward and put his fists on the table. "Thank you for your patience. I have sent a message to Puerto Maldonado asking the other two members of your team to return. Once they are present, I would like to interview each of you separately. But first, with your permission, Sergeant Garcia will search your rooms while I relate what happened in Lima. After the interviews are complete, I'd like you to take me to the place where you captured the sloth."

"Certainly. You have my consent to search the lodge." Denys had managed to compose himself. In fact, he seemed in full control—almost back to his bombastic self. He puffed on his meerschaum and stroked his mustache.

Montoya didn't miss a beat. "My sincere thanks, sir. Now please, will you all take a seat?" The sergeant ushered Hector and Winston in and took up a stand by the door. The two guides sidled past him and remained plastered against the wall.

The detective walked around the chairs and stood, his back to the windows overlooking the river. Over his shoulder, Petra saw a pair of macaws fighting over a Brazil nut. A swallow-tailed kite sailed by, a small fish dangling from its talons. "When I got your call, I immediately notified the Lima police, who searched the airplane. Rook could not be found, but they spoke to the baggage handlers. Two of them admitted helping him take the crate off the plane and putting it in a truck. The truck was unmarked, but one of the handlers recognized the driver." He broke off. "Lima is in many ways just a big village."

Denys showed signs of increasing impatience. "So

they traced the truck?"

"Yes. And located it at a storage facility just off the airport grounds. Rook had left the box in one of the units. One deputy was deployed at the facility and the other one dispatched to locate Rook. He found him in the general aviation terminal arranging his flight to Kansas City."

"What did they do?"

"They arrested him on the strength of my report—and the fact that the box was shaking and the thing was bellowing."

"Their first clue that a large animal was inside."

"A large animal in a crate marked Machine Parts."

Nick snickered. "Under the circumstances, their skepticism was understandable."

"Yes." Montoya did not laugh.

Felicity let go Kelly's hand. "Did they open the box?"

A range of emotions crossed the detective's face, the most obvious one being anger. "No, which may have been a serious mistake. They weren't sure if the three of them could handle whatever was inside, so the sergeant made the decision to leave it in the storage unit while they transported Rook to the police station."

Emory spoke up. "They left it unattended?"

"Yes. The sergeant needed his deputies to escort Rook. He told the manager not to let anyone open the unit. They planned to return with animal control agents." He pounded a fist into his palm. "It seemed the safest way to proceed. Unfortunately, they hit a huge traffic jam on the highway, and while they were at a standstill, Rook jumped out of the van and ran off."

"Oh, my God! Is that when they shot him?"

"They didn't shoot him."

"But you told us he was dead."

The policeman sat down. He pressed his lips together. "The rest of the story is quite shocking. Perhaps the ladies would prefer to retire?"

Several titters were quickly stifled. And those were from the men. Petra said sweetly, "It's very considerate of you, but we'd prefer to hear you out."

"Very well." Capac slid a cup of coffee onto the table in front of Montoya. "*Gracias.*" He spooned half the bowl of sugar into the coffee, then resumed. "The police reckoned Rook would try to double back to the storage unit, so they returned to the airport. They hit another traffic jam on the way back, which slowed them up for half an hour." He sighed. "Lima's population has outgrown its road system, I'm afraid. They arrived too late."

"Too late for what?"

He took a long sip of coffee. "Rook had indeed returned and persuaded the manager to let him into the locker. Once inside, he apparently decided to open the crate. We don't know why. Maybe he thought he could tranquilize the sloth more easily. The unit is a small room about twenty feet square, and Rook had locked it from the inside. When the men got there, they could hear the animal roaring and Rook screaming. By the time they were able to break the door down, Rook was dead. They cornered the animal." He paused. "The deputy described it as about ten feet high and covered with dark hair—like a gorilla or a bear."

"It's a giant land sloth. Thought to have died out ten thousand years ago." Denys spoke resignedly.

"Sloth?" Montoya knit his brows. "Aren't sloths

vegetarian?"

"Yes."

He tapped his empty cup. Capac refilled it. "Well, this fellow wasn't. He was ripping into Rook's body, tearing pieces off. And eating them."

John turned away. They heard a gagging sound. Petra raised her eyebrows at Emory. *So it did evolve.*

"What did they do?"

"They shot it."

Denys gurgled, "Shot it? They *shot* it?"

Montoya seemed perplexed. "What would you have done?"

Denys slowly rose with his color. His breath came in short, sharp stabs. "You…you killed possibly the only living link to what was thought to be an extinct animal. You destroyed what would have been my…our…greatest discovery, a discovery for the ages." He lunged at the detective, his hands reaching for his neck.

Montoya leapt to one side. Nick and Emory grabbed one arm each and pulled Denys back. Sergeant Vasquez drew his service revolver.

Denys howled, "Assassin! Butcher! It was in our grasp, so close…so close." He collapsed on a chair and put his head in his hands. Montoya cocked his head at Vasquez, who put his gun back in the holster. Denys's muffled voice sifted through his fingers. "And now the institute will go under."

Petra asked curiously, "Why do you say that? You must have other projects, other sources of funds."

He lifted his head, revealing a face flushed with despair. "This was our last hope. If we could find one new species—it didn't matter what—our charter would have been extended. And the sloth…such an incredible find…think of the money that would pour in! It would have more than made up for the embezzlement."

"Embezzlement!" Felicity peered at the man. "What are you talking about?"

He dropped his eyes again. "Someone drained our accounts of two hundred thousand dollars. It's the real reason we're in such dire financial straits. We were near bankruptcy when I was offered this project."

"This project? You mean the Mapinguari? Then you lied to us about the original mission?"

"What? No." He nodded at John. "John received a prospectus in the mail detailing the availability of a large grant to study this area. I told him to check it out, and we were awarded the money. He informed me of the Mapinguari sightings as I was preparing for the expedition."

Nick was curious. "Who offered the grant? Where did the funds come from?"

"The name escapes me. Some corporation based in the Caymans. John?"

John looked nervous. "The Castle Group."

Petra cried, "Of course—the anonymous donor—Rook."

"I can confirm that." Kelly interrupted. "The Castle Group is a subsidiary of Rook Enterprises."

Emory sat back. "So we were right. He was behind this all along. You know what that means."

"He must have known about the Mapinguari before we did."

Nick added, "Maybe he planted the stories of sightings to get our attention."

Petra protested, "The stories weren't made up,

though. Huayna and Acarapi saw *something.*"

"Then what about the hair? Could he have had Aguirre plant that?"

She shook her head. "The hair is real."

"Your swatch, yes, but did Aguirre actually find any?" Nick wasn't ready to let his theory go yet.

"I think so. She gazed thoughtfully at Emory. "He was genuinely upset that it was missing…and genuinely surprised when you found my bag in his pocket."

"Rook again?"

"Uh-huh. Remember when we saw him loitering outside Aguirre's door? I bet he'd gone in and stolen the specimen while Aguirre was sleeping."

John said eagerly, "Then planted yours—"

"Which he'd stolen from my desk."

"—in Aguirre's pants…But why?"

"To discredit Aguirre. He always had it in for the man." Nick stated it flatly.

Petra was reminded of the last argument between the two men. "Did he? Are you sure?"

Nick stared at her. "No other explanation. He was trying to get rid of Aguirre." He stood up. "Tramposo was a loose cannon—running away like that. Coming up with all the cockamamie decoys. Rook had had it with him and wanted him gone."

"It doesn't matter what his motivation was." Emory took the floor. "He must have heard the stories of the Mapinguari and wanted to capture it for his menagerie. A scientific expedition would make a great cover."

"But why risk us finding it first? Why not just come here on his own?"

"A good point. I—"

John interrupted. "No, no. He needed our expertise." He scratched his head and said bluntly, "You don't suppose he was behind the embezzlement too? To make us more open to his proposal? And not ask too many questions?"

Emory nodded. "Makes some sense. He spies out a small, relatively unknown nonprofit desperate for funding." He glanced at Denys. "A more prominent research organization wouldn't be so vulnerable."

Kelly nodded. "He gives Ffoulkes carte blanche. Then, when it's up and running, he appears on the scene."

Montoya mulled this over. "Are you suggesting Mr. Rook stole your money? To what purpose? He is very rich."

Nick added, "Besides that, you wouldn't need to be hurting for cash to take it on. The project would obviously be attractive to you anyway."

Denys stared at him. "I suppose."

Petra thought about the director's single-minded pursuit of glory. *Could he have stolen his own funds to finance some crackpot enterprise?* "Maybe it wasn't Rook. Maybe—"

Emory held up a hand and leveled a searching gaze at Ffoulkes. "Denys? Did you by any chance embezzle the money yourself?"

"What? No! What a ridiculous notion. The ITR is my life—I would never do anything to cripple it. I'd accept any grant, take any action...Um."

Never mind.

Nick had been muttering to himself. He stepped in front of Ffoulkes. "Any action you said. For example, would you steal a Peruvian artifact?"

"Me! What are you talking about?"

Nick swung on Petra. "Remember when we first flew to Iquitos from Lima, back on October third? I told you I saw Ffoulkes."

"That's right. First at the ruins, then at the airport."

"Right. He was talking to a man at the general aviation desk. I know who it was now. Igor Havel."

"Havel! The pilot?"

"The very one. I thought he looked familiar when he showed up here." He turned back to Denys. "You were arranging to fly to Pacaya with him, weren't you?" When Ffoulkes remained silent, he went on. "At that point, you'd only just heard of Aguirre's fossil. You hadn't seen it. You didn't know it was a fake. Your first thought was to get your hands on it and whisk it out of Peru."

A tear welled up in the older man's eye. "John had just informed me that the accounts were emptied and that the anonymous donor conditioned his gift on speedy results. I was petrified. I...I fear I lost my head. We had to have something to proffer, and quickly. Havel said he couldn't get to Pacaya for another two weeks. By then, we'd learned the truth about the fossil, and I told him not to come." He brushed the tear away.

Felicity frowned. "Well, who do you think stole the money? You must have a theory. Do you have an accountant?"

"No. We hired an outside firm."

"How about staff? Board members?"

"We're operating on a shoestring at the moment. No board." He stopped at the exasperated sniff from Emory. "Yes, I'm afraid I exaggerated our size and significance a *teensy* bit. In fact, my secretary, the IT guy, and John are pretty much it. John has been my right-hand man throughout all our difficulties."

This declaration was followed by a short silence. Petra considered the chubby man. His customary carefully groomed presence seemed a bit askew today. Neither the meticulous comb-over nor the safari ensemble unstained by contact with a jungle vine or a splash of silty water—*except by accident*—were quite as immaculate as usual. *Something's raised his hackles.* She looked to Emory for guidance. The latter pressed his lips together, his eyes troubled.

Nick said thoughtfully, "Right-hand man?"

John turned crimson. "What are you insinuating, Steele?" He trembled with rage. "You odious troublemaker. You've had it in for me ever since you invited yourself along. Always making snide jokes at my expense. Mocking me behind my back." He wiped his nose with a finger. "Goes for all of you. You all think you're better than me, don't you? Bunch of loony scientists." He tossed his head at Denys, dislodging one of the long hairs from his pate. It danced in the slight breeze. "But you. You're the worst. Dumbass Victorian groupie."

Felicity intervened. "Take care, John. Don't say something you'll regret."

Denys, who seemed to have been lost in thought during John's rant, looked at Felicity, then turned slowly to John. "You dealt with the accounting firm. You received their report. You were the one who found the irregularities."

Emory stepped between them. "You confirmed it was the fault of the accountants, didn't you, Denys?"

He hesitated. "No...I...Well...John seemed to

think…" He stared at his assistant with new eyes. No one spoke.

Kelly's voice struck a harsh note. "Why didn't you go to the police?"

"We did….Or rather, John did. He said he'd take care of it."

Another short silence. The policeman broke it. "Mr. Dillinger? Do you wish to make a statement?"

In response, the little man moved like lightning. He grabbed Sergeant Vasquez's revolver from its holster and backed to the door. "Happy to." He waved the gun at them. "Why don't you all stand together there in the center?"

Denys stiffened, but Montoya raised a hand. "Do as he says."

They obeyed. "Thanks." John nodded with satisfaction. "Sure, I took the money. This old fool was squandering it all on wild goose chases. He'd fall for any rumor, any tittle of gossip about some hitherto unrecorded insect or salamander." His face crumpled. "This job was supposed to be my salvation. I'd been unemployed for three years. My wife left me. My son's in the penitentiary." He chuckled painfully. "For embezzlement. Go figure. Fred always was a loser." He curled his lip. "Takes after his mother. His old man's a lot smarter. I knew how to do it."

"How did you manage it? In such a small office, someone was bound to notice missing funds." Nick kept his tone neutral.

"Simple. Took over more and more responsibilities while Charles Darwin here spent his time writing his memoirs and posturing in the mirror in his plus-fours. Siphoned it off in thousand-dollar increments."

Petra thought she detected movement behind John. *Keep him talking.* "Where were you going to go with the money?"

"Belize. Nice sandy beaches. Good food. No extradition treaty. I was ready to decamp when Rook's proposal plopped in my lap. Claimed he'd heard of the Mapinguari's existence and wanted it for his zoo. Offered a hundred thou to find it, but he insisted he remain anonymous. What a whack job." He smoothed the recalcitrant hair back over his head. "I knew Ffoulkes would leap at the money without asking questions. Gave him a song and dance about the Castle Group acquiring a pharmaceutical company and looking for new species of medicinal plants. I waited until I got down here to let slip the rumors about *Mappie*." He gave Denys's nickname a venomous skirl. "I sent him reports about a mysterious Sasquatch seen roaming the jungle." John shot Ffoulkes a withering look. "He bit like a snake on a rabbit. It was almost too easy."

Emory followed his gaze. "So Denys was fixated on the quest for the Mapinguari even before he got down here."

"Yeah, but I wanted to erase any doubts. To seal the deal, I found a native willing to claim he'd seen the creature."

Petra remembered a hunched-up figure sneaking off in his canoe. "Huayna."

He smirked. "Man after my own heart. Willing to diddle anyone for a few soles."

Hector clenched his fists and rose on his toes. At a word from Montoya, he settled down.

"But why go to all this trouble? I thought you were

ready to split with the money. Didn't this interfere with your plans?" Felicity seemed genuinely stumped.

He snickered. "I'm nothing if not flexible. I rearranged my schedule. Figured we'd get down here and I could take my…winnings…and melt into the undergrowth."

Nick had been drumming his fingers on the back of a chair. "So you had everybody on board with the Mapinguari, and things were going smoothly. Suddenly, Aguirre drops the bird bomb into your party. We know now that he wanted to distract us from the Mapinguari so Rook could capture it—but did you have any clue then what his motive was?"

John snorted. "No idea what the little twerp was up to. At first, it bugged me to hell and back—I was ready to scram and didn't need more complications—but then I figured, why not throw a little grease on the fire?"

Nick jerked and knocked the chair over. "The guinea pig. You killed Esteban's pet, didn't you? And planted the feather next to it. Aguirre knew nothing about it—he wasn't even here when it happened."

"Bingo." His eyes crinkled with mirth.

Petra realized he was beginning to enjoy his narrative. *With any luck, he'll relax and lose his concentration.*

"I was outside Tramposo's room one night and saw him dying feathers—trying to get one that would pass muster, I suppose. Would you believe it? The fathead left his discards in his trash can. Plucked one out"—he snickered at the pun—"and dropped it by the hutch." He wrinkled his nose. "Shouldn't have rats in the kitchen anyway. Disgusting."

"But weren't you worried people would start to ask

questions?" Nick seemed confused. "Felicity and Denys were still studying the one Aguirre found. If they decided it was a fake—"

"Everyone would blame Aguirre. Nothing would come back to me."

What a bully—to kill a child's pet. Petra could hardly control her indignation. *And he expects us to feel sorry for him.*

Montoya, who had been listening to the proceedings without a word, straightened. "We now know the Mapinguari—the land sloth—exists. You thought you'd lured these people out on a lie, but once the news came out, Pacaya would be crawling with scientists and tourists. How did that fit into your scenario?"

"Oh, I'd be long gone by then. After all"—he sneered at Denys—"I knew he'd keep it a secret as long as he could. I'd have plenty of time to get to Belize."

Emory coughed. John swung the gun around and pointed it at Petra. "One move and she gets it in the forehead." He winked at Emory, a gesture that sent nauseating chills down her spine. "You wouldn't like that, would you, lover boy? Oh yeah, I know you two have been shacking up. I guess any port in a storm, eh?" At Emory's sudden movement, he cocked the hammer. "Did I mention I happen to be a crack shot? Take after my grandfather, the gangster. I had a great gig at a shooting range in Miami, until they fired me." He shook his head. "Just because I peppered an obnoxious customer with a little buckshot."

Felicity cried, "Mr. Dillinger, what are you doing? What makes you think you can get away with this? You're way out in the wilderness. You've shut yourself up in the lodge all this time. How will you survive out there?"

"That's where you're wrong." He patted his pocket. "While you all went traipsing after whatever dinosaur caught your fancy, I've been socking away a few necessities for life on the run. I have camping supplies and"—he glanced toward the kitchen— "enough food to last me a week. They're stashed in a safe place."

Denys's brow furrowed. "There's no room in the lodge for that much material. Where did you put it?"

"For that matter, where did you hide the money?" Nick probably didn't expect an answer.

He would have been wrong. John smiled. "Those kapok trees are huge, aren't they? Enormous roots. That fellow Manuel showed me one maybe half a mile from here. Some animal had dug a handy little burrow underneath it. Big enough for a man and all his loot."

"Is the stuff still there?"

"Of course." He frowned. "Almost had to move it once, though."

"The animal came back?"

"No."

Petra had an inspiration. "Someone else discovered it."

John, lost in thought, paid her no attention. "Finding another hideout that convenient wouldn't be easy." He looked up. "So I was forced to take other measures."

Chapter Thirty
Mutation

November 9

"Measures?"

His face scrunched up with old frustration. "Damned Lewis. Nosey creep."

"What are you talking about?" *Oh no, tell me he didn't...*

"The SOB was snooping around and stumbled across my cache. He knew about the missing funds because Denys can't keep his trap shut. When Manuel blabbed that the stuff belonged to me, he put two and two together. I had to eliminate them." He beamed at Felicity. "See, I do have some survival skills. Did my homework. I knew about the Chullachaqui. Got my trusty Huayna to leave the pegleg marks around Manuel's banana garden. Then it was a simple matter to get some cuttings from a curare vine, make a decoction of it, and rub it on a spike I hid in the banana leaves. Manuel never saw what killed him." He scratched his neck with the barrel of the gun, then trained it on Felicity. "For scientists, you're pretty easy to deceive. Mythical creature on a murderous rampage? Sure! One-footed imp laying a trap? Why not?"

Petra hissed, "Them. You said 'them.' You poisoned Lewis too, didn't you?"

He made a slashing motion with the gun. "Cut a little nick in a branch to make the sap flow. Then all I had to do was slip and fall, catch Gordon's wrist, and leave some nice, deep scratches with my fingernails." His mouth twisted in a grimace. "Being *accident-prone* as I am, who would question it? And who would suspect I'd been with him? Little John, who never leaves the lodge? Nah."

"You pushed him onto the vine."

"I knew the poison wouldn't take effect for a while, so I had plenty of time to nip back to the station and no one the wiser." He nodded in satisfaction.

Nick was gazing at him in wonder. "Why did you hollow out his organs?"

"Oh, that. Another little nod to the Mapinguari. It made a nice touch, didn't it? Huayna did a bang-up job. You all immediately assumed it was our jungle Yeti. I used your smug superiority against you. So convenient. And you never suspected the fat man, the nobody, the stumblebum." He glared at Montoya. "Until you stuck your ugly mug into it. Here I'd convinced them all to bury him before anyone looked too closely, and along come these jokers tracking some no-account thief. Even so, I could have gotten rid of the police if you'd left me to it, but nooo. This asshole"—he snarled at Emory—"had to go and invite them in."

"You wanted his death to remain a secret. A mystery. To keep us sidetracked."

Denys murmured, "That's why he offered to let Lewis's next of kin know. You never did contact them, did you?"

Dillinger scoffed. "You're no rocket scientist, are you?"

Denys drew back, affronted. "Well, I nev—"

Petra, who had been thinking about her first day at the lodge, interrupted him. "You took the chips out of everyone's phone, didn't you? So they couldn't contact the police."

"I thought of everything, didn't I?" Luckily, John didn't wait for an answer. "Slipped 'em back later when you were being interviewed. Piece of cake. Snipped a wire on the radio, too, just in case."

Hector spoke for the first time. "I assumed an animal had eaten through the wire, and I repaired it."

Emory asked, "Did you tell Rook about Gordon's death?"

"Him? Yeah. Well, I ginned it up a bit. Told him we suspected the Mapinguari. He was as much a fool as the rest of you, but I thought it would goose him—get him down here even quicker. Worked." During his monologue, he'd been slowly backing farther and farther into the hall. "And now…I think I'll just hop on the launch and take my leave."

He whirled and ran smack dab into the officer Montoya had sent to search the rooms. The policeman snagged John's gun and popped handcuffs on him before he could move. "Señor." He said something in Spanish to the lieutenant.

"Well done, Sergeant Garcia. Take him to the police launch."

"Wait a minute. What about my Miranda rights? You have to read them to me. You can't arrest me until you do."

Montoya was unmoved. "Señor Dillinger, here in Peru we have a constitution which enumerates many human rights. We do not, however, have a Miranda equivalent." He turned to the waiting scientists. "We'll transfer him from Iquitos to Lima after I radio the details ahead."

John didn't struggle, which Petra found odd. He took a step toward the detective, his expression mocking. "Like hell you will. You don't know, do you?" He taunted, "Backwoods hick of a cop. You can't hold me. I'm an American citizen. Wait'll I call the embassy. Teach you to mess with the US."

Montoya was unimpressed. "Perhaps you are unaware, sir, that—unlike Belize—we have had an extradition treaty with America since 2001. It has functioned very well." As his words sank in, John's jaw dropped.

I guess he didn't think of everything after all.

"And anyway," the lieutenant continued in a friendly tone, "you committed the murders on Peruvian soil. We are perfectly within our rights to charge you with those crimes. Vasquez, Garcia. Take him away." As the men and their prisoner left, he called, "You'll find our jails most accommodating. I believe one of your comrades had the pleasure of staying with us only recently."

They watched as the two officers escorted their prisoner to the boat, John sagging between them. Petra asked Montoya, "What's going to happen to him?"

"I shall notify the authorities in Lima, who I'm sure will be in touch with the American embassy and the Florida police. They can decide jurisdiction. I shall return as soon as possible." He rose. "An interesting day. I'll see myself out."

"Interesting? Is that the best you can do?" Nick threw up his hands. "If this whole expedition weren't such a disaster, it would be hilarious."

Petra and Emory moved closer together. "Not a *total* disaster."

The sound of a body slithering to the floor caught everyone's attention. Denys lay prostrate, a hand on his chest. His eyes had rolled up into his head. Felicity rushed to him. "Oh, my God, is he having a heart attack?"

Denys tried to speak but only garbled sounds came out.

Kelly was grim. "A stroke, I think. Quick, catch the police before they leave."

The launch was just pulling away. Hector yelled. The pilot put it in reverse and returned to the dock. Hector ran down to explain. One of the policemen returned with him. Together, they lifted Denys and carried him to the boat.

Felicity said, "Thank God they were still here. Otherwise, who knows how long he'd have had to wait for medical attention?"

Emory said heavily, "That would have been the least of his worries."

"What do you mean?"

"Well, he's run the institute into the ground while at the same time destroying its fledgling reputation. We—Nick, Alex, and me—signed contracts with him. Any of us could sue him. He could also be held liable for the fact that the embezzlement wasn't reported. And he's got nothing to show for this expedition except one faked species and one dead one."

"Other than that…" Nick was, as usual, irrepressible.

"Nicky!" Aware her remonstration would have no

effect, Petra turned to Emory. "What do you propose we do now?"

Before he could speak, Kelly said, "I presume Montoya still wants to interview all of you. Nothing to do but wait for him to come back."

"That likely won't be till tomorrow."

Petra remembered something. "Aguirre and Alex. He said they'd been asked to return from Puerto Maldonado for questioning. I wonder when they'll get here."

"We're here."

The two men fought each other to shimmy through the door first, laughing. "Winston picked us up in Nauta. We saw the police leaving with John. What happened?"

Emory gave a quick recount of recent events.

Alex goggled at him. "John? An embezzler? A murderer? *John*?"

"Also—according to him—a crack shot." Nick tittered. "Turns out his last name should have been a warning to us."

"He certainly played his part well. I'm wondering now if all those accidents—the pratfalls, and everything—weren't just to make him look the buffoon so we wouldn't take him seriously."

"He sure had me going. Remember when the snake fell on him?" Nick chortled.

Emory said grimly, "He as much as admitted it was an act."

Petra disagreed. "If so, he could have had a career with the Cirque du Soleil. No, I'm guessing he used his natural awkwardness to his advantage."

"You know," mused Felicity, "he really is a loser,

though. He said he hadn't had a job in three years. Nothing had gone right for him. He made rather a pathetic figure."

"Bad luck doesn't excuse murder."

"No."

Aguirre looked around. "So where's Rook?"

"And Denys?"

"That's another long story. Grab a beer and make yourselves comfortable."

"A little early for alcohol, don't you think?"

Somehow I don't think Alex means that.

Emory shook his head. "Not when you hear what we're about to tell you."

They were on their third beers when Emory finished. Alex whistled. "Whew. Looks like we left before all the fun began."

"So Rook was murdered too." Aguirre's voice shook. Petra glanced at him quickly and thus observed the anguish in his eyes before he could extinguish it.

"It was his own fault, though." Petra wished Nick hadn't said that. She watched Aguirre carefully. His face remained blank.

Felicity gazed outside, where a couple of spider monkeys were roughhousing. "I'm not sure you can be murdered by an animal. Murder implies conscious and rational decision-making. Not hunger."

Kelly scooped up a handful of the toasted corn called *cancha* and munched. "Between Dillinger and Rook, Rook was the greater criminal as far as I'm concerned. Who knows how many animal deaths he's responsible for? How many species are gone because of him?"

"But if you're right and he was acquiring

endangered species, wouldn't that serve to protect them?" Petra wasn't ready to condemn the man yet. "Zoos do the same thing."

"My job is to make sure that wild animals remain in their natural habitat. Zoos are okay but not optimal for a self-sustaining population. Anyway, zoos have the proper equipment and facilities. We don't know what sort of installation Rook had."

"I do."

They all looked at Aguirre. "I've been there. It was state of the art. Over the years, he's brought specimens of some twenty endangered species there. They were all healthy and content. At least at first."

"Was it just for his own amusement? Like those guys who buy stolen art and keep it in their vault?"

Aguirre gulped the last of his beer. "Can I have another?" Capac gave him a bottle. "Thanks."

"Well?"

He closed his eyes as if he were rehearsing his words. "Victor Rook was brilliant, but he was also slightly insane. He had been totally ensnared by the global warming movement. For one thing, he was even more convinced that the earth was rapidly heating up than even the most passionate proponents, and that it was a hundred percent due to human activity. He had no patience with scientific studies that indicated a twenty-year hiatus in the warming trend, nor in the theory of respected researchers that sun spots were the real culprit for the very slight rise in temperature we've recorded. He called them all 'climate change deniers.' " Aguirre rolled his eyes. "It became his religion. He reminded me of those messianic cults who proclaim the end of the world is near and, when it doesn't happen, denounce the rest of us for our cynicism." He stopped. "Did you ever hear of the Voluntary Human Extinction Project?"

Petra caught Felicity's eye. "We were just talking about that."

Nick asked curiously, "What is it?"

"An organization that thinks they can persuade people not to reproduce. Man will eventually die out, and the planet can go back to its pristine, pre-human state."

"Huh?"

Alex scratched his ear. "If all the humans are dead, how would we know the earth had improved? And how do you define 'pristine'? With or without slugs, for instance?"

"Or cockroaches?" Nick's shoulders shook. "Or—"

As usual Nicky takes a rational discussion and jumps right off the high dive with it. She interrupted. "Was Rook connected to the project?"

"He was a charter member. But…"

"But?"

"They had a falling out. Rook became less and less enthused. He contended that humans would never voluntarily choose death, even for the good of the planet."

Emory snorted. "He's got my vote on that."

"He decided he had to take direct action to give Gaia—"

"That's Mother Earth," put in Nick, and nodded wisely. Petra pinched him.

"Yes. He wanted to give her back to the animals. In his eyes, animals were pure, uncorrupted, clean. You know he had one of those hand-washing fetishes."

"Yeah, we noticed."

Kelly sat up. "We're getting a bit far afield from his zoo, aren't we?"

"Agreed." Alex went to the door of the lounge. "Before we get into that, I'm going to see if Capac has lunch teed up. I'm starved." He was back in a minute. "He says if we'll go along into the dining room, he's ready to serve."

They filed in, retrieved the requisite beers, and sat. Petra felt a bit ridiculous—like a German burgher waiting impatiently for his bratwurst and sauerkraut. She half expected Nick to start banging his knife and fork.

Capac trundled in looking grumpy. Petra checked her watch. *Oops. We're ten minutes late. We're lucky he's feeding us at all.* He handed around plates of fish stew. Esteban placed a basket of cassava bread and a salad of fava beans, red onion, corn, and tomato on the table. "*Solterito.*"

Kelly took two bites and leaned forward. "The zoo?"

Aguirre uncapped his beer. "Yes…those endangered specimens I mentioned? They weren't pupfish or northern spotted owls or gopher frogs. They were what are called apex predators—animals at the top of the food chain. The snow leopard, the cougar, Bengal tiger, red wolf. Vicious, smart, big."

"*Hmm.* Why only them? I thought you said he loved animals."

"Love? No. I'm not sure he loved anything. Hate, now there's an emotion he practiced daily. He loathed humans. As for the animals he had in the zoo, I guess you'd say he considered them a useful weapon."

"A weapon?" Alex put his fork down. "He wanted to exploit them?"

"Uh-huh. I said the animals were healthy. That's because they were fed prodigious portions of meat." He stopped.

Alex spooned more salad on his plate. "What's so odd about that? They *are* carnivores, after all."

"A particular type of meat."

Felicity held a hand to her mouth. "Oh, my God."

Petra choked. "Not...not..."

"Human meat. Yes. His intent was to turn them into man-eaters."

Nick pushed his plate away, shocking Petra. *He must really be floored.*

"In other words, he was deliberately engineering the mutation of these beasts." Kelly's voice was low and ominous.

"Yes."

Emory clucked his tongue. "Human flesh is hardly easy to come by. Did he raid morgues or something?"

"Didn't have to. You know what a killing zone Chicago has become? Almost eight hundred homicides in one year. Due to incompetence, political correctness, liberal policies, and corruption, the city administration is completely overwhelmed. Now and then the body of some nameless punk shot in the crossfire goes missing. No one pays any attention." He gulped his drink down. "Rook found a conduit."

Emory spoke suddenly. "How do you know all this?"

Aguirre looked around at them, a profound sorrow clouding his eyes. "I'm his son."

Chapter Thirty-One
Inherited Traits

November 9

"*What?*" Even Alex seemed surprised.

"His bastard son. You see, Victor felt nothing but contempt for the wealthy New York princesses in the upper crust circles in which he ran and so never married. A friend of his—a man named Eckles—had a private island to which he brought young girls for his rich pals to enjoy. My mother, Gabriela Tramposo, was one of those girls. A child of fourteen who spoke no English—an urchin plucked from the streets—suited my father's needs well. When she became pregnant, she was simply flown to Spain and dropped off in a Barcelona slum."

Felicity breathed, "The man was a *monster*."

Petra agreed. "More of a monster than any of his man-eaters."

Aguirre's face twisted. "Do not blame him. This was standard procedure for Eckles—a truly depraved human being. To his credit, when Victor learned what his friend had done, he located her and provided for her needs for the rest of her short, horrific life. After she died, he sent for me. I grew up in a mansion outside of Madrid. He paid for my schooling all the way through graduate school. When his company moved to Kansas

City, I went with him. He put me on the staff of one of his research institutes."

That would explain the Midwest twang salting his Spanish accent. "Why did he name you Aguirre?"

He almost smiled. "He didn't. My mother did. She thought I was the spawn of Satan—the wrath of God." A tear welled up in his eye. "She didn't know how right she was."

"So you supported his sick goal to turn the predators into man-eaters?"

"No!" He pounded the table.

Esteban came running in. "You want?"

Petra realized she hadn't eaten anything. Aguirre's revelations had ruined her appetite. Felicity's meal was also untouched. "Esteban, could you take the food away, please?"

Only Nick held onto his plate. "Not mine! I haven't finished!"

Emory stood. "Let's continue this in the lounge."

"I'll be there in a sec." Nick picked up a fork.

The rest walked single file down the hall. The sun was just dipping behind the trees. From outside came the catcalls of howler monkeys and the occasional splash of a dolphin breaching. Felicity turned on the lamps, and they settled in. "Go on."

Before Aguirre could start, Nick came skidding into the room. "Did I miss anything?"

His sister snapped, "Sit."

He sat.

Aguirre paced the center of the room. "I knew my father kept a private zoo, but it wasn't until a few months ago that I discovered its purpose. I happened upon a panel truck delivering meat for the animals. The delivery man was dressed in one of those haz-mat suits. It made me curious. I mean, what was he afraid of? What kind of infection could he get from butchered beef?"

"I dunno—maybe he only ate kosher?" No one laughed at Alex's joke.

"I asked the man what kind of meat it was and where it came from. He told me, 'From a chop shop.' "

Nick coughed. "You know, there's a really good butcher shop in Florida called the Chop Shop. Maybe that's what he was referring to."

"But the zoo's in Kansas City."

"Still…"

Capac put a bowl of *cancha* on the coffee table. Petra nibbled on one. "You say it bothered you, but why? What made you suspect they were involved in something shady?"

"The guy told me the meat came from a special source in Chicago. He dropped hints that led me to think it was human flesh. At first I guessed someone was operating a human-trafficking ring. Maybe a street gang, or the Mafia."

"Did you go to your father with your concerns?"

"No. I didn't have a chance. He spends…spent…a lot of time traveling."

"What did you do?"

"I started keeping an eye on the operations at the zoo. If criminal activity was indeed occurring, I wanted to have indisputable proof to take to him."

"What did you see?"

"Well, over time the animals were becoming increasingly agitated. The tigers paced constantly, and the red wolf spent hours banging his head against the plexiglass. The hyenas yipped all night long."

Kelly shrugged. "That's not abnormal for animals kept in small cages."

"But these animals weren't in small cages. Like I told you, the complex was state of the art. Each inmate had at least three-quarters of an acre of space designed to duplicate their original habitat. The most advanced principles of zoological architecture were applied. They should have been reasonably content."

"But they weren't."

"No."

"And you think it was due to their diet?"

"That, and I had evidence that the technicians were applying behavioral modification techniques to render the beasts even more bloodthirsty."

Emory leaned forward. " 'Evidence'? Such as?"

"I found mangled dummies in the dumpster. Bloody clothes. I also noticed that the feeding schedule changed often—"

Kelly pursed his lips. "It's good policy to vary the routine—keeps the animals from getting too complacent."

"Ah, but in this case, sometimes they wouldn't be fed for a week or longer. By the time the keeper brought their meals, they were tearing up their enclosures."

Felicity wrapped her arms around her chest. "You must have been beside yourself. Why didn't you call or text your father about it?"

"I couldn't decide what to do. If he was involved or—"

"But you didn't know that. If it was going on under his nose, he'd want to be informed."

Aguirre's tortured face said it all. "He took the decision out of my hands."

"How?"

"He called me to his office one day. He said the zoo director had complained about me spying on the employees."

"And you told him why you were monitoring them."

"I did. At first he dismissed my notions and ordered me to stay away from the facility and the staff. He told me I was too soft—that I needed to toughen up—like his zoo animals. Then he launched into this long diatribe about filthy humans polluting the planet. I knew he was pro-environment. Until then I didn't realize just how radical his views were."

"What did you do?"

He hung his head. "I told you, I'm his bastard son. He's always made it very clear that I'm there on sufferance—that if I ever cross him, he'll chuck me out on my ear."

He stopped. Petra, pretty certain she knew what he was going to say, murmured encouragingly, "Just tell us. It's okay."

"I started repeating some of the bilge he'd been spouting about humans and Gaia. I made sure he overheard me talking about how something should be done to reduce the population. I jabbered on and on about how revolted I was by man's degradation of nature."

"Who did you say these things to?"

"No one, really. When I knew he was within earshot, I'd talk into the phone as though I were speaking to someone."

Emory's voice was surprisingly neutral. "Tell me this, Aguirre. Did you do this to protect yourself?"

"At first, yes. I admit it. I'd always been dependent on his largesse. I was terrified he'd throw me out and I'd have to survive on my own. But—" He held up a hand to keep Emory from erupting. "But when I saw how he responded to my comments, I began to think that he was actually directing the project. So I decided to test him."

He leaned forward, his hands on his knees. "We were heading to a business conference in Las Vegas. He was, as usual, condemning the urban sprawl, the artificial lights, the street scum. He said the only act he enjoyed was those lion tamers." He gulped.

"Go on."

"I saw my chance to prove whether he was innocent or not and tossed out the proposition that the lions be used to take care of the problem. He…he confessed that was what he intended to do. He thought…he thought I would react positively."

"Did you?"

"I managed to cover my shock and pretended to share his passion. I kept my revulsion to myself." He wiped away a tear. Alex put a hand on his shoulder and squeezed.

"Surely you went to the police then?"

"With what? He'd been building his collection for years. He had all the mechanisms in place and left no trail. On the surface, my father had created a utopia for these animals—far superior to most zoos. Can you imagine if I walked into a police station and announced that my father—the great *humanitarian,* known for his generous donations to the arts and medical research—

was training endangered predators to attack humans? They'd brush me off as a vindictive ingrate."

Kelly stirred. "I would have believed you."

"Why?" Aguirre seemed to notice him for the first time. "Who *are* you anyway?"

Felicity took Kelly's hand. "This is my fiancé, Kelly Chisholm."

"Oh, you're the guy who was supposed to bring the scope."

"Yes, but instead, Rook sent him off to Turkmenistan on a trumped-up story to get him out of the way."

Aguirre turned to Kelly. "You worked for him?"

"Ostensibly. I'm actually an undercover enforcer for the US Fish and Wildlife Service."

Aguirre's mouth dropped open. Alex offered him another beer. He waved it away. "Did you know about his project?"

"Only that he was purchasing endangered animals. We didn't know what kind or what for." He stood and took out his phone. "I have to report this as soon as possible to the authorities."

"Yes. You'd better do it quickly. They may not know of his death yet. You could surround the compound before they have time to seal it off."

"Seal it off? Perhaps," said Emory gravely, "or they might even set the animals loose."

Petra shivered. Kelly punched in a number and walked out to the hall.

Aguirre had remained slumped in his chair, thumbs rubbing his temples.

Petra studied him. "You haven't told us why you joined the expedition."

He looked up, his face brightening. "Ah, I had an idea! See, I'd been at my wit's end trying to figure out what to do. When he told me about the Mapinguari and his plans to come down, ostensibly to test his new telescope, I persuaded him to let me come ahead and check you all out."

"The fake bird—was that to distract him?"

"Him? No. A bird wouldn't suit his project; I only hoped to delay him. If I could plant obstructions in his path, maybe he'd give up and go home. I didn't want him to collect another apex predator, especially one as vicious as the tales implied."

"I suppose he saw through your little ploy?"

"I'm afraid so. He kept trying to trip me up— expose me as a fraud."

"To get rid of you?"

He threw his hands up. "I don't know what he wanted. I'd always found it impossible to know from one day to the next what he was thinking. Sometimes he was affectionate—almost loving—and the next disparaging, even hostile."

Alex blew out his cheeks. "A madman."

That's why his motives were so unclear even to his son. "Well, it's over now."

His face drooped. "Yes. I wonder what's to become of me?" He rose. Alex rose too, and they walked out together.

When they'd gone, Nick asked, "What now?"

"I guess we wait for Montoya."

****

The idea of hanging around for the rest of the day did not sit well with anyone. Finally, Felicity and Petra went for a swim. The rest retired to the laboratory. Alex

411

and Aguirre went on a hike to look for orchids.

It wasn't until evening that Kelly called them together. "It took a while to get through." He held up his phone. "These chips don't get very good reception."

"You're sure there's one inside?"

"Of course." He realized what Petra was suggesting. "Oh, yes. Yes, I checked."

"What did Fish and Wildlife say?"

"My boss is contacting the Kansas City office, but before they can act, he'll have to send Tramposo's information up the food chain to the director in Washington." He glanced at Aguirre. "I impressed upon him the urgency of the situation, but there will still be a lot of red tape involved before permission is granted to enter the premises."

Aguirre flushed deep red. "They must hurry— before something dreadful happens!"

"Believe me, I couldn't agree more."

Capac came out. "Dinner is served."

"Great, I'm starved."

"Nicky!"

He shrugged and followed the cook. "What are we having?"

"*Chirimpico*."

He looked to Hector. "It's a stew made of part of a young goat." He pointed at his stomach. "Very good. Spicy."

Felicity leaned forward and whispered, "Tripe."

"Golly, after the recent events, you'd think we could have something vegetarian...or at the very least unrelated to internal organs."

Petra knew her brother was kidding. *I always said his brain was not connected to his stomach.*

Later that night, Petra lay in Emory's arms. She didn't really want to talk about Aguirre's story but had to ask, "Do you believe Aguirre? I mean, that he didn't know what his father was doing?"

"I think so. I never would have guessed he was his son—the undercurrent of antagonism was pretty stark."

"Yes…but I also sensed a unique—maybe freakish is the better word—kind of affection." She brought up the two faces in her mind. "They definitely had the same nose." She moved restlessly. "But why stay? Why work for him?"

"Maybe he had no choice."

"Maybe…or maybe there was love hidden somewhere in the morass of hate."

Emory rolled over to face her. He kissed her nose. "Fine, you work on your love story. Right now, I have something else to study."

She giggled. "And that is?"

"Human anatomy."

Chapter Thirty-Two
Social Darwinism

November 10

Emory and Nick were on the dock fishing when the police cruiser came around the bend in the river and pulled in. Montoya jumped off. Petra saw him from the hammock room and came down. "What's the news on Mr. Ffoulkes?"

"If you would please gather everyone, I will give a full report. Did Tramposo and Bönickhausen arrive?"

"Yes, and Aguirre gave us some very—how do I describe it?—disturbing information."

The others filed in from different parts of the lodge. The detective sat down at a desk in the lounge. "I'd like to see you one by one, please. The rest can wait in the dining room."

Felicity held up a hand. "We all want to know Denys's condition first, if you don't mind."

"According to the hospital, he is resting comfortably. It was a mild stroke, but he will require some time to convalesce. When he's stable, he can return to the United States. I believe his nephew is on his way here."

"Nephew! I didn't know he had any family." Alex raised his eyebrows.

Petra knew he was thinking that the old man

probably didn't deserve any loved ones. *Yes, he's a pain in the ass, but...*She couldn't bring herself to condemn him, after all that had transpired.

Felicity remarked, "He had a sister, but he told me she had just been diagnosed with brain cancer and wasn't expected to live more than a few weeks."

"She must have passed away, then. Mr. Ffoulkes told the nurses the young man was his only kin. Name of"—he checked his notebook—"Darwin Ffoulkes. Did I pronounce that correctly? He's coming from England."

Petra kept a straight face with difficulty.

Emory, his voice vibrating slightly, said, "Well, I'm sure he'll do wonders for his uncle."

"Now, shall we get started?"

Alex pointed at his friend. "Perhaps Aguirre should go first. He can tell the lieutenant his story."

The policeman looked about to reject the idea, but Petra interrupted. "If you want a full picture of everything that happened up to Rook's death, you'll need to hear what he has to say."

"All right." He motioned Aguirre to sit.

The others shuffled into the dining room. Capac brought out beers. A half an hour later, Aguirre appeared. He sat down hard and rubbed his eyes. Before they had a chance to ask how it went, Montoya appeared in the doorway. "Well, that was most informative. Now, Mr. Emory Andrews? This way."

One by one, they all told their stories to the policeman. He reacted very little to Petra's responses but took extensive notes. Kelly was the last. Montoya followed him to the dining room, wiping the back of his neck with a handkerchief. Capac offered him a beer, which he declined. "A Moche Kola would be most welcome, though." When he had been supplied with a bottle, he resumed. "Now, tell me. Which of you went back to retrieve the beast once it was trapped?"

Emory thought. "Let's see—we took the launch. We tied three canoes to the stern for a makeshift float to carry the crate. There was Denys, Rook, Nick, Hector, Winston, and me."

"All right, I want you to lead me to the site."

Kelly stood up. "I'd like to go too, if you don't mind."

"Certainly."

Aguirre and Alex spoke together. "Detective?"

He turned to the two men. "What is it?"

"Um…are we free to go? When you summoned us, we were in the middle of negotiations for a gentleman's shed."

Alex added eagerly, "The roof bears a strong resemblance to the panels on the Catedral de Santa María that my ancestor designed for the town of Chiclayo, Peru."

"We'd managed to whittle him down to three hundred soles." Aguirre seemed quite proud.

The detective sighed. "Fine, but I insist you leave your contact information here in case I have further questions. And you may be called to testify at the inquest."

Hector said, "Winston will have to remain at the lodge, then, in order to take Mr. Tramposo and Mr. Bönickhausen to Nauta."

"Fine, fine, fine." He gestured for the other four to follow him.

When the police boat had disappeared down the

416

river, the two friends went off to pack. Petra and Felicity saw them off an hour later. "Don't forget to write when you get there!"

Alex mouthed, "Will do," and they both waved with gusto.

The sun was just beginning to set when the launch with Montoya, Kelly, and the others returned. Nick kissed his sister on the cheek. "See you at the bar in two secs." He peeled off to the darkroom.

Petra and Felicity met Emory at the entrance. "How did it go?"

"Rook just left all his junk there on the ground." He shook his head. "You should have heard Kelly on the subject of litter." He sang, "Pack it in, pack it out."

"He's right, though. For someone who claimed to revere Gaia…"

Nick appeared. "He probably expected one of his minions to pick up after him. I'm ready for a drink." He slid around them and headed toward the lounge. "Come on, Hector. I'll buy you a beer." After a second's hesitation, Hector followed him.

Felicity looked after them. "The atmosphere is so much more genial without Rook and Denys, don't you agree?"

"Felicity! That's not nice."

"Well?"

Petra didn't want to encourage her, but she had noted with pleasure the addition of Hector to their socializing. The commingling of upstairs and downstairs—another modern concept which Denys, the sturdy Victorian, would have decried. *Were he here.*

Kelly was the last to leave the boat. As he stood on the dock, the police sergeant began to cast off. Petra ran down. "Wait, Detective Montoya! What about the carcass?"

The sergeant pulled the boat back, and Montoya hopped off onto the dock. "You mean of the sloth?"

"Yes."

Kelly gasped. "You didn't dispose of it, did you? If it's what we think it is, it's an extraordinary find, and Ffoulkes should be allowed to study it."

Emory came up behind Petra, Felicity at his side. "I doubt whether he's in any condition to do that."

The lieutenant answered, "You are correct. That is why we sent the remains to the University of Lima. Professor Wanapaku is a specialist in sloths and anteaters. There is also an internationally renowned paleontologist on the faculty. I do not exaggerate when I say they are extremely excited." He offered a slight smile. "Dr. Calvo is already talking about mounting a new expedition to search for more of the animals."

"But if they're endangered, he can't remove them from the wild." Kelly was growing perturbed. "It's against international law."

The detective replied gently, "I understand it is your duty to defend such species as have been listed as endangered or threatened. We here in Peru are perhaps even more wedded to the conservation of our precious wildlife. However, I must remind you that this animal is not designated endangered"—his voice rose to drown out Kelly's angry shout—"since we had no proof until now it even existed. Be assured, great care will be taken if one is found alive."

Felicity took Kelly's arm. "He's right, my dear. Perhaps—if you can keep your temper under control— the professor will allow you to observe his examination of the body. If it is the *Megatherium*, they will need the full resources of a university. You yourself insist that it's preferable to keep the animals in or near their habitat." She smiled winningly at him.

"Besides," added Emory, with a less winning smile, "you don't have any power here."

"But—"

Petra had an idea. "On the other hand, you may be able to do something about Rook's facility. Have you received an update from your superiors?"

"Yes." Kelly's agitation increased. "Headquarters is trying to expedite, but they can't do anything without a court order. It could be days."

"Wait!" Felicity clapped her hands. "You're still on Rook's payroll, aren't you?"

"Ye-esss."

"If you get there quickly, you might get inside before they have a chance to dismantle it."

Kelly's eyes lit up. "And I can report back to Washington before Rook's people can organize a legal defense." He took a deep breath. "Okay, you win. Lieutenant, I apologize for my rudeness. My work is not just a job—it's a calling. Sometimes I get a little…er…prickly."

"Quite understandable." The policeman turned back to the boat.

Emory touched his shoulder. "What about Tramposo? Why didn't you arrest him?"

"Arrest him? What for?"

"He worked for Rook."

"Yes, I questioned him extensively. I saw no reason to detain him." He started to board but then paused and said something to the sergeant, who handed him his briefcase. He pulled an envelope out and gave it to Emory. "I almost forgot. I have a letter here from a lawyer in Kansas City. It is addressed to Aguirre Tramposo. The post office knew I was coming out here and asked me to bring it. Can you make sure he receives it?"

Felicity said, "Alex gave me a forwarding address. I'll send it on."

"Thanks."

"So…" Petra wanted to make doubly sure. "Aguirre is off the hook for aiding and abetting Rook?"

Montoya grinned. "As I understand it, during the events in question he was in Puerto Maldonado, reenacting Fitzcarraldo's heroic effort." His eyes twinkled. "The Amazon brings out the adventurer in many men. Did you ever see the movie *Aguirre: Wrath of God*?"

Chapter Thirty-Three
Survival of the Fittest

November 17

"Emory, where are you? Come here! We have mail."

Petra took the pile from Winston and carried it into the lounge. Emory stood up. "I'm right here. Anything interesting?"

"A letter from Alex…and one from Felicity as well! Our cup runneth over."

"Read the one from Alex first. I want to know if the lawyer's letter reached Aguirre."

"Okay." She slit open the envelope and skimmed it quickly. "He says Puerto Maldonado is a pretty dreary place—not as many restaurants or historic buildings as Iquitos. I guess it never really took off even with Fitzcarrald's celebrity."

Emory pointed at the map of the Amazon on the lounge wall. "It may have more to do with the demise of the rubber industry. That was his claim to fame, after all—finding a way to get the rubber to ports in Brazil."

"The overland passage to the Madre de Dios River, yes. They named it the Isthmus of Fitzcarrald to honor him." She giggled. "Felicity thinks every immovable object in the Amazon is named after him—except Puerto Maldonado itself."

"He founded the city, though, didn't he?"

"No." She put down the letter and picked up a magazine. "Hector gave me an article that says he actually drowned five years earlier. They built the city on the spot where his ship sank."

"A tribute of sorts, I guess."

"Yes."

He poured himself a cup of coffee from the carafe. "All those tales you hear of the great Fitzcarrald moving mountains. Funny how these legends get so distorted over time."

"Like the Mapinguari." She thought of the creature she had never actually laid eyes on. "Still, there's always a kernel of truth in every legend, isn't there?" Petra opened the letter again. "Alex says the town's nothing more than a jumping-off point for all those Amazon boat tours now. There are more and more of them every year." She looked out the window. "I'm so glad Pacaya's off the beaten track."

Emory kissed her. "If it weren't for Capac, we could run around naked all day."

"He is a bit of a prude, isn't he? By the way, when does Hector get back?"

"His sister's wedding was this past Friday, I think. He should be here any day."

"Poor guy. I'm sure it was an ordeal—constant hints and nudges about his sorry single state."

Emory added, "If not outright demands that he find a wife ASAP."

"At any rate, I hope he brings those supplies from Iquitos. I need that extra lens and the developer fluid, since Nick took all his stuff back to Florida." She paused. "Speaking of Nicky, did you read his email? I can't believe he's decided to throw in his lot with Denys. They make an odd couple, don't they?"

"No more than Aguirre and Alex. Let's hope young Darwin Ffoulkes has a level head. He's taken over the business end of the institute."

"Really? That's good news. Denys...well, if *John* could hoodwink him, anyone could. And I can't remember the last time my brother balanced a checkbook."

Emory sat down on the sofa. "So what else does Alex say?"

"Good news and bad news. That shed they bought—"

"The one they got for only three hundred soles in that shrewd deal?"

"It wasn't even iron. The guy had painted it with some kind of black varnish to make it look like metal."

"Aw. So the news of their quest must have preceded them. Too bad."

"Huayna isn't the only native to take advantage of the gringo."

He prodded the paper. "And the good news?"

She continued to read. "He says they were walking around the main plaza, and Aguirre noticed a couple of decorative pilasters that had fallen off the rear of the old city hall. They were propped up with some rusty old panels. Alex is convinced the panels belong to the iron house. They're negotiating with the city to buy them."

"Sounds like a big job."

She said dreamily, "Wouldn't it be spectacular if Alex could prove Eiffel designed the Casa de Fierro?"

"Sure, sure." He picked up a magazine and began to leaf through it. "Anything else?"

She read on. "There's a postscript...Oh, my God." She looked up. "The letter we forwarded to Aguirre?"

"He got it? Good. Why?"

She gazed, wide-eyed, at her lover. "Apparently, Rook designated Aguirre as his sole heir. He bequeathed him his entire fortune!"

Emory whistled. "I guess your female intuition is good for something."

"Huh?"

"You knew there was more between them than animosity."

"I guess so." She was thoughtful. "I wonder..."

"What?"

"Now I look back on it. The whole song and dance with the hair. It's possible that Rook wasn't trying to discredit him, but to extricate him from this mess. Force him to leave. He may have actually loved him, in a deranged kind of way."

"If so, the whole relationship was really, really screwed up."

She thought of her own father. "Rook must have been seriously conflicted—I mean, after all, he hated humans in general, but found himself feeling affection for his child. He didn't know how to handle it."

Emory shook his head. "Aguirre used the fake bird to derail Rook's plans for the Mapinguari, so I'm guessing the warm feelings weren't mutual."

Petra remembered the look of anguish in Aguirre's eyes at the news of his father's death. "Oh, I don't know. We'll have to see what Aguirre does with his inheritance."

"Maybe he can use his newfound wealth for good—atone for Rook's misdeeds." Emory put the magazine on the coffee table. "Which begs the question: now he's in charge, what's going to happen to the zoo?"

"It was seized by the Feds. It'll be taken apart"— her mouth twitched—"very carefully."

"Wait a minute. So Aguirre gets bupkis after all that?"

"No. Rook's other enterprises were legit, so it's unlikely his assets will be frozen for long." She read further. "Assets which include—brace yourself—this research station."

He gaped at her. "Don't tell me. Rook wasn't merely the anonymous backer of the expedition?"

"It began that way, but the day he got here, he called his real estate agent. He bought the whole thing—lock, stock, and monkeys."

Emory tapped his index finger on his empty coffee cup. "That way he wouldn't have to deal with any nosy landlords."

"Uh-huh."

"He was just toying with us, then. He could have thrown us out at any time."

"No reason to do that. Like Nicky said, renting it out is very lucrative."

"And a good cover for his activities. He may have even envisioned bringing his zoo down to Pacaya."

"Or operating a second one here. Remember, he came himself because he'd never been to the rainforest before. He likely planned to capture more than just the Mapinguari."

Emory went to the bar and poured himself a glass of water. "So when does our new landlord come back to claim his property?"

"Let me see...not yet. He's having too much fun playing Diego to his Fitzcarrald. He requests that we hold the fort for now." She looked at Emory with shining eyes. "He asks if you'll consider taking the post of director of the station. Oh, Emory! A real job!"

"I'm going to take that in the spirit in which it was intended."

"What? Oh, you know what I mean. Aguirre obviously has great respect for you—and it will definitely restore your reputation." When he didn't respond, she said tentatively, "Alex writes that Aguirre is going to arrange to have the parts you need for Rook's telescope sent here."

"Great!" He smiled, his mood restored. "We're lucky Victor forgot to take it with him. It's his only positive legacy. I'm getting amazing shots. There's a flock of crested guans over by the oxbow lake. And I think that motmot might very well be a new species. I'm running tests now..." He realized she wasn't paying attention to him. "What is it?"

She put the letter down. "That reminds me. My two-week extension was up three weeks ago."

"I thought you'd extended it again?"

"Only on the condition that I get Phoebe three chapters by November 25." She swatted his hand away from her breast. "It's been harder than I thought to settle down and work on it." At his snigger, she stuck her chin out. "Perhaps I need a sabbatical from my sabbatical."

"You mean..." His eyes registered alarm.

She kissed him. "No, no. Just a little one-on-one time with a laptop instead of a lap."

He pretended to sigh. "Happy to oblige. It'll give

me time to get a bead on that passerine I saw downriver. It could be—"

"Could be what?"

He smiled. "Never mind. I'm not going to jump the gun again."

She sat down and snuggled under his arm. "You want to jump something else?"

His hands squeezed her middle. "What do we tell the laptop?"

"He can wait."

"Sounds reasonable." He pinched her bottom. When she tried to rise, he caught her and pulled her back down. "But first, let's hear what Felicity has to say."

"You want her blessing?"

"I already secured that lady's approval. She only asks that our standard day include lying in the hammock and popping grapes in each other's mouths. Now read."

She opened the second letter. "Okay...She says they were able to sit in on Professor Wanapaku's autopsy of the sloth. The paleontologist thinks it's definitely related to the giant land sloth but had evolved from pure vegetarianism to an omnivorous diet."

"Like chimpanzees. They're primarily vegetarians but have been known to eat meat. As we surmised, loss of habitat required adaptation to a broader array of food types."

"Last I checked, the Amazon basin is pretty big."

"Yes, but our cryptid was quite a large animal— probably needed to eat its weight in leaves every five minutes."

"True." She stopped, thoughtful. "Maybe it wasn't

loss of habitat, but lack of companionship. There can't be many others out there. You know how some people eat when they're lonely..."

He stared at her. "Now I'll bet a dollar *that's* a theory that's never been considered. I can see the headline: 'With no females around, the giant land sloth takes solace in surf and turf.' "

"Very funny." She gave him a severe look.

Chastened, he asked, "So how long will Felicity and Kelly be in Lima?"

Petra went back to the letter. "Looks like they left today. They're heading to Kansas City."

"To Rook's zoo?"

She nodded. "Kelly's been given the lead on the Fish and Wildlife effort to release the animals back to the wild. He's thrilled."

"It will be a long process. They'll have to wean the beasts off human flesh. What about Felicity? Will she stay with him or go back to Cornell?"

"She's commuting back and forth for now." She read on. "Oh, no!" She checked the date on the envelope. "This has been in transit a week!"

"So?"

"So...Professor Wanapaku has organized an expedition to come to Pacaya and search for more sloths. Hector is accompanying them. Emory, they're arriving tomorrow!"

"Does Capac know?"

The cook stuck his head in. "Missy Petra, Mister Emory, I forget to tell you. Hector is escorting two *científicos* from Lima. Famous professors from university." He beamed. "They will expect my caiman *chicharrónes*. Luz is preparing their rooms now."

Petra sighed. "Just when I thought I was done with the Mapinguari."

****

November 18

Professor Wanapaku proved to be a jolly little man with a jolly crew in tow. He leapt from the launch when it was still five feet from the dock, skipped up to Emory, and vigorously shook his hand. "Thank you mightily for accommodating us! May I present my team? This is Professor Calvo." The paleontologist turned out to be a tall, raw-boned, dour man, his bald head shiny with sweat. "He's an expert on the *Megatherium*." He beckoned two more men. "Juan Ortiz—our recorder. Raul Ramos is our photographer. And this, this—come here, my dear—is my daughter Elena. She's at university studying history. It is the winter break, and she asked to come. I know she will be a great help to me, her only father." He chortled and followed Capac past them.

Petra greeted Elena, a lovely girl with brilliant black hair swept back in a long braid. She shyly acknowledged Emory before turning back to Hector, who was tying up the boat. He looked at her, his expression so soft he could have been melting inside. Petra touched Emory's hand. "I see nuptials in the offing. Hector's family will be thrilled."

He didn't answer for a minute, then whispered, "Soon, yes, but not before ours."

She turned to him, surprised. "What did you say?"

"You heard me." He straightened and said more boldly, "I figure we'll get married here in the lodge, then take a cruise down the Amazon, escorted by pink dolphins."

"Oh, really?"

"Uh, yes. I've already arranged for the wedding feast—roast *cuy*. Esteban's new guinea pig had a litter, and he has offered us two as a gift." He paused, and in a slightly less steady voice, said, "In fact, I have a gift of my own." He handed her a small box.

Expecting a ring, she opened it with trembling fingers. Something soft lay in the tissue. She held it up. "What is it?"

"A rabbit's foot."

She stared at him. "Why on earth?"

"You once told me you always wished on Orion's foot. They thought I was crazy when I requested it on a keychain. This was the best the store could offer." He kissed her. "You know, come to think of it, I'm glad they couldn't make one. Too much lust, murder, and power associated with him. Rabbits are much more benign."

"You do know there aren't any rabbits around here."

"Yes—that's why I specifically ordered one made in China."

Rook loved Orion the hunter. "Orion boasted he could kill all the animals on the earth, didn't he? And that's why Gaia sent the scorpion?"

"Yeess." He pursed his lips, his eyes uncertain.

"So why would Rook name his gun Orion X?"

"*Hmm.* A perverse desire for retribution? His gun would kill humans, not animals. He could give the planet back to Gaia."

Makes sense. "I guess…"

He stroked the rabbit's foot. "So what do you say?"

"I think…yes, I think I won't ever wish on Orion's

foot again."

"Okay." He quavered, "Does that mean you don't want this then? Shall I take it back?"

"No!" She held the box tightly.

He threw up his hands. "I don't understand."

"What don't you understand?"

"What's holding you up? Is it my proposal? The boat? The dolphins? The *cuy*?" His voice began to rise.

"I…uh…"

He gazed at her anxiously. "Would you prefer goat to guinea pig?"

She pondered his features, features that had become so familiar in such a short time. His green eyes cooled her, and his long, slow smile warmed her. They'd already been through so much. She was ashamed to tell him what really worried her. *What happens if it's all dull routine after this?*

"Petra…am I way out in left field? Are you saying…are you saying—"

They were interrupted by cries and shouts coming from the river. A swarm of natives paddled their canoes furiously up to the dock. The man in the lead canoe waved wildly. Petra peered at him. "Isn't that Huayna—John's sidekick?"

"You mean the fellow who cooked up the fake Chullachaqui?" He shaded his eyes. "Yes, it is."

The canoes pulled in to the shore, where Winston waited. Huayna spoke rapidly and breathlessly, pointing back down the river.

Winston held up a hand and strode to where Petra and Emory stood waiting. "He says he saw something."

"Let me guess—the Mapinguari."

"Why, no." He gave her a look that all but said,

"You silly creature, that's old history." "No, he says he was fishing and a mermaid surfaced right next to him. She was dark and very beautiful. She tried to pull him out of the boat, but he beat her back." Winston pointed at Huayna. "He says he can take us back to the very spot."

And so it begins again. Contentment washed through her and settled like fine mist over her heart. *No worries on the routine front.*

Emory was still huffing and puffing. "Put him off for now, Winston." He turned to Petra. "Well, what *are* you saying?"

She took Emory's hand. "I'm saying...yes, the boat, the dolphins, the *cuy* are all fine."

"But? You want something else? Diamonds? A rubber tree? Your own pet tapir? I'll give you anything. *What do you want?*"

"I want, my dear, to marry you."

A word about the author...

Although M. S. Spencer has lived or traveled in five of the seven continents, the last thirty years were spent mostly in Washington, D.C., as a librarian, speechwriter, literary editor, professional staff at a U.S. Senate committee and at the Dept. of the Interior, non-profit director, and parent. She holds a BA from Vassar College, a diploma in Arabic Studies from the American University in Cairo, and Masters in Anthropology and in Library Science from the University of Chicago. All of this tends to insinuate itself into her works.

Ms. Spencer has published thirteen romantic suspense or murder mystery novels, with two more on the way. She has two fabulous grown children and an incredible granddaughter. She divides her time between the Gulf Coast of Florida and a tiny village in Maine.

http://msspencertalespinner.blogspot.com

Thank you for purchasing
this publication of The Wild Rose Press, Inc.

For questions or more information
contact us at
info@thewildrosepress.com.

The Wild Rose Press, Inc.
www.thewildrosepress.com

To visit with authors of
The Wild Rose Press, Inc.
join our yahoo loop at
http://groups.yahoo.com/group/thewildrosepress/

www.ingramcontent.com/pod-product-compliance
Lightning Source LLC
Chambersburg PA
CBHW070800030726
47504CB00003B/630